THE
FIRMAMENT
OF
FLAME

ALSO BY DREW WILLIAMS

The Stars Now Unclaimed

A Chain Across the Dawn

THE
FIRMAMENT
OF
FLAME

Drew Williams

A TOM DOHERTY ASSOCIATES BOOK
New York

THE FIRMAMENT OF FLAME

A Tor Book
Published by Tom Doherty Associates
120 Broadway
New York, NY 10271

www.tor-forge.com

Tor® is a registered trademark of Macmillan Publishing Group, LLC.

The Library of Congress Cataloging-in-Publication Data
is available upon request.

ISBN 978-1-250-18620-1 (trade paperback)
ISBN 978-1-250-18619-5 (hardcover)
ISBN 978-1-250-18621-8 (ebook)

Our books may be purchased in bulk for promotional, educational, or business use. Please contact your local bookseller or the Macmillan Corporate and Premium Sales Department at 1-800-221-7945, extension 5442, or by email at MacmillanSpecialMarkets@macmillan.com.

First Edition: February 2020

Printed in the United States of America

0 9 8 7 6 5 4 3 2 1

For Leo George Barnacastle—Welcome!

ACT
ONE

CHAPTER 1

Esa

This is *not* my fault!"

"This. Is. Entirely! Your! Fault!" Jane wasn't just shouting because she was angry with me—though she was, she was *very* angry with me—she was shouting to time her words between the cracks of her rifle shots, the echoes of the gunfire booming down through the great vaulted chamber we found ourselves suspended above.

Even shouting between the reports of her rifle, her words were almost drowned out by the crackling bolts of electricity that kept soaring over our heads, not to mention the roar of the belching flames jetting from the exhaust pipes below. Underneath all that chaos, there was also the tramp of dozens of steel boots, that particular sound coming from the automatons left behind to maintain this space station, automatons now trying to kill us instead. The service bots were clambering out of the piping that curled down the walls, boiling from vents and ductwork, emerging from every possible crevice like mechanical maggots bursting out of metallic internal organs, an image from some station mechanic's body-horror nightmare.

How many machines did you need to keep a space station running? A few hundred, apparently, and they were all very interested in killing us, even though we were trying to stop the station from self-destructing, which would have vaporized all the automatons right along with everything else onboard. "Self-preservation" didn't rank high on non-sentient automation's programming.

"It's *not*!" I protested to Jane, tracking the targets rushing toward us through the steam and flashes of chaotic light, though I was saving my rounds until they were closer. Meanwhile, I kept arguing, because . . . well, because that's what I did. "We're on an intelligence-gathering mission! I was gathering intelligence!" *Now* the machines were close enough to hurt, and I punctuated my sentence with a staccato burst of small-arms fire from Bitey, my submachine gun; timed it just as Jane stopped to reload. Even my lesser-caliber rounds punched right through the automatons, carving pathways through their steel exoskeletons; these things went down easily enough, but they just kept *coming*, more and more of them flooding from the crevices and cracks in the station's framework.

"We're on a very specific intelligence-gathering mission; that means gathering *specific* intelligence! It does *not* mean—Sahluk! Ammunition!" Jane shouted her interjection further back the reactor core, to where the big Mahren— seconded to us for our current wild goose chase—was holding the center span of the catwalk, along with Sho. The mismatched pair—the massive stone-skinned security officer and the only half-grown Wulf, his fur slick with sweat in the heat—were laying down fire as well, defending both our position forward as well as Javier and the Preacher, further back; Javier was covering the Barious as the synthetic tried to hack her way into the mainframe of the suicidal AI running the station, trying to get us access to its core.

The machine intelligence hadn't been suicidal when we'd first come onboard—it had been perfectly welcoming, then. It was only after Schaz tried to access some of its internal databanks—to track down who had been here before us, otherwise known as "the entire reason we were out here"—that the machine had gone, well . . . insane. It had been a trap, the AI wired to self-destruct as soon as someone came asking—that someone being us. Fortunately, it took time to overheat a station's fusion core, time that we could hopefully use to stop that incredibly catastrophic thing from happening— but the machine knew that was what we were trying to do. Hence the army of repurposed service bots.

Sahluk was a little busy to respond to Jane's request, given that he was trying to pull his big rock fist out of the center of one of the automatons, but Sho acted in his stead, pulling a magazine from the big bag o' bullets the Sahluk toted everywhere with him. Winding up like he was pitching in some sort of sport with a very odd-shaped ball, Sho hucked the magazine through the snapping connections of electricity with a *surprisingly* good arm. The young Wulf had spent several years paralyzed from the waist down; he was mostly better now, thanks to some exobraces wired directly into his nervous system, but he still had the upper-body strength he'd developed hauling himself around without the use of his legs.

I fired Bitey dry, trying to hold back the horde as Jane grabbed the thrown magazine and slapped it into her rifle; of course, even while she was doing that, she took time to berate me. "'Intelligence gathering' does *not* mean haring off to investigate every Golden Age relic we come across!"

"I had the watch," I responded hotly, beginning to back up toward the others even as I swapped out magazines myself—our position was going to be overrun; it was just a matter of time. "It was my call! We knew the cultists had been through this system, and it only made sense that they would have stopped here: plus, clearly—I was right!"

"And if we all die here, I hope you take a great deal of solace in that fact! You should have woken me; you should have woken Marus, or the Preacher, or Sahluk! Hell, you should have woken *Javi!*"

"Wait, why am *I* last on the list?" Javier asked, from far enough away that his voice was coming through the comm rather than over the sound of fire and electricity and explosions that filled the cavernous reactor. Even through the patchy connection, though, I could still make out his incredulous tone.

"We are *off the maps*, Jane," I said through gritted teeth—that wasn't just my anger, it was also a side effect of me gathering up my teke; I let it loose in one big blast, the telekinetic force smashing into the wave of enemies charging up the catwalk at us. That sent them crashing backward into the ranks of the machines behind them, creating impacts that sent limbs clattering across the pipes and into the fire-filled exhaust ducts below. "We're out of leads—this was the last system where we had any sort of vector for the cultists' transport. I *had* to—"

"Ladies, perhaps save this conversation for once you're off the death-obsessed space station," Marus said calmly—of course, he could afford to be calm: he was still safe onboard Khaliphon, in orbit around the station, along with his own apprentice, a young Avail called Meridian. Granted, the two of them were still helping—along with the AIs of our networked ships, they'd been diverting energy to other parts of the station, the only reason the reactor core hadn't already overheated—and granted, they'd still *die* if the entire thing went up in a ball of atomic fire, but at least Marus didn't have dozens of reprogrammed maintenance machines trying to tear his head off his shoulders.

"No!" Jane replied, her voice still just as hot as Marus's was cool. "She only ever *listens* to me when she's—"

"Through!" the Preacher shouted, cutting off whatever remark Jane had been about to make and stepping back from the panel. With a sharp jerk, the Barious unplugged herself from the access port, the connections still trailing sparks. "Esa, Sho—you're up!"

I fired Bitey dry—yet again—then turned, already running, the catwalk shivering under my boots as the entire station began to quake; we were close to a meltdown now, as evidenced not just by the shaking, but by the marked increase in fricking *lightning* singing over my head and flames belching out of exhaust ports around us. Time was . . . definitely of the essence.

As I passed Sho, he was already dropping to one knee—counting on Sahluk for cover, and the Mahren was doing just that, achieving said cover by bashing together two automatons until they came apart in his fists—and the Wulf's eyes were sparking like thunderstorms at sea; he was channeling the electrical currents from the atmosphere into himself, filling his body up like a battery. Granted, that wouldn't have been *hard* at the moment, given the sheer amount of electrical energy surrounding us, but it would still take him some time to draw it all into himself, and I still needed to be in place before he did.

I ran faster. The big blast doors at the end of the catwalk were sliding open, the Preacher's hack giving us access; the AI core was visible now, hanging over the reactor furnace itself like a giant mechanical heart—you'd need a vertical leap of about twenty feet to get up there with the access ramp retracted, which, of course, it was. I didn't *have* a vertical leap of twenty feet.

What I did have was telekinesis.

I passed Javier and the Preacher, both firing down at the automatons still trying to overwhelm our positions, and I *pushed* at the catwalk beneath me just as I reached the edge; pushed hard. Newton's third law kicked in, and I went sailing upward, toward the AI core. I was going to make it. I was going to make it. If I didn't make it, I was going to fall into atomic fire and vaporize, moments before the station itself did the same thing, taking my friends with it. I was going to make it.

I *hoped* I was going to make it. Propelling oneself across a deadly drop into atomic fire with a bone-rattling push of telekinetic power that came from being born soaked in radiation nobody understood wasn't really an exact science.

I made it, barely; hit the edge of the core hard enough to bruise, then clung to the exposed piece of piping on the bottom with the tips of my fingers just before I slipped, fell, and got vaporized by the heart of the reactor. Gritting my teeth, I tightened my grip until I could free a knife with my other hand—all the time I spent arguing with Jane aside, I was always glad she'd drilled into me very early on to never go anywhere without a knife—and used the tip to jimmy open the access hatch on the side. With that done— still hanging over an *atomic furnace*—I plunged the blade in between two of the connections, at the precise spot Marus had told me to look for, the information gleaned from the schematics he'd been able to download before the station shut him out.

Golden Age AI tech, and we were going to do a hard reboot with a conductive knife and about a megajoule of direct current. There *had* to have been a better way to do this.

Too late to think about it, though: that megajoule was headed my way, courtesy of Sho—he'd gathered up all the electric energy he possibly could, then sent it leaping into the catwalk at his feet, headed my way like a lash of current. It was already racing along the metal in cresting waves. The rest of our team were grounded thanks to their combat gear and the catwalk itself, but I was hanging in the air, completely exposed to all that power—and that was very much the plan.

The energy arced up off the catwalk, snapping above the glow of the atomic furnace beneath me—a bright line of azure lightning cutting through the orange blaze of the reactor—and I reached out with my free hand to grab hold of it with my teke, letting it build and build and build and build until I couldn't hold any more.

That was when I poured *all* of it into the knife.

For a moment, I didn't think it was going to work. I was sure it wasn't, in fact—I was going to lose my grip, or the core would just explode, and either way I'd go tumbling into the atomic fire, and that would be it; our search for the cultists who worshiped the Cyn would be done, our search for answers would be done, and all we might have learned, all we'd learned already, would be gone. We'd never return to Sanctum, we'd never be able to tell the rest of the Justified what we'd found, as it had been months since we'd last been able to send them a broadcast; we'd never know if there had really been a cure for the Barious, a cure for the pulse, a way to turn the fact that the Cyn could *eat* pulse radiation into something we could use to do good.

Maybe Jane was right; maybe I shouldn't have altered our course.

Then everything around us shut down: everything but the fire of the furnace beneath me—the lightning, the belching flames, even the automatons—it all just . . . *stopped,* ground to a halt like a Golden Age piece of tech being exposed to pulse radiation. There was a moment of silence, deep and still, and then the AI core came blazing back to life.

Steel shutters slammed closed over the reactor core beneath me; I let myself drop, slowing my descent with another burst of teke. The crushing horde of automatons began to jerk back to awareness, their homicidal tendencies wiped along with the reset of the AI, and they went wandering off one by one—those that still had limbs—presumably looking for brooms or whatnot, to clean up the mess we'd made on the way here. It had been half a millennium since the end of the Golden Age; hell, maybe they'd be happy to have something to do for once, even if that was just sweeping up rubble and shell casings and their own blown-off limbs.

"Welcome to the Raizencourt Observatory, travelers," the AI voice said brightly, restored to the friendly, welcoming tones she'd used before whatever trap Scheherazade had triggered had sent her into a suicidal algorithmic crack. "How may I help you today?"

Just don't try to *murder us all* again, machine; that would be a good start.

CHAPTER 2
Esa

The observatory's externally induced suicidal tendencies averted, our little troop—including Marus and Meridian, who had joined us from Khaliphon, now that there was markedly less murder happening on board—gathered in the station's lobby, just off the docking bay where we'd set down our ships. The lobby's walls were decorated with tasteful images of worlds and systems taken by the Raizencourt telescopes, a somewhat . . . bizarre collection of perspectives, given that those same worlds and systems might not have looked anything like those images any longer, assuming they even still existed at all: this station wasn't just a pre-pulse relic, it was pre–sect wars, too, from a time period before the primary occupation of most beings in the galaxy had become the eradication of every other being in the galaxy who didn't think exactly like they did. Odds were, at least a handful of the worlds in those picture frames had been destroyed completely, wiped off the galactic maps.

Marus and Meridian, the two "intelligence operatives" (read: "spies"), had joined us so they could pore through the data the Preacher had accessed from the observatory, once a thorough scan had revealed there weren't any *more* traps of a suicidal nature hiding in the AI's code. The spies made a mismatched pair, Marus with the bright green coloring and slim-shouldered frame of the Tyll, and Meridian—like all Avail—with skin like cut obsidian, so dark it seemed to swallow the light around her.

Still, they were no more mismatched than Javier and Sho, the fur-covered Wulf already broader through the shoulders than his human partner, despite the fact that Sho still had a few years before he hit full maturity. And mismatched species or not, there were reasons Sho had been assigned to Javier, and Meridian to Marus: "boundless curiosity" was the first descriptor you'd reach for when it came to the pair of explorers, whereas "emotional stability" was probably what you'd be more likely to apply to the pair of intelligence operatives.

I kind of hated to wonder what that meant for Jane and me, what commonalities someone might find in us, but we'd been partnered up for over three years, and whatever similarities we now shared that we wouldn't have otherwise, I was comfortable with them.

While the spies worked their way through the data, the rest of us argued about the trap we'd wandered into; that was . . . kind of what the Justified did. Argued, I mean.

"So. They know we're on their trail," Sahluk said, his usual understatement still sounding like a minor rockslide.

"Or they're just paranoid," Jane shrugged; Jane always thought people were paranoid, mainly because that's what she saw when she looked in the mirror. I'm not complaining—her paranoia had kept us both alive, on several different occasions—it just meant she tended to see it, even when it wasn't there.

Sahluk shook his head, rubbing at the fringes of crystal "beard"—a sign of advancing age, one Mahren started to develop once they slid into their second century of life—that lined his jaw like stubble. "They were using this place as a staging ground, as a processing area," he replied. "Nobody else knows it's here, or it would have been picked clean by now, and it's too damn useful to destroy just on the off chance somebody came along—this was aimed at us, specifically."

"He's right," JackDoes agreed; the little Reint engineer had also steered clear of the fighting earlier, though he'd been onboard Bolivar, Javier's ship, in the docking bay, because, among all of us, he had the least combat training. I understood why the Sanctum Council had sent him along: with four ships on an open-ended mission, they'd known we'd need a starship engineer to keep us all flying—already had, in point of fact, several times over the last six months—but he was still the one I worried about when violence erupted, as it always seemed to. Sho had grown up in a war zone; Meridian, at least, had several years of Justified field training under her belt, if not practical application; JackDoes was the only one of our team who wasn't rated for combat of any kind. Violence just wasn't in his nature.

"This was a trap, and it was set for us," the Reint continued, his wide-set reptilian eyes blinking rapidly as he leaned forward to turn his viewscreen around so we could see. I had no idea how to actually read what he was showing us—I'd grown up on a heavily pulsed world, so computer programming was very much not my area of expertise—but his tail was swishing behind him in excited emphasis, so I just assumed the data proved his point. "It was put in place recently; very recently. As in, the recruitment vessel—the same one whose vector we followed here—left it behind after they exited the system."

Six months of searching, and that was the best lead we had: a single cargo vessel, jury-rigged to haul people rather than heavy machinery, one we'd tracked from a heavily pulsed world, a world often visited by cultists who came offering salvation . . . salvation that came in form of "shining beings who could wipe the pulse away." The cultists called themselves "the Bright Wanderers," but the beings they had described during the recruitment session we'd infiltrated—described in tones that bordered on worship—sounded exactly like the Cyn, and it was the Cyn we were after.

Jane and I had run into one of the forgotten species almost entirely by accident, during a routine mission to pull a gifted child—Sho, as it turned out—from a pulsed world. The Cyn had been after him as well, but we were less interested in *why* the Cyn were collecting gifted children than we were in the biological anomaly that the Cyn themselves represented: namely, as beings of pure energy, they subsisted on radiation, which meant they could eat pulse radiation, could "cure" pulsed worlds, or at least pockets of them. Even if there were somehow billions upon billions of their kind, hiding somewhere in the galaxy, they couldn't cure the whole universe, of course—but just a handful, on just the right worlds in just the right places, could make a massive difference.

Yet none of them had tried. In the hundred years since the pulse—and nearly five hundred since the Cyn vanished from any historical record—no Cyn had been seen, not until Jane and I had been attacked by one of the glowing bastards. *He'd* been a homicidal maniac with a zealot's fervent belief in some form of apocalyptic religion—the sort of thing these "Bright Wanderers" also seemed to buy into, which wasn't a good sign—but just because he'd been a murderous lunatic didn't mean all of them were, and finding just one of the Cyn willing to eat the pulse around, say, a Barious factory would mean the reversal of the slow-motion extinction of the synthetic race, an extinction the Justified had unwittingly set in motion when they'd detonated the pulse bomb in the first place.

That was why the Preacher was with us, at least. "The Cyn you met on Sho's homeworld—he worked alone," she mused, leaning back against the wall, her metallic exoskeleton gleaming in the overhead lights. "Yet these Bright Wanderers seem to worship his kind as some sort of . . . saints, or demigods, as avatars of some greater force."

"So did the Cyn we met on Odessa," Javier reminded her. "Kept going on about a 'goddess.'"

"Which is not a phrase we've heard the Wanderers use, yet," the Preacher pointed out. "These 'Wanderers' worship the Cyn; the Cyn worshipped something else. I don't know that we can safely assume they're part of the same collective. That doesn't mean"—she held up a palm to forestall Sahluk's objection—"I don't think we should be following the cult; just that we should keep in mind that the maniac who . . . desecrated . . . Odessa Station might not have been in league with these . . . believers." The electronic glow behind her eyes flared a bit at the mention of Odessa, the station where I'd been born, the station where the Preacher had conducted experiments to try and cure her people of the pulse—experiments that had resulted in me, a gifted child exposed to much more powerful doses of radiation than most, and so with much stronger gifts to match.

The Cyn had arrived on Odessa shortly after the Preacher had fled with me in tow; he'd butchered his way through her former colleagues—a massacre she hadn't known about until we'd returned from our confrontation with the Cyn, and told her what had happened just after she'd exiled herself. She couldn't take a Cyn on directly—their ability to manipulate energy meant destroying the fusion core in her chest would be as simple as thought to them—but given the anger that constantly threaded through her voice at the mention of the Cyn, that was probably a good thing . . . for the Cyn, at least.

"In league with him or not, they're still selling snake oil to poor pulsed worlds that don't know any better," Sahluk grunted. He'd been born into the Justified, and spent most of his life on Sanctum—he tended to view pulsed worlds as blighted, benighted war zones, because if he set foot on one, that's likely what it was: somewhere harboring the enemies of the Justified, enemies he'd been sent to root out. As a result, the Bright Wanderers' recruitment spiel—"Join our cult, and we'll deliver you from the pulse forever"—sat especially poorly with him: it seemed like grifters running cons on those who already had nothing left to lose.

As someone who'd grown up on a pulsed world, though, I knew there was always more to lose. "Not if they can deliver," I reminded him. The Cyn could eat pulse radiation—we'd seen one do so, and there was no reason to believe he was some sort of anomaly. They couldn't do it on the scale the Wanderers were promising, but it still wasn't as though the cultists had pulled the idea from thin air.

"You know they can't," JackDoes said to me, his words coming out in a hiss—he didn't mean it as an insult; the way his mouth was shaped just made everything sound that way.

I shrugged. "I know that if somebody landed on my world, offered to get me away from the violence and the pulse both at the same time, I maybe wouldn't look too hard at what sort of conditions were attached. Given that's how I met Jane—and how Sho joined the Justified, as well—I would say it makes a certain amount of sense, people buying into the Wanderers' line."

"All the more reason to stamp it out," Sahluk answered with gravelly surety.

"Not our mission," the Preacher reminded him. "Our mission is the Cyn."

He shifted uncomfortably—his age meant Sahluk had been Justified since before the pulse, back when the Justified stood for something more than "trying to stop the pulse from returning." He still *thought* like what the sect had been back then—peacekeepers, soldiers, police. Jane and Marus and Javier, all of whom had operated outside the limits of Sanctum for most of the past century, had grown accustomed to the notion that the galaxy was a crueler place than that, had the notion that trying to help everyone just got you killed, but that way of thinking was still alien to the Mahren: as far as he was concerned, the Justified did right, and what the Bright Wanderers were doing . . . there were a lot of words for it, but "right" wasn't among them.

"In that case, we're in luck," Marus said, turning away from his own screens to face us. Like every time he looked at me, I felt a twinge of sick guilt at the ruin the Cyn had made of his face: the lunatic had taken his eyes as he screamed, while I was lying on the floor just feet away, helpless to do anything but watch. Marus had been given mechanical implants at Sanctum, of course, but they weren't *him*, stood out from his green face like metal lesions, and they meant he could never descend to a heavily pulsed world again— the rads would melt them right inside his head.

He'd never given me a reason to feel guilty, of course—he'd dealt with the injury with typical Marus stoicism—and now those eyes turned toward his apprentice, who was grinning up at him, revealing teeth just as black as everything else about her, from skin to hair to irises. Marus smiled back, and gave her a nod. "Meridian managed to crack the station's own scan logs," he said, "and reverse engineer the data locks on the radiation telescopes, searching for different patterns than it ordinarily flags. She's reading Cyn energy signatures; the same ones our ships picked up from Odessa. The Bright Wanderers aren't just serving the Cyn—there's one on board their vessel. We've found what we're looking for."

CHAPTER 3

Esa

One of the niftiest inventions of the Golden Age? Entropically null store-rooms, the sort of thing where you could stick, say, noncomplex food-stuffs, seal them up, and have them come out exactly the same several hundred years later. One of the less nifty failures of inventions from the Golden Age? Not building their goddamned service robots to be reprogrammable—or, at least, not by us.

We were on an open-ended mission, which meant "catch as catch can" where supplies went, and Jane was thrifty enough that she wasn't going to overlook the protein-and-carbohydrate nutrients (the sort of stuff Sho called, disparagingly, "food-drink") the observatory's long-dead masters had left behind in their storerooms. We had the Bright Wanderers' vector, and from the information Marus and Meridian had turned up, it looked like it was their final destination: apparently they'd been using the observatory as a kind of stopover point from their various "recruitment drives" before heading to . . . wherever the hell cultists who worshipped insane Cyn laid their heads.

There wasn't anything to glean about the cultists themselves onboard the observatory—they'd left surprisingly little sign of their passage—but there was the station itself to ransack. We were in no real hurry—in fact, a bit of a wait was probably advisable, to let our quarry think their trap had killed us off—which meant Jane had decided it was time to raid the observatory's storerooms.

Which meant Sho, Meridian, and I got to engage in good old-fashioned manual labor, all because we couldn't figure out how to reprogram the god-damned machines that had been built to do exactly this sort of thing.

"Why . . . why isn't Sahluk helping with this, again?" Meridian panted. Avail didn't so much "sweat" as they did "mist"—they'd evolved in caverns, deep underground, and I think it had something to do with cooling the air around them actually being more useful than cooling their skin—and she was barely visible in a cloud of not unpleasantly citrus-scented fog as she leaned on a dolly stacked high with the heavy crates of foodstuffs. "He could lift these . . . could lift these . . . one-handed."

"Javier says manual labor builds character," Sho grunted, wrestling his own crates onto a similar dolly. The damned things didn't even have wheels— they fit into special grooves in the floor instead. I was pretty sure the Golden Age had come about long after the invention of the goddamned wheel, so I didn't know what the hell the grooves were about. "Javier lies."

"You three are . . . junior, yes?" JackDoes was watching, an amused flair to his nostrils. Watching—not helping. "Apprentices. Rookies. You are . . . paying your dues. The engineers at Sanctum would do much the same thing; give hard-cold work to the newly assigned. I remember when I was new to the operative maintenance pool—I was made to clean the inside of Scheherazade's engines. Blindfolded. While her sensors were active."

"That doesn't sound . . . so bad," Meridian said, finally getting her dolly into position; I started pulling my own load along the grooves, heading toward the docking bay.

"That's because you haven't spent much time onboard Scheherazade," Sho replied dryly, the servos in his exobraces whirring as he began to pull as well, the motors in his prosthetics coming alive to cope with the excess load. "Schaz can be . . . vocal . . . about her maintenance."

"Hey," I objected, in defense of Jane's ship. "Schaz is just . . . particular. 'Fastidious,' like."

"Obsessive," JackDoes corrected, following along behind us.

"Do *you* want to help?" I growled at him.

"Not really, no. I came along to fix engines. This is not a 'fix engines' problem."

"Esa came along to shoot at stuff, and break things with her mind," Meridian pointed out. "This isn't a *that* problem, either."

I felt like I should object to that, too—was that really what she thought Jane and I did?—but given the amount of time I *did* spend shooting at things and breaking others with my mind, I didn't have a great deal of ground to stand on.

"But I am *not* junior," JackDoes cackled. "I am not a rookie. So I do not *have* to do heavy lifting."

"Esa . . . can't you just . . ." Meridian managed to free one hand from her dolly, and made a sort of swooping motion toward Scheherazade, whose cargo bay doors were already lowered as we approached the bay.

"A little mental shove would make things easier," Sho agreed through gritted fangs.

"No shoving!" Schaz said through our comms, sounding horrified at the thought. Even under ordinary circumstances, Jane's ship had a sort of maternal bent to her voice, but at that moment, she sounded *exactly* like a terrified mother, one who had just found her offspring planning something incredibly dangerous and set on making her objections . . . stunningly clear. "The *last* time Esa tried to push something heavy across my interior—"

"Yeah, my fine control with my teke isn't . . . perfect," I admitted, wanting to cut her off as much as anything else—Sho and Meridian didn't particularly need to hear that specific story. Especially not the way Schaz told it, where I almost cracked the containment wall between the living quarters and her fusion core and risked melting Jane and myself into pools of radioactive soup. "If you wanted these crates sent all the way through one of the bulkheads, I could do that—but setting them down . . . gently"—I grunted again, struggling to do the same thing with the dolly using just muscles rather than teke—"is still a little bit beyond my capabilities."

"It's all right, Esa," Meridian grinned at me, reaching out to touch my elbow; she started to glow, just a bit, as she did. Another one of the Avail genetic curiosities, left over from their subterranean evolution: when they felt "safe"—which often translated to "happy" or "content," in a non-hand-to-mouth existence—they tended to give off a pale luminosity, meant to alert other Avail that a particular cavern was someplace to try and reach. Unlike Sho and me, Meridian hadn't grown up on a heavily pulsed world—hers had been pulsed, yeah, but only to just pre-spaceflight—so she was less used to this kind of labor than we were, but she'd set her shoulder to the dolly just the same, and here she was, glowing at me, actually enjoying the work.

It took a certain kind of someone to become a Justified operative, especially when they came from the ranks of the "next generation," like us; the gifts all three of us had been born with came from the pulse, but the decision to leave the safety of Sanctum, to put our talents to actual use, trying to better not just the Justified's home system, but the worlds beyond as well? That was a decision all three of us had made, and I don't think any of us regretted it.

Even when Jane made us do manual labor while she snuck off to have a cigarette or engage in carnal stress relief with Javier, or whatever it was she was doing that wasn't *lifting crates*.

"That is not the only reason they make you—the three of you, the young ones—do the hard work," JackDoes added, almost as an afterthought. "You are the 'next generation,' after all, in more ways than one. When I was sent into Scheherazade's engines, blindfolded, to be berated—"

"I did no such thing," Schaz objected, but I think even to her it sounded half-hearted, and JackDoes ignored her.

"—I was not sent alone, either. Other engineers—also . . . untested—were sent with me. So we would learn to endure together. One day, Marus will retire." He looked at Meridian as he said it, then turned to Sho. "One day, Javier will dock Bolivar for the last time." My turn, next—and he grinned, unexpectedly, his mouthful of needle-sharp fangs open wide as he said, "And one day, Jane Kamali will die in some sort of massive explosion, one woman holding off an army, because that is the only way death will find her."

"She will most certainly *not*." Schaz sounded, if possible, even more scandalized than before, but I just grinned back at the Reint; I knew what he was getting at.

"And one day, Meridian will be Marus," I said, still grinning, but nodding my understanding. I tended to underestimate the little engineer—he was atypical of his kind, more interested in engines than in other sentient beings, but that didn't mean he wasn't paying attention, it seemed. "And Sho will be Javier, and I'll be Jane. And we'll have to work together, like they do. So they put us together now—make us do the scut work—to forge that bond, the same bond they have. So that it'll be there, when we need it."

"And you will need it," JackDoes agreed. "I have patched up . . . much damage, to the ships of the Justified operatives. This is not an easy life you have chosen."

"A fun one, though," Sahluk commented, the big Mahren wandering by and—predictably enough—lifting one of the carts, crates and all, right out of Sho's grasp, swinging the heavily loaded dolly around and setting the whole thing down in Schaz's cargo bay just as easily as I might have moved a chair around. A light chair. "Not a bad find, this," he said, rapping his knuckles against the foodstuffs and purposefully turning the conversation from the rather grim turn it had taken. "Thousand-year-old powder or not, protein is protein."

"Did you have your taste buds burned out on some op or another, Sahluk?" Sho made a face at him. "This stuff is awful."

"I came along to find exciting new things to shoot at, Sho," the Mahren grinned back, giving Meridian's dolly the same treatment as he did. "Maybe even be shot *by* exciting new things, though that part's not—strictly speaking—necessary. Nobody said there'd be gourmet eating along the way."

"Why *did* you come along, really?" Meridian asked him. Maybe it was her training—"spy" and "diplomat" were terms used pretty much interchangeably by the intelligence corp—but she always seemed very interested in the people around her. She wasn't glowing anymore, which probably meant . . . something, but I was too worn by all the lifting to try and figure out what. "Marus told me that you—both of you"—she nodded at JackDoes—"volunteered for this operation. An open-ended cruise, out past the edges of the Justified maps, well past the point where we can call back to Sanctum for aid, just hoping to find an alien race that's been wiped out of all the records, one that no one had even seen for five hundred years until Esa and Jane, you know . . ."

"Killed one?" Sho suggested brightly, turning toward me. "Still proud of you for that, by the way," he added.

I nodded, though I kept my expression neutral. He might have been; I wasn't. I'd killed the Cyn because he had been a threat, because he had been about to kill me—and, partially, because of what he had done to Marus, to the other gifted children we hadn't been able to rescue, to Sho's mother. But in the end, he had seemed so . . . alone. The Cyn hadn't been the first being I'd killed, but he had been the first one I had *wanted* to, and that need—the cruelty I'd felt in that moment—still kept me up at night, sometimes.

Ultimately, I hadn't pulled the trigger; the Cyn had ended his own life. But I'd put the knife in his heart—I'd forced him into a corner where he felt he had to make that choice.

"It's a lot to take on faith," Meridian said again, still speaking to Sahluk. "That there are other Cyn out here, in the direction the other one came from; that we won't run into something we can't handle."

"We've done all right so far," the Mahren shrugged.

"We've survived so far," JackDoes corrected. "I have patched . . . much damage to the ships. And our medical bays have patched much damage to each of you."

"We've found the Bright Wanderers," Sahluk said. "That's a lead."

"But it's not what I'm asking," Meridian shook her head. "I'm asking why *you* came. Why you volunteered."

"To shoot at things, like I said," Sahluk replied with a laugh—a laugh that sounded like a rockslide, granted, but still a laugh. Maybe not an honest one, though.

"That's the easy answer," she replied calmly, not buying it for a second. "It's not the truth. Or not all of it, at least."

He made a little sound, almost like a snort—but he kept looking at her, reappraising, through his one good eye. The other had been torn out by a devolved Reint during the battle of Sanctum—a reminder that, no matter if he'd spent most of his career with the Justified stationed close to home, he'd still paid his own set of dues for the good of the sect we all belonged to. Unlike Marus, he preferred to wear an eye patch rather than a prosthetic; his HUD could expand the field of view of his remaining optics to compensate during combat, and Sahluk had no interest in looking like anything other than what he was.

"Right," he said finally, the one good eye still fixed on Meridian. "These last six months since we left Sanctum, I keep thinking of you three as kids—mainly because I've known you, the two of you, at least"—he nodded at Meridian and me—"since you both were. But you're not anymore, are you?"

I shrugged; of the three of us, I was the oldest, at eighteen, though Sho's maturity was rapidly approaching my own, since Wulf aged faster than humans. Meridian was only slightly younger, less than a year shy of me—

THE FIRMAMENT OF FLAME ✳ 27

the same age I'd been when I'd faced off against the Cyn in Odessa. I hadn't felt like a "kid" since that day; I don't know that I was fully an "adult," either—I wasn't Jane, not yet, just like Sho wasn't Javier, nor Meridian Marus—but that had also been the day I'd seen the face of my mother, for the first and last time; the day I'd watched the Cyn try to burn my friends alive from the inside out; the day the Cyn had cornered me, alone, and I'd fought the fuck *back*: I hadn't felt young after that. The sort of person who could see—or do—those things: they weren't a "kid" anymore. They just weren't.

So a kid probably would have said something snotty to Sahluk when he said what he did, would have found a way to say something sarcastic, something they thought was witty and impressive and was really just obnoxious. I didn't say anything. I just waited, to see what he'd say next; so did the other two. None of us were as young as we'd once been. Though I guess that was true for everyone—sometimes it just seemed to happen faster than it did ordinarily.

Sahluk noted the lack of response; nodded his approval. He'd been testing us, seeing if we'd snarl and yap—apparently we'd passed. In the corner, JackDoes hissed uncomfortably—Reint were culturally sensitive to conversational silence—but Sahluk ignored him, looked at me instead. Not even at Meridian, who'd asked the question, but at me. "Mo," he said finally. An answer, of a kind.

Mo—Mohammed. Jane's mentor in the Justified. I'd only met him the once—he'd long since exiled himself from our sect, his version of penance for his part in the detonation of the pulse bomb—but he'd . . . made an impression.

And then he'd died, holding back the Cyn that had been trying to get to us.

"You knew him?" I asked, though I didn't need to.

"I did," he nodded. "When I was just a kid . . . he was the Mahren all the rest of us looked up to. An elite; the operative's operative, the best of the best. What we were supposed to be, the same way the Wulf in the Justified look up to Criat, the way the Reint"—he looked over at JackDoes—"do with MelWill."

"Everyone looks up to MelWill," JackDoes said in reply; he wasn't wrong, but I took Sahluk's point. Mohammed had been to him what Jane was to me—something to aspire to. Though you'd never catch me telling her that.

"Mohammed was the ideal of what the Mahren amongst the Justified could be," Sahluk continued, a slight dip to his rocky head punctuating the words. "Strong, smart—ruthless, when he had to be—but decent, too. There's a part of me, I guess, that's still trying to be him. Even after he left the way he did. And when I heard one of your bogeymen took him down . . ."

"Not revenge," Meridian said quietly, watching his face. "That's not what you're looking for."

"No," he replied, sounding surprised she'd even suggest it. "That Cyn's gone, and even if he wasn't—revenge isn't the Justified way."

"You just want to fight the same battle he did." It was JackDoes who said it this time, his forked tongue testing the air as he spoke. "To fight his . . . war. His last war."

"To fight it? No. To win it?" Sahluk grinned. "Yeah. I'd take that."

A hint of music drifted through the air, manifesting from nowhere—a Mahren vocal piece, a warrior's dirge, the sort of thing composed on their homeworld back when the height of martial technology had been "a sledge-hammer." We all looked at Meridian, Sahluk raising an eyebrow, and she ducked her head, nervously brushing her jet-black hair back behind her pointed ear. "Sorry," she apologized with a murmur. "Slipped."

Meridian's "gift"—her next-generation answer to my telekinesis and Sho's ability to control the flow of energy—was a sort of highly specific telepathic empathy: she could "read" a person's emotional state, and manifest that same state as music. Not very useful in combat, but all sorts of useful for a spy—one of the reasons, I'm sure, she'd been sent to Marus for her apprenticeship when her training at Sanctum was done. She'd been accidentally "reading" Sahluk, translating his emotional state—his admiration for Mo, for the Mahren virtues he'd exemplified, regardless of his human faith—into a complemen-tary piece of music. It was something she had to work *not* to do, just . . . a part of her, like breathing, ever since her gifts had manifested at puberty.

"Looks like Esa's not the only one who needs to work on her fine con-trol," Sho said mildly.

She stuck her tongue out at him; he crossed his golden eyes in response, and she laughed, glowing a little bit again. So much for maturity, I suppose.

CHAPTER 4
Jane

I sat in Scheherazade's cockpit and watched the stars stream by; we'd left Raizencourt Observatory well behind us, with a firm lead on the Cyn—our first in months—ahead, in the form of the Bright Wanderers. Our supplies had been restocked, we'd stripped the observatory of as much mapping data as we could manage, and, hopefully, those very same cultists thought we were dead, taken out by the trap they'd left behind. I should have been happy, or as close as I got to it; Esa was pleased as anything, talking animatedly to Schaz back in the living quarters. I should have felt the same. I was brooding instead.

Oh, if Esa had asked, that wouldn't have been what I would have called it. I would have told her I was thinking about tactics, planning our next move or something similar—strategizing how to take down the next Cyn we encountered. We'd learned a great deal from the fight on Odessa Station, theoretically enough to, if not level the playing field between us and the Cyn, at least make it slightly less tilted, but "theoretically" was different from practical application; until the metal met the . . . whatever the hell it was inside the Cyn's armor, we wouldn't know for sure.

Still, that wasn't what I was doing: thinking about tactics, I mean. I was most definitely brooding. Cultists. Fucking cultists. Some of the others—Marus, especially, despite what the Cyn had done to his eyes—still hoped for a peaceful resolution to all this; hoped that we'd find some Cyn who just hadn't known about the pulse, who would happily return to one of the Barious factory worlds with us, reverse the unintentional genocide we'd set into motion. I knew better. You didn't send your . . . minions . . . out to seduce people with hope for a better world, with a promise held out before them that you couldn't deliver, not unless you needed them willing to die for you.

I should know. Once upon a time, I'd been one of those minions. The "sects" in the sect wars had been a great many things—governments, ideologies, species-purity obsessives—but most of them had been focused on belief, in one form or another: the sect I'd grown up in had been no different. "Do what you're told, and salvation awaits." Therefore any enemy that stood between you and that salvation was subhuman, evil, unworthy of the mercy you'd been promised awaited in the next life, a mercy you'd rush toward with open arms—and a bomb strapped to your chest, if necessary. I'd never bought into it; not really. But I'd seen the toll it could take, and I'd still hated the enemy on the other side of my gun, because they'd *put* themselves there, and I'd needed something to hate.

That was what we were going to find, wherever these "Bright Wanderers" were headed, and I'd known it, ever since the first Cyn we'd encountered had started going on about "goddesses" and "destiny." Regardless of the hope they might offer the Barious, these Cyn—and the cultists they controlled—represented a clear and present danger to the Justified, to the universe at large, even if they themselves didn't know it yet. It was the same reasoning that had led Mo to pluck me out of my own sect, to turn me against my people before they even knew they were on the Justified's radar, and it had been sound reasoning then, just like it was now.

Take out the threat before it even knows it's a threat. Neutralize; contain; eradicate, if necessary. For the greater good.

The Bright Wanderers were expanding their reach across the galaxy—I knew that, from every rumor and story we'd heard about them on worlds off the edges of our maps. Our trek had taken us into the uncharted space where the Cyn's ship had come from, seventeen years ago, before he'd hit Odessa Station. All we'd had to go on when we started this mission were the data recorders we'd salvaged from his ship, but those rumors, those stories, they all confirmed the same fears: the cult was growing more powerful, growing hungrier, and using the devastating combat abilities of the Cyn as the stick to match the carrot that was their "salvation from the pulse" pablum. Sooner or later, that hunger would curl around Sanctum, where they'd expect us to bow to their goddess as well, or face annihilation.

The Justified didn't bow. Never had. Never would.

So: what would we find, when we reached the end of the line, the place where the Wanderers took their new recruits? I wasn't sure what form it would take, but I knew what it would be: trouble, and ours to deal with. Same as it ever was.

When I finally stopped brooding and stepped back into the living quarters, I found Esa, and as it turned out, she knew all that too. She'd been talking to Schaz, yeah, as I'd sat in the cockpit, and she'd been excited while she did it, looking forward to the next step.

But she'd also been cleaning her gun.

Good girl.

"You think there's going to be a fight," she said, feeling me enter the room but not looking up from the pieces of her weapon, just as studious at this task as she was with every other. "You *always* think there's going to be a fight, but this is . . . different."

I nodded, stepping past her to the armory in the airlock, so I could retrieve one of the spare energy rifles there. "I think, best case," I answered her, "we're going to find ourselves storming a compound full of true believers, the sort who will throw themselves in front of a bullet just for a chance to please those that said such an act was the shortest distance between them and salvation." I put the gun on the table beside her own and started stripping out the housing, taking a seat beside my younger partner as I did.

"And worst case?" she asked, still hard at work.

"You heard Meridian; their scans said there was a Cyn on board."

"And that's why you're rewiring the energy rifle." She'd noticed which weapon I was working on, despite the fact that she hadn't looked up. "Even though you hate energy rifles."

I smiled at that; she wasn't wrong. The fancy, cutting-edge tech that made the weapons work also meant they were useless on nearly every pulsed world, and given that the vagaries of distance, friction, and atmospheric conditions meant you never knew how *much* each shot would drain the battery, they always seemed to crap out on me about three seconds before I thought they would, even when I did manage to take one into combat in an atmosphere that wouldn't chew through it immediately. Still, the rifles were our best chance if we came up against another Cyn; Esa had been the one to discover that the energy matrix that made up the bodies of the forgotten species vibrated at a certain frequency, and if we rewired the rifles to match, it should burn right the hell through them.

"I know you don't want to hear it, Jane," she said slowly—choosing her words with care, like she'd been thinking about this for a while—"but if we *do* come up on another one of . . . them . . . you need to let me take the lead. I'm . . . built . . . for fighting them. You're not."

"If we *do* come up against another one of them, I'm going to fire this laser directly at their flaming head from the absolute limit of accurate distance," I said, still not looking up from the rifle. "The Preacher and Marus still want to capture one alive, but we're not going to be able to do so; not if they're all like . . . him." True believers; zealots. "So we put them down, and we learn what we can from what they leave behind."

"Fair enough, but if it gets closer than that—you let me take the lead. You tried to fight him, on Odessa. You lost." I'd lost because I couldn't *hit* the bastard. With her ability to channel energy through her telekinesis, Esa could, which was the point she was trying to not-so-delicately make. What she didn't get was that, no matter how much she'd grown, I would always be her mentor, her trainer, the closest thing she had to a parent; she would always be my student, my ward, my daughter. I was never going to do anything but put myself between her and those who would do her harm; that was just the way things were.

Still, I'd trained her well, and her victory on Odessa had given her confidence, if nothing else; between that and the improvements to her intention shielding she'd had built in during our debriefing on Sanctum—an improved battery pack, wired into her spine, one that not only strengthened her shields but also allowed her to channel more energy through the energy matrix with her teke—I had no doubt she *could* take on another Cyn, provided that new enemy was the equal of the last.

What we didn't know was if that part would be true. Another Cyn—the one in charge of these Bright Wanderers, perhaps, the same one Meridian had read on the scans of the cultists' vessel—might make the last one we'd met seem a tame puppy in comparison. And if she went into a fight forgetting *that*, she'd lose, and lose badly.

So I said nothing; just kept working on the rifle. After a moment, she shook her head and went back to the submachine gun; if nothing else, the nearly four years we'd spent together meant we were both good enough at reading the other's moods to know when continuing an argument would simply be a lost cause.

That was when the destination alarms started going off: we were approaching the end of our hyperspace route.

We both snapped our weapons back together; I wiped my hands off, then tossed Esa the rag to do the same. As she finished up, I made my way back to the cockpit, sliding in behind the stick. She followed me shortly and took up her position at the gunnery chair, both of us waiting to see where the Bright Wanderers had been running to.

Before us, the stars were still flowing like liquid past the viewscreen; even after nearly two centuries of life, I still half expected them to actually splash across the reinforced glass of the cockpit canopy, like waves might breech over a submersible when it broke free of the surface of an ocean. It was still a beautiful sight, no matter what horrors awaited us once I pulled us out of the flow of the stars. I reached for the lever to pull us out of hyperspace, taking a deep breath before I did: we had no idea what we were about to emerge into.

"Do it," Esa said, a note of quiet assurance in her voice, one that I felt a not-so-small sense of pride in having helped instill there.

"Get ready to throw on every stealth system we've got, Schaz," I said; we didn't know what, exactly, was waiting for us, but even if it was just the recruit transport, sitting on a barren moon somewhere, they'd notice another vessel emerging from hyperspace: they'd left the trap behind in the observatory for a reason, after all. We needed to disappear the instant we hit real space, and hope nobody was looking real hard in the few moments it would take for the stealth systems to come online.

"Roger," Schaz agreed.

I cut the hyperspace engine and pulled us out of the current of the stars.

There had only been one system on the observatory's maps that matched the precise vector of the recruiters' exit from the otherwise empty Raizencourt system; the Wanderers' only possible destination had been a backwater during the Golden Age, notable only for its relatively rare trio of stars, all in tight orbit around each other. As far as actual planets went, there were only a handful of gas giants—any terrestrial worlds had likely long since been eaten by one star or another, or even the giants themselves.

Most of the planets had a few rocky moons, all of which had been in the very early stages of terraforming at the time the observatory had taken its scans. That information was centuries and centuries out of date, though, which meant we had no idea what to expect as the liquid stars dropped away—

—and despite that, I was *still* shocked at what I saw.

We'd emerged from hyperspace close to the largest gas giant in the system, a golden-hued beauty with lavender storms swirling through the heights of its atmosphere. That much hadn't changed from the observatory's data, but its two moons were both unrecognizable—one of them was now surrounded by a massive web of arches and cables, the sort of metal scaffolding used for building enormous structures in zero gravity, and the other just wasn't *there* anymore, not as a planetoid, at least: it had been cracked open entirely, the remains held in place by lines of magnetic force as mining ships blasted rare metals out of what remained of its core.

Zero-gravity construction and obliteration-level mining operations: together, they added up to exactly one thing, a sight I hadn't come across since well before the pulse, when the sect I had been born into had finally taken our war off-planet to strike at the heart of our enemies' strength. It was a *shipyard*, a military shipyard, and on a massive scale. These Bright Wanderers weren't recruiting followers so they could bring them back to some sort of agricultural commune, or even to become soldiers, trained to carry their fight across the continents of whatever planet they called a home—they were recruiting slaves, laborers, a workforce for the yards whose scope had only one possible explanation.

Building starfighters didn't take obliteration mining; zero-g scaffolding wasn't required to make hyperspace-capable craft like Schaz, or even large-haul cargo freighters. Not even military frigates required that combination of resources and effort. The Bright Wanderers weren't just making themselves a fleet, one to replace aging craft that had sailed the stars ever since the pulse: they were building dreadnaughts. Superbehemoths, crewed by thousands. The kind of ship that only had one conceivable purpose—war.

War, or annihilation.

CHAPTER 5

Jane

Well," Esa said, swallowing, as she stared out the cockpit with me. "That's . . . yeah."

It was, granted, one hell of a sight—an entire system converted into industrial purpose. I'd seen its like before, though not in a century; she hadn't.

"Yeah," I agreed, taking the stick and bringing us into a slow curve toward one of the more distant planets in the system—another gas giant, much smaller, this one with no moons at all, possibly because its orbit passed within a few thousand miles of one of the much larger celestial spheres once every decade or so. Schaz shuddered a little with atmospheric chop as I dove into the crimson-hued atmosphere, passing through clouds that looked like nothing so much as ruffled velvet; a warning light popped up on the console as one of our sister ships came out of hyperspace as well—Khaliphon.

"Transmit our location to Marus," I told Esa, still holding Schaz steady against the turbulent pressure of the gas giant. Luckily, gas giants were significantly less likely than terrestrial worlds to have picked up anything but the lightest traces of pulse radiation, and Schaz could hide out among those strangely dense maroon-tinged clouds for as long as we had fuel to keep her airborne, which would be for quite a while, given the low gravity this high up.

Khaliphon didn't have nearly as good a stealth suite as Schaz did—though still better than Bolivar or Shell—but he had enough of one that, even if the Bright Wanderers came to investigate anomalous pings on the edges of their system, they likely wouldn't find anything. We'd have to hide out for a while in the atmosphere of the smaller giant, but that was fine by me; I needed time to digest exactly what in the hell we were looking at anyway.

It wasn't just the shipyards, or the dreadnaughts themselves that were bothering me—though they bothered me plenty—it was the design of the things, the sweep of the half-built hulls we'd seen tethered to the scaffolding, nearly half a dozen, at my count: familiar, all of them, in a way I couldn't quite put my finger on.

"Something . . . Go back," Esa said. She wasn't talking to me—which was good, because I had no intention of bringing us out of this atmosphere with the Bright Wanderers still investigating the possibility that we'd survived their trap—but to Schaz instead, sweeping her finger across the datascreen on her console. "There." She looked up at me. "They're not just building ships, Jane. There's something inside the giant itself, down in the atmosphere, some sort of . . . I don't know." She slid her hand toward me, "throwing" the image over to the helm console; I settled us into a flight pattern and let Schaz take control, examining Esa's findings myself.

Barely visible, climbing through the golden clouds and lavender storms of the planet, there were towers, jutting like spikes from the aureate glow; actual buildings, rising up from the dense fog of the world. The only reason I knew of to build structures in the atmosphere of a gas giant was if you wanted to harvest rare gases, and nothing in the composition of the world implied anything worth harvesting—in fact, it was mostly oxygen, more or less breathable to most of the sentient species.

"Some kind of . . . training facility, maybe?" I asked, though "training" wasn't the first word that had come to mind: that would have been "indoctrination," like the reeducation camps I'd spent most of my childhood doing everything in my power *not* to be sentenced to, a fate worse even than the war-choked fronts where I'd grown up.

"Don't see why they'd need buildings in the planet's atmosphere for that—it could be done just as easily in the living quarters on the construction sites," she replied, sounding almost distracted, still studying the scan. "Maybe even easier; no horizon, total control of the environment; complete reliance on the station AI for anything and everything." So Esa *had* realized the likelihood of what would be happening to the "recruits" the Bright Wanderers ferried off the pulsed worlds like the one where we'd picked up their trail, worlds so much like hers. She didn't sound happy about it, either.

"I'm counting five hulls, under construction," Marus said, his voice coming in over our encrypted frequencies, as Khaliphon fell into place behind Schaz. "Ranging from 'almost complete' to 'superstructure still being lashed together.' Based on the differential between the five craft—Jane, they could be a completing three dreadnaughts a year with this operation. Maybe even faster."

"Which begs the question: where are the completed craft?" Javier asked; Bolivar had arrived as well, and was diving for the crimson world. "The odds that we showed up just before their very first monster took its maiden voyage . . . well, I wouldn't take them against a hot meal."

I considered the question as I kept an eye on our scanners: there was indeed a flight of patrol craft, heading out from the shipyards to investigate the interspatial disturbances left behind as our ships emerged from hyperspace. It would be a race to see who would arrive at the vector first: the Preacher, with Shell, the former Pax vessel she'd ripped the AI out of so she could run it herself, or the cultists. I started plotting a course to reach her, just in case— though starting a firefight here, where there were almost certainly larger craft in the shipyards themselves, frigates or carriers that could pound us to dust, would not be my first choice of strategy—but Shell came through with more than enough time to spare; I bounced the Preacher our location and she dove for the red-tinged atmosphere of our distant world, slipping into the velveteen clouds well before she came into range of the patrol crafts' scanners.

"Based on the material missing from the mass of the cracked-open moon, it's possible they've built dozens of dreadnaughts already," the Preacher added her own observations to the conversation; despite the fact that she'd just arrived, she'd guessed at exactly what we'd be discussing, and she was right, though it was still a very Barious thing to do. "And also, the design of the things: they *are* Atellier-designed *Nemesis* class vessels, correct? Does that strike anyone else as one enormous coincidence?"

That's where I'd recognized those lines from—I hadn't recognized the superstructures themselves since they were still under construction, but once the Preacher said it, I could absolutely see it in my mind's eye, a "completed" version of a *Nemesis* laid over the bones of the still-being-laid hulls. "No coincidence at all," Marus said grimly. "One of the lingering questions of the Pax invasion has always been where they got their fleet. I think we've just found our answer."

"But . . . that makes no sense." Esa was shaking her head. "The Pax were—
in their own way—just as zealous as these Bright Wanderers, just as rigid in
their beliefs. Why would a cult claiming they can banish the pulse give dreadnaughts to a society obsessed with *strength*, one that saw the pulse as their
deliverance?"

"Cash money's always a good bet," Javier replied, his voice dry.

"The Pax would have had to sell most of their worlds' populations to the
Wanderers to even afford half the dreadnaughts they flew against Sanctum,"
Marus said in response. "No—Esa's right. They were . . . a gift. It's possible,
perhaps even likely, that the Pax themselves had no idea of the original origin of their crafts. 'Don't ask the trajectory of a free supply drop' and all that."

"Besides, the Pax were egomaniacal enough to assume they just deserved
to discover a dozen dreadnaughts, all in perfect working condition," the
Preacher agreed. "But the question remains: why would the *Wanderers* want
to arm the *Pax*?"

I was only half listening to the discussion; the other half of my attention
was still riveted to my screens, where the patrol craft were investigating the
rough area of the void where we'd slipped out of hyperspace. They'd branched
out into a search pattern, overlapping their scans. Depending on what kind
of gear they were equipped with, Schaz's own flight path would almost
certainly go undetected, but some of the others might not be so lucky.

"Us," Sahluk replied, something grim in his tone. "That's the common
denominator; the Justified. The Pax hit us, and the Cyn from Kandriad was
seeking out gifted, just like we do. We're the competition. The Wanderers
gave the Pax the vessels because they knew, somehow, the Pax were about to
come into conflict with us—hell, they may have been the ones to tip them
in our direction in the first place. The Cyn you fought; he made clear inti-
mations that he knew about the role the Justified played in the origins of the
pulse. Arming the Pax might have been an attempt to take us off the board,
to stop us from sweeping up gifted kids before they could get to them—"

"Or, at the very least, to tie up our attention with rebuilding and recon-
struction." Marus was nodding; I could tell by the tone in his voice. "Leaving us unlikely to realize what they were up to until it was too late."

"Which it may well be already," Javier said again. "If they could afford to just give the Pax—what, a half dozen dreadnaughts? More? At least some of the supercraft the Pax flew against Sanctum would have been owned by them originally, but still—if the Bright Wanderers have enough craft they could afford to just hand that many over: how many do they have total?"

"And why does *no one else* seem to know about it?" Esa asked. On the screen, the patrol craft were disengaging, though two had been left behind, on-station, to observe, and I let myself relax, just a bit—that was probably the best we could have hoped for. "We're off the Justified maps, yeah—"

"Pretty damn far off," Sahluk agreed.

"But it's not like there aren't any sects out here; there are power struggles, worlds only lightly pulsed that can still trade, still send ships out to the stars. It seems impossible that no one would have, you know, noticed a cult growing this . . . this . . ." She stopped, momentarily at a loss for words—a rarity for Esa.

"Goddamned terrifying?" Javier guessed.

"Relentlessly industrial?" JackDoes put in, from the bridge on Khaliphon.

"Aggressively evangelical?" I could hear the ghost of a smile in the Preacher's voice, as even she chimed in on the joke.

"Point is," Esa continued with some asperity—I don't think she had any idea how much she sounded exactly like me in that moment, the same tone in her voice that *I* took when she and Schaz thought they were being clever— "the worlds we visited, where we heard about the Wanderers—even the ones where they'd been recruiting—all of them said that their interest was in *people*, converts. Not industrial materials, not— They thought of the recruiters as a curiosity; a nuisance, at most. Not as an army." And that was exactly what we were looking at: an army. An army that could have just taken, at gunpoint, whatever or whomever they wanted. So why the charade of the poor religion with good intentions; why do their recruiting in knock-about cargo ships like the ancient hulk we'd been pursuing?

For the same reason they'd armed the Pax indirectly, rather than coming at the Justified themselves: because they didn't want to tip their hand to the rest of the galaxy. Because they were playing a much, *much* longer game.

Which meant they were after a much *greater* prize.

CHAPTER 6
Jane

I leaned back in my chair, relaxing a bit now that the patrol craft hadn't blown our location; hopefully, they thought it was just a false positive, and four "arrivals" in-system in a row with nothing to show for it was more likely to read as a software glitch than anything else. Even with the trap they'd set for us, we'd been careful to stagger our arrivals into other systems when we were on their trail—what Esa called my "relentless paranoia" paying dividends again—so they didn't know how many of us there were.

"So," I said, trying to put the pieces together in my mind—"working the problem," Mo used to call it—"they build the dreadnaughts here, and probably also make this the first step in their indoctrination efforts: brainwash the new recruits on-site, where there's only hard labor and no chance of escape for those who get cold feet. Then, they send those who—they probably have some bullshit term for it, 'ascend' or something like that, but what it *really* means is 'won't question orders'—they send those recruits, along with the completed dreadnaughts, to a second location, their staging ground, wherever that is. Those who don't make the cut never see different suns than these; they get to spend the rest of their lives here, building weapons of war."

"Meaning this isn't actually their . . . home, their origin," Sahluk followed along. "We haven't found the heart, is what you're saying—just the fist."

"More like 'the spleen,' biologically speaking," JackDoes hissed. "The 'fist' would be wherever the dreadnaughts are going."

"The big question remains," Marus said, "how does all this tie in to the Cyn, and their hunt for the gifted? If the Bright Wanderers can actually deliver on what they're promising—a galaxy free of the pulse—why are they preparing for war? Most of the still-functioning governments out there would surrender unconditionally to an outside force that could lift the pulse from their atmosphere."

"Even my world would have done so," Meridian agreed, sounding just a little hesitant to be chiming in on the comms. "And we were less affected than most. Still, a return to the Golden Age, offered in an instant. Marus is right—they wouldn't need warships. So why . . ."

"Because it's bullshit," the Preacher said flatly; of course that was her opinion. If what the Bright Wanderers were offering was true, that would mean they could revitalize the Barious factories on Requiem and elsewhere in a heartbeat—bring the Preacher's race back from the brink of extinction. There were only two ways for a person to react to someone offering them a miracle: to weep and assume it was divine intervention, or to flatly deny even the possibility of the act, to look for the sharp blade hidden in the offering palm. The Preacher had very much taken the second assumption, ever since the first Cyn had shown up, because the only other possibility was that the race of glowing beings *could* have stepped in, at any time, to prevent the Barious's slow-motion erasure, and had not.

"And what they'd be offering wouldn't be a return to the Golden Age anyway," I reminded them all. "That era fell apart centuries before the pulse, remember? And maybe that's what they're preparing for: not a return to the peace and prosperity they're promising—even if they could deliver it—but what would actually happen instead."

"The return of the sect wars." Marus took a deep breath; I could hear it over the comm. "A return to all of that." All the indiscriminate killing, all the hate, all the pain; entire worlds, lost in an instant. Say what you like about the pulse the Justified had—inadvertently—released onto the galaxy; it had at least slowed the pace of violent death that had been omnipresent across the galaxy before we—I—had triggered the bomb.

"And every world would be like my home," Sho said softly. Kandriad, Sho's home planet, had never learned of the end of the sect wars, had been locked in sectarian conflict for generations, as the rest of the galaxy moved on.

"Worse," I told him. "At least on Kandriad, the weapons were determined by the pulse. Your people never had access to orbital laser platforms, or black-hole missiles, or core-melting fracture bombs."

"No; just guns, and awful determination," Sho replied. I didn't really have an answer for that; he was right. Hate was hate, regardless of the scale.

"Best way to win a war, though," Sahluk mused; I could hear him rubbing his chin, even through the comm, stone scratching against crystal. "Don't let the other side know they're even at war before it's too late." He was right: if the Bright Wanderers really were planning to bring the sect wars roaring back to life, they'd have . . . distinct advantages, just in being prepared for the return of the bloodshed, when the rest of the galaxy was not.

"We need to know more," Javier said simply. "Out here in unfamiliar territory, we've had few enough chances to broadcast our findings back to Sanctum, and we don't know when the next time we'll happen across a broadcast tower will even be—we need to find out as much as we can before we send the next packet out."

"And your suggestion as to how we would do that?" Marus asked.

"How do you find out anything?" Javier asked, and I could hear the grin in his voice, the grin that meant he was about to do something stupid, but before I could do anything to stop him, he'd answered his own question: "You look." And then he was pulling Bolivar out of our flight pattern, arcing his little ship upward through the crimson atmosphere.

"Get *back* here," I hissed at him, with no results. If he'd been standing right beside me, I would have grabbed for his arm, but there was nothing I could do—short of having Schaz shoot his ship out of the sky, which would draw just as much attention as anything he might be planning—so instead I simply ground my teeth as, *per fucking usual*, Javier acted without thinking of the greater consequences.

"Calm down, Jane," Esa said, and I could hear a smile in her voice, "your sweetie knows what he's doing."

"My *sweetie* is going to get us all *killed*," I hissed back, not bothering to cover the comms channel as I said it. The two patrol ships were still out there, scanning for any sort of movement; Bolivar had the least stealth tech of any of us outside of Shell, and I reached for the control stick, ready to blast the two smaller craft out of the sky the instant they locked onto Javier's position—maybe, just *maybe*, if I could take them out quick enough, they wouldn't have time to send a warning to the shipyards: instead, the shipyard control would just know that its two patrol craft had disappeared once they didn't check in, which wasn't much better—

Except Bolivar had barely broken free from the gravity well of the gas giant before Javier brought him around in a tight loop, diving right back into the smooth clouds of velvet, the patrol ships none the wiser. "Relax, sweetheart," he said evenly. "'Var's got the best long-range scanners of our little convoy, remember? I just wanted to take a more . . . focused . . . look at the network data surrounding the yards. We need information, and the network's where the information lives."

Relax? *Relax?* I'd give him "relax"—I'd give him—

"What's the setup?" the Preacher asked calmly, as if he *hadn't* just risked giving away our position entirely, and bringing down the wrath of god knows how many vessels on our heads.

"Not great," he admitted, dropping back into position and sharing out the data with the rest of us. "Each of the dreadnaught superstructures is tied in to a single network hub down in the planetary atmosphere—that's probably what those towers Esa picked up are for—but the network itself is locked down, tight. Feel free to prove me wrong," he added hopefully, "given that I'm not the most tech-savvy member of this little crew . . ."

"Unbreakable," JackDoes replied succinctly, already studying the new information himself. "Shifting encryption derived from purposefully chaotic algorithms. They must generate a passcode, then share that passcode—likely physically—with the AI on each dreadnaught core before even they can access the larger network. And even if we did—somehow—get access to one of the AI's central controls, a thing that would require us to be physically present on one of the dreadnaughts, they'd simply shift the passcode again, at the network's hub: here." A region of the gas giant's golden surface was highlighted on our maps as JackDoes transmitted the data: one of the spires Esa had seen on our first pass through the system. "The AI we'd accessed would be locked out from that point on."

"And if we accessed the hub directly?" Javier asked him; the whole idea was ludicrous—we had no idea what sort of defenses the Wanderers had in place—but I let it play out, even so. If there was some sort of way to hack into the network hub, we'd have access to the answers to all of our questions: the Cyn's relationship with the Bright Wanderers, the purpose of this armada, maybe even why the Cyn were kidnapping gifted children. The thought of all those answers, hidden on the world below: it was a tantalizing idea, but getting to it would still require us to pull off one hell of a heist, hitting the fortified shipyards and cracking their network open.

"Same problem," JackDoes replied to Javier. "In order to access the network, we'd need access to the hub itself—physical access—as well as a passcode, which we could likely only get from one of the dreadnaughts' AIs. And even if we sent two teams, more or less simultaneously, in the time it would take to hack the AI core of whichever dreadnaught we chose, even if we were physically at that location, that dreadnaught could be cut off from the network by any of the other AIs present on the system."

"So the only way to do it would be to gain access to an AI without taking the time to hack it," Javier mused.

"I'm good, but no one is that good, no matter how weak-willed their . . . machines . . . are." The Preacher had gotten better, but she sometimes still slipped into a certain level of haughtiness when comparing herself and the Barious to other, more recent AIs.

"Maybe not, but what if we accessed one of the dreadnaughts that was *on* the network—but didn't actually have an AI installed yet?" On the screen, a circle appeared around one of the hulls still under construction, Javier indicating what looked like the newest of any of the dreadnaughts. All there was of the craft was a sort of hollow shell, great gaping holes in its superstructure giving away the emptiness inside. "Judging from the network scans, that one's not drawing enough power to even run an AI, and they haven't completed her reactor, either. We could retrieve the password from her computer banks without the effort of cracking open the AI."

"And then what?" I asked, intrigued despite myself—it was still *impossible*, given the level of resistance we'd be likely to meet, but not so impossible it couldn't even theoretically be achieved. And we'd done the impossible before.

"We'd still need a second team, at the hub," he admitted. "Working in concert with the dreadnaught team. One group to secure the password from the dreadnaught hull, and the other to plug that password into the hub at the tower. Then we could lock the rest of the AIs out of the system, and download as much of their data as we had time to. Before they, you know, kill us."

"I can reach the towers without being detected," Schaz said confidently. "I don't know that any of the others could, but *I* can."

"Khaliphon can't reach the network hub, no, but he could at least get an assault team onboard the dreadnaught before he was spotted," Marus said.

"But as soon as he was, wouldn't they just change the password?" Sahluk asked.

"Not if we shut that dreadnaught off from the network completely, which I can do from any terminal on board—assuming their terminals are up and running," the Preacher said. "Alternately, the hub team could do the same— bring the network down, before the dreadnaught team even landed. Granted, the dreadnaught team would still have to deal with any workers and any security on the ship, but the rest of the system wouldn't even know there was a problem. They'd realize the network was down, of course, but that would seem like a software glitch rather than an assault. That sort of scheme wouldn't be possible on a dreadnaught with an AI—even cut off from the network, it could scramble the password on its own recognizance—but if Javier is right that there's *not* an AI installed, then it's . . . doable."

I examined the plan from every angle I could think of. It was *insane*, but "insane" was a definite downgrade from "impossible." The difficulty was that we just didn't know what sort of resistance we'd face, either at the hub or on the dreadnaught: if it was just cultists armed mostly with the machinery they'd be using to work on the superstructure, then it was doable, but if—like every other cult in existence—there were armed guards, unobtrusively watching to make sure their own people stayed in line, the difficulty would skyrocket. And that was only taking the dreadnaught into account: we had no idea what the hub team would encounter.

"Send Sho and me to the hub," Esa said, her voice rising the way it did when she got excited. "That's your best bet. We *know* the other team will hit at least some form of resistance, so you need all the gunhands we can spare—

we don't know that about the hub. It could just be technicians maintaining the equipment—"

"And it could be a small army," I reminded her. "Based down there to handle any insurrections among the new arrivals who maybe decide they don't want to build dreadnaughts for the rest of their natural lives."

"A small army, maybe," Esa shrugged, "but a small army protecting a tower built to generate a massive, planet-wide data network. That sort of network requires *power*, and that much power means they must have a reactor. And where there's a reactor—"

"There's energy for me to draw, and channel to you," Sho said as the realization of Esa's full plan dawned on him. "Esa, that's *brilliant*."

"With access to that much raw energy, they'd *need* a small army to stop us," she said firmly, and I frowned—confidence was one thing, but this was skirting dangerously close to arrogance, and that could get her killed.

"So you and Sho slip into the hub—hopefully unnoticed—and you take the central control room," Javier was summarizing. "Meanwhile, the rest of us hit the dreadnaught, and once we're on board, the Preacher cuts it off from the network. Then, once we've reached the core where the AI *would* be installed once the ship was finished, the Preacher retrieves the password, and broadcasts it to you. One problem."

"Shoot," Esa said.

"I don't mean to be insulting—"

"Neither Sho nor I know the first thing about computers or hacking; we can barely operate the holoprojections on board Scheherazade." She was right—they'd both been raised on deeply pulsed worlds; neither of them had even seen a working computer until they'd joined the Justified. But Esa had seen this coming, which meant she had a plan. "We can't even ask Schaz to do it remotely, because—to stop the other AIs from changing the passcode— we'll have to bring down the network as soon as we reach the hub."

"Correct."

"Which means we'll need to take Meridian with us."

Oh, Marus wasn't going to like that at *all*.

CHAPTER 7

Jane

No," Marus said flatly, his tone brooking no disagreement. "Esa, she is *not* ready for this—"

"Neither was I, when Jane took me off my home; neither was Sho, when we pulled him from his. Like it or not, Marus, combat is part of being Justified—and violence is part of being gifted. There are just too many people in the universe trying to use us for it to be otherwise."

"She's right," Meridian said, the first she'd spoken up. "I knew when I signed on to serve outside Sanctum I'd likely have to fight. I went through the operative training; I know how to handle weaponry, tactics."

"Theoretically," Marus said, his voice almost a growl—more emotion than the Tyll usually showed. "Theoretically, you know all of that."

"When you agreed to take me on—as your apprentice, on this mission—you knew there would be violence. You and the others keep throwing Esa, Sho, and me together so that we can learn to work as a team: this is why. Esa's plan needs each of us to succeed—and the other operation needs the rest of you. I *want* to do this, Marus."

"No," he said again. Then, to Esa: "Take JackDoes."

"We need JackDoes on Scheherazade, writing a virus," I replied instead. Believe it or not, Esa had thought this through, and she was my partner: I could see the same connections she'd already made. "Once he has the passcode data to base it on, we'll need something to introduce into the hub, something that will shut down production here, at least for a little while. Even spiting their production for just a few days could save countless lives."

"Also, JackDoes *really* doesn't know how to fight," the Reint hissed. He wasn't wrong—Reint, the smallest and the lightest of the seventeen species, were in general ill-suited to modern infantry combat. They'd evolved as apex predators on their homeworld, and facing a Reint in hand-to-hand combat was a daunting experience, given the claws and the teeth and the razor-sharp tails, but a melee wasn't a gunfight: very few of our weapons, for example, would fit comfortably in JackDoes's claws—the recoil of even the smallest handgun in my collection would likely put him on his scaly hindquarters.

"I want to do this," Meridian said again to her mentor. "This is the job, Marus; this is why I'm here. I'll be with Esa—I'll be with Sho. They won't let anything happen to me."

Marus sighed, something like regret in the tone of the sound. "They all grow up eventually, Marus," I told him quietly. I remembered the resistance I'd felt, sending Esa into combat on her own for the first time—and she'd done me proud. Meridian would do the same for Marus.

"That doesn't mean they have to grow up into *us*," he replied evenly. "Fine. But Meridian"—he turned to his ward, though we could still hear him over the comms—"if shooting breaks out, you do exactly what Esa and Sho tell you to do; you keep your intention shields raised at all times; you—"

"I *have* studied basic tactics, Marus," she said, the sarcasm in her voice hiding a quiet note of anxiety. "I know how to—"

"No, you don't," Sahluk put in. "But soon enough, you will."

"And don't be afraid to hide *behind* Esa," Marus added.

"Hey," Esa objected mildly.

"What? It's your mission—so I'm holding *you* responsible for bringing her home."

"Plus, you do have the heaviest intention shields of all of us," Sho pointed out reasonably. "And, you know . . . telekinesis."

"Fair enough," Esa sighed. "So. It's Sho, Meridian, and me on Scheherazade, to the hub. The rest of you can cram into Khaliphon: he can get you closer than any of the other ships, maybe even drop you onto the dreadnaught skeleton itself before alarms start going off."

"There is another risk, you know," Javier said quietly. "Just so someone says it: the Bright Wanderers are our best lead on finding the Cyn. Maybe antagonizing them isn't the way to play this."

"You want to play nice with people who abduct and brainwash their re-cruits?" Marus asked him.

"I don't *want* to, no, but I've made deals with the devil before. When it was necessary. Devils—quite often—have more to offer than angels do."

"No," Sahluk rumbled. "No deals. This isn't just about the Cyn any longer. These Bright Wanderers—if they have this many dreadnaughts, if they're building more—they're a threat. And we answer threats."

I agreed with him, wholeheartedly, though that was inevitable: it was what I did, what I'd been trained to do, the same as Sahluk. The job meant eliminating threats against the Justified before they could materialize at our doorstep, hitting them before they could hit us. It was what Mo had been doing when he'd recruited me, and it was what I'd done *with* him, right up until the point where we failed, and the Justified wound up with a weapon of planetary destruction pointed at our home. That was part of the reason I'd volunteered for the pulse-bomb mission in the first place—because it had been my job to prevent that kind of threat from ever reaching the Justified, and I hadn't done it well enough.

The guilt of what had come after—the inexplicable spread of the pulse, the worlds locked away from the galaxy—had driven Mo to the empty spaces of the universe, looking for God; it had driven me to throw myself into new work, the missions to rescue the next generation, so that I could try and put something good back into this universe, rather than constantly taking away from it. But when push came to shove, my answer was always going to be "Hit. Hit first, hit harder, hit them so they can't hit you back." And these Bright Wanderers *were* our enemy. They were a cult with warships: everyone who wouldn't join them would be their foe.

"What would you suggest instead, Javier?" the Preacher asked him. "Do you want to fly Bolivar right into the center of their shipyards, see if you can open a channel to negotiate before they blast you out of the sky? You *saw* those patrol craft they sent to investigate the telltale signs of our exit from hyperspace—they were bristling with guns."

"Well, sure, but would the security craft we'd send, if it seemed like someone had discovered Sanctum, be any different?" He asked the question honestly, rhetorical though it was, and he had a point. "They've made no aggressive moves toward us—"

"The trap, in the observatory," JackDoes reminded him. "They drove the station AI mad, so that it would try to kill us. Us, or anyone who came looking into what they were doing."

"Look—I just want to make sure the question is raised. If the agreement is we should go in hot, we go in hot. I just want to make sure we consider all our options first."

I shook my head. "We've seen this all before, sweetheart," I told him. "The population brainwashed into believing there's only one path to salvation, and that path leads through their enemies; that's no different from the Pax, from any number of doomsday cults you or I have run into on the fringes. It's not all that different from the sect I was raised in, and I still think the Justified made the right call there, as well." Javier and Marus were the only ones who knew what had happened to my homeworld, the aftermath of my recruitment—but the rest knew it hadn't been pretty.

And still: I'd make the same decision again. Every time.

"They're building *weapons*, Javier," Marus said quietly. "Regardless of . . . the Cyn, or the pulse, or their religion, if we don't do anything, those weapons will wind up turned against innocent populations. JackDoes can write a virus that at least delays that, and if we can find out what they want with the gifted, whether their goal truly is to bring the pulse back as the Cyn on Odessa intimated: stopping *that* from happening is worth an ocean of blood, and I think you'd agree with me there."

The world Javier had been raised on—in the absolute chaos that had followed the spread of the pulse—had been a . . . very bleak place, from the stories he'd told me. Of all of us, he might be the most committed to making sure the pulse *never* returned, which was why he was willing to deal with the Wanderers in the first place, a dark means justified by a brutally necessary end. Still, Marus was right: stopping the pulse meant protecting the next generation, the only bulwark we had against its return, and the Wanderers were the enemies of the gifted, in league with the Cyn that were hunting them.

"Okay," Javier said, and I could tell just by the tone of his voice he was spreading his hands in defeat. "I just wanted to make sure we discussed it—now we've discussed it. So let's get the ships linked up, and get everybody on their respective vessels; we've got a dreadnaught to storm. Again." He sighed, this time theatrically. "Why is this *always* your plan, Esa? Every time your back's up against the wall, it's 'Send Javier to storm the dreadnaught.' You—and I mean no offense—"

"Yes, you do," she sighed, but she was grinning as she said it, and he laughed.

"I really don't. I'm just saying: you have the worst plans. The *worst*."

CHAPTER 8

Jane

We linked various airlocks only briefly enough for everyone to shuttle onto their respective assault craft, hauling their combat gear with them—Sahluk took the longest to prepare, even though he wasn't swapping ships, since he had to power up and strap on the armored exosuit he'd lugged all the way from Sanctum. This would be his first chance the entire trip to use the damn thing, since we'd successfully managed to avoid fighting in full-scale *wars* up until this point, and I think he was looking forward to causing some real chaos.

As I entered Khaliphon's airlock from Scheherazade, Javier was sealing the final clamps of the exosuit in place, wrapping Sahluk's already hard skin in even harder metal; I raised an eyebrow at the automatic plasma launcher the big Mahren had rigged to a belt-feeder on the mechanical exoskeleton, a weapon even he wouldn't have been able to lift otherwise.

He grinned when he saw my expression, though it was a little hard to read through all the armor plating now surrounding his face. "What?" he asked. "You afraid I'll melt through the hull of the dreadnaught we don't want them to finish building anyway?"

"Fair point," I shrugged, checking to make sure my own grenades were secure. On the far side of the airlock, back inside Scheherazade, Marus was giving all kinds of advice to Meridian, most of which would likely fly right out of her head as soon as the shooting started; I caught Esa's eye, and grinned. She just grinned back; I'm sure I'd been just as useless the first time I sent her into combat. They were ready for this, all three of the rookie operatives. They had been, for a while—if not when we'd started out six months ago, then during the various scraps and scrapes we'd seen on our journey outward, chasing the trail of the Cyn, and then the Bright Wanderers themselves. Marus just hadn't been forced to realize it yet.

"Stay safe," Esa told me, barely having to raise her voice despite the fact that we were standing in two separate ships.

"You too," I said right back, my grin not dropping a jot. Whatever else I'd taught her, good or bad, she was *talented* at this sort of thing. She knew how to enjoy it, as well. Right or wrong, that was the only way to stay sane doing the kind of work we did.

"Both of you will stay safe, of course," Scheherazade said, as if there were no doubt in her mind that would be the outcome. "And Khaliphon?"

"I know, Scheherazade," Marus's ship replied, his voice carrying the same aristocratic Tyll accent that JackDoes had inflicted on Schaz a while back. "I'll be careful with your captain."

"Actually, I was going to say to make sure she's careful with you. She tends to be rough on the paint job."

Thanks, Schaz.

Then Marus was back across, and we detached. From Khaliphon's cockpit—which would only fit Marus and me, but if something went wrong, I was who he wanted on the guns, so I got the second seat—we watched Schaz disappear into the thick red clouds of the gas giant, her hull shimmering as her stealth systems engaged; I couldn't help but feel like she was sailing through a sea of blood, and I hoped it wasn't an omen.

"Mission timer on," Marus said, all business now that he'd seen his ward off. "We'll give them a seven-minute start; that way they'll reach the atmosphere of the gas giant just about the same time we hit the dreadnaught."

"You up for this, Khaliphon?" I asked Marus's vessel.

"What, sailing into the middle of a cultist shipyard, dropping my entire crew onto the hulk of a half-built dreadnaught, then sailing right back out and trying to lose the inevitable pursuit, all in *this* soup? Sounds like fun." Every time I complained about Schaz's rather dry sense of humor, I remembered what Marus put up with—though it was true what they said, that after sailing long enough, starship AIs took on certain characteristics of their captains.

"I hope you know what you're doing, sending the children off like this," Marus said quietly, checking his gauges one more time, the statement addressed at me.

"They can't stay children forever, Marus," I told him. "They're not even children now, not really. Not after what they've seen. When you met *me*—"

"When I met you, you already had a dozen sectarian campaigns under your belt. Meridian comes from a different world than you did, Jane. A better one."

"And she's willing to fight to protect it. That should make you proud."

"Mostly it just makes me scared."

We waited out the rest of the timer in silence; nothing else I could really say to that.

Finally, it was our turn to engage Khaliphon's stealth systems and lift off from the smaller gas giant's atmosphere—as soon as we were clear, we could see the glint of the distant suns shining against the edges of the metal that wrapped like a web around the sole remaining moon. That wasn't just because the two worlds—including the broken one—were in close orbit: the shipyards truly were massive, maybe even bigger than anything I'd seen during the sect wars.

A question, whining at the back of my mind since we'd first dropped out of hyperspace in this system and seen the cult's hive of military construction: had the Bright Wanderers *found* this place, already built, then abandoned for one reason or another? Or had they actually put the whole thing together, after the pulse? Even with the relatively low amounts of radiation on the two moons—low, but not nonexistent—just finding the components to hang all that scaffolding in high orbit would have been one hell of an undertaking. The Justified couldn't have done it—we'd actually discussed the possibility of building a shipyard in our home system, and decided that the amount of resources it would have taken to do so would have been better spent just flat-out *buying* new craft when we needed them.

"We're on approach," Marus reported through Khaliphon's internal comms, for the benefit of our other passengers back in the hold. "Khaliphon will have to break stealth for us to disembark, so it'll be a zero-g drop, possibly under fire—everybody double-check your mag boots." I'd known that was how we'd have to board the enemy dreadnaught, but just hearing the words made something tighten in my stomach, like someone was wrapping wire around my guts; ever since the sinking of the Ishiguro, I'd *hated* zero-g operations.

"Stealth systems are holding up," I said, ignoring the tension in my abdomen and checking Khaliphon's scans; the two patrol craft were still engaged in their automated circuit, hadn't seen us lift off from the crimson giant.

"I may not be Scheherazade, you know, but we *do* have a pretty decent stealth rig," 'Phon said, a little defensively. I grinned—both Khaliphon and Bolivar had their specialties, but neither of them could hold a candle to Schaz for insertion *or* combat, and she'd never let her counterparts forget it.

"Just get us there in one piece, 'Phon, and I'll tell Schaz she has to play nice for a little while," I told him.

"Will she listen?"

"Probably not, but she'll at least feel guilty after."

Marus laughed at that, and then we were both silent; we were approaching the great lattice of metal, and I didn't want to interrupt his concentration as, with the flick of a switch, the viewscreen filled with thousands of unbroken bright threads, the crescents of light describing parabolic arcs through the void around the shipyards—holoprojections of the various security systems we'd have to slip past, displayed on the window of the cockpit itself. *That* wasn't a module Scheherazade had, and I made a mental note to ask JackDoes if he could copy it from 'Phon's database and install it on my own ship when we had time. Handy thing to have.

With a light hand on the stick, Marus slipped us through the outer defenses; given that no one started shooting at us, I figured we didn't trip any alarms Khaliphon *hadn't* been able to detect, either. "I've got it from here," 'Phon said confidently; Marus just nodded, and we both headed down to the hold to join the others.

Javier and Sahluk were already sealed up in their spacesuits—Sahluk had put his on before he'd even gotten into his exosuit—and the Preacher, of course, didn't need one; Barious could survive in the void indefinitely, or at least until their internal batteries wore down without exposure to the solar radiation and kinetic friction resistance that powered their systems. Without comment, Javier helped me into my own suit, and the Preacher did the same for Marus. "Final approach," Khaliphon said, just as I was checking the hang of my two rifles on my back—yes, I was taking the energy weapon as well. Just in case. We'd read a Cyn signature on the freighter full of recruits, after all: that meant at least one of the energetic beings was somewhere in the shipyard, and with my luck, "somewhere" would turn out to be "right in our path."

I'd lost a fight to a Cyn before; doing so had almost gotten Esa killed. I hated losing, but I hated losing a second time even more. The next time I met a Cyn, I was going to be ready.

The cargo door slid open, and there it was, passing below us like a land-scape: the dreadnaught skeleton, a hulk of elongated metal that looked like someone had carved apart a city and was reassembling it haphazardly in the nothing of the void. Once completed, Nemesis were a streamlined class of vessel, all flowing lines and sweeping curves, but at the moment, there was nothing streamlined about it—the exposed ribs of the framework glowed in the refracted light of plasma torches from the robotics doing automated work, and the outer hull was only half-completed, giving the whole thing a patchy, almost piebald sort of look: in places, we could see all the way to the ship's "ribs," massive girders that made up the endoskeleton of the design.

"That's our best bet," Marus said through the comms, pointing to one of those open patches on the hull. The gap he indicated was just beneath the framework of what would become the ship's conning tower, the half-built spines of their comms array sticking up like the defenses of some Reint-extraction sea creature. Marus was right: the hub of the ship's internal net-work would likely be close to that tower; should have been just three floors below, in fact, unless the Wanderers had changed the specifications of the Atelier design we'd all brushed up on earlier.

Khaliphon soared toward the breach at nearly full speed—stealth tech didn't actually mean "invisible," not entirely, and if one of the workers weld-ing or wiring or doing whatever else inside the exposed hull happened to look up, they'd see the flare of our engines passing overhead, though hope-fully they'd think we were just a new design of patrol craft—and Javier took hold of the descent cable. "I'll set the anchor," he said, and then we were in place: Khaliphon hadn't even completely stopped moving before Javier was diving out into nothing, actually diving headfirst, like he was some ancient mariner hunting for pearls at the bottom of a coral reef, except the sea in that particular metaphor was the cold black of the cosmos, and the reef was one of the most destructive weapons ever built.

God, I *hated* zero-g.

As soon as he hit the superstructure of the dreadnaught—executing a textbook flip before landing just as the artificial gravity generated inside the hulk caught him—he was anchoring the magnetic clamp of the line onto the hull itself; the Preacher followed, gripping the metal cable directly in her steel palms as Sahluk gave her a push to speed her passage, and she went sliding out into the void as well. Then it was my turn, and I took a deep breath inside my helmet—yes, I was aware of the fact that I was already breathing suit air, it wasn't as though I were *actually* diving into a cold and airless sea, but I did it, all the same—and I clamped my harness over the metal wire.

"Watch the landing," Sahluk said as he gripped the back of my suit, preparing to shove me toward our destination as he had the Preacher. "It looks like Javier—"

Then there was the sound of metal whining on metal: we were taking fire, hyper-accelerated small-arms rounds singing up from some security team below to snap off sparks inside Khaliphon's hold, the guards aiming at where we stood on the ramp. I barely had time to get my intention shield up—raised in front of me, where the shots were coming from—before Sahluk was shoving me out along the cable, and I went sailing out into the void.

CHAPTER 9
Esa

Scheherazade guided us through the holes in the shipyards' defenses like the protections weren't even there, somehow finding every single gap and dead zone in their security, even as her own various pieces of stealth kit hummed merrily away, keeping us invisible to more active detection measures. I sat behind the control stick—not that there was much I could do in the cockpit, if things went south; I wasn't the pilot Jane was, and we'd likely be better off with Schaz making flight decisions and me on the guns if it came to trouble—and I just watched as the massive steel dreadnaught hulls passed us by.

Seeing the different ships that came looming out of the void in various stages of completion was like watching the skeletons of some gargantuan cosmic superpredators going through a kind of reverse decay: bones rising from dust in the hulls just beginning to be constructed, then internal systems being filled into the craft further down the line of production before we passed the nearly completed ships where the whole thing was covered in thick alloys and plating, like new skin.

Beyond the craft-in-progress, the gas giant was approaching, and fast: I dialed up Schaz's forward scans to see if I could get a better view of the facility that housed the network hub. As we closed, I could tell there was significantly more to the structure than just the spire I'd seen on our first fly-by: there was a whole web of the things, tall towers interlinked by the curve of long spans, the whole complex—dozens of those spires, all told—floating in the atmosphere of the golden clouds like something out of a fairy tale. Somewhere far below, there must have been one hell of an anti-gravity generator keeping the whole thing airborne—it was too low, and in too much of a relatively fixed position, for its stabilization to be explained by orbit.

Then Schaz hit the atmosphere and we were diving deeper into the aureate gas giant, the lower sections of the tower coming into view. Definitely not a military installation—or even an industrial one, despite the lattice of shipyards that were now stretched above the upper atmosphere like a steel mesh holding down the sky. The design of the tower was too open for that, great archways and windows looking out over balconies and landing platforms exposed to the clouds, and it was also too . . . well, too *pretty*, frankly, something sumptuous and almost indulgent about the structure, all marble cladding and gilded edges that caught the light diffused through the golden clouds just right, making all the walls seem faintly edged in fire.

It reminded me, more than anything, of the ancient, crumbling pleasure houses we'd seen on the Jaliad preserve world, except that, where those had been long neglected—the Jaliad aristocracy having been purged from the galaxy during a brutal coup near the very beginning of the sect wars—these were still maintained. So whatever else these Bright Wanderers were, they had an eye for aesthetics, at least.

Or at least saw the benefit in using those aesthetics to cow their recruits— this place *looked* like a city of the gods, and that would almost certainly have been part of its appeal to the cultists. I needed to keep that at the center of my mind: what these people were doing, what they believed. The promises— the lies—they had told, in order to bring people off of pulsed worlds, to turn them into slaves in all but name.

"We're approaching our destination, Esa," Schaz said, and I nodded, unfolding myself from Jane's chair. The towers were passing by us on the right and left now, stretching to either side like a skyline partially hidden in fog— every time we passed one, another would rise out of the mist ahead of us, shining in the constant dawn brought on by the three suns of the system.

Trusting that Schaz knew, from her scans of the local network, which of the towers held the hub—*I* sure as hell didn't—I retreated to the armory at the rear docking bay, where Sho was finishing up strapping body armor onto Meridian. She looked nervous, and excited, even if she was sweating out citrus-y fog again—body armor was heavy stuff—but that was as it should be, and the hands she had wrapped around a spare shotgun were only barely shaking, which I took as a good sign.

Still, I reached out and gently removed the scattergun from her grasp, placing it back in one of our racks of many, many weapons. "Shotgun's her best bet," Sho said skeptically—I'd bet good money he'd been the one who had suggested it in the first place.

"I know *you're* a fan," I said, looking pointedly at the double-barreled sawed-off he wore on his waist—of the bad habits he'd been picking up from Javier, a love of street cannons was . . . one of them—"but she doesn't know *how* to fire them, and she's not as strong as you. A shotgun'll break her shoulder." I couldn't keep a smile from my face when I said it—Jane had said much the same thing to the Preacher when she'd first met me. "Take this instead." I reached for a submachine gun on the rack, the same basic design as Bitey, without the bells and whistles.

I showed her how to change the fire selector, and how to change out the magazine; she nodded, watching carefully—she'd learned the basics of this sort of thing in training, but each weapon was different. Still, her eyes occasionally darted up to my face, the faint widening of her pupils—even darker than the rest of her eye—the only hint of the nervousness she was carefully trying not to betray. "You've got this," I said, putting a calming hand on her shoulder; she glowed slightly in response. "Just stay behind Sho and me, do what we tell you to do, and you'll be fine. I don't expect you to actually kill anybody today, Meridian; you're here for the network core, and that's all. At most we may need you to lay down some suppressing fire—just shooting in the general direction of the enemy will do the job."

"But if I'm shooting at the enemy, won't they be shooting *back*?" she asked nervously, laying her hand over mine, on her shoulder, even as the momentary glow faded. "Isn't that—isn't that what 'suppressing fire' kind of entails?"

"You've got your intention shield, you've got us—you're good," I told her again, ignoring that—correct—little piece of supposition. "This is what you wanted, remember? Why you came along—a chance to be part of the adventures." I grinned, just a little. "This is how adventures feel."

"I *feel* like puking."

"Sounds about right, yeah."

"We're almost in position, Esa," Schaz warned.

"Got it." I moved to the airlock, taking a deep breath to steady myself.

"Wait, that's it?" Meridian asked, sounding confused. "Don't we need— we're not landing, not setting down, shouldn't we have . . . anti-grav gear, or descent cables, or *parachutes*, at least?"

"You don't need parachutes," I told her, having to raise my voice to be heard as the door began to slide open and the golden atmosphere began to rush in: it tasted . . . strange . . . metallic and almost sweet, like licking burnt sugar from an aluminum plate, but was perfectly breathable otherwise. "You've got me."

I didn't even look as I threw myself out the door. Partially that was bravado for Meridian's sake—the more confident she thought I was, the less afraid she'd be—but mainly it was because this shit was *fun*.

Schaz was hovering about thirty feet up from one of the marble-plated balconies, and there were no sentries in sight; a good sign. As I fell, I pushed *out* with my teke, the downward force "crunching" a bit as it met the marble, then exerting an equal and opposite amount of upward push on my descent, slowing my fall until I touched down with . . . only a *bit* of a stumble.

I did absolutely ruin the fancy floor underneath me, though, cracking the marble apart into splinters that glimmered in the light.

Nobody in view; Schaz had chosen our insertion point well. "Come ahead," I said, touching the comm bud under my jaw as I did so.

"Alreadydidlook*up*!" I whipped my head upward and reached out just in time to grab Sho with my telekinesis, catching him just in time to prevent him from breaking half a dozen bones on landing; he was laughing as he rolled off of the invisible platform I'd "built" beneath him. I bopped him on the side of the head with my knuckles as he came to kneel beside me with his shotgun raised, his tongue hanging out in a Wulf grin; then I looked upward for Meridian, who I could see standing at the edge of Schaz's ramp.

You can do it, girl. Just one step. Just one step into nothing.

And if you *can't*, I'd rather know now, before we actually got into combat. We could figure something else out for the network—if you were going to freeze, freeze *now*. All the training in the world wouldn't stop that from happening if it was going to happen, and it if was—

She didn't freeze.

I slowed her descent much more elegantly than I had Sho's—mainly because I'd had more *warning*—and she set down as gently as a feather, only a slight hesitation as she raised up her own submachine gun (though there was a moment where she got her elbow tangled in the strap). All the same, she was grinning too, a little bit of light shimmering again from her obsidian skin. "That was *fun!*" she said, and I grinned back—I had a feeling we were going to be—

"You! What the hell are—" There was a Bright Wanderer sentry who'd just . . . *wandered* into view on the other side of the archway from the balcony, staring at us with wide, glittering Tyll eyes, probably drawn by the sound of my descent cracking the marble floor apart; for just a moment, we froze, all four of us, and then the sentry was going for her gun and I didn't even think, just grabbed her arm with my teke and *pulled,* and she went flying over the railing, disappearing into the golden glow of the clouds beneath us.

"Now, her?" Sho said to Meridian, stepping to the edge and looking down. "She *definitely* needed a parachute."

CHAPTER 10

Esa

"Y ou just . . . you just murdered that woman," Meridian said, staring with wide eyes toward the balcony where Sho was still looking downward, following the path of the Wanderers' sentry. Meridian wasn't glowing any longer.

"Probably," I agreed. Almost certainly, in fact—even if she hit one of the anti-grav generators buried beneath the cloud cover beneath us, she'd have reached terminal velocity well before then. It was a long way to fall.

"She was reaching for her weapon, Meridian," Sho said as he stepped back from the ledge, apparently satisfied the cultist sentry wasn't going to sprout wings and make a return. "Esa was justified."

"She was reaching for her weapon because we showed up out of *nowhere* at the tower she was supposed to be guarding—"

"You saw all those warships they're building in orbit, Mer." I shook my head, checking the action on Bitey for the fiftieth time—it was what my hands just did when we were in a potential combat scenario and they didn't have anything else to do. "Dreadnaughts may not be planet-killers, but they *are* city-killers, at the very least. I've seen what a dreadnaught can do to a civilian population that doesn't have any defenses against it—seen it in the skies over my own hometown. These Bright Wanderers aren't planning to unite the galaxy through peace and goodwill."

"She was brainwashed, desperate, just like those people—"

"And desperate people will kill us if we give them half a chance; she'd bought into this cult nonsense bullshit, at least to the point where they trusted her enough to put a gun in her hands and tell her to *shoot* at anyone she doesn't like the look of—up to and including the other desperate souls who arrived with her. Whether they've done that convincing with a cocktail of drugs and a healthy dose of groupthink, or whether she came to that decision of her own free will, that's where she was at—and it's where any others we see will be at as well. So we're going to kill them before they kill us, and I need to know: are you up for that?" I was channeling Jane, and I knew it—a part of me was marveling that I could be so cold, asking myself if I really meant what I was saying. But I needed Meridian to get past this; it didn't matter that she was young or pretty or unprepared, we didn't have *room* for anything else.

For the first time, I knew what it must have been like for Jane and the Preacher during the flight from my homeworld, surrounded on all sides by the Pax, with me desperate for answers they didn't have time to give in the middle of a firefight.

She nodded, once, even though there was still something a little shell-shocked around her eyes—though I didn't know what she'd expected; she'd been through combat training, seen the guns we all carried, seen us return to Scheherazade and Khalipon and Bolivar with empty magazines and blood-stains on our clothes the few times we'd seen action on our little outward-bound journey. I mean, I got it, I understood—seeing the aftermath of the thing and seeing the *thing* were very different—but all the same, we had a job to do.

She was at least trying to move past it, though, which was good; what was *also* good was that Schaz had apparently managed to set us down on the very balcony of the network hub: I could see it pulsing in my HUD in the very next room, sending information flowing out through the invisible ether.

We stepped inside the tower, underneath the soaring archway from the balcony, and if I thought the exteriors had been ostentatious, they had nothing on the interior: it was all one big room, the domed ceiling rising at least four stories over our heads, and absolutely all of that ceiling was covered in a kind of shimmering, scintillating material that was at least a synthetic re-production of crushed Klitek pearl, if not the real thing.

The walls looked like they had at one point been covered in tall hanging tapestries—you could see on the marble where some places were darker than others—but those had long since been torn down, replaced with a kind of looping, archaic script, painted directly onto the cladding in a language I couldn't read, but recognized all the same: it was the same as the etchings on the Cyn's armor and the robes of the proselytizers for the Bright Wanderers, those we'd watched—from a distance—as they recruited from pulsed worlds. The designs were as much schematic as they were linguistic, seeming nearly arcane, or at least alchemical: the vertically oriented script was bizarre purely in the fact that it seemed to share no common root at all with the universal system of writing and language developed during the Golden Age.

Still, that meant the designs were ultimately meaningless to me, so I turned back toward what lay at the center of the room: the network hub, weirdly out of place on a raised dais, all computer banks and whirring machinery where there clearly should have been some kind of throne or altar instead, the center of power for whatever skyfaring people had built these soaring towers.

I mean, I supposed it still *was* that—the center of power—just in a very, very different way.

"Take a look for the network router," I said, bringing up an image in my HUD of what a router for this sort of system ought to look like. "It should be kind of . . . kind of tube-y, and . . . sort of *blinking*-ish—"

"Okay, yeah," Meridian sighed, shaking her head and running a hand through her long black hair, "this is why I'm here." She pointed a finger at a random piece of machinery halfway across the room, instantly recognizing the stupid thing among all the *other* tall, tube-y, blinking pieces of machinery. "That's the router. Shut that down, and the AIs onboard the various dreadnaughts will be cut off from the network. Then all the other team has to do is retrieve the password from—"

A sharp cracking sound, and the smell of electrical ionization, followed by melting plastics and metal in an acrid tang that made me wrinkle my nose; Sho lowered his paw as the network router gave its last gasp. "Shut down," he said simply, the fur on his palm still standing on end from the static of the charge he'd thrown into the electronics.

I grinned at him. "I take it there *is* some sort of reactor, lower in the tower?" I asked; he couldn't generate electricity, just harness it, which meant the energy from that blast had come from somewhere.

"Oh, yeah," he replied in the affirmative. "More power flowing through these walls than there was at Raizencourt Observatory. I've got juice for *days*, when you need it."

"Right," Meridian nodded, taking Sho's . . . rather drastic interpretation of "shut that down" in stride. She moved quickly up the dais, kneeling in front of one of the many, many monitors on the hub. "Let me try and get—"

A massive clash from behind us, coming from the balcony: the sound of metal on marble, with real *weight* beneath it. Even without turning, I knew that sound—had been, in equal parts, dreading it and desperate to hear it again, ever since I'd put a knife through the Cyn that had killed Sho's mother. It was the sound of the metallic exoskeletons the Cyn wore, crashing down as they dropped out of flight.

I turned, slowly, already building a telekinetic burst into my palm; Sho fed a slow trickle of energy in my direction, and I made a link between that flow and the intention-shield capacitor built into the base of my spine. He had recognized the sound as well, and knew all hell was likely about to break loose.

The Cyn was kneeling, out on the balcony, in the crushed ruin his landing had made of the marble floor, deepening the cracks I'd made in my own descent. The metallic wings of his exosuit were still spread behind him, haloed by the golden glow of the suns peeking through the clouds, and despite myself, something caught in my chest: fear, yes, but also exhilaration. Rumors were one thing; even scans could be faked, somehow. But here one was, in the "flesh," so to speak, confirmation that the Cyn I'd killed hadn't been alone in the galaxy.

The first one had beaten the hell out of our crew; we'd fought him, lost, fought him again, fought him again, *nearly* lost, and then I'd faced him alone, and barely scraped out a win. But we'd learned from that fight—that was what we did. We'd modified our tools, our arsenals, had been preparing for this moment all during the outbound trip: I'd spent plenty of time during the long stretches of hyperspace between systems going through the last fight in my head, learning from the memory. I wasn't going to lose again.

Sho and I both took a step down from the dais; we separated out, just a bit, each giving the other room to work.

"What's—"

"Don't turn around, Meridian," I told her flatly, beginning to spin the energy from my shields—energy replaced by Sho's flow as quickly as I was siphoning it off—into the teke burst vibrating between my fingers, until I was holding a whirling storm of light in my palm. "Just keep working. We'll deal with this."

We were ready to deal with this.

The Cyn kneeling at the entranceway didn't say anything. Didn't move, didn't draw a weapon—much like his brother, he was wearing a heavy exosuit, a way for him to interact with the physical world around him, since the being *inside* the suit was comprised almost entirely of light and fire.

Whereas the first Cyn we'd seen had been relatively sleek, the metal of his suit almost seeming painted onto a slim, well-built bipedal physique, this one was markedly heavier: at least as broad through the shoulders as Sahluk, and nearly as tall, like he was wearing plate armor to the first Cyn's sleeker chassis. Even his *helmet* was more aggressive: curling metal horns curved upward from the sides of the head to meet again like a tangled crown above, and the carven eyes were trapped in a narrow glare.

We simply stood there for a heartbeat, then two, Sho and I flanking Meridian, staring down the Cyn. The first move would be his, and all three of us knew it—he studied us for a moment, just as we studied him, the air thick with energy and the potential for a great deal of violence.

"*Heretics,*" the Cyn said finally as he stood, slowly, his voice coming over our comms channels, "broadcast" along the spectrum of energy that was reserved for radio waves. "*Defilers. Your very presence in this holy place is—*"

So that was his first move—a fucking speech. I wasn't impressed.

I hit him with the full weight of the teke burst I'd been building in my hand: there was enough strength there to crush a tank, and never mind the weave of electricity I'd buried in the center, a burst of energy that washed over him like a wave of pale fire. It did exactly *nothing* to the Cyn—didn't even make him furl the metal wings that rose behind him like sheets of razors.

He cocked his head to the side, an expression that seemed less one of curiosity—given all the hate carved into his armored face—and more of mean amusement. *"So. Three martyrs, come to offer themselves up. An imitation among your number. Unexpected—but useful."* As he spoke, he reached with both hands to the small of his back; reaching for a weapon, no doubt, but slowly, like he had all the time in the world. *"All the chaplains and all the inquisitors have worked for decades to seek your kind out, and now three of you deliver yourself right to our door. I feel the goddess's will, in that. Is it possible that you, imitation"*—he was speaking directly to me, now, his mask tilted just slightly in my direction—*"that you shall be the one to open the way to the Palace, where all the other martyrs have failed? I think so. I think you shall open the doors with your sacrament, with your pain."*

None of that sounded friendly, though I hadn't expected much else.

His hands came back into view, now that his speechifying was done: he held a pair of axes in loose grips, held them like he knew how to use them. The Cyn I'd encountered had been armed merely with a pair of razor-sharp claws, but this one had actual weapons to go along with his exosuit.

I'd assumed the Cyn we'd fought—on Kandriad, on Valkyrie Rock, on Odessa Station—had been their best, the warrior sent out into the galaxy to retrieve the gifted from wherever he could root them out, a twisted knight-errant trusted to survive far from the safety of his home. That had been a flawed assumption; I realized that now. Rather than a soldier, the Cyn we'd fought had been the Bright Wanderers' version of Marus—an intelligence gatherer, a spy, trained to cover his tracks rather than for out-and-out conflict. Now, we were facing the Cyn version of Sahluk—a warrior, Bright Wanderer security, a true combat operative.

I'd assumed, because I'd been able to take down that first Cyn—with jury-rigged systems I'd since replaced with dedicated implants, and an only theoretically possible plan of attack I now *knew* would be effective—that I'd be able to take on any others that came at me.

That arrogant assumption—that Cyn were all the same, were all trained the same, in a way humans or Tyll or Wulf were not—might be about to get me killed.

The Cyn started forward across the marble, picking up speed with every crunching step.

CHAPTER 11

Jane

I couldn't *hear* the bullets snapping past me as I went sailing out into nothing. Somehow, that made it worse. I knew they were there—I could see the bright flares of muzzle flashes below, where a security team was crouched on one of the catwalks that surrounded the dreadnaught hull; they were firing both at me, sliding down the line, and at where Javier and the Preacher had taken cover on the hull itself—but with no atmosphere to carry the sound of the bullets' passage, there was nothing for me to *hear*, no sharp "crack" of distant gunfire to make the rest of my body tense up, no "snap" as one of the rounds passed close to my head. I couldn't even fire back, because if I did, the recoil would kill my rate of descent. So I just held tight and went flying down the wire—

—right until one of the unseen bullets hammered directly into my intention shields. I was knocked backward and nearly jarred off the line, all my momentum killed. No time to *think*—I was hanging nearly still now, an easy target—so I just reached up with my knife and cut my harness, then pulled my rifle off my back and fired: not down toward the security team, but upward instead, so that the recoil pushed me in the opposite direction, down toward the hull of the ship.

It also sent me into a spin, given that the butt of the rifle had been held tight against my shoulder; I drew my sidearm and fired off another round to counteract that, and I was actually *doing* this—"falling" in roughly the right direction, the hulk of the dreadnaught's chassis rising up to meet me—when another round hit my intention shields, and I could actually see the energy field crack apart, like I'd been surrounded by panes of glass and now they were shattering.

No more protection—another round would punch right through my suit. And me. Of course, the impact from the bullet that had just *broken* my shields had also sent me spinning again, and—

"Jane! On your left!" It was Javier's voice on my comm; I holstered my sidearm and flailed in that general direction, until the back of my hand brushed against some sort of cable he'd sent flying out toward me. As soon as I grabbed it, my arm was almost jerked out of its socket: the cable was retracting, attached to some kind of winch, and as I reoriented my perspective—my guts sloshing around behind my ribs like they were floating in a sea of caustic acid; if this kept up, I was going to puke inside my helmet—I could see Javier, kneeling beside the winch, firing back toward the security team.

Then Sahluk touched down beside him—*he* hadn't been knocked off the goddamned descent cable—and the big Mahren was firing his grenade launcher, the bright green flares of plasma rounds making burning, comet-like arcs over the weak gravity of the hulk, falling in almost slow motion before they smashed against the catwalk at the enemy position, blazing like phosphorus as they melted through metal and cultist alike. Screams didn't carry through the void either, but all the same: I knew there'd be screaming.

The gravity of the dreadnaught grabbed hold of me, and I reoriented myself, making sure my magboots clamped onto the hull—yes, there *was* gravity, but it was weak stuff, both because of the nature of the artificial generators and because the construction crews wanted it that way: made it easier to lift heavy pieces into place—and I was clomping my way toward the others, muttering a continuous stream of "Fuck, fuck, *fuck!*" as I went.

I *really* didn't like zero-g.

"Well, they know we're here," Marus said with a sigh as he touched down. He nodded his suited head toward the great gaping hole in the superstructure through which we would make our entrance. "I'd say we should get inside, sooner rather than later. The hub team should have cut off the wider network by now, so hopefully the security personnel on board can't summon patrol boats or reinforcements, but all the same: I would still like to be off this exposed hull as soon as possible."

"You are not wrong," I agreed, and without waiting for anyone else, I dropped through the exposed skin of the dreadnaught, landing in an unfinished corridor inside. Pieces of it looked almost completed, then there would be missing bulkheads exposed to the shining stars beyond, or simply the steel ribs and alloy spines of the dreadnaught's superstructure below.

Cables of bright lights had been hung along the passage, and they followed a very specific course along one axis or another, stopping every once in a while to run along the walls and reorient themselves. It was an old void construction trick, one I recognized: the lights indicated where the nearest artificial gravity generator was, and thus which way was "down." They were hung so that they'd always be "above" the workers, a kind of warning system to prevent someone from taking a wrong step and breaking their neck when they swapped gravity fields, not that the gravity inside the hulk was really strong enough to break a bone if you fell.

I approached the first switching of the lights; it took a kind of "hop" to swap between the fields without risking your ankles, but thankfully, I'd done this sort of dance before, and I knew the steps. The others were dropping into the corridor behind me, and since from their perspective I was now walking on a wall at a ninety-degree angle from where they were standing, they noted the shifting gravity as well.

The Preacher moved immediately to a nearby terminal, typing on its keypad in a blur of metal fingers, and soon enough, the screen glowed to life: she was in, and even though Esa's team had already cut off the network, she wanted the dreadnaught's local systems under her control, which would only be possible if Javier's supposition had been right and there wasn't already an AI running things onboard.

"No AI," she reported. "Just data storage and dummy programs at the core—the other AIs on the network were running things here until construction was further along and this craft could sustain a full intelligence on its own. Also, yes, Esa and the others have successfully taken the network down"—a small smile on her face; she was proud of their work, just like I was—"and up until that point, there wasn't any sort of alert going out over the system. The other craft in the shipyard have no knowledge that we're here."

"All according to plan," Javier said. "Just means something's more likely to fuck up down the line." Always the optimist, my sweetheart.

"How far are we from the empty AI core?" I asked Marus. I theoretically had that information stored in my HUD, but with the network down, I wasn't getting a good reading on where we were currently on board the hull, and my mapping data was confused as all hell, trying to place me in about seven different areas of the ship at once.

"Not too far, relatively speaking," he said, making his own little "hop" to join me, standing on the wall. "But given the lack of interior completion, it's likely to be cut off from the finished corridors." The two of us approached one of those great gaps in the superstructure beneath us, peering over the edge: we could see all the way to the lower bulkheads from here, nearly half a mile to fall if we went through—I wasn't lying when I said dreadnaughts were big, *big* ships—though in between us and the far side of the ship were more spines of metal, the ribs of the endoskeleton leading toward the dread-naught's reactor and its AI core. I twisted my head, but I couldn't actually see all the way to our goal, thanks to the angle.

"Why do I have the feeling that the best way to get there is going to be dropping onto one of those spines and approaching that way?" I sighed. The spines weren't even catwalks—though a few had those built alongside them—they were just massive pieces of metal, the superstructure of the hull, usu-ally hidden from sight in a completed craft behind interior bulkheads. Part of the reason dreadnaughts required zero-g shipyards was because assem-bling pieces of steel and alloy that size would have been physically impos-sible in a true gravity well; here, where the gravity generators could be powered up or down at will, it was . . . not *easy*, but at least doable.

"Your call," Marus shrugged. "But heading forward from our current position"—he pointed down the hallway we were standing in, which got fuller and fuller as it went along, until you could barely tell you were stand-ing in a half-finished spacecraft at the far bulkhead—"means we'll have to pass through the more finished areas of the ship, and as I recall the Nemesis design—"

"Which you should, given that we were running around trying to seize control of one from the inside during the battle of Sanctum," I added.

"Which I do," he nodded, "then the areas between us and the core are the barracks and the armory. I doubt they've been fully completed yet, but it's still likely where the security teams are stationed, and right now, they're likely inside, gearing up to hunt us down."

"Whichever direction we're going in, we need to make a choice, *now*," Sahluk said. He and the Preacher were facing backward, their guns trained on the hole in the ship's plating where we'd slipped through, both of them waiting to see if any of the security teams topside—or at least, any of those that had avoided being melted by the Mahren's plasma fire—decided to follow us down.

"He's right," Javier agreed. "If Sho and the others have already shut the network down, that means they're in the hub already, and they're going to have to hold it until we can send them the passcode."

"Actually, I meant because we're probably about to have more security forces pouring in here and trying to blow our heads off," Sahluk shrugged. "But sure: that other thing too."

Javier had freed the descent line we'd used to get between Khaliphon and the dreadnaught's hull—he was affixing it to the barrel of his shotgun again, the magnetic harpoon's utilitarian design allowing it to be fired from his weapon just as easily as it might have been affixed manually. "So who wants to go first?" he asked, stepping to the breach in the hull and lining up his shot on one of the exposed girders beneath us.

"Me," I sighed, stowing my rifle on my back again. "Hopefully I won't get shot off a descent line twice in the same mission."

"Sweetheart, I love you, but you know you've never had the *best* luck, right?"

"Just fire the damn line, Javi, and let's get this over with."

CHAPTER 12

Jane

Thankfully, our passage along the second descent line didn't involve gunfire—just the "descent" becoming "ascent" about halfway through, as we moved into a different gravity field. My stomach did another backflip as I was momentarily pulled in two directions at once at the overlapping edges of the fields, but I gritted my teeth and started hauling myself up the line instead, telling my stomach to sort itself out, not that it particularly helped. Human bodies—or Tyll, or Wulf, or any organics, for that matter—just weren't built for negotiating this kind of rapid shift in gravity; our physical evolution was still tens of thousands of years behind our technology.

Still, nothing to do about it but tough it out and continue the climb. At least the gravity wasn't exceptionally strong, meaning that hauling my relative body weight—not to mention all my various guns and body armor—wasn't as strenuous as it might have been.

I climbed to the "top" of the metal skeleton and took a knee, looking forward with my rifle raised up to my eye. That was just instinct and habit—I didn't have a scope on my gun, because I didn't need one; my HUD did all the zooming and scanning for me, which meant raising the weapon didn't help me see any farther. Still: always better to have your gun ready to fire.

The dreadnaught's AI core was a cube of solid metal in the far distance, with several completed hallways branching off it; between here and there, though, there was mostly just emptiness, the bare skeleton of the dreadnaught's superstructure still waiting to have bulkheads and corridors and machinery and cladding applied to massive girders of unadorned metal. More of the lines of glowing filament had been wrapped along that exposed endoskeleton, all of them set at different angles from each other, meaning the gravity fields would continue to shift and warp as we moved across the exposed bones of the dreadnaught toward the distant cube that would eventually house the AI.

Great. More low-g gymnastics in my future; we'd have to make our way across several of the long spines of metal, swapping gravity fields along the way, before we reached the finished corridors leading into the core. At least we weren't being shot at.

As soon as the thought crossed my mind, of course, a laser swept across the spine I was standing on, the heat blistering the metal as it passed. I scrambled backward, shifting my view upward (downward): that was the *other* thing about fighting in differentiated gravity wells—it meant attacks could come from any quadrant, because your enemy wouldn't necessarily be constrained to the same axes you were.

Sure enough, there was another team of security officers, standing on a half-built catwalk about a hundred yards away to my right—of course, from my perspective, they weren't "standing" at all, but glued to the side of the catwalk by their boot heels, since they were at about a ninety-degree angle off-gravity from me.

The ruby-red beam of the laser was sweeping again toward my position—it looked like one of the security team had taken control of a cutting laser, a heavy, mounted thing; they were using it to attack me likely because lasers, unlike ballistic rounds, wouldn't be affected by the shifting gravity fields.

I eyeballed the beam for just a moment, forcing myself to breathe and calculate its trajectory as it swept toward me—move too soon, and the cultist manning the cutter would compensate and catch me; move too slowly and I'd wind up missing a limb—then I feinted to the left, a good old-fashioned head-fake, and he took the bait, sweeping the laser toward where the feint would have taken me; I responded by rolling to the right instead, right through the vector it would have cut through initially. I popped up on the other side of the beam, swapping out rifles as I did; they'd been smart to use the laser cutter, but two could play at that game.

I fired three energy blasts into the cutter itself; it shorted out and exploded, sending the other cultists scrambling for cover. I tried to blast through their ad hoc barricades as well—mostly piles of crates and cladding meant for the eventual bulkhead walls that would be raised around the spine—but it was no good; of *course* materials used in dreadnaught construction were sealed against energy attacks.

Sahluk had pulled himself up onto the spine behind me, and he sent a trio of plasma grenades arcing toward the enemy's position, but he had the same problem traditional ballistic rounds would have had; the shifting gravity played merry hell with the parabolic arcs of his aim, and the grenades splattered their sizzling cargo across several different pieces of the dreadnaughts' exposed construction, landing pretty much everywhere except the catwalk where our attackers were tucked into cover. Streams of molten metal, liquefied by the plasma, dripped and twisted as they fell through multiple gravity wells, but outside of creating a truly spectacular light show, Sahluk hadn't achieved anything beyond forcing the security team to keep their heads down.

The big Mahren frowned at their dug-in position. "Fuck," he said succinctly.

"Yeah." I nodded down the length of the girder we were standing on; there was a pile of crates that we could use for cover just before the spine ended, the same sort of stuff the cultist security team was hiding behind. "Let's move."

The two of us hustled in that direction; about two-thirds of the way there, bullets started dropping toward us, the sound of the gunfire coming from our distant aggressors oddly muted by the shifting gravity. Of course, the enemy was having just as difficult a time compensating for the differing ballistics as we were, and what few rounds landed anywhere near us felt random and chaotic at best—only one actually impacted against my intention shields, which had fully recharged after the excitement during our boarding.

Still, I was happy to slide into cover behind the crates—running across open ground while under fire was still *running across open ground while under fire*, otherwise known as "possibly the worst thing you can do in combat"—and that meant we'd closed a little bit of the distance, but our enemy still had forward cover from our angle of attack, just like we had from theirs.

We laid down suppressive fire as the Preacher, Javier, and Marus came to join us, but we couldn't move forward without giving them enfilade on our position: for one thing, there was no more girder for us to move forward along, and for another, doing so somehow anyway would still expose us to their attacks. That meant we'd have to use another descent line to reach another spine, one that continued forward toward the core, and we'd be perfect targets during the climb. A stalemate.

Thankfully, I was good at breaking stalemates.

I stopped firing for a moment, swapping out magazines—jamming the half-empty one into the autoloader on my belt; there was a clicking sound as the loader filled new cartridges into the magazine from my bandolier—and looked to the left of our position, away from the enemy, tracking the lines of glowing filament that indicated the shifting wells: there.

If I could make the next spine over, the gravity would shift again, and a hanging rat's nest of cables and wiring should hide my movements from the enemy. From that girder, I could reach a further spine, one that would put me at a full one-eighty degree of gravity difference from the enemy, directly above them, well past the hanging mass of material I was hoping would veil my approach. Their cover wouldn't help them at that point.

Of course, all of that was assuming I could make the next spine at all.

I'd gotten too used to having Esa as my partner; with her beside me, she could have "pushed" a telekinetic shield in front of me to deflect the enemy's attacks, then just picked me up and hurled me at the girder I wanted to be on. Or just smashed the enemy position with her teke, and forget all the other nonsense—telekinesis wouldn't have been affected by shifting gravity. No gifted tricks here, though; just me, and a gun, and even more ground to cover.

"Everybody hold position," I said to the others; Javier, the Preacher, and Marus had all reached our barricade. "When I say, give me covering fire."

"What are you going to *do*," Javier asked, though his tone made the words less of a question and more of a resigned moan.

"Dig them out of there. Hand over the descent line."

The Preacher looked past me to the left, analyzing the spikes of rebar and steel that made up the dreadnaught's in-construction superstructure, finding the path I was planning to take in an instant. "If you're going to try that route—you should let me. You might pull your shoulder out of your socket."

I shook my head, taking the descent line—shotgun and all—from Javier.

"I fired my energy rifle dry; it'll take a moment to recharge. I need you here, to pick them off once I scatter them out of their position." I stuck my head up over the crates—winced as an enemy round, likely a ricochet, skimmed across my intention shields just above my head—and fired the descent line; it pulled taut, attached to the spine to the left and "beneath" us, and I handed the shotgun back to Javier.

"Good luck," Javier told me, taking his weapon back. "I think you'll need it."

"Thanks," I replied dryly. Then: "Covering fire, now!"

As my team unloaded toward the enemy's position—compensating decently for the shifting gravity fields between them and their targets, though they couldn't do much about the crates their targets were hiding behind—I leapt over the pile of construction detritus we'd been using for cover, wrapping the slackening descent line around my hand and throwing myself off the spine.

I fell. Then I fell *sideways*, the tangle of cables cutting off my view of both the enemy and my own team for a moment as I did. My shoulder didn't quite pull itself out of its socket when I hit one of the sharper shifts in gravity, the way the Preacher had thought it might, but it was a close thing.

Then I was falling *up*, my initial momentum carrying me through the gravity now pulling me back in the direction I'd come from, and I was swinging past the line's anchoring point. That was when I let go of the cable.

I passed into a new gravity field—this one pulling me forward, toward the empty AI core—and that gave me just enough momentum to reach the spine I was aiming for, letting me scramble up into the exposed metal ribs of the ship. Another leap into nothing—now aiming for the third girder, the one that would put me a solid hundred feet above the enemy position—and the gravity pulled me to the left again before I landed; I hit, hard, tucked into a roll, then looked up: I was where I wanted to be, one hundred and eighty degrees rotated from the enemy, the girder "beneath" my boots about a hundred feet above their heads.

And they hadn't seen me move. Before I'd even stood I was pulling a concussion grenade from my belt; I popped the pin loose with my thumb, holding the explosive tight to cook its detonator down as I judged the distance between my position and the enemy "above" me. I gauged the angle and the differing wells one last time, then I threw the grenade, as hard as I could, straight up.

If it didn't make the edge of *my* gravity field, it was going to come right back down and explode in my face, and the whole point of a concussion grenade was to overwhelm intention shields and force an enemy out of cover; mine wouldn't be able to eat the force of the blast, and I'd be thrown right off the spine, to fall . . . quite a long way. There was no cover for me to take, nothing I could do but trust in the strength of my own arm, and my calculations—based on the wrapped lines of filaments—as to where the fields overlapped.

The grenade twitched as it sailed through the fields, then it was dropping again—though still rising, from my perspective—as it sailed toward the enemy position; I'd timed it damn near to perfection, and the detonator went off just before it hit the deck, the explosive throwing the security forces against the stacked crates that made up their cover—and throwing those crates right off of the girder in the bargain.

That left them exposed to the pinpoint blasts of energy fired from the cannon installed in the Preacher's right arm. She ripped them apart with the sort of mathematical precision only a Barious was capable of.

Sahluk stood from behind my team's position—now at a weirdly skewed angle from me—and tossed off a salute, grinning as he did. I saluted back, then pointed down the long stretch of metal ahead of me. "I don't think I can get *back* to the rest of you," I said dryly into the comm. "Just start making your way to the AI core; I'll meet you there."

CHAPTER 13

Jane

The rest of the run along the unfinished spines of the dreadnaught was . . . not one of my favorite things ever. Running firefights were always chaotic at best; running firefights through shifting gravity, cut off from the rest of my squad, with my "path" through the interior void of the supercraft splintered and broken depending on how far along construction was, well . . . I don't think "chaotic" was a good enough term.

Thankfully, bringing down the network seemed to have scattered the cultists' response, and given the fact that I'd inadvertently split our group, that meant we had multiple angles of attack available each time we came across another batch of enemies trying to lay an ambush. Equally working in our favor was that, no matter what fatalistic views the cult held, they hadn't seen *this* coming, and the most dangerous weapons their security were armed with were the cutting lasers appropriated from the construction teams: twice more I had to dance through glittering beams of focused fire, drawing the attention of the bright lines of energy until Javier or the Preacher could get around behind the enemy position (or above, or below, given the shifting nature of gravity along the spines) and take the gunner out.

Still, when I finally reached the inner passages to the AI core—those corridors I'd seen in the distance, leading into the gleaming cube at the center of the dreadnaught like veins to a heart—they at least had actual walls, solid bulkheads rather than just great emptiness where walls might eventually *be*, and I was more than happy to leave the shifting gravity and the wide-open dangers of the ship's unfinished interior behind. At least this way, there were only two directions attack could come from: forward, and back.

Some of the enemy's security team had realized where our assault was directed: as always, the scanning elements of my HUD were useless inside a dreadnaught, the walls sealed against exactly the sort of infrared scans I used to detect enemy movement through solid matter, but I could still hear them around a bend in the corridor, a clanking of heavy machinery that sounded definitively ominous.

I holed up in what was probably going to wind up being a maintenance closet when construction was done, complete with wire racks to store supplies and terminal access to reprogram service bots; the only thing missing was the *floor*, which was . . . a pretty important part of any good closet. "I'm close to the core, I think," I said into the comm, reaching out to the rest of my team as I closed the door behind me and stepped—very carefully—over the gap in the plating beneath my feet. "ETA on your arrival?"

"If by 'close to the core' you mean you can see the dozens of cultists building barricades to prevent us from getting access, then you know our arrival might be just a little delayed," Marus answered; I couldn't hear gunfire from his side of the channel—nor, for that matter, from the mass of cultists just around the bend in the corridor—so my team hadn't stumbled into the firing solution of the enemy position yet, which meant we had time to plan.

"Any ideas?" I asked.

"We hit them," Sahluk grunted.

"That part's pretty much a given," I told him dryly. "I was looking for more specific ideas, like a *way* to hit them, preferably one that doesn't include getting half our team cut into pieces by ad hoc laser positions."

"I, for one, support that approach," Javier added. "I like my pieces where they are."

"So do I, sweetheart," I answered, a grin on my face; I couldn't help it.

"The core's sealed off completely, except for the access corridors—it looks like it's about the first thing they built after they raised the superstructure," the Preacher reported. "There's an entrance on the far side, as well, but if we try to circumvent *this* exit and push in that direction, the enemy will likely just fall back through the core, and we'll be doing the same dance on the other side."

"Still: easier to hit an enemy on the move than one dug in like a parasite under a Wulf's fur," I mused. I could feel a plan starting to take form—unfortunately, having Esa as a partner for the last four years meant it was kind of an insane idea. I really did need to examine the notion that she'd been almost as big an influence on *me* as I had been on her.

"What are you suggesting?" Marus asked.

I was standing on a thin beam of metal, supported over the nothing that made up most of the interior of the dreadnaught. "The core has its own gravity generators, yes?" I asked the Preacher instead. "So inside, 'up' is always 'up'?"

"*Inside*, up is always up, yes," the Preacher agreed. "But outside, there are generators operating on each face of the core, meaning the core itself is always 'down.'"

That's what I'd wanted to hear. "Stay in place, if you can," I told them. "I'm going to draw off the defenders by making my way to the far side, and trying to get access over there. They'll think that's all of us, attempting a breach, so when they start to move—"

"We fall on them from behind." I could feel the nod in Marus's voice as he saw the rough pattern of my—admittedly relatively simple—plan.

"Exactly. Unless anyone else has a better idea . . ." I would *not* have objected if someone else had a better idea.

"Stay safe," Javier told me, and that was that.

I took another breath, then dropped through the floor.

I hit the shifting gravity field almost immediately, drawn beneath the "floor" of the corridor I had occupied as it became a "wall" instead, gravity pulling me toward the AI core as I clung to the struts in the construction—which meant a brief climb put me directly beside the enemy position, only a thin sheet of metal separating us, their "floor" my climbing wall. No use wasting a good ambush: I affixed a few remote charges before I finished the climb down, then transmitted the charge sequence to Sahluk, ready to be activated once the enemy tried to pull back inside the core.

After that, it was down to the core itself, down and around, and even given that this was what the security teams were protecting, it didn't seem to have occurred to them that someone might try to scale the outside. There was a reason for that, of course—AI cores were one of the most well-armored positions inside any dreadnaught, second only to the reactor itself: even with a high-powered cutting laser like the ones that had been aimed at my head a little bit ago, it would still take me hours and hours to open a breach big enough to slip through.

"Through," though, wasn't my destination; "around" was, and outside of navigating the shifting gravity at each corner it was relatively easy going, ducking through the tangle of pipes and wires that hung loose and unconnected around the core itself, waiting for exterior pieces to be finished before they were plugged into the currently empty AI socket.

I made the other side in relatively short order, and started looking for a way back up: much like the aft side of the core, the corridors and hallways here had been built outward from that position, meaning there was open superstructure a ways forward from me, but closer to the core itself everything was closed off, a maze of unfinished metal.

Well, the whole point of being on this side was to draw attention to myself, so rather than looking for another open floor where some lazy cultist had forgotten to finish up their work—like the closet I'd used to sneak into this maze to begin with—I affixed nearly every explosive charge I had remaining on the underside of one of those hallways, then took cover behind a tangle of alloy wiring and triggered the detonation.

Dreadnaught corridors were made of thick stuff, but not so well armored they could shrug off multiple military-grade explosives. Before the smoke had even cleared—swirling in strange eddies as it tried to find *which* twisting pathway of gravity to follow—I was through, reorienting myself to the new gravity in the hallway and approaching the core from this unguarded side.

"Well, they heard *that*," Sahluk confirmed over the comms. "Didn't seem to like it too much, either."

"Just wait until I start fiddling with the access controls," I said, dropping to one knee in front of the maintenance panel and jimmying it open with the point of my knife.

"Do you actually know how to hack open that door?" the Preacher asked me. "Even without the AI in place, the systems will be—"

"I've got only the vaguest idea," I admitted, attaching electrical clamps to the wiring, "but it doesn't really matter—as soon as I—"

Another blast, one I could hear but not feel, the heavy material of the core dampening the force of the vibrations: Sahluk must have set off my ambush charges. "What?" he said, I think more to the others than to me, despite the fact that the comms channel was still open. "They started moving!"

Then the channel was cut off, my team with better things to do than talk to me, and all I had to go by was the crack of distant gunfire, distorted by the thick metals of the core and the shifting gravity fields around it. I pulled back from the panel, put the corridor wall to my back, and waited.

Waiting was never my favorite part of combat. I knew it was absurd, but I actually preferred the "getting shot at" part of a fight to the bit where you weren't getting shot at, but you knew you were about to be. The instinct was a remnant of my—

"Act, don't react—when you have a shot, you fire."

What the hell was *that?* I'd heard it, over my comm—actually jumped a little, my gun coming up. I'd been so focused on the corridor ahead of me, waiting on the Bright Wanderers' response, that the voice seemed to come out of nowhere—

—except I *hadn't* heard it, I couldn't have. Only the other Justified operatives had access to this channel, and that voice . . . that voice hadn't belonged to any of them. That voice had belonged to a woman who'd been dead for a hundred years.

I hadn't heard it. I'd *imagined* it. I'd been thinking about my years on the front lines of my own sect war, the war I'd fought before I'd even joined the Justified, and I'd been thinking about *her,* and so I'd heard her voice in my head. That was it. That was all.

Bullshit. I knew the difference between a comms broadcast—even a subaural one—and the sound of my own—

A pair of security officers came hustling toward the core from deeper in the vessel, guns drawn and eyes up, not paying any attention to anything but the door I was supposedly trying to hack; I shot them in the back as they approached the panel I'd broken open, then I turned, aiming back the way they'd come, looking for more. Nothing.

The voice of the ghost still echoed in my head.

"Marus, is this comm channel clear?" I asked, opening up the comm again, but I got no response: either they were inside the core already, which would block broadcasts, or they were in the middle of a firefight, and Marus didn't have time to answer me.

I'd imagined it. The corridor ahead was silent, motionless down the barrel of my gun: I tried to slow my breathing, to slow my heart rate, my pulse hammering far too fast for something as simple as the ambush I'd just pulled off. My body wasn't reacting to the violence: it was reacting to that voice, the one my subconscious had whispered into my ear—why *now*? A hundred years since I—

The doors behind me—the entrance to the core—started grinding open; there was still nothing moving in the corridor ahead of me, and I turned, fitting my rifle tight against my shoulder. Regardless of imaginary voices in my head—combat did weird things to your mind sometimes, I *knew* that, and that was all it had been—there very well might be a full combat squad of the enemy inside the core. If they'd repulsed my team in their attack from the other direction, then I was very much alone, and about to be—

I found myself staring down the sight of my rifle at Javier's grinning face. "Come on in," he beckoned. "The place is a little messy right now, but—"

"Oh, shut it," I moved past him, growling a little more than I meant to, my reactions still thrown off by the fact that my brain had decided to fuck with me for no apparent reason, just for a moment there. "Is the Preacher in, has she got access?"

"She's in," he confirmed. "We—" He paused; was looking more closely at me. "You all right?" he asked, his voice quieter now, not broadcasting to the others. Whatever he was seeing in my face, he didn't much like it. "You look . . ."

If he said "you look like you've seen a ghost," I was going to hit him, sweetheart or not—my nerves were still stretched that taut—so I interrupted him instead. "I'm fine," I told him shortly. "Do we have—"

"Broadcasting the password to Meridian now," the Preacher said, from the far end of the cavernous core. "It should give the hub team full access to the Bright Wanderers' databanks."

Javier grinned at me, knowing better than to press the other thing.

"Then we're grand," he said. "We know they're in place thanks to the network coming down; all they have to do now is empty the databanks. So long as the Wanderers don't hit them with something they can't handle—and between Esa and Sho, that won't be much—it's clear sailing from here."

CHAPTER 14

Esa

I've heard it said that combat—violence—is always defined by your first experience with the thing; that how you approach any given scrap is a direct response to how your first fight found *you*. My first taste of life-or-death struggle had been against the Pax, fighting off wave after wave of disposable infantry, paradoxically prepared to die just to prove how strong they were. True to the form of the aphorism, I favored hit-and-run tactics, the combat of attrition; mobility and precision.

On the other hand, *Sho's* first taste of combat—of actually being in the fighting, not just near the front lines like in the factory city where he'd grown up—had been against a Cyn. And just like me, he'd let that define *his* training, with Javier.

As I faced down the heavily armored opponent, trying to figure out the best way to peel him out of his armor—because once he was out of his armor, I could take him on; once he was out of his armor, I could *hurt* him—Sho took another step forward, swapping out the shells of his double-barreled shotgun. I had just a moment to look at him, to wonder what the hell he thought he was doing—Sho could channel energy, yes, but the Cyn's armor was energy-neutral; it had to be, otherwise the energetic body of the creature held within would melt right through the stuff—and then the Wulf raised up his shotgun, and he fired.

Typical shotgun pellets wouldn't do a damn thing against that armor, not unless you were at *really* close range, and Sho wasn't. But the new shells he'd loaded in weren't typical shotgun pellets—they were something . . . else.

The Cyn simply kept moving, shrugging off the blast like it wasn't there, but the rounds Sho had fired weren't meant to inflict ballistic force—the pellets were just a delivery mechanism. Instead of ricocheting off the hard surfaces of the armor, they clung to it—magnetically charged, somehow—and then they began to glow, at first giving off a pale, almost pleasantly pastoral green, then swiftly brightening to a flare of witchfire bright that hurt to even look at.

Radiation rounds. The Cyn's exosuit began melting around those specks of burning viridian glow, the metal running like liquid from the intense heat of the radiation; the Cyn howled through our comms—not in pain, just in anger; radiation couldn't do a damn thing to the Cyn itself, the bastards *ate* radiation, quite literally—but we could already see bright blue shining through the cracks in his protection: his actual body, inside the armor. He started moving faster, but Sho was already changing out shells—he'd be able to get off at least one more shot before the Cyn closed the distance.

So our enemy tried to use his other advantage instead, snapped his wings open and fired his jetpack, soaring up toward the scintillating ceiling, where the reflective surface was awash in the bright glare of the jetpack's engine and the pinpricks of green and blue shining through the cracks of the Cyn's armor. That was the moment *I'd* been waiting on, though, and as soon as he started upward, I reached out and "grabbed" the top corners of both his wings with my teke, and I pulled downward, as hard as I could.

My telekinesis was strong enough to hold a gunship in place. The Cyn's thrusters were powerful, but they weren't *that* powerful. The sudden shift in momentum fractured his exosuit, right along the weakest point: the joins where the wings met his back. I ripped the razor-edged wings right off him, and then I *hit* him, as hard as I could, with a burst of sheer telekinetic force right to the center of that cracking armor, and he was still in midair—there'd be no anchoring himself against the blast when he had nothing to anchor himself *on*. He went fucking flying, even without his wings, sailing right back out over the balcony, over the edge.

For a single, heart-pounding instant, I thought we'd done it—that it was going to be just that easy. He wouldn't be able to get out of the armor in time, and it would carry him down and down and down, into the golden atmosphere of the clouds below. I almost believed it.

Then, just before the wingless metal exosuit went sailing out of view, the whole thing split apart—like a snake shedding its skin in an instant—and the Cyn leapt free of the metal cage. The empty exosuit kept falling, sailing out into the golden clouds, but the Cyn landed safely on the balcony, his form, like the other Cyn I'd fought, shifting and almost liquid: fire, then electricity, then back to fire, a kind of molten blaze of bright blue shaped like a man.

He knelt on the cracked tiles of the balcony, staring up at us on the throne room steps, the glow of his body reflected in the shattered marble beneath it, like the inverse of a shadow. *"You've fought my kind before,"* he said, the words still buzzing in our comms rather than carrying through the atmosphere between us—because even without the fancy tech in his armor, Cyn still "spoke" by vibrating radio waves, manipulating energy the same way organics could manipulate matter. *"You are the ones that took the fourth chaplain off the board."*

Sure; probably; whatever. I hadn't known the bastard had a title, and I didn't care—beyond the fact that such a title meant there were at least three other "chaplains" out there, somewhere, hunting the gifted. I didn't say anything—just started warping my intention shields around me, using my teke to pull the energy into position, twisting electric fire around my wrists and knuckles like barbed wire made of flame. My shields vibrated at the same frequency the Cyn did; if I could hit him, I could *hurt* him—which he wouldn't expect.

Or maybe he would; we'd carved him out of his armor, after all. He knew we knew at least *some* of his tricks.

He stood, started toward us, slowly, like azure wildfire spreading through a forest of cool marble and golden light. *"I think the Palace seeks you, little one. What you think of as bravery, you don't—"*

Sho hit me with a wide-open channel, pulling as much energy as he could muster from the reactor core in the tower below us; it *burned* as I took hold of it, burned inside my mind, but I just let it, held on to the pain, then redirected that lashing channel of energy, making use of its chaotic, unrefined rush as I transmuted it into a whip, slicing across the golden distance between us and the Cyn.

Our enemy reached up, instinctively, to let the lash wrap around his arm rather than his head—whatever the Cyn had once been, they still had the vestigial instincts of organics, instincts like "protect the head," even if his head was no more a central part of him than any other limb at this point—and then he *did* scream, in pain this time, as the whip seared right into his energetic flesh. If he'd been organic, I would have said it "burned" him, except something already *made* of fire couldn't really "burn," and anyway I was too busy for metaphors: I was already running, charging right at him, Sho still channeling raw energy to me even as I shifted that energy into a shield, held out in front of my bull rush.

The Cyn dodged away from the ram of force, but manipulating energy wasn't the only trick I had up my sleeve—I threw a telekinetic push against the opposite wall, hard enough to crack one of the murals there, and the resulting force redirected my charge, throwing me right back toward him even as I swung the shield of fire around in that direction. It only clipped him, but that much energy made even just a glancing blow devastating; it warped and darkened the blazing brightness of his shoulder, and then I was in close, and close quarters was where I fucking *ate*.

It wasn't a fight about metaphor any longer—wasn't about what sort of clever things I could transmute with the energy Sho was throwing my way—but about actual, tight-in training; in a fight against an organic opponent the Cyn's size, I wouldn't have stood a chance, his mass lending too much force to his blows, but "mass" wasn't a question here: it was the amount of energy behind our strikes, mine trying to push through his energetic skin and strip away the electric fire that protected his core, his trying to overwhelm my shielding and scorch my *very* vulnerable flesh and bone into atomized dust.

I hit him. He hit back. The reverberations of those impacts were like thunderclaps inside the great hall; above us, the reflections of both our forms—mine nearly as bright as his, thanks to the twisting lines of energy that wrapped like blazing tattoos around my forearms and legs—glowed in the crushed pearl of the ceiling even as they scattered and shattered where cracks appeared from the force of the impacts below.

I hit him. He hit back, again. As we broke apart, another stalemate, his hands dropped to his sides, and at the speed of thought he re-formed his axes, this time out of the energy of his own flesh—focusing a piece of *himself* into the sharpness of the blades, so that they would scorch hot enough, fast enough, to get through my shields—and I took another step back, glaring at him across the burning glow of his weapons. That was a trick the "chaplain" I'd fought on Odessa hadn't known—if he had, our fight might have ended very differently.

Still, anything he could do, I could answer. I focused my will on the pull of my own intention shields and the energy Sho was still feeding me, tightening and sharpening the projected field until it wasn't barbed wire wrapped around me any longer, but a riposte to his challenge, instead: a pair of knives coalesced out of the bright flare between my palms, manifesting ex nihilo and flame until I held a curved, guttering crescent of fire in the grip of my right hand, and a sharp triangle of light was jutting from the knuckles of my left.

"*You* are *the one*," he said, something almost like awe in his voice, as we stared at each other across the emptiness of the throne room—and somewhere behind us, Meridian was frantically working, trying to make all this posturing and combat *mean* something. "*I can feel it in the synapses, in the very neurons, of the brightness beyond. You even feel like she do—*"

I came at him, hard.

I didn't really *give* a fuck what place I filled in his cosmology.

CHAPTER 15

Esa

The Cyn had carried axes in his armored form as well—that meant he knew how to use them. After just a few passes—passes where I came within an inch or so of losing my head to shining edges of bright fire—I knew he was better than me. I could keep him off, but not forever: even with Sho channeling all the energy I could possibly use, it took *effort* to warp that torrent to my uses, took *will* to keep my knives manifested and sharp. I would run out of reserves well before the Cyn did, and when that happened, I'd get sloppy, and in a fight like this, it would only take one sloppy move for me to wind up in separate pieces on the floor, glowing gashes of fire bisecting what remained of my body.

Not the ending I was hoping for.

I needed a way to distract him, to throw him off his game. Level the playing field again.

"Meridian." I spoke through gritted teeth, trying to suck in as much oxygen as I could as we sprang apart again, the Cyn and I circling each other in the great hall, both of us throwing off bright reflections that made the twisting alchemical murals on the walls seem to shift and run like liquid shadow. "I need you to read me."

"What?" To be fair, she was just a little busy scouring the Bright Wanderers' database, setting up a broadcast antenna, and hoping I didn't get us all killed. "You want me to—"

"Just *do it!*"

Like when she'd read Sahluk earlier, on accident, Meridian's gifts manifested music, drawn from the subconscious of her subject: reading *me*, I'd expected her to broadcast a burst of the down-and-dirty honky-tonk cludge that Javier listened to all the damn time inside Bolivar—I'd heard so much of it on this trip, taking a break from Schaz and Jane on certain hyperspace legs, that it seemed like it was always in the back of my mind. Either that, or maybe Marus's more classically inclined chamber pieces, Tyll harpisvaria winding through Klitek percussion and human electric guitars. Either one of those would have made *sense* for Meridian to channel out of my subconscious.

What I got instead was a full-volume blast of flat-out *opera*, an unseen chorus of seraphim scream-singing at full volume high above me, reams of dead language tumbling through major-chord descents like the entire world was about to be on fire. I don't know that Meridian had ever read me before, and so I hadn't really known what to expect—but apparently, my subconscious was gothic as *fuck*.

Still, it worked: the Cyn *definitely* hadn't been expecting an angelic chorus to start a goddamned a capella aria within the golden tower, and he took a step back, searching for the new threat, shifting his guard to meet it—and that meant he wasn't fully prepared to meet me when I lunged at him again, sliding under his haphazard return swing and then rising up from my lowered center of gravity, spitting him right through the center with the blade of electric fire that jutted from the knuckles of my left hand.

The Cyn stared at me, somehow glaring even with the no-face of flame he presented to the world; I stared back, and I was definitely glaring back at him as I pushed the blue line of pain further into his chest. The fire that made up his body was flickering, weakening, his axes evaporating into heat, but he wasn't dead yet—just wounded, badly.

If I gave him half a chance, he'd use his control over the energy of his own body to collapse his atomic structure, ripping the very molecules of his being apart to create an atomic blast that would kill all of us, himself included. I didn't intend to die that way: the chorus of angels screamed again, *I* screamed to match them, and then I ripped the blade free, "dropped" the knife in my right hand, and grabbed hold of his *face*, ignoring the charring, blistering agony against my palm and in my *mind* as my telekinetic field struggled to protect me from the blaze of his body.

I didn't have to shout for Sho—he'd been waiting. He opened up the floodgates, let *all* the energy he'd been siphoning from the reactor below come screaming across the channel between us. He'd been keeping the full force of it back; without anywhere to go, all that energy would have burned out my intention shields and fried me where I stood, but with the Cyn actually in my grasp, all I had to do was hold tight to the son of a bitch, and an entire fusion reactor's worth of output flooded through me and into him, making the Cyn's form jutter and stutter and *shift* as wave after wave of electric energy poured into him.

The lights in the great hall actually dimmed as Sho pulled the entire reactor's output away from the power grid and into himself—and from there, into *me*, and from me, into the Cyn.

Our enemy didn't last long, not under that kind of assault. His form began to melt and fade, and that was all the chance I needed: I saw the beating organ that lay at the heart of him—the only piece of any Cyn that still remained organic, touchable, killable—and I pushed my electric blade inside him again, widening the gash in his fiery form until I could shove the makeshift weapon all the way through him, my hand deep enough in his sternum that I could wrap my hand around his heart and rip it right the fuck out of his chest, sparks of his body following as if I'd pulled an ember from a dying fire.

The chorus of angels screamed in triumph, the climax of whatever opera Meridian had been channeling. I screamed as well, just a little, as I smashed the thing into bloody pulp—not with the atomic energy Sho was already cutting off to a trickle, and not with my telekinesis; just with the muscles in my hand.

Meridian cut off the unseen chorus; Sho cut off the flow of power, and I was left standing, sucking in as much air as I could, one of my hands still a *little* on fire, the other covered in the blood and pus that was all that remained of the second Cyn I'd ever met.

We'd been ready for you, you son of a *bitch*.

We'd been ready for him—and he'd been ready for me. Or at least, been expecting me. Some of the things he'd said . . .

They thought I was some sort of, I don't know, a messiah, some sort of prophet, meant to lead them to the promised land? They thought that's what *all* the gifted were—dumb animals that they could prey upon to achieve their own salvation? I was *no one's* prophet; I was *nobody's* salvation. How many kids like us had their "chaplains" *killed*, trying to steal us from our homes, trying to force us to fit into whatever insane religious rapture they were building toward?

Well, I'd show them that some of us could fight back: I'd show them that some of the lambs they were herding to the slaughter had claws and muzzles and sharper teeth than they'd expected from simple-minded prey. I'd show them what it meant to *fuck* with me and mine.

I shook out the fire in my hand, looking toward Sho and Meridian both, who were staring back at me across the golden hall of the tower. For a moment, we just . . . stood there, looking at each other, like we were all unsure of what we'd actually just witnessed, what we'd just heard, except we *weren't*: the Cyn—and their cultist followers—wanted to use us somehow, to make us unwilling "martyrs" for their cause, to seek this "Palace," whatever that was. That was why they were hunting us down, combing the universe for the next generation so they could harvest us like crops, cull us like cattle. They'd forgotten why they wanted us in the first place: because we could achieve something they couldn't. The reason they needed us at all was because *we were more powerful than they were*.

And unlike all those other kids who had died—unlike the face of the poor Vyriat girl I still saw in my nightmares sometimes, the one who had taken her own life in a cage rather than face whatever terrible future the Cyn that had stolen her away from her family had to offer her—we *knew* it. We knew it, and we were going to fight *back*.

Starting with whatever data was on the computer banks up on the dais.

CHAPTER 16

Jane

"We're receiving the broadcast from Esa and the other team now," Khaliphon said calmly as he swung around to pick us up, his unruffled demeanor unchanged even with the scattered fire being directed his way from more of the industrial laser cutters, repurposed from arm emplacements off the superstructure's hull. The things were meant to cut through dreadnaught plating—they could burn through his shielding just as easily, but Khaliphon was always calm, somehow.

As soon as the Preacher had cracked the passcode out of the empty AI shell, we'd loaded up the core with the bespoke virus JackDoes had broadcast to us from the relative safety of Bolivar, and we'd gotten the hell out of there. The Bright Wanderers may not have known exactly what kind of attack they were under—they may not have known they were under attack at all, not really—but they knew *something* was going on: their network was down, their AIs were cut off from the hub on the tower below, and then there was the matter of the several small explosions they must have been able to detect within the interior of the half-built dreadnaught, the sort of demolitions not even supercraft construction could adequately explain.

That meant the orbital yards were full of patrol ships, all flying back and forth seemingly at random, most of them cut off from their superiors and trying to figure out what they should do, and so mainly adding to the chaos. Honestly, we'd been lucky Khaliphon had so far only been scanned by some of the engineering teams on board the dreadnaught itself: if one of the patrol craft picked up his scent—or if one of the engineering teams on one of the nearly *completed* dreadnaughts managed to wonder what was happening in the other yards, and started turning their functional guns toward the chaos—we'd be in . . . significantly worse trouble.

Khaliphon had almost reached our position—he was already lowering a descent line toward where we were dug in on the top of the dreadnaught's conning tower, trading potshots with the Bright Wanderers' scattered security teams on the supercraft's hull—when the first missile sang directly past his port engine, exploding against the dreadnaught below us in a silent flare of flash and fire.

So *someone* had noticed the unregistered ship in their midst.

The rest of the team fell back into the airlock, but I saw my chance, and I took it: Khaliphon's evasive roll sent the descent line swinging right past the tower, and I pushed off the metal rather than falling back, making a wild grab for the trailing line as it lashed past, trying *real* hard not to think about what would happen if I missed and just went floating forever, doomed to suffocate inside my suit when my oxygen supply ran out.

I grabbed hold of the steel cable just as it pulled taut, Khaliphon rolling away, and then I hauled myself hand over hand up toward his cargo bay, buffeted as I went by the bursts of flak fire coming from the patrol craft in pursuit. "What the hell are you *doing*?" Javier hissed into my comm.

"'Phon could use some help," I said, pulling myself into the hold and shutting the door behind me. "We'll draw the patrols off—call in Bolivar to pick the rest of you up."

Yeah, it was definitely possible Esa had a point when she said she'd picked up a certain impulsiveness from watching me in action. "Act, don't react": that was what the voice in my comm—the voice in my *head*—had said, in the empty corridor before the core, and it had said it for a reason, my subconscious reminding me of where I'd come from. That phrase had been one of the earliest dictums of my training, something I'd learned well before the Justified, well before the pulse, back when I was just another soldier on the front lines of an ugly, endless war: in that kind of fight, "reacting" meant you were already bending to the enemy's will; "acting" meant bending them to yours.

And it was always better to be the one doing the bending. Because will, like anything else, could be broken.

"'Phon, where do you want me?" I asked, pulling off my suit's helmet and tossing it to the side; god, it felt good to be able to really breathe again.

"Rear turret, please, Jane," he answered, his voice still full of the unflappable sangfroid Marus prized so highly. "There are several . . . interested parties back there."

Thankfully, six months of travel—most of it spent in hyperspace, with our crews trading off between legs, just so we didn't drive our usual partners crazy with the enforced company—meant I knew 'Phon's layout nearly as well as Scheherazade's, and I knew there was an access hatch directly from the hold to the turret. As I slipped up the ladder and then behind the controls, the big gun was already thumping away methodically, Kaliphon unable to shift enough processes away from flight control to do anything more than throw off regular patterns of turret fire at the pursuit craft.

I didn't toggle the big gun over to manual control right away; instead, I just watched, and waited for my moment. There were three patrol craft behind us, their pilots easily evading the predictable patterns of the turret's firing solution, and I waited until one was halfway through a textbook barrel roll—slipping above the turret's line of fire so he could lock on with another missile—before I flipped the toggle and hauled the turret out of position, cutting the little patrol craft in half and then sweeping the gun's targeting back toward his comrades.

They scrambled in opposite directions, the destruction of the third craft making them swiftly aware that "directly behind Khaliphon" was no longer the safest place to be, and I hauled myself up out of the turret, letting 'Phon take control again and heading for the cockpit instead. It would take our pursuit a moment to realize his turret was back to more orderly fire; for all they knew, its return to predictable algorithms was just a ruse to catch them off guard again. I'd forced them to react to my play, and that bought me time to try something new. "Has the broadcast from Esa and the other kids finished yet?" I asked 'Phon as I moved.

"It's still continuing—there's . . . quite a lot of data there," he replied. "And given that the header title of the file is 'Esa 2–Cyn 0,' I think it's safe to say they met at least *some* resistance in the midst of their operation."

So: Esa had taken on—and taken *down*—another Cyn. Good girl. If we'd needed any more confirmation that these Bright Wanderers were somehow linked to the Cyn—beyond the promises the cultists were making, the scans Meridian had picked up on the transport, and the fact that following the original Cyn's vector was what had led us out here in the first place—well, we had it now. "Is Schaz en route for their exfiltration?" I asked Khaliphon even as I slid behind the stick in his cockpit, 'Phon manually adjusting the settings of the pedals and the stick to match my preferred positioning, data he'd pulled from Schaz.

"She's already picking them up," he confirmed. "The broadcast doesn't need them in place anymore, and Scheherazade still hasn't been detected by their patrol craft. Unlike us." This last was said somewhat pointedly—there were still bright lines of laser fire singing past the cockpit.

I took manual control, pulling 'Phon into a tight spiral and throwing everything he had into the rear thrusters, aiming us for the tangle of hanging steel and solar reflectors that was the shipyards' power station. Those thrusters didn't have the same "kick" as Schaz's would have—over the years, Schaz, JackDoes, and I had reworked her engines until she could go from full maneuverability to speeds just under sublight in an instant, even if it did nearly rip the stick out of my hands every time I pushed her that hard—but the maneuver still threw our pursuit off their game, and by the time I pulled up on the throttle, skimming just over the solar panels so we'd be difficult to find against the reflected light, the enemy patrol craft were too distant to get a clean shot, their lasers refracting off the panels beneath us to slice harmlessly back out into the void.

I found a gap in the panels ahead of us, then pushed the stick forward, spinning us down into the tangle of the understructure of the power station, juking and sliding past whirring arms and thrumming power lines (many of which Khalipon targeted with his rear turret as we passed: no reason *not* to fuck up as much of the Wanderers' infrastructure as we could). The patrol craft, despite being smaller and theoretically more nimble than 'Phon, declined to chase me into the maze, and as soon as we breached the other side, I found out why: there were another half dozen enemy ships waiting for us, and they all opened fire as soon as we shot free of the machinery.

I rolled clear—well, mostly; 'Phon's shields took a hit or two—and pushed the thrust to max again, even as the patrol crafts' barrages sang past us and collided with the power station instead: let them finish up the work we'd started, destroying their own machinery. As they tried to come around to follow, I was already diving us toward the atmosphere of the gas giant itself, aiming directly for one of the lavender storms lashing tendrils of lightning at the golden clouds below. "If you take us into the atmosphere, the hyperdrive will have to cool again,"'Phon reminded me, his voice not . . . *worried*, exactly, but definitely unsure of precisely what I was planning.

"Don't worry, 'Phon—that's not where we're headed," I told him, though I didn't change our course one bit—our rear shields were melting fast under the combined fire of the patrol craft, but if I tried to roll away again, I'd just be exposing the completely unshielded pieces of Khaliphon's underbelly to their withering fire. With the stick vibrating in my hand—Khaliphon was *really* not built for combat operations at maximum speed—I held our course, cuing up 'Phon's forward missiles as I did.

That was when Scheherazade came roaring out of the storm beneath us, her forward batteries blazing, tearing into the pursuit craft on our tail with a hail of combined ballistic fire and stuttering laser rounds. As the enemy ships scattered before the barrage Esa was letting loose from her cannons, I wheeled 'Phon around, locking targets and launching the missiles after the handful of ships that had escaped Schaz's sudden assault. "Break for the debris belt around the crushed moon," I ordered Schaz over the comm. "We can lose them in there until your hyperdrive has cooled."

"I was already *doing* that," Schaz said, a little petulantly. "Also, are you on Khaliphon's stick? Khaliphon: give me back my captain. Give me back my captain right now."

"Scheherazade, we're a little *busy*," I reminded her, making one last pass to frighten off the few patrol craft left, those still intact enough to make a try for arcing past us and coming around to strike at Schaz from behind.

"Fine—but don't get too comfortable over there," Schaz said, a note of possessiveness still lingering in her voice. "And don't get any *ideas*, either, Khaliphon. You sneak."

"I wouldn't dream of it," Khaliphon said mildly. "Marus is a much less . . . exciting . . . helmsman, anyway."

"I know! That's why I said it!"

I shook my head, matching Schaz's course as she dove for the cracked-apart moon—once a starship had entered an atmosphere, its hyperdrive needed a certain cooling period before it could engage, but the mined-out husk of the former satellite didn't have any atmosphere left. We should be able to lose the Bright Wanderers' patrol craft in the canyons and chasms of the smashed-apart crust, at least long enough to reengage our stealth systems and give Schaz's hyperdrive time to cool.

"So you took on another Cyn?" I swapped my comm channel over to Esa's personal frequency. "Well done."

"I'm pretty proud of myself," she replied nonchalantly. "But no big deal."

"Yeah? You still have all your skin?"

". . . Most of it."

"Then I'd call that an improvement over the last time you tangled with one of those bastards. Baby steps, but still."

She sighed. "Couldn't let me just have the win, could you? Anyway— Bolivar reports he got the others out: he and Shell are about to jump away, they'll meet us at the rendezvous point. Also"—a missile soared between our two ships, then vanished in a ball of flame as Esa expertly targeted the munition with Schaz's port-wing cannon—"we've got more patrol craft closing on us."

"Then let's go spelunking; see if they like chasing us through the wreck they've made of their own moon."

"I really don't think it's still 'spelunking' when you're in a spaceship."

"It is the way I do it." I pushed Khaliphon's thrusters to the maximum again—Schaz gave an undignified squawk as we overtook her—and dove for the detritus of the mining operation, aiming to lose our pursuers in the debris field and the broken chasms of the shattered celestial orb before the enemy could get a tracking lock on our engines.

It shouldn't be hard—for Esa and me, at least, this was just another day on the job.

ACT
TWO

CHAPTER 1

Esa

I stood from Scheherazade's gunnery controls and stretched, fighting back the absurd desire to yawn; despite everything I'd just gone through, I could feel the adrenaline crash closing in already, stiffening my limbs and sapping every ounce of strength I had left. This was what happened when you pushed yourself too hard, too fast. Of course, sometimes that pushing was necessary: I'd call coming face to face with a Cyn—and coming out on top—a "necessary" reason to push, even with the resulting headache and muscle fatigue.

"Everybody okay?" I called out, still stretching; Meridian was in the living area behind me, and Sho was down in the rear turret, where he'd been picking apart the attacking patrol craft before we'd jumped to hyperspace.

"I'm good," Sho called up, though from the sound of his panting, I could tell I wasn't the only one crashing; he'd pushed his gifts just as hard as I had in the tower, maybe even harder, and that was bound to be taking its toll. I frowned when I didn't hear anything from Meridian, and I crossed back into the living quarters to check on her; she was curled up in a chair, staring at one of Scheherazade's display screens . . . or rather, staring *through* it, not really seeing whatever it was displayed in the glowing lines of text scrolling past, likely the data we'd pulled from the network hub.

"Hey, you okay?" I asked her softly, touching her shoulder as I approached.

She actually jumped a little; either she'd been *really* engrossed in the data on the screen, or she was going through an adrenaline crash of her own. "I'm . . . I'm good, yeah," she said, shaking her head, then immediately grimacing and making the statement a lie, reaching behind her to grip my wrist:

thankfully, it was the one that belonged to my uninjured hand. "No, I'm not. I'm still terrified. Esa—that thing . . . it was . . ."

"Yeah, they're not . . . easy to get a handle on." The first time I'd seen a Cyn, his energetic body glowing through the holes we'd punched in his exosuit, I hadn't believed my own eyes—hadn't wanted to. Across the whole breadth of the galaxy, every single known species had certain physiological traits in common; all of them but the Cyn. Some things were just supposed to be true, and "a sentient being made of energy" wasn't one of them.

Of course, at the time, that particular Cyn had also just set off a nuclear blast that had leveled Sho's hometown, and come soaring out of the resulting mushroom cloud on steel wings like some sort of harbinger of the apocalypse, so I'd had multiple reasons to feel the icy grip of fear tightening in my gut.

"I thought I understood," she shook her head, leaning back in her chair, though she still kept her tight grip on my arm. "I read the reports from all four of you who were on Odessa, plus the Preacher's observations from Jaliad—I thought I knew what they . . . I thought I knew what it would be like. But I was wrong. I was wrong." She was quiet, for a moment, so quiet she seemed like maybe she was done; I sat in the chair next to her, pretty sure that wasn't actually the case. I just gave her time, a trick—a tool—I'd learned from Jane.

It worked; she started speaking again, for no real reason at all, but it would all come back around. She was just trying to process, any way that she could. "There's a . . . story," she said. "A fairy tale, really."

She was staring off into the distance now, into the blank space between everything—that first shock of combat affected everyone differently, and without Marus here, it was my job to walk her through it, so I kept hold of her hand, prompting her with a quiet "What sort of story?"

"A folk tale, from my people. It's like every other folk tale"—she shook her head—"probably based on nothing but superstition, meant to explain *why* my people evolved underground, why the surface of our lost planet was so dangerous. Why the sky was so far out of our reach. And even on *my* homeworld—where we didn't live underground, where we had . . . towers and highways and aerocraft—they still told the story, to children. Because it was part of our culture, you know?"

I nodded—it made sense; not even the sect wars had completely erased the fundamental cultures of the seventeen species—not for most people, anyway. Still, I said nothing: for whatever reason, she *needed* to tell this story, needed to use it to make sense of what she'd just seen, and there was no point in me jumping in and trying to "help" by pushing her when she wasn't ready to be pushed.

Jane, again.

"In the story . . . I read it in a book, when I was young." I could tell she was seeing the pages behind her eyes; "hearing" the words as she'd first heard them in her mind. "The story said the people of Avail angered the Princes of Fire, somehow—I don't remember how—and so they set the land alight and burnt the sky, and we fled below." That made a certain amount of sense, from what little I knew about the lost Avail homeworld: it had a very slow axial rotation, well off from most of the planets where the other species had evolved, and "days" would last as long as seasons on more typically terraformed worlds. The heat would have grown unbearable, very quickly. "But underground," Meridian continued, "we met the Princes of Winter, and they, too, were angered by our incursion into their lands, and so we were trapped: close enough to feel the sky, but never to see it; allowed to go deep enough that the heat was bearable, but not so deep the winter would snatch us away." I'm sure that part made sense as well; before being transmuted into a fairy tale for children, there would have been dangers, deep in the caves where her people evolved. "Princes of Winter" was as good a name as any for those dangers.

For a moment, she was silent again; I was on the edge of saying something else when she shook her head, still staring into the middle distance. "I used to *hate* that story." The words came out with a fierceness I hadn't expected. "It gave me nightmares. Princes of Fire, Princes of Winter, and us trapped in between. I could *see* them, in my mind's eye, very different from the charming illustrations of the storybook: tall, and regal, and hateful, wreathed in flame or ice. Still, I grew up, and I mostly forgot about it, you know? Until that Cyn came out of his armor. And then I knew: here was my nightmare, become real. A Prince of Fire, come to gobble me up for trespassing on his domain. And I was *terrified*.

"But you fought him. And you *beat* him. And not with the cold of winter, but with his own electric flame. I wonder: did none of my people ever think to try *that?*"

"Sho helped," I added quietly. "So did you."

She shook her head. "I just . . ." She turned toward me, and there was a vulnerability in her face, an openness, that made me ashamed, just a little. Maybe Marus was right. Maybe she didn't belong in combat at all. Training or no training, this life took a toll, and I didn't want to see that openness taken away. "I just wanted to—" Then she gasped, staring down at my side with her jet-black eyes grown as wide as saucers. "God, Esa, your hand!"

I raised the offending appendage up, and frowned at it; the adrenaline spike hadn't quite worn off completely, so I wasn't feeling nearly as much pain as I should have been. Grabbing a being made of fire by the *face*—then channeling a fusion reactor's worth of output into said visage—hadn't exactly done wonders for my skin, it was true. My telekinetic shielding had blocked most of the energy, but there were still blisters and second-degree burns all across my palm and my fingers, and of course, now that Meridian had pointed that fact out, I *could* feel a great deal of hurt radiating up my wrist; even the air stung against the injury.

"Yeah," I said weakly. "Ow."

"That's . . . 'ow'? That's what you have to say? I'm here telling useless stories about my childhood, and you're . . . just . . . just—Schaz, your medical suite, please, *now!*"

"Is someone hurt?" Schaz asked anxiously, even as she lowered the table down into her floor and folded the infirmary out of the wall. "Is Esa hurt?"

"Nothing I can't live with, Schaz," I said comfortingly, grimacing as Meridian grabbed up an injection gun and pressed it against the flesh of my wrist—the nearest she could find any undamaged skin.

"You even *sound* like Jane when you say that," Sho shook his head as he climbed up the ladder from the turret; I didn't know if he'd been listening while Meridian told her story, giving her the space she needed to deal with her reactions to the combat, or if he'd had his own fears to work out, in the privacy of the capsule below. Now, though, he was as calm as ever. "Lie back, Esa—let Schaz take care of you."

I obligingly obeyed—though I didn't think it was a *bad* thing that I sounded like Jane sometimes, and anyway, what did they expect? I had spent large chunks of the past four years with only Jane and Schaz for company, after all.

Schaz unfurled her robotic manipulator arms, and they began delicately peeling away the damaged tissue from my hand even as a barrage of needles began poking me in all sorts of places, injecting various solutions and compounds that would kick the medical nanotech swarming through my blood-stream into high gear. Once that was done, further instruments began lowering toward my arm, preparing to repair the damage nanotech alone couldn't.

"So," I asked Meridian, more to take my mind off the minor surgery be-ing performed on my appendage than anything else, "did you take a look at the goods? Was there anything useful in all that data? Because I'd really hate it if we went through all of that for nothing."

"It's too early to say, really," she pursed her lips, pulling up a different screen, this one mounted on the wall, since Schaz had sunk the main terminal in the floor to make room for the medbay. In order to not watch what was happen-ing to my hand, I was watching Meridian instead, the skinny Avail girl who hadn't even unstrapped her body armor yet, and I couldn't help but notice the slight tremble in her fingers before she clenched them tight; she was be-ing very brave, but this *had* been her first combat experience, and as far as those went, it had been a bad one.

"We pulled a great deal of data off of their databanks," she continued, that tremor in her hand not reaching her voice, "and most of it's at least partially encrypted—Schaz is running decryption algorithms now, based on the Preacher's work on Jaliad, the original algorithm she built to get the Cyn's course to Odessa—but the information is still going to be . . . fragmented, scattered, even once the decryption is done; we were pulling files damn near at random, and the decryption itself is scrambling the headers. We may well have come away with the Bright Wanderers' 'entire master plan for galactic conquest,' but even if we did, it'll *still* be all jumbled up with the Bright Wan-derers' 'entire master plan for what the mess hall will serve over the next six months.'"

"Probably something bland," I yawned—some of the many, many drugs recently introduced into my system included a few intense soporifics; I wasn't supposed to fight them, but I was going to anyway, because that's just what

I did—"like . . . Klitek tubers without any butter. Rice served with slightly different rice. Cults like order, regularity, predictability: they don't want their adherents getting any ideas about making things exciting. Or peppery."

"Drugs are kicking in, all right," Sho said mildly, watching my expression melt as I began to lose my fight against the injections. I made a rude gesture in his general direction with my good hand—he made it right back with one furry paw, and I grinned, albeit in a sleepy kind of way. "Before you slip off to dreamland," he continued, "is there anything we need to know? About the rendezvous when we're meeting up with the other ships?"

I shook my head, lying back against the pillow. "Schaz knows the course. We'll have to make . . . make multiple little jumps, each a couple hours apart, just to throw off any pursuit the Wanderers might . . . might have . . . might have . . ." I about cracked my head open with a yawn; I wasn't doing so good at the "fighting the sedative" bit anymore. Not that it really mattered. In my current state, not very much mattered at *all*—another Cyn could have materialized in the middle of the living quarters, dripping like liquid flame down from the light fixtures, and I would have yawned at him, too, and then fucked right off into dreamland all the same. "It'll be a few days, at least, before we can meet up . . . can meet up with the others."

We'd set a rendezvous point before we'd begun the operation, knowing full well we would all likely be leaving the cultists' system on different trajectories at different moments. Our little crew was currently all mixed up across the ships—Jane was alone on Marus's vessel, Sho and Meridian were on mine, and poor Bolivar was having to play host to everyone else, even though he was the smallest craft in our fleet next to Shell. "I hope he . . . brought enough snacks along," I muttered sleepily.

"Snacks? Esa, what are you . . ." Meridian turned to Sho. "Is she hallucinating? Is that . . . like . . . a code phrase?"

"Bolivar. For . . . for . . . houseguests," I explained to her, though for the life of me I couldn't bother to remember why I was keeping my eyes open at all. It seemed a silly thing to do. "A good host . . . always . . ."

And then I was gone.

CHAPTER 2

Esa

I woke to the sight of the ceiling above the medbay table; I was depressingly familiar with the particular contours of that part of Scheherazade's hull. Sho was sitting at the kitchen counter, working his way through . . . some kind of meal, something likely high in protein heaped in mounds on a platter: young Wulf grew fast, which meant they ate a lot. In the six months I'd known him, he'd grown—and matured, emotionally—as much as a human might in a few years. In *another* six months, he'd be roughly at his full size, and the emotional equivalent of a young adult, the same as I was. For now, though, he was still caught in that somewhat awkward period between adolescence and the beginnings of real maturity.

"Welcome back," he said dryly, keeping his voice low. "How was dreamland?"

I grimaced, levering myself off the table, careful not to use my injured hand, not that I could have even if I tried: Schaz had worked her miracles, and while it didn't hurt anymore, I couldn't feel anything at all beneath my elbow, like my arm just . . . stopped somewhere beyond my shoulder. Everything from my wrist down was wrapped in shiny foil; it looked like the covering Sho had pulled off his meal before he popped it into Scheherazade's reheater.

"Medsuite drugs give me weird dreams," I told him, testing out my other limbs for stiffness.

"Beings made of fire, great towers of shimmering gold? A moon cracked open to its core, and a chorus of unseen angels singing opera in a dead language while you poured atomic fire through your body and into the face of your enemy? Sorry, big sister"—he gave me a Wulfish grin around a bite of some kind of meat—"that's just our lives now."

"One of these days you're going to get that sense of humor all bruised and battered, you keep abusing it so much," I said, taking a seat beside him—and grabbing an extra fork to steal some of his meal. Wulf-ecology allidon meat, slathered in spicy barbecue sauce. Synthetic, of course—allidon, like nearly everything else native to the Wulf homeworld, were too vicious to domesticate—but still tasty.

"Now you *really* sound like Jane. And get your own dinner."

"Tastes better when I steal it from you. Where's Meridian?"

He nodded to the far side of the main table, where Meridian was fast asleep, her head on her arms. I hadn't even noticed her there, she was curled up so tightly in on herself. "I tried to get her into the private cabin," he said, nodding toward the small room at the far end of the living quarters—Jane and I usually reserved it for when we had passengers, like the gifted children we rescued, but it hadn't seen much use on this particular trip, except when Jane and Javier needed some alone time. "But she was just . . . out. She waited until you were patched up—watched the whole time, like she thought Schaz was going to make a mistake—"

"Like I would," Schaz sniffed.

"—and then she went down damn near as fast as you did, no sedatives required."

"Well, it was a long day," I said, keeping my voice low to avoid waking her.

"You can say that again. Esa: can I ask you a question?" His earlier complaining aside, he leaned back, pushing what was left of his platter toward me—I didn't need a second invitation to dig in, even with only one working arm.

"Sure," I said around a mouthful of allidon. Fancy table manners were not a prerequisite for space travel, or not for a berth on Scheherazade, at least.

"Are you attracted to Meridian?"

I stopped chewing my bite of brown-slathered meat. "Come again?" There probably wasn't a great deal of dignity in my response—if nothing else, I was pretty sure I had barbecue sauce smeared across my chin—but I couldn't help it; I had not been expecting *that* particular question.

"I know humans and Avail are . . . compatible, in that way. Humans actually have the widest sexual compatibility of any of the seventeen species. Interesting, huh?"

"Hey, it's not my fault nobody else is furry enough for the Wulf."

"The other species' coats *do* lack luster," he admitted, taking a sip of water. "But you didn't answer my question."

I finished chewing and leaned back, really thought about what he was asking. *Was* I attracted to Meridian? She was very sweet, and funny, and smart, and there was something undeniably . . . *appealing* about her Avail features, like she was a statue hewn from onyx, only much softer, very . . . touchable.

"I don't *know*," I shrugged, a little uncomfortable; I wasn't very good at self-scrutiny, another habit—or lack thereof—I'd picked up from Jane. "*Maybe?* Why do you ask, anyway?"

"You just seem very . . . solicitous of her."

"And I wasn't solicitous of you, when you came on board?"

"You were, but that was different. My mother made you my sister." Sho's mother had died in the Cyn's attack on Kandriad—or perhaps even just before, a victim of the sectarian conflict that had raged across his homeworld—and she'd known her end was coming, known that her son would have to make his way in the galaxy without her guidance. She'd sent him with Jane and me—to heal the injuries to his spine, to give him a better life than what he'd know otherwise—but before she had, she'd made me promise to take care of him, to make him part of my "pack." Wulf culture took family bonds very seriously: as far as Sho was concerned, I *was* his sister, and I reciprocated the connection—I'd always wanted a little brother anyway.

Though if he kept tucking into the allidon, the term "little" wasn't going to apply for much longer. When he finally finished growing, he was going to be *big*, even for a Wulf.

"I don't know, Sho," I shrugged, still a little uncomfortable with his line of questioning—little brother or not, this wasn't the sort of thing I'd spent a great deal of time thinking about *myself*, let alone considering sharing with anyone. "I really don't. We've got . . . a lot going on. We're stuck on a convoy months and months from our home, exploring far beyond the edges of everything we've known, and likely to face off against horrors and wonders we couldn't imagine. I don't know that trying to form a romantic connection with someone else right now is really the best time for that sort of thing."

"Or maybe," he offered a differing perspective, "it's exactly the *right* time."

"Easy for you to say—we don't have another Wulf on board. And now you sound like Javier."

"Thank you," he grinned.

"Oh, stuff it, will you?"

He raised up his paws. "I'm just asking a question, sister. You didn't have to answer, you know. But it never even occurred to you to lie, did it?"

I shrugged again—I seemed to be doing that a great deal in this conversation. "Look: do I find Meridian attractive? Yes. Is that attraction just . . . aesthetic, or is it something deeper? Sho, I promise you—I've been so busy, not just these last six months, but these last few *years*, that 'interrogating my own sexuality' hasn't exactly been high on my list of priorities. Does that satisfy you?"

"I think it satisfies *you*, maybe. Or at least you think it does." He grinned at me again. "But *I* think you're attracted to her."

"I'm getting that, Sho."

"I think you're attracted to her, and you know what?"

"What?"

"I think *she's* attracted to you right—"

"You two idiots know I can hear you, right?" Meridian didn't raise her head up off the table when she spoke, but I groaned all the same, dropping my head in my good hand and running my fingers through the fuzz of my slowly returning hair.

"Can we just pretend you *didn't*, though?" I asked her plaintively. "For all our sakes?"

"Sure thing." She yawned, and snuggled deeper into the crook of her arm, not opening her eyes once even as she started to glow, just a little. God help me, I found it *cute*.

"Good. Thanks. Great." I wasn't looking at her anymore—I was too busy glaring daggers at Sho, who was still grinning back at me, like an idiot.

"Hey, Esa?" Meridian asked, her voice still sleepy.

"Yeah?"

". . . You think I'm *pretty*."

". . . Shut up and have sweet dreams, Mer."

"'Kay."

CHAPTER 3

Esa

Once I was finished with my breakfast and Meridian had officially decided she was awake now—and not just pretending to be asleep to eavesdrop on people's private conversations, private conversations those people, like *idiots*, started right in front of her—we got to work, diving into the data we'd pulled out of the shipyards.

Meridian had been right; there was a lot of it, and the very decryption process we used to unscramble the files had completely rearranged their storage order, so there was no rhyme or reason to any of the file locations. Still, it was something to do other than focusing on my horribly embarrassing breakfast, and putting that out of my mind wasn't made any easier by the behavior of my shipmates: Meridian was just . . . there, being pretty, Sho kept grinning at me when he thought I wasn't looking, and Schaz occasionally interrupted my research by opening new tabs on my screen—mostly with fragments of early records from the first human explorers who had encountered the Avail, or sexual health guides on human-Avail couplings. I honestly couldn't tell if she was attempting to be helpful or just wanted to get in on the joke.

I ignored all three of them—even Meridian, who couldn't really help the "being pretty" thing—but I wasn't getting anywhere with the data, either. I sighed, leaning back in my chair. "This isn't working," I said, somewhat waspishly. "There are *millions* of pages of data here, everything from the cooling cycles of the mining equipment used to core out the moon to indoctrination procedures for newly arrived 'recruits.'"

"I've come across some pieces of that stuff myself," Meridian admitted with a grimace. "The indoctrination routines, I mean, not the mining equipment. It's . . . an ugly business."

She wasn't wrong; if we'd had any doubts about the true nature of the Bright Wanderers, they'd been put firmly to rest by some of the procedures they subjected recalcitrant recruits to. Isolation, pharmacologically induced psychosis, even invasive neurosurgery had all been on the table to "reorient" those who "struggled in their commitment." "Point is," I said, "we need some way to . . . sort it, to make sense of it. It's not like high-level communication from the leaders of the sect—or even just the commanders of the shipyards— are going to be labeled as such, since Schaz's decryption algorithms seem to have *eaten* all the file headers."

"Not my fault," Schaz protested hotly. "It's the Preacher's decryption program, after all."

"Yeah, but it was designed to work through the databanks of a single Cyn's records—the records of one of their 'chaplains'—not the collected archives of an entire shipyard. If we—"

"That's it," Meridian snapped her fingers, a quick pulse of light highlighting the veins in her arm—she'd had an idea.

"What's it?" I asked her.

"'Chaplain': that's what the Cyn said, the term he used for one of his kind that sought out the gifted. That was it, right?"

"It was," Sho nodded.

"And we also heard him say 'inquisitor,' and 'martyrs,'" Meridian continued. "He even called us 'heretics,' before he realized we were all gifted, all next generation. Your reports from Kandriad, Valkyrie Rock, and Odessa, as well." She was busy poking at her screen, likely pulling up the exhaustive reports we'd written—and then rewritten, and then rewritten again, until Criat was satisfied he'd wrung every bit of information out of us, even things we'd forgotten or initially overlooked—after the Odessa incident. "The Cyn you met there used religious terminology too: 'goddess,' 'crusade,' 'sin.' Even the stories we've picked up about their proselytizers, their recruiters: almost all of them referred to the Wanderers using phrases like 'salvation' and 'damnation.' They're *obsessed* with the language of religious eschatology—the notion that we're all being punished somehow, that we're living in a kind of apocalypse, one only they can avert."

"The Cyn on the tower—he called me an 'imitation.'" I shifted uncomfortably in my chair; something about that word had struck a little too close to the bone, for some reason. "That's not religious terminology."

"Not to any religion *we* know, but that may just be the exception that proves the rule," Sho pointed out, before turning back to Meridian, Javier's influence making him take the devil's advocate position for both of us. "Still, Mer, it's a little thin—a great many cults use eschatological language in their recruitment; I don't know that it *means* anything, necessarily, besides the fact that it's easier to bring people into your ideology if you convince them the rest of the galaxy is somehow lesser, or at least unaware of some impending doom."

"I still think it's worth a look," Meridian said, her jaw set, stubborn. "Schaz, can you do a keyword search through all these files? Highlight and separate any religious terminology, and prioritize the terms we've already heard the Cyn use."

"Will do."

"Once you've run that, cross-reference with two more terms," I said, sitting up in my chair; Meridian's theory might not have been airtight, but it had the ring of truth to it nonetheless, and besides, we didn't have any other leads to go on. "Add 'palace' and 'open the way.' He said that's what we were going to do, once he'd captured us; what we were going to be . . . used . . . for. I have a feeling maybe that's what the Cyn, the . . . chaplain . . . we fought on Odessa—maybe that's what he was trying to achieve as well."

"They were kidnapping the gifted to try and get them to *open* something?" Sho frowned. "But he was also killing them, killing *us*. Can't open something if you're dead."

"Only as a last resort," I shook my head. "The killing, I mean. His priority was retrieval, but maybe they think there's something to be gained by . . . studying . . . our remains." The word wasn't nearly ghoulish enough for what it implied, but I couldn't think of a better way to put it. "I still got the impression that taking us alive would have been the first priority—both for the chaplain and for the Cyn we fought in the tower."

"Done," Schaz said. "Isolating for religious terminology leads to fifty-seven thousand, six hundred and two separate files; further isolation for the specific terms we've heard Cyn use cuts that down to twenty-one thousand, nine hundred and twelve. Cross referencing with either 'palace' or 'open the way' narrows it down to six hundred and forty; cross-referencing with both isolates one hundred and eighty-three."

I groaned; those results weren't nearly as narrow as I'd hoped they'd be. I guess the Bright Wanderers really enjoyed their end-of-days rhetoric. Still, it was a start. "Divide the six hundred and forty into groups of three, please, Schaz, and break them out to our three terminals," I said glumly. "Start us off with the isolated pages that use both terms together."

Schaz would be scanning the documents herself, of course—had been doing so, over and over again, since we'd first downloaded them—but an AI, even as talented as we could make them, still couldn't understand nuance or pattern recognition the same way a *truly* sentient being could: simply put, their minds weren't chaotic enough to make the leaps of intuition required for this kind of work, or even to follow the similarly chaotic impulses of the organic beings who had put all this down in the first place.

"There's something here," Meridian said confidently, already starting to sort through the information on her screen. "I know there is."

"Even if the religious obsession is merely a facet of the indoctrination of their cult, it's worth a look," Sho agreed. "Learning more about them, even if we don't learn where they've come from, can't be considered wasted effort."

"I don't think it's been wasted at all." I barely whispered the words; sometimes, you just got lucky.

The first page. The very first fucking *page* Schaz had pulled up for me: *the martyrs will restart the fires of the Dead Furnaces, and once their light again illuminates the cosmos, the way to the Palace itself shall finally be made clear. Only once the goddess opens the way beyond those gates will she be able to purify the first sin from the very void itself, and the last echo of heaven shall return as a chorus of flame.*

"You've got something?" Sho asked me.

I read the passage out loud to the others; the rest of the text was a similar jumble of sermonizing and eschatological rhetoric—I couldn't tell if it was some sort of public address given by the station commander, or perhaps part of the indoctrination ritual used once the cult's adherents "ascended" to a higher level of their faith—but "martyrs" had been the term the Cyn had used in reference to the gifted. That meant that *this*, this act of "restarting the fires of the Dead Furnaces"—which was a phrase that didn't sound ominous at fucking *all*—this was what they wanted us for.

"Schaz: cross-reference everything we have for 'Dead Furnaces,'" Meridian said immediately. "And scour the rest of the documents as well. Prioritize anything that might be a map, or a location."

"There's . . . nothing else," Schaz said as she scanned the databanks again. "No other references at all to that specific terminology, either in the samples we've already set aside, or elsewhere. Perhaps—"

"Eliminate 'dead,'" I told her—another shot in the dark, intuition, more than logic, guiding my thought process. "Just look for 'furnace.'"

"One other hit," she said immediately. "'The Furnace's Gate.' Esa: it's a planet. And it's on a *map*."

CHAPTER 4

Jane

I frowned at the map displayed on Scheherazade's holoprojector, Meridian's hand-coded notes floating in glowing script over the world the Bright Wanderers had designated "The Furnace's Gate."

Khaliphon and I had finally rendezvoused with the others in the unremarkable system we'd designated as a rally point—there was almost literally nothing here; just a supermassive red star that, if it ever even had planets, had long ago swallowed them up as it grew—and baleful red light was thrown across Schaz's interior through the portholes, making the flickering green of the display seem weirdly malevolent as well, a sickly marshlight glow in the face of that external hellfire glare.

"It's the best we've got," Esa replied firmly, and she was right: none of the rest of the team onboard Bolivar—or I—had come up with anything anywhere close to a lead while going through the data Schaz had broadcast to us all before we'd jumped. There were a few worlds designated as "high priority" by the Bright Wanderers, but that was about it, and we didn't know *why* those worlds had been so keyed: they might have been important industrial, agricultural, or cultural sites already under the Wanderers' control; they might have been the homeworlds of *enemy* sects the Wanderers were preparing to take over, through infiltration and recruitment of the populace, or just by the expedient tactic of dropping several of their brand-new dreadnaughts into orbit.

The "Furnace's Gate" was not among them. Esa had done her due diligence, checking and cross-checking her new findings against the rest of the data we'd pulled from the shipyards' network—the map Scheherazade had found was the only reference in all of it, either by name or by the stellar co-ordinates of the system. It didn't show up on the maps we'd taken from Rai-zencourt Observatory, either, so whatever it was, it wasn't some relic of the Golden Age.

Which either meant the world *wasn't* as important as Esa thought it was, or the Bright Wanderers were keeping it hidden, even from their own fol-lowers. Given the basics of how cults worked—something I knew all too much about—I was willing to bite on the idea that it was the latter.

"You're not wrong," I agreed with her, leaning back from the map and turn-ing to look at the others, all equally transfixed by the data, all looking slightly sickly in the red glow of the soon-to-die star. "Thoughts?" I asked.

"Her logic is sound," the Preacher agreed, somewhat surprisingly: I thought she would have been keen to focus on the Cyn, rather than the religious ramblings of the Bright Wanderers, but I wasn't giving her enough credit, I suppose. "And we know there's a direct link between whatever these . . . chaplains . . . are doing with the next generation, and whatever they're trying to achieve with the pulse."

"Investigating this 'Furnace's Gate,' though," Marus pointed out, "will take us even further off the projected course of our original target—the back-trail of the Cyn we met on Odessa." He reached up and expanded the map again; the bright line of our best guess as to the Cyn's course arced away from the cluster of space Esa would have us head into, further into the unknown.

"We have to adapt to new circumstances," Javier shrugged. "That's what being Justified is all about."

"That's what being *Javier* is all about," Sahluk said dryly.

"Yeah, that too. It's why I'm so damned good at my job."

"I'm not saying we shouldn't look into this new information, necessarily," Marus shook his head. "Just making sure everyone realizes that if we do, and it doesn't pan out, we're going to be quite a ways off from any of the other worlds that the Bright Wanderers labeled as significant." He nodded at the map, and he was right: the coordinates of this "Furnace's Gate" were in a sea of dark on the display. There was just nothing out there, nothing in any of the surrounding systems, even. Not even a terraformed moon spun within a dozen light-years of Meridian's marker.

"These Bright Wanderers—whether they realize it yet or not—are a direct threat to the Justified, a direct threat to Sanctum," Sahluk said. "I hate to agree with the mapmaker—"

"I . . . still have a name, Sahluk—" Javier protested mildly.

"You do, and you're right. We need to adapt, just like you said. We need to head to this 'Furnace's Gate,' not because it's our best bet of figuring out where that original Cyn came from, but because at this point, our mission parameters have changed. I think the Bright Wanderers—and their fleets of dreadnaughts—have to take priority. You don't build weapons like those unless you plan on using them—"

"Or on selling them," Marus put in. "Though that could be nearly as destabilizing as a full-on invasion, depending on who they sold them to."

"They won't sell them," I shook my head. "That's not how cults work. They wouldn't trust that much power in the hands of someone not themselves. Everyone else is an outsider, and every outsider is an enemy of the faith."

"They sold them to the Pax," the Preacher reminded me.

"They *gave* them to the Pax, and I'd bet anything I own inside this ship that they also provided the Pax with the location of Esa's homeworld as a target ripe for plucking, *and* with the location of Sanctum."

"Please don't gamble with my things, Jane," Schaz said primly; I ignored her.

"That wasn't a risk on their part," I continued, "that was a calculation—they knew the Pax would move directly against the Justified once they were told we had gifted children, and I'd wager—"

"Not with *my* stuff you won't—"

"I'd wager they knew we'd find a way to win, too. They just wanted us distracted, off balance."

"I think you might be forgetting how close we came to losing that fight, Jane," Sahluk reminded me. "It was by no means a sure thing."

I shrugged. "Fair. But either way, they would have known we would have cut apart the vast majority of the dreadnaughts they 'gifted' the Pax—even if the Pax had won, their strength was always going to be greatly diminished afterward, because they'd thrown everything they had against Sanctum. It was always an overreach on their part, and it's never quite made sense that the Pax would make that play: not unless they were goaded into it, goaded by the same people who handed them the dreadnaughts. Make them feel powerful by giving them all these fancy new ships, then give them a target to use all that power on. And when the fighting was done, both the Pax and the Justified are diminished, if not wiped out all together. Two birds, one stone."

"So long as we're making bets—who's willing to take the odds that they didn't 'give' the Pax the dreadnaughts at all?" Javier added. "I'll bet they just abandoned them in some out-of-the-way system, then fed the Pax the location of that system, sideways-like. Pax philosophy would mean they wouldn't look twice at such good fortune—they were powerful enough to deserve a whole fleet of dreadnaughts, so the universe just . . . manifested them, for the Pax to find."

"And on those dreadnaughts' databanks, the location of Sanctum, and Esa's homeworld, both," Marus nodded. "And the Bright Wanderers are never directly involved—if we hadn't been all the way out here, been all the way out here *and* stumbled across their shipyards, we never would have known. Hell, Justified forensics teams went over every inch of the few dreadnaughts that were still floating after the Battle of Sanctum, and none of those teams ever found a hint of where the ships had come from originally."

"All of which leads us back to the question of the day," Sahluk nodded again at the map. "The data we pulled from the shipyards shows the various dreadnaughts heading off in different directions once they're completed. Whatever these Wanderers are doing with their supercraft, they're not centralizing them in one place, not unless they're taking a very roundabout way to get there. So we don't really have a way to track that threat, not unless we break from our mission entirely and spend the next year following up on each of those vectors one at a time. But we do have a line on what the Wanderers want with the next generation, thanks to Esa and the rookies," he nodded at Esa, who nodded back; I couldn't help but notice that, to Sahluk, at least, Esa herself was no longer one of the "rookies." "So again: my vote's for following her instincts, and heading to this 'Furnace's Gate.'"

Esa herself had been very quiet for all this; that was suspicious in and of itself. Whatever else she was, "unwilling to speak her mind" was *not* a character trait she'd ever had, and that had been true even before she'd come under the influence of watching me exercise my own not-inconsiderable temper. I turned toward her again. "Well, partner?" I asked. "It's your plan; you've had longer to weigh the pros and cons than the rest of us. What do *you* think?"

She shrugged. "It took us three days to get here from the shipyards—three days that Meridian, Sho, and I spent every waking hour of, almost, going through that data. And I'm willing to bet the rest of you did much the same on your trip."

"We had to," Javier said dryly. "Bolivar wasn't built to hold that many people, not for extended periods of time, and certainly not when one of those people is six hundred pounds of rock."

"Six hundred pounds of rock that's perfectly willing to knock you into the next world, mapmaker."

"You take up a lot of space, Sahluk, that's all I'm saying. Point is—we *had* to spend the trip staring at screens, otherwise we'd have been at each others' throats."

"And *my* point is," Esa continued on, "in those three days, none of us found anything else in the shipyard data that looks like a solid lead. Reaching the Dead Furnaces isn't just our best bet, it's the only one we've got. And, yeah, the connection between 'Dead Furnaces' and 'Furnace's Gate' is a tentative one, but it's still the only connection any of us pulled out of all that data, in all that time." She nodded. "I think we go, yeah. But I think we go cautious, and we go quiet. Our little assault on the shipyard will likely have the Bright Wanderers' collective noses to the wind—they know we're out here now, even if they didn't before. The trap on the observatory might have been a reaction, a defensive move, but now . . . now they're going to be the ones hunting *us*."

She had been watching me, the whole time she was talking, even as the rest of the crew were watching her. I nodded, just a little bit, and gave her a small, approving smile, when what I *wanted* to do was pick her up, spin her around, and shout "You really *have* been listening!" at the top of my lungs.

My little girl was finally growing up.

She smiled back, then rapped her knuckles twice against the metal of Schaz's holoprojector, a habit she'd picked up from Criat. "So—we've got ourselves a course," she said. "Now will everyone please get off of Scheherazade and back to your respective ships? Having three messy teenagers onboard over the last few days has driven Schaz close to a nervous breakdown when it comes to her floors."

CHAPTER 5

Jane

Wait, you're into Meridian? I didn't see that one coming." I frowned, a little bit, playing it up for her sake more than my own. It wasn't actually all that surprising, but Esa had been surprised by it, and I was—always—on her side.

"I didn't even know you liked girls," I added, like an afterthought. That was a lie too, of course—once she'd grown out of a little bit of a schoolgirl crush on Javier, which was only natural, she'd been drawn like a lodestone toward women, but there was no real reason to point that out, either, since I didn't know that she'd fully figured it out for herself yet. Until, apparently, being stuck in close quarters with the young Avail spy for three days had rather forced the revelation.

Right on the money. "Neither did *I*, I don't think!" Esa threw herself down on her bunk, producing a dramatic "flump" in the process. Our course set in, we'd started the long hyperspace jump toward our destination—it would take us nearly a week to reach the Furnace's Gate—and almost as soon as the airlock was sealed, this had come bubbling out of Esa like a teapot on the boil. She'd started by telling me what I'd missed during her mission to the network hub, but she hadn't even gotten around to detailing her fight against the second Cyn before she'd come out with *this* particular piece of information instead. It was clear what she, at least, considered far more important. "Jane, what do I *do*?"

"You're asking *my* advice? After what you know about the long, strange courtship Javier and I went through?"

"You're still my partner," she growled—an impressive trick, that growl, given that she was also staring forlornly up at the ceiling at the same time. "And my mentor. So come on . . . mentor me! Give me some of that good mentoring gleaned from your long, long, looooong—"

"You do realize I forgot Javier's birthday last month, right? Bolivar had to remind me. I'm not exactly the *best* at interpersonal stuff, is my point."

"I don't give a damn about your problems; come *on*, Jane! Advice me."

"You should *kiss* her." This came, of course, from Scheherazade. "Right now."

"We're in hyperspace right now," I reminded her gently. How my own ship could forget that particular detail, I wasn't sure.

"Right. As soon as we reach our destination, then," Schaz amended, a little petulantly. "The first time you see her, go sweep her off her feet: just go march right up, grab her, and—"

"Keep in mind, of all of us, Schaz is the most incurable romantic," I told Esa.

"Marus," they both said at the same time.

"We're literally a thousand light-years from home," Esa moaned. "We're going to be stuck out here for a long, long time—even if we turned around right now, which we're not going to do, we'd be out here for another six months. This is *weird*, and anything I do's just gonna make it weirder—"

"But you get the reward of happy make-outs if everything works out!" Schaz chirped enthusiastically. "People like happy make-outs, Esa. I have the data to prove it. You can use the spare room, if you like—"

"Thank you, no." She wrinkled her nose. "I'm not doing anything in Jane and Javier's sex dungeon. That room is *rank*."

"'Dungeon'?" I asked mildly.

"Fine. 'Sex pit.' Does that make you happier?"

"You could stand to clean up a little better in there," Schaz reminded me. "I mean, the shower's *right* next door—"

I shook my head, cutting Schaz off. "You know I like her, right?" I told Esa. "You know that—all joking aside—I think you two would be a good match. She's smart, she's significantly more . . . even tempered—"

"This implying that I'm not."

"Anyone who's ever *met* you can infer that, and pretty quickly, kiddo. Yes, I'm implying that you're not. I'm saying—you want my advice? Don't make the mistake Javier and I did. Don't wait until it's almost too late, and don't get derailed by all the . . . insanity and nonsense around us. There's always going to be insanity and nonsense—that might as well be the official description of the wider galaxy, on all of our maps: 'here lies insanity and nonsense.' We're dealing with a crazy cult now, yeah, but after that gets handled, there will be another paramilitary strike force, or a 'genetic purity'–obsessed death squad, or something equally horrible; there always is."

"Your faith in the better angels of the various sentient species in the galaxy is always just so life-affirming," Schaz told me dryly.

I ignored her. "But that leads me to another conversation we need to have— one we've been needing to have for a while now, and I've just been looking for the right time to have it."

Esa sat up in her bunk. "You just swapped over to your serious voice. Why don't my relationship woes make you use your serious voice?"

"Because you're interested in her, and she's interested in you—that math's easy, Esa; it's fairly cut and dried. Scheherazade is right. You should kiss her."

"That's the sum total of your advice?"

"Yep. And I've moved on now."

"Fine," she sighed, still a little theatrically. "Go ahead with serious voice."

"You took the lead on the strike mission on the tower—and you didn't hesitate. You faced down a Cyn, yes, but more importantly, you *volunteered*— and both Sho and Meridian followed you without hesitation. They'd follow you into a full-blown stellar collapse, and that doesn't have anything to do with Meridian's fairly obvious romantic feelings for you."

"Seriously? Now you're just—"

"Yep. Past that, you put together the information on the Furnace's Gate— yes, you needed the help of the others, but *you* took the lead, you connected the dots. And even back there, with the rest of the crew looking on: you laid out your plan, you waited to see what the others could contribute, then you took all of that into account, and you made an argument for your course of action. Do you see what I'm saying?"

"That I'm impressively persuasive?"

"That you're a Justified operative. Not an 'operative in training,' not my second in command: you're not learning the ropes anymore. You don't need them anymore. I'm saying we're past the point where the ropes can come off entirely."

Esa frowned at me. "It's entirely possible I don't know what 'the ropes' are in this metaphor, Jane. Did I miss some lesson about ropes, or tying things?"

I smiled, slightly. "And a few years ago—or even six months ago—you would have kept that lack of knowledge to yourself, and just tried to bluster through. I'm saying you're ready, Esa. You're my partner—you'll always *be* my partner. But the Justified needs more operatives in the field; we always do. I'm saying keeping you on board Scheherazade—with me—beyond a certain point is a poor allocation of resources."

"No. No. No. No no no no no no *no no.*" This little outburst did not come from Esa; it came from Schaz, of course. "You can't just . . . *give* her away, Jane! She's mine, she's *ours!*"

"She's grown up, Schaz," I said quietly, watching Esa's face—she'd been listening, intently, as I spoke, but she was schooling her expression, which meant she was feeling *something* about what I was saying, but whether that was agreement, excitement, despair, I couldn't tell, and that in and of itself spoke to the fact that she was ready. "She's trained. It would be . . . selfish of us to try and keep her, when the galaxy needs her elsewhere."

"So . . . what does all that mean?" Esa asked quietly. "Are you saying— when we finally get back to Sanctum, whenever that is, you go to Criat, and you—"

I shook my head. "He's already come to me. Several times, actually. The first time—well before Kandriad, before the Cyn—I told him you weren't ready. The last time, before we took off on this venture, he wasn't asking anymore, and he knew I'd changed my mind. Relax, Esa." I gave her what I hoped was a comforting smile. "It's not like as soon as we get home I'm toss-ing you out on the street. All this means is that, right now, John Henry and Bathus are busy building an AI for you. It'll be done by the time we get back to Sanctum. That's the *last* step in an operative's training, before they get their own ship; you'll have to train her, to raise her, just like I did Schaz."

"Oh, *no!*" Schaz wasn't just being theatrical this time—she was legitimately horrified by that idea. "I am not letting some other AI—the same AI that's going to steal my Esa away—on board this ship! I am *not!* Do you remember how *horrible* I was to Al-Kindi when you were raising me?"

"I do—I think they call this 'karma,' Schaz." Al-Kindi had been Mo's ship, my mentor among the Justified, and Schaz *had* been pretty horrible to him, all things considered—unlike organics, AI were born "mature," with their databases full and their processes in place, but they didn't have the lived experience or emotional spectrum to make use of all that knowledge. The combination made them remarkably similar to teenagers—highly intelligent, deeply self-absorbed teenagers—for the first six months or so of their existence. It was Justified policy to make an operative spend that time "raising" their starship AI, so the bond between them was more than just data and programming—it was a "real" thing, forged by experience and shared respect.

"You really think I'm ready?" Esa asked me softly, and her expression wasn't schooled then—or maybe it was, and I could just see through it. She was afraid, and she was excited, and she was proud, but trying not to be: she was a lot of things, all at once, and just trying to muddle through as best she could. Best any of us could do, I suppose.

"I really do," I told her, reaching out to take her hand. "I think you have it in you to be one of the best, Esa—but more important than that, I think you have it in you to do a lot of *good*. And that's what matters most."

She swallowed, and nodded, and brushed a tear from her cheek, suddenly not trying to be stoic anymore, as if, just by taking her hand, I'd given her permission to let the mask slip. That was fine; I could admit that I'd been crying a little as well. "So long as we don't get killed on this op first," she amended my statement.

"Well, yeah. Obviously."

CHAPTER 6

Jane

J avier," I asked slowly, "what am I looking at?"

The planet beneath us, the very last solid world on the edge of an otherwise unremarkable system, was a small marble of swirling chaos. Storms—*a storm*—blanketed the entire surface, making the atmosphere seem nearly alive, a crawling, spasming thing in constant motion, like a blue-black swarm of rain and wind and thunder. Blue-black, that is, until crimson lightning split the skies, and then massive patches of the storm system would glow bright red, even pink at the edges, like an algae bloom that faded almost as soon as it had appeared.

There was nothing about those storms that hinted at why we were here; nothing about the world to indicate why the Bright Wanderers had such an interest in it. Just those constant spinning tempests, exploding into brilliant light shows every few seconds. The only good news so far was that there didn't seem to be any Bright Wanderer presence in the system, either—no dreadnaughts, no stations, no tech of any kind. Just the squall-choked world that had been flagged on the piece of the map Esa had found as the "Furnace's Gate."

"Yeah, that's . . . that's a place, all right," Javier answered through the comms. I'd been hoping for something a little more concrete—Bolivar had, by far, the best scanning equipment of any of our ships. Javier, however, was apparently so impressed by the hurricane-cloaked world he hadn't actually used any of that equipment yet.

"Why would anyone build something *here?*" Esa asked, staring through the cockpit from the gunnery seat. Our four ships were just out of range of the world's gravity, all angled down to stare at the constant swirling of the light-splashed rain clouds below.

"It's all ocean underneath the hurricanes," Javier said, getting around to actually reading his scans. "I mean, there's crust down there somewhere, of course, but it's entirely submerged, and submerged *deep*. Cold as hell, too; the seas are mostly liquid neon, the rainfall and the storm clouds as well—that's what's causing those flashes, whenever the lightning strikes. The atmosphere's breathable; mostly just oxygen and more gaseous neon, and neon's inert. Assuming you didn't freeze to death so quickly you couldn't even take a breath, you'd be fine."

"Who the hell would terraform a place like this?" Sahluk asked, apparently studying the scans as well, on board Khaliphon. "There's no terra to form."

"I don't know that anyone did," Marus replied to him. "The oxygenated atmosphere may simply be a byproduct of the storm, or of the atmosphere's basic composition. It's not *so* rare in the galaxy, after all—all the organic species originated on planets with oxygen-rich atmospheres that came about naturally. We're just used to equating oxygen with terraforming because ninety-nine percent of worlds we set foot on were created that way, rather than coming about their atmosphere naturally."

"Marus is right," Javier said. "I think it's a natural occurrence."

"You're picking that up from your scans?" the Preacher asked him.

"No, just experience—why would you terraform *this* world, and not any of the others in the system?" He broadcast his data over to our ships, the information on the other planets in the orbital chain, sweeping outward from the fairly normal sun that made a distant orb of fire at the center of the alignment. "Look: the second world in; it has more than decent mineral deposits. It definitely would have been worth terraforming, at least back when that was possible—it's pulsed all to hell and back now—but no one ever did. The fourth world's the same. Even a few of the gas giants out past us would support refinery platforms. The old corporations could have made a fair bit of cash in this system, but nobody ever did—because nobody ever found it, maybe? I'm not sure." The universe was a big place; even after the several-millennia-long span of time encompassing the Golden Age and the sect wars both, there were still more systems unexplored than otherwise, so it wasn't impossible no one had been here until the Bright Wanderers arrived.

"So why are *we* here?" Sahluk asked. "Or, more specifically—what is it about this place that caused the Bright Wanderers to flag it, to name it? There's nothing down there, nothing but storm."

"Oh, there's something," Javier disagreed. "I'm picking up energy fluctuations from near the equator—the storm's causing all sorts of interference, making it hard to pinpoint exactly where the readings are originating from, but *something* down there is generating a great deal of energy, significantly more than just the lightning. Energy, and heat. It's in a fixed position, too, inside a hundred-mile radius or so. The planet rotates at a pretty good clip—almost three full rotations every standard 'day'—but that signature stays steady. Hell, it may even be responsible for the storms, or at least their severity: that much heat in one portion of the upper atmosphere, meeting the colder air from the night side as the planet turns, is a recipe for meteorological chaos."

"How is something *generating* that much energy at all, though?" Esa asked. "Unless Bolivar's reading something different, our scans aren't picking up reactor radiation. That means it's not fusion, and you couldn't exactly build a solar array down there, not underneath all that."

"Wind power, maybe?" Sho joked.

"You might not be wrong," Marus mused, taking the notion seriously, despite Sho's tone. "Whoever chose to build something here—and ignored all the other worlds—was thinking way, *way* outside the box. Again, we're so used to power being generated by fusion reactors or solar arrays—because they're both so cheap, relatively speaking—that we forget there are other means of producing energy. Wind, combustion, geothermal—"

"Yeah, it ain't that one," Sahluk told him. "Any 'geo' down there is buried *deep* under water, which is in turn buried by a whole lot of storm."

"But you could, theoretically, harness that very storm energy, if you needed to—or the churning of the waves below," Marus answered. "Anything in motion can spin a turbine, and both storms and waves are a source of motion. It would be a . . . complex working—especially if Javier is right, and the generator is simultaneously producing the storms—but it is doable."

"Perpetual motion on a planet-sized scale." JackDoes sounded impressed by the concept. "A machine, generating a storm, powering a machine. There's an . . . elegance to that, no?"

"It may be elegant, but what would be the point?" I asked. "I mean—"

"That might be the most 'you' thing you've ever said," Javier interrupted dryly.

I could hear the grin in his voice; I ignored him. "I get that the act of building a fusion reactor in all . . . that . . . would be dangerous," I continued, "but they've been built in worse places, and once you got the thing built, it would be stable as solid rock; they always are." Stations and big starships were powered by fusion reactors for a reason: unless they took a direct hit, they could go through almost any kind of stress without the risk of catastrophic failure—the sort of failure that would be immediately lethal for everyone on board. I doubted the same could be said for the complex workings of a planet-sized meteorological hurricane turbine, or whatever the hell it was we were looking at.

I could hear the shrug in Marus's voice as he replied: "Maybe this place is far older than we think," he said, slipping into his historian's cadence as he warmed to his subject. "Fusion reactors weren't perfected until early into the Golden Age—part of what allowed that age to prosper to the extent that it did was because the seventeen species shared technology, information, overcame certain obstacles together that none of them had been able to surmount alone. Shrinking the window of terraforming from centuries to decades to years; stabilizing planetary rotation and axial tilt; miniaturizing hyperdrive tech—all of those were based on technologies that had been discovered *before* the Golden Age, but weren't perfected until after the species came together, and brought their various knowledge with them."

"So you're saying this place is *pre*–Golden Age?" I asked, just to make sure I was hearing him right.

"It's . . . a working hypothesis, but yes," he admitted. "As you said: nothing we would build, especially in a place like this, would generate that much waste energy, which means it's either very old, or the waste energy has a purpose—creating the storms, in order to power the generator through the very atmospheric churn the energy creates. A kind of ad hoc perpetual-motion engine in the form of an entire planet, like JackDoes said. And that's still not something that would be necessary, not if a fusion reactor—or even a magnifying solar array—could simply be built in orbit. Ergo, it must be older than perfected fusion tech; that's the only explanation I can think of."

"So this was built by one of the seventeen species before they encountered any of the others," Javier said, something close to awe in his voice. I could understand why: the homeworlds of most of the sentient races had been lost forever during the chaos of the sect wars—either figuratively, when their locations had been wiped from all known databases in an attempt to protect them, or, in the case of the Klite, the Vyriat, and the Grailt, quite literally, when the worlds had been destroyed by the very same sort of planet-killer weapons the Justified had built the pulse to prevent.

And if we were truly hovering over a world—over a machine, somewhere in the atmosphere—that had been built by one of the seventeen, that meant we were at least relatively close to one of those lost homeworlds. Early hyperdrive tech had been extraordinarily cumbersome, and comparatively slow when held against the engines we used today; the territory "claimed" by the species before they encountered one another would represent a relatively small slice of the galaxy, not very distant from where they'd each originated. Still hundreds upon hundreds of systems, of course, but not the millions upon *millions* that were reachable now.

"Whatever it is—whoever it *was*—that built this place, that's a question for academics and intellectuals," Sahluk reminded us all.

"I *am* an academic," Marus reminded him, a little wounded; he'd been a historian with the Justified before he branched out into field duty.

"And I consider myself something of an intellectual," JackDoes added, something almost breezy in the little Reint's tone; I couldn't help it, I barked out a laugh, and heard JackDoes hiss in reply, gratified by the fact that somebody finally found him funny.

"My point is," Sahluk continued, "the Bright Wanderers came here for a reason, and we're here to find out what that reason was. So what's the plan of attack, here? What's the approach?"

"It'll have to be Schaz," I told him. "Maybe Bolivar could handle those storms, but neither Shell nor Khaliphon can. Plus, whatever it is that's causing them is also causing a great deal of disturbance in the planet's magnetic fields, and that means we'll have instrument troubles before we even hit the atmosphere: the same reason Bolivar can't lock onto that energy source's signature. That means once we're *in* that mess, we'll have to rely almost entirely on dead reckoning. I mean no offence, Marus, Preacher—"

"—but you and Javier are better pilots than we are," I could hear Marus nodding as he said the words. "No offense taken."

"If I had a better ship than this Pax reject, you might think differently," the Preacher grumbled at me; apparently *she'd* taken offense, at least a little. I just grinned, and took no offense my own self—the Barious hated admitting someone else was better than her at something; it was just in her nature.

"So—an expeditionary team, then?" Marus suggested. "Jane and Esa on Scheherazade, Javier, JackDoes, and Sho on Bolivar? And the rest of us stay on-station in orbit, feeding you information—if we can—on the storm's patterns, and keeping watch for anyone else arriving in-system."

"Oh, you're not taking any kind of expeditionary team out minus me," Sahluk said. "That's my job description, remember? I'm no good in a space fight, but I can blow shit up real well on the ground."

"I don't know that you'll have anyone to shoot *at* once you reach your destination, Sahluk," Marus told him. "There's no hyperspace radiation in the atmosphere, no hot vectors leading in—if someone's been here, it hasn't been in the last few weeks, at least."

"All the same—still more useful down there than up here. Maybe they'll need something, I don't know, picked up. Or crushed. Those are . . . those are pretty much my two skill sets, outside of 'explosions.'"

"I'll join the expeditionary force as well," the Preacher offered. "Sahluk, join Bolivar—I'll go with Jane and Esa on Scheherazade. That way, between JackDoes and myself, each team has a qualified mechanic on board, in case we hit trouble in the storms."

Now it was my turn to frown in the general direction of the comms systems. "Who the hell do you think has kept Schaz flying all these years?" I asked her. "I'm a *perfectly* qualified mechanic."

JackDoes just started hissing again, in Reint amusement; I regretted laughing at his joke earlier, the little bastard. "You're . . . adequate, Jane," the Preacher said primly, sounding for all the world like she was a schoolmarm dealing with a difficult student, one who thought she was smarter than she was. "At least, adequate for emergency repairs and for when your ward manages to overload the hot-water system on board—"

"That happened *one* time!" Esa protested weakly—she was lying; it had happened twice. She was mildly obsessed with hot showers, I think because they'd been a paradisical luxury on her homeworld.

"But at best," the Preacher continued, ignoring Esa entirely, "you can manage to keep your vessel limping, not soaring. Without regular maintenance at Sanctum, we both know Scheherazade would have fallen apart years ago."

"I mean . . . she's not wrong, boss," Schaz told me. "I pretty much always feel, like, worlds better after we've had, you know . . . actual mechanics work on me."

"Fine," I said sourly—Esa was trying not to grin at me, the hot-water jab forgotten in *my* sound rhetorical beating, and she was failing miserably in doing so. "Get over here," I told the Preacher, "and get on board; slave Shell's systems over to Khaliphon when you do." That way, the Preacher's ship—lacking an AI of its own without the Barious on board—could be controlled by Khaliphon if something happened. Not controlled very *well*—Khaliphon would be too busy dealing with whatever was happening to spend too much processing power trying to fly the former Pax craft—but more so than if it were just . . . floating. "Marus, Meridian, you offload Sahluk to Bolivar, then hang tight, and keep a close eye on the approach vectors. Once we're down there, we'll be blind; we'll be counting on you to react if someone else drops out of the stars."

"Good luck," Meridian said softly, one of the first times she'd ever felt brave enough to pipe up on one of these comms sessions, and now it was my turn to grin at Esa, who was scowling right back at me. We both knew it wasn't *me* the pretty Avail girl was wishing good luck to.

"Descending into a tempest-cloaked, pre–Golden Age storm world," Jack-Does said moodily. "Why do I feel like my talents are going to be needed very, very soon?"

I would have tried to come up with some sort of rejoinder to that, but the truth was, he probably wasn't wrong.

CHAPTER 7

Jane

Oh, *god*, I'm *blind!*" Bolivar wailed.

"Calm down, buddy," Javier said soothingly. "You're not blind. You're just not used to flying with most of your sensors down."

"I am, I'm like . . . three-fourths blind! That's more blind than not-blind!"

I hated being right. We hadn't even hit the atmosphere proper yet, and the strangely warped magnetic fields were already playing merry hell with our instruments. Schaz didn't have it quite as bad as Bolivar, mainly because Bolivar had a much more precise—and therefore delicate—suite of sensors to begin with, but it was still disconcerting; we were flying into a raging tempest using only dead reckoning, and all we had to guide us was the fixed equatorial position of the heat output coming from whatever theoretical facility had been built in the atmosphere of the storm-choked world.

Still, nothing else for it: I tightened my grip on the stick and dove us downward, toward the cyclonic churn of the blue-black atmosphere. "Schaz, I want full shielding, even if you have to steal output from the engines to do it," I told her, the command provoked by another bloom of shining red, a hellfire glow on the edges of the clouds: the aftereffects of storm-born electric discharge coursing through the neon skies. If one of those lightning strikes hit *us*, we might as well have been targeted by a frigate's laser battery. "And cut the running lights on, too. Give Bolivar something to follow."

"Like a nightlight for a frightened child," the Preacher said with the inflection of a smile in her voice; I smiled as well, just a little. Despite the Preacher's occasional tendencies toward your typical Barious superiority complex, it felt good to have her back on board Scheherazade: with Esa in the gunnery chair and the Preacher behind the (currently useless) navigation console, it felt just like old times, especially with Bolivar at our wing, a reminder of the pell-mell chase we'd led when I'd first met the two of them, trying to beat the Pax to Sanctum.

Esa, meanwhile, was quietly humming to herself as she primed the weapons panel in front of her—we weren't expecting trouble, but I'd trained her to always be ready for it, regardless. The song, barely audible under her breath, was something I couldn't quite place, a strange, lilting tune, one I'd heard her sing to herself before. Out of the corner of my eye, though, I could tell that the Preacher *did* recognize the music, and she was looking at the teenager quite sharply. "How do you remember *that?*" she asked Esa.

"Remember what?" Esa asked, still focusing on the instruments; she hadn't even realized she'd been humming.

"It was . . . never mind," the Preacher shook her head, and let whatever it was lie.

"Brace for turbulence," I told them; the storm clouds were coming up fast, the outer edges of the atmosphere full of massive breakers of boiling vapor. The rain-swept storms were as tall as cliff sides, each split by pillars of collapsing fronts and valleys of dead calm, the whole mess shot through with the neon blooms left in the wake of the near-constant lightning.

"That might be the understatement of the year," Esa told me; my smile stretched to a full-on grin in response.

God help me, I *loved* this sort of thing.

We dove right into the storm, our running lights illuminating the cloud banks around us, making sculptures and faces rise out of the churning walls of tempest. Rain spattered across the cockpit, sometimes glowing slightly as it struck the edges of Schaz's shields; the neon in the liquid was channeling the electric charge. "You on us, Javier?" I asked.

"Like a Reint on a fresh-killed merioc carcass," he replied, then added, belatedly, "Sorry," presumably to JackDoes.

"What?" the little mechanic replied. "I *do* love merioc meat. It's tangy."

"Focus, guys," I told them, their nervous chatter receding as I searched out pathways through the clouds, finding twisting avenues between the storm heads, barely able to see farther than we were flying, except when the whole atmosphere came alight in the neon burn. I was starting to find a kind of rhythm there, though—not in the lightning strikes themselves; those were chaotic, random, leaving blooms spreading in their wake like ripples after a stone that had been skipped across a pond—but they came often enough that I could glance ahead to try to predict the movement of the storm, and thus keep us clear of the worst of the buffeting.

"Four-fifths blind," Bolivar moaned softly, into the quiet that had stolen over the comms. Schaz's instruments, as well, were dancing and leaping like mad every time we hit a wave of magnetic interference; I reached down and shut them off entirely, a distraction I didn't need. Dead reckoning—it was how I'd been taught to fly, when my sect was still locked in combat on our homeworld, kept from the freedom of the stars beyond by orbital strikes and anti-aircraft cannons, and instruments would have been a dead giveaway to the scans of our enemies. If I could fly bombing runs on enemy fortifications— coming up under the defilade of their AA fire to drop refitted seismic charges right on top of the walls of their fortresses—I could do this.

"I'm going to start pulling us a few degrees port, every chance I can get," I warned Javier. "We've been shifting away from our heading, away from the energy readings, thanks to the path we've had to carve through this mess." I was actually sweating—or maybe that was just the beads of rain rushing past the cockpit glass, making me *feel* like the same liquid was running down my skin. I grinned again; I hadn't had this much fun at the stick in years.

Esa was humming again, the Preacher still staring at her, and it wasn't ex- actly distracting—actually the opposite, in a way, the sad little tune calm- ing, almost meditative—but I was still zoning out a little, focusing too much on *finding* the course through the storm rather than what was around me cur- rently, and that was when another one of the crimson lightning spikes splashed bright glowing pools of light through the cloud heads. I thought I saw some- thing in the burst of the lightning, but it wasn't until the bloom of neon that came afterward that I was sure—sure, and not sure at the same time, because what I'd seen had been . . . impossible.

"Pull *up*, Javier!" I shouted into the comm, doing the same on my stick. Impossible or not, there was *something* there: something *big*. "Pull up *now!*"

I hauled back as hard as I could and pushed the throttle to full reverse thrust; all the same, it was a damn close thing.

We soared over the top edge of the massive monolith that had come looming out of the storm, rising from nowhere—if I hadn't caught the edges of it, silhouetted against the swirling clouds in the bloom from the lightning strike, we would have smashed right into its surface, and that wasn't *just* because I'd been zoned-in a little too far: the few of Schaz's instruments still working should have warned us of an obstruction that close, and they hadn't.

I didn't need to see the strange glyphs carved into the monolith beneath us—though I could, as lightning again spiked through the storm—because I already knew what we were looking at: it was a forerunner relic, a floating remnant of the cosmos-faring race that had existed well before any of the current sixteen organic species, the same lost species that had been the creators of the Barious. I'd seen the monoliths before—miles-long stretches of floating stone that seemed to obey no laws of physics at all—during our approach to Odessa, and even there, without the magnetic soup currently making a hash of her instruments, Scheherazade had utterly failed to recognize their existence; she hadn't been able to pick them up on any sort of sensors at all.

"That's . . . not possible," the Preacher whispered, and I could hear the metal of the console creak as she tightened her grip reflexively around it. She knew what forerunner relics were, of course: her sect had operated Odessa Station, before she'd fled with Esa, and so she'd be able to recognize them.

"Possible or not, it came damn close to smashing us apart and spreading the wreckage all across the ocean below," I growled, leveling off and looking up for our rear projector feed—sure enough, there was Bolivar, right behind us, Javier tipping his wings back and forth to make the running lights dance, just so I knew he was still back there.

"Of course it is," Esa said, her humming stopped, now, forgotten—she was leaning forward in her seat instead. "Of *course* it is," she repeated. "The Bright Wanderers—the Cyn—they're obsessed with the pulse, and the tech to build the pulse bomb, at least some of it, came from forerunner relics. It makes sense they'd note the location of a world with forerunner relics—"

"But what does that mean the 'Dead Furnaces' are?" Sho asked her over the comm. "And if the Wanderers were here studying the relics, where did they *go*?"

"These are all very good questions," I told them. "And once we fucking find whatever it is that's flooding the atmosphere with heat and creating these storms, hopefully we'll find answers. But until we get there, do me a favor and keep it the fuck down, so I can concentrate on avoiding the massive hunks of floating metal that I can't fucking *see*." Where there was one relic, there were more—they'd been found on dozens of sites across the galaxy, and that had always held true.

Sure enough, no sooner had we finished passing above the rain-slick, weirdly even surface of the first monolith—it seemed like it went on forever, even bigger than the dreadnaught-sized relics in Katya—another one loomed out of the storm front, a lightning strike's illumination coursing through the liquid neon that ran down its sides, making the whole thing look like it was dripping electric blood. It was like something out of a nightmare—ungraspable, unknowable, something beyond our very comprehension, massive and alien and terrifying.

I wasn't having nearly as much fun anymore.

CHAPTER 8

Jane

The good news is you're closing in on whatever it is that's pumping energy into the atmosphere, Jane, but the bad news is that . . ." With a crackle of static and a high-pitched whine that made me wince away from the comm, I lost Meridian's voice; that was it, our eyes in the sky were gone, or at least blinded, temporarily.

"Can you clear up the interference?" I asked the Preacher, who had swiveled to the comm console set against the far bulkhead.

"Not possible," she said; she'd already been trying. "Jane: this isn't interference from the magnetosphere—it's an active jamming broadcast. Whatever . . . facility is at the heart of all this, it's blocking all transmissions out of this location. Unless we hit a dead zone in the signal, we're on our own."

We were still soaring in between the forerunner monoliths, great hulks of not-quite-metal that slowly rose and fell through the storm clouds, the lightning sometimes crawling along their flanks and leaving neon tracers through the wash of rainfall sweeping over their edges. There was a truly massive storm front to our port side, and I had a very bad feeling what the "bad news" Meridian had been about to deliver might have been.

"Hold on, everyone," I said, and I was speaking through the comm as well—short-range communications, at least, were still holding.

"Oh, tell me you're not doing what I think you're doing," Javier sighed; he already knew the answer.

"I am. I think the . . . whatever it is we're headed toward—I think it's in the eye of that storm. See how the storm wall isn't moving?"

"It's . . . moving plenty. It's moving a *lot*."

"It's *rotating*, yeah, but it's not shifting out of position—it's . . . anchored, somehow, tethered in place, maybe because that's where all the heat is coming from. We've got to go through the storm front."

"I hate this."

"I know. Just follow my lead." I waited until we'd passed another one of the massive relics—that was the seventh we'd seen, and there were more, waiting just inside the storm, I was sure of it—then cut hard to port and plowed right into the side of the boiling cloudbank. The thermal push of the rising heat—relatively speaking—that was sustaining the storms made the air currents chaotic around me, but I wasn't fighting their pull any longer; I should be able to feel it, in the stick, if those storm channels came up against another monolith. The resistance of the pull would fade away, giving me just a tiny amount of warning before—

—there. I pulled hard on the yoke, angling us up and away, and we soared clear of another monolith, Schaz's wings mere meters from the adamantine material; we passed so close I could see her running lights reflected in the liquid streaming over the surface. The rain splashing against my cockpit was a constant flood now, and I couldn't risk ionizing the glass to clear it off—I had a feeling that would just draw the lightning strikes. I checked my rear projection; Javier had followed my lead, and he'd cleared the monolith as well. Just a little bit more now . . . just a bit more . . .

We broke clear of the storm, or at least of the massive cyclonic storm wall we'd been pushing through. There was still plenty of rain, and still thunderheads boiling above us, but the eye was calmer than anything else we'd seen in the atmosphere. All we needed now was—

—another flash of lightning, triple-pronged, spreading neon blooms through the storm, the color rising up like mushroom clouds following a carpet-bombing. In the flood of light, I could see another monolith beneath us, this one *not* moving, anchored in place somehow just like the hurricane was anchored around us, and rising off the leading edge of the relic: a glint of metal, something made of different material than the monolith itself.

"What the hell is that?" Esa asked, leaning forward in her chair. I shook my head; I had no idea, even as I pulled us closer, bringing into view some sort of . . . *ring*, a massive circular construction, metallic and complex. This wasn't relic construction—it was later, the product of one of our species, the tech at least something we could comprehend, if not recognize—but still . . . old. Very, very old.

Whatever it was, it was big, big enough to fly a dreadnaught through, not that you could get one into this atmosphere. The ring was anchored to the top of the monolith itself somehow, though I'd never heard of tech that could even pierce the strange material of the forerunners' construction. Cables and stays traced down from the ring to tie into a facility clinging to the top of the relic like a barnacle, its mundane nature—squat, utilitarian, almost military—weirdly out of place amid the alien construction of the monolith it was built upon.

Those cables and trailing wires continued out to the side of the facility as well, leading to three pillars that rose up out of the storm, surrounding the relic like a triangle, electric blue light crawling up and down the complex machinery of their construction. Even as we watched, another lightning strike hit, and it was drawn into the pillars themselves, the pinkish glow of the charge slowly subsumed into the blue.

"I don't know," I answered Esa as I was pushing Schaz's nose down, drawing us closer even as I cut thrust: I actually had to fight to do so; there were great, sweeping thermals coming off those pillars, trying to carry Schaz upward and back into the raging storm behind us. We'd found the source of the heat energy, and more besides.

Whoever had done this—created the storm, created those pillars—they'd caged a forerunner relic. The pillars, and the ring, they were creating some sort of field, holding the monolith in place, forcing it to obey mundane principles of gravity and magnetic attraction, the sort of principles forerunner relics tended to completely ignore. I'd never heard of such a thing, not ever.

"I do," Javier said as Bolivar fell in behind us. "The ring, at least; I've seen a few of those before, out on the fringes. It's called a 'direct rift': very, very old tech. Marus was right—this place predates the Golden Age, by a fair bit."

"What does it do?" Sho asked him.

"In theory, it opens a single, stable hyperspace rift in orbit above the world—a point-to-point jump," Javier said. "In theory. I've never seen one working, though. I've *heard* there's one still operational in Shear territory, but

I've never seen it, nor met anyone that claimed they had. The Shear aren't exactly . . . friendly."

"Javier is right," JackDoes agreed. "Direct rifts are a . . . dead avenue of tech, largely abandoned during the Golden Age. Before the miniaturization of hyperspace drives, they were the only way to achieve interstellar travel. But why would it be *here*? There's nothing in this system, and for a direct rift to have value, there would have to be another rift, aimed at this world from somewhere else, another system. They're like doors, doors that only open one way—if you build one as an exit, like this one, you have to build an entrance somewhere else."

"Doors?" Esa asked, and I knew what she was going to say next—I'd had the exact same thought. "Or 'gates'?"

"The Furnace's Gate," Sho breathed. "This is why the Bright Wanderers made note of this world's existence: whatever these Dead Furnaces are, this rift is what led them there. But once they arrived at that location, *this* place was useless: once they had that system mapped, they could reach it with conventional hyperdrives. No need to deal with all this . . ." He made an uncomfortable hacking sound, the Wulf equivalent of a snort, indicating the storm around us.

Something about the name of our final destination still made my skin crawl, and it wasn't the "dead" part. Furnaces were good for two things: powering something, or incinerating something. Whatever the Bright Wanderers were after, neither one of those would be good outcomes.

"So can we open the rift again, do you think?" I asked Javier. "Follow them through?"

"I mean, the ring's intact, and there's clearly power running through the system," he answered. "That's more than I could say about any of the others I've seen. Plus, if Sho and Esa are right, the Bright Wanderers *have* opened it, and in the relatively recent past. So I don't see why not."

"You don't sound too sanguine about our odds, though," the Preacher added dryly.

"I'm a cartographer," he replied, and I could hear the reluctance in his voice. "I like to map things as I go along—so that I can follow my path back if I have to. A direct rift could spit us out halfway across the galaxy, out of any kind of known space, Golden Age era or otherwise. If we open the rift and fly through, we could be in hyperspace for months, or even years, and there's no guarantee there's another rift in that location, pointed back this direction. See how big that thing is? It was designed for ships much larger than ours, ships that could carry supplies for *much* longer jaunts. We could very well starve to death before we even came out of the rift."

That was a cheery thought—our four ships, sailing through hyperspace as we wasted away inside, finally tumbling out the other end crewed only by the dead—but I pushed it aside: we needed to deal with *this* place first, and we could worry about the rift after. "We at least need to check the facility out," I said firmly. "We'll leave the next step for the next step. If nothing else, if we can get into that complex, we can unjam our communications, get Marus's input." Plus make sure everything was good topside—with our long-range comms cut, Khaliphon could be in a dogfight against a frigate right now, and we'd have no idea.

"Certainly we're going to check it out," the Preacher said, sounding surprised, as though it wasn't even possible someone might have suggested anything to the contrary. "Regardless of the rift, that's a forerunner relic beneath it, a forerunner relic somehow . . . chained, anchored in place. Those that built my people also built that thing, and no one has ever been able to study them this closely before." Regardless of what else she was, the Preacher was a scientist first, and all Barious shared a certain . . . veneration . . . of the lost race that had created them. It wasn't *quite* a religious deification, and most Barious would scoff at the idea that it was even related to the various faiths of the organic species, but it was closer than any of them would like to admit.

"There's a landing platform, just outside the facility," Javier said; I had seen it too, a circular platform slick with the wash of the rain. "Let me set down first, Jane—in case something comes out and tries to eat us, Schaz has better anti-personnel weapons than 'Var."

"I have better weapons than Bolivar, period," Schaz said, a little smugly.

"Yes, dear, you're very deadly," Esa told her, reaching out to touch the console like she was stroking an already purring pet.

I pulled Schaz into a slow circle as Javier sat Bolivar down on the platform— whatever had been meant to fly through the ring, it hadn't been meant to land at the facility itself; there was enough room for half a dozen ships our size, but not for any sort of larger vessel, though I supposed frigates or dreadnaughts all had launches they could use to ferry people to and from the facility if it had been necessary.

"All right, we're down, and nothing's trying to kill us yet," Javier reported, his figure a silhouette against the light of 'Var's cockpit. "There's power to the facility, but no—hey, *hey*!"

"Let go of me!" Bolivar shrieked; I pulled Schaz back to get a clean shot even as Esa swiveled the laser batteries on the wings toward them, ready to target whomever the aggressors were, but there was no one emerging from the facility, just strange cables, snaking around Bolivar's landing gear, anchoring the ship to the platform.

"False alarm," Javier reported, though I could tell from his voice he'd nearly had a heart attack. "It's just an anchoring system, meant to make sure whoever lands here doesn't get blown off the platform by the winds. It's the sort of thing we'd do with magnetic fields and pinpoint gravity generators, but again . . . this is old tech."

"Can you get them off you?" I asked him.

"Not from out here—I was about to say, there *is* a wireless network emanating from the facility, but it's encrypted well past 'Var's ability to crack. Which doesn't make a lot of sense, given how old this place is, but it's true anyway. I'd guess we'll have to go inside, shut the anchors off manually."

"Do that, then," I said unhappily. "We'll stay topside." I wasn't loving the idea of Bolivar's crew entering the facility without us, but I was even less happy with the notion of grounding both ships before we figured out how to release them from the landing platform.

"Finally," Sahluk grunted. "Room to stretch. And maybe even folk to kill."

"I really, really hope you don't get your wish," Sho told him.

"If anything goes wrong in there," I told them, "you just—"

That was when something hit us from the side; a barrage of machine-gun fire, strafing across Schaz's shields, the ballistic impacts hard enough to knock us out of our circling pattern and drive Schaz into one of the upward thermals. If I hadn't had the shields raised to ward off lightning strikes, we would have been torn apart.

Something *had* gone wrong, just not on the facility below. There was someone else inside the storm, another ship—those shots had come from the storm walls around us, not from within the facility itself.

Our comms crackled to life again, but this time it wasn't Javier, or Sho, or Sahluk on the other end. Instead, it was an impossible voice, a voice I'd never forget, the same one I'd *thought* I'd heard in the shipyards, and this time, there was no doubt: I was really hearing it, the voice of a woman who'd been dead for a hundred years. "I always told you, Jane," the ghost said. "You spend too much time looking forward—not enough watching your flank."

And then we were under fire again, the mystery ship with the impossible pilot filling the clouds with bright orange bursts of fire as she dove out of the storm, aiming right for us.

CHAPTER 9

Jane

I hauled hard on the yoke and cut thrust, bringing us into a tight corner and aiming Schaz in between the metal rings of the rift projector. I figured the enemy wouldn't risk firing on the ancient tech—blowing apart pieces of the ring might have a cascading effect through the entire facility, which would in turn likely destroy the pillars, and maybe even the forerunner monument—and I was right, but her reaction still wasn't the move I'd expected her to make: I was trying to force her to circle around, to come at us from the front where I could target her with our forward guns, but instead she followed my hard turn, staying tight on our tail as I passed through the rings.

She was good.

A burst of static on the comm, and suddenly Marus's voice was coming through, as clear as a bell as we hit a pocket of atmosphere that was a dead space for the jamming signal: "Jane, a ship just dove out of hyperspace—it passed right by us, made straight for the world, straight for *you*. Jane, can you *hear* me—" Then he was gone again as we left the pocket behind, the jamming back in full force.

Better late than never, Marus.

"I've got a shot lined up with the rear turret," Esa said, her fingers flying over the console. "We'll give her something to—"

"Esa, no!" I shouted, but it was too late—a lance of azure fire shot out of the rear gun, and it was immediately followed by three bolts of lightning striking out from the wall of the storm, each aimed right at Scheherazade and the origin of the blast: their paths carved through the rainstorm, lighting neon trails behind them, drawn by the ionized atmosphere around the barrel of the turret. I pulled us out of range—barely—but if we'd been any closer to the clouds where the bursts had originated, that would have been it; we would have been done.

"Right," Esa swallowed; I could hear the fear in her voice. "*Don't* fire the lasers. Got it."

Thankfully, the bolts of lightning had also shaken our tail, but all that meant was that I'd lost her again—she wasn't behind us, and without instruments, I didn't know where she was going to come from next.

I pulled up on the yoke, describing a slow loop back toward the facility, but the comm crackled to life again, Javier shouting through, "Go, get out of here! She can't hit us on the platform—destroying Bolivar would level the whole facility. Make a run for it, lose her in the—"

Another signal came across the comm, cutting into Javier's voice, but it wasn't Marus this time: the ghost again, slipping into our comms channel like she belonged there. "Yes, Jane, by all means," that impossible voice purred, "do what you do best: look to the horizon, and to hell with whatever you leave in your wake. Maybe I won't risk destroying the facility, or *maybe* I'll—"

The Preacher shut the comms off with a slap. "She's baiting you," she said firmly. "Don't listen."

She wasn't wrong; it was good advice, and I tried to heed it—to block out the memories that had come roaring out of my subconscious just from hearing that voice again. It wasn't easy.

I dropped Schaz into another dive, this time down the side of the relic, pushing her into the magnetic fields that warped between the pillars and the strange metal of the forerunner monolith—at least that way, port was one direction I knew our enemy wouldn't come from, unless her ship could phase *through* the monolith somehow.

"She knows your name," Esa said softly, staring out the cockpit as we barreled down the side of an ancient forerunner monument, into a rising storm, toward an ocean of freezing neon far below. "She knows—"

"She doesn't know a damn thing," I snapped back, my anger aimed more at myself—for letting that voice shake me—than at Esa. "It's a trick; a voice sampler; a scrambler." Though where the Bright Wanderers could have retrieved fragments of that particular voice, I had no idea—any records the sect had kept would have been destroyed when Hadrian's Gambit had—

The ship came blazing in from the far side of the pillar, the machine guns spitting lead toward us—the rounds ricocheted off the surface of the monolith, striking bright sparks from the not-quite-metal even as I twisted out of the firing path, pulling away from the relic and diving into the storm itself. The enemy ship had anticipated the move, was right on our tail again, giving us a clear view of the craft through the rear projection: a sleek, aerodynamic piece of killing tech, and no matter that it had come out of hyperspace *after* us, the ship looked as if it had been hand-designed for combat in exactly this sort of atmosphere: that was why she didn't have any lasers to fire. Still, reading the design of her craft—even as she opened fire again and I danced us away from the hail of lead—I would bet good money she wasn't as *fast* as Scheherazade, and I reached for the throttle.

I pushed us to top speed and kept both hands on the yoke, sending us cutting into tight spirals as we passed two more monoliths looming up out of the storm. I was counting on the bursts of lightning and the spreading pools of neon they left behind in the rainfall to give me just enough warning to—

—*close!* I pulled up on the yoke and barely scraped over another of the rising relics; Schaz's underbelly would need yet another new paint job whenever we finally got back to Sanctum. "If I had my landing gear lowered, we wouldn't *have* landing gear anymore," Schaz muttered.

"You think she's using a voice sampler?" Esa asked me. "Jane—do you *recognize*—"

"Not now," I said, and I cut our thrust entirely, letting the air currents of the storm carry us off to one side, further away from the monolith, even as I reached up and switched off the running lights, even the interiors. No instruments—not even those purpose-built for this atmosphere—would work in this mess; for a moment, we simply drifted in the darkness of the storm, Schaz's cabin silent, still, quiet enough I could hear Esa's breathing, could hear my own heartbeat behind the patter of the rain across the cockpit glass as we were carried through the dark.

Then, brightness: the engine of the enemy craft, soaring past us, a little above our position. I cut the thrusters back on and rose upward even as Esa let the forward machine guns off the chain—the forward guns were the only tool we had that wouldn't call the lightning or be otherwise useless: all the turrets were lasers, and the missiles' guidance systems wouldn't make it ten meters in this soup.

The tracer rounds dashed through the storm clouds, chewing apart the rear shields of our enemy, but unlike Scheherazade, *she* had a secondary layer of ballistic protection over her engine cowling, and before Esa could do any real damage, more tracer fire was arcing back toward us, flashing through the red lightning—she had a rear turret as well, and it was outfitted with more ballistic cannons.

She was safe on our tail; we *weren't* on hers.

I pulled us off into a barrel roll before the turret fire could chew through our forward shields the way she had our port and rear defenses; Schaz's drive core was already working overtime to replenish our shielding, but the more damage she took, the longer the drive would take for her to patch over the holes. Was there *any* angle of attack I could use to hit her from?

Another one of the monoliths came rising up to meet us—how many of the damn things were there?—and I skimmed down the side, more tracer fire singing through the rain to strike bright sparks against the relic's surface as our enemy fell in behind us again, like she'd known not only that I'd turn away, but which direction I would head: whoever she was, she was good, almost as good as—

—no. The Preacher was right—it was a trick. The woman that voice had belonged to had been dead for a hundred years, more: even if she'd survived the crash, she wouldn't have made it through the devastation that had followed, when the entire atmosphere of Hadrian's Gambit had melted down on top of the—

Focus, damn it. Ghost stories are for children. The *here*, the *now*—the enemy craft on your tail, the monoliths rising out of the edges of the storm clouds like rocky shorelines appearing from a mist—those were what mattered, that—

—a shoreline. That was it; that was my best shot. I pulled off the side of the monolith, letting the tracer fire chase me across the open storm, and pushed Schaz to full thrust again as I leaned hard on the stick, this time heading straight down, deeper into the atmosphere, deeper into the planet's gravity well.

"Jane?" Esa asked. "Are you planning on pulling up any time—"

She didn't manage to finish the sentence; we finally broke free beneath the storm's ceiling, and there it was: the endless ocean of the world's surface, crashing waves of liquid rolling forever toward a horizon that was just more storm. The sky was too low, like a tight lid on the world, and when I finally pulled up on the yoke to level out from our dive, Schaz actually smashed *through* a few of the waves before we found the horizon, the clearance between the storm and the sea was that minimal. The liquid washed over us in waves of lit brightness, the neon flaring to life against our shields as I pulled us back up, skimming over the top of the sea.

I reached out and wrapped my hand around the throttle, but I didn't punch it; not yet. "Esa, when I say, fire the electric chaff, right toward her; three deployments ought to work."

"The chaff? But won't that—"

"Just *do* it. When . . . I . . ."

The other ship came bursting out of the storm front behind us, and pulled out of her own dive much more cleanly than I had—either she'd known the rough elevation of the ocean below, or she was just that much more maneuverable than me—and her guns were already spinning up, spitting lines of bright fire above the waves, the orange tracers mirrored in the chaotic sea.

Ahead of us, another monolith, this one rising up out of the ocean, extending all the way up into the storm: the "shoreline" I'd been looking for. I dialed up the magnification on my viewscreen as much as I could; there had to be—

There was. "Esa, *now!*" I barked, even as I rammed the throttle home.

The chaff was designed to emit electrical impulses that would throw off the guidance systems of enemy missiles—to be fired backward, giving enemy munitions something to track other than Scheherazade. Of course, those same electrical impulses would draw the lightning just like the lasers had; that's what I was counting on.

We roared forward; the other ship gave chase, the chaff arcing backward from Schaz's tail beneath the bruised sky. The lightning strikes came just as our enemy reached the point where the chaff was dropping toward the sea, the tines of electricity forking out of the storm toward the falling metal cylinders, with the enemy craft caught right between the bolts and their targets—

—except then she just *wasn't*, had danced her ship between the forks of lightning in as graceful a piece of piloting as I'd ever seen. The bolts struck harmlessly into the neon below, spreading a glow across the entire face of the ocean—all I'd really accomplished was to throw off her targeting solution for a moment.

But a moment was all I needed.

"She's firing missiles!" Esa warned; of course she was. They wouldn't have fancy guidance systems, either: likely just heat-seekers, drawn to the warmth of our engines. And we were *both* moving at top speed now—Schaz putting distance between us and our hunter even as I wove between the threads of her ballistic fire—so the chaff trick wouldn't work again, not that it had really worked the first time.

I was running low on my bag of tricks. Low, but not empty.

There had been a crack in the side of the monument ahead of us—a crack, or a tunnel, bored right through the center of the thing. Hopefully, it came out the other side. *Hopefully,* I wasn't going to hit a dead end at damn near the speed of sound. If I did, Schaz's shielding would barely even slow us down before we were spread all over the monolith walls in a mess of drive-core eruption, burning starship parts, and miniscule portions of flesh.

Here's to hoping.

I hit the breach and cut my running lights on again; the missiles behind us impacted against the side of the relic, their primitive guidance chips unable to recognize the very existence of the monoliths, just like Schaz couldn't. After being in the rainfall for so long, the sudden absence of it was jarring, making the cockpit seem almost tomb-like in its silence; I eased back the throttle a little, just enough to—

—*turn!* I barely missed an outcropping of . . . had that been some kind of a statue, maybe even a *building*, rising up from the wall? Didn't matter. All that mattered was the next turn coming up, and then the next, and then the next; I really was sweating now, sweating buckets, but I couldn't take my hands off the stick long enough to wipe my brow, couldn't blink, was barely even *breathing*—anything that broke my concentration would mean I might miss the next shift in the passage, and we wouldn't even feel the impact that would kill us we were moving so fast.

I almost missed anyway; it was a close thing. The crack in the surface of the relic suddenly widened out: we were out the far side, and the edge of the monolith stretched above us, but there was another wall ahead, a second relic, the clearance between the two making a chasm rising up toward the storm. As I pulled us up into a tight climb between the walls of the relics, rain began spattering on the cockpit again; there was barely enough room between the two monoliths for Schaz to claw her way upward, into the curtain of the downpour sweeping off the distant edges high above.

"Is she still behind us?" I shouted; I couldn't take my attention off the twists and turns of the rising chasm, not even for just a moment—not even long enough to glance at our rear projection.

"She is, but she's not firing," the Preacher informed me, sounding as calm as if we were plotting some lazy hyperspace jump from one nowhere system to another. "I think she's afraid she'd fly right into the ricochets—and into our wreckage, if she did manage to shoot us down."

"Good," I said with a nod. I could tell by the neon light spreading above us that we were approaching the opening of the canyon, right where I wanted us to be: this hadn't been my plan, I hadn't even had one of those, not really, but I didn't need one—don't "react," just "act."

I pushed Schaz's forward thrust again to full, and we broke out into the storm—then I immediately cut the thrust all the way back and pulled us into a tight loop, aiming Schaz's nose right into the chasm we'd just left behind.

"What the hell are you *doing?*" the Preacher howled, not so much calm anymore: the enemy was headed right for us, rising out of the darkness below with her guns spinning up—she hadn't expected me to head straight for her any more than the Preacher had—but I ignored both of them, and screamed, "Esa, *now!*" even as I punched the thrusters to full again and twisted the stick in my hands, matching our position against the tiny clearance between the enemy ship itself and the hard walls of the relics.

We scraped past the enemy ship—literally *scraped* her, Schaz's undercarriage striking sparks against her own—just as Esa fired three more chaff canisters. The enemy ship sped past us, past the canisters rising from Schaz's aft, even as the charged particles in the chaff called the lightning down from the tempests above. The blaze of electricity swarmed inside the chasm like it was being pulled into a vacuum, the neon rain blooming to light as the blades of lightning forked toward the pull of the electrical impulses of the canisters—and found the enemy ship instead, caught in between, the lightning overwhelming her shields and frying her internal systems all to hell and gone.

Nowhere to *dodge* in a goddamned *canyon*, was there?

I cut the thrusters to reverse and pulled us into a kind of awkward sideways lateral turn—no way to loop, not with the walls this tight—trying to give Esa a shot with the forward machine guns, in case pieces of the enemy ship were about to come raining down on us, but it wasn't necessary: she was still flying—that was one tough ship, built for this atmosphere or no—one engine sputtering, the other out entirely, but still capable of climbing over the wall of the relic, and making for the storm beyond.

I followed her. Of course I did. But when Esa reached for the guns, I said, "No," and shook my head. Esa looked at me—read something on my expression, I'm not sure what—and nodded, drawing her hand back again.

Our would-be ambusher was making for the facility; trying to reach the landing pad. Even with one engine out and the other fried, she was still fighting the storm to reach that relative safe harbor—even though she had to *know* that Javier and his team would have taken control of the facility entrance by now. Of course, she didn't have a lot of other options; it was that, or fall.

The voice she was using—the voice that couldn't have been real—that woman never would have given up, either. Survival, above all else.

Anyway, she didn't make it. She came close—got through to the eye of the hurricane, got the anchored relic and the facility actually in sight—but then her last engine gave up the ghost, and she started dropping, losing al-

titude too fast to reach the pad, the storm winds circling around us too chaotic for a full glide, even with the rising thermals.

She managed to ditch it into a skid anyway, the craft scraping across the
metal of the relic itself, finally coming to a rest teetering on the edge of the
monolith, perhaps thirty feet below the landing pad. I knew what I was looking for, even as I set Scheherazade onto the platform—she shook slightly as
the anchoring cables took hold of us as well, but I didn't care, getting away
from this place was the furthest thing from my mind at the moment—and I
saw what I needed, through the rain: a ladder, leading down.

The enemy pilot *couldn't* have been the woman who belonged to that voice.
She couldn't have. But she'd known my name, and she'd known my history,
or at least enough of it to make a guess at the rest—she'd implied knowledge, referenced conversations, that not even the Justified could have known.
There was only one person who could have known all that, beyond myself:
Julia Doniger, the woman who belonged to that voice, the woman I hadn't
seen in over a hundred years.

But she couldn't have been Julia Doniger, because Julia Doniger was dead;
I'd killed her myself.

Still, I had to know. Just hearing that voice again, the ghosts that it brought
swarming up out of the long-dead tombs of my history—if there was any
chance, any, that Julia was still alive . . . I didn't have any other choice. As
soon as we set down, I headed for the airlock, not even bothering to retrieve
my gear—my pistol was all I'd need for this, even if the pilot, whoever she
was, had survived the crash. And if—somehow—the woman in the storm-
skipper ship *was* Julia, dredged up from my ancient past and put in my path
again, well: I'd killed her once.

I could do it again.

CHAPTER 10
Jane

I came down Scheherazade's ramp with my gun already in my hand. The "warmth" coming off the pillars beneath us was a relative thing—it was still nearly freezing cold on the landing platform, but even that temperature differential was enough to turn the intermittent neon raindrops into a low mist, one that occasionally shimmered into a red phosphorescent scatter of light when it caught a stray burst of electrical discharge from our ships or the facility. Thankfully, the pillars seemed to be drawing all the lightning from the swirling storms, which was why the whole place hadn't been fried centuries ago or more.

Questions about the facility could wait, though: I headed straight for the ladder that led down off the landing pad, the metal rungs slick with wet until they reached the surface of the relic below. Sahluk was already standing on the edge, right beside the ladder, the big Mahren immobile, like a statue. His gun was in his hand, trained on the sparking ruin of the enemy ship. "Watch your back" was all he told me. I didn't know if he'd caught part of the conversation over the comms, or if he was just doing what he would want me to do, if our positions were reversed: let him take the final shot at someone who'd tried to burn him down.

I nodded. "Tell Esa to stay up here," I said—I knew she'd be right behind me. Then I grabbed hold of the ladder and slid downward, toward the monument itself.

My boots hit the not-quite-metal of the forerunner monolith with a sound that wasn't quite the clang of a hollow structure, but wasn't far off, either: I was actually *standing* on a forgotten creation of the race that had come before all the others, the race that had built the Barious and left clues to dozens of different advanced technologies scattered throughout the galaxy, and I couldn't care less.

All *I* cared about was the airlock to the damaged ship.

I started forward down the sloped surface of the relic, watching my step on the incline; all I needed now was to put one foot wrong, slip on a pool of liquid neon, and go careening off the edge of the damn thing, carelessness and gravity finishing what a thousand or more different enemies had never been able to. Carefully, I made my way toward the enemy vessel that had slid to the edge of the relic in its skid, now teetering like one stray burst of wind in the wrong direction would send it crashing down to the seas far, far below.

I was almost to the crashed vessel when a crack appeared on the relic itself, the metal between me and the ship splitting apart like tectonic plates, spilling a wall of pale light from the breach. I cursed and rushed forward, footing be damned, but I was too late—the light rose up and curved into something almost like a bubble, sealing over the fallen craft. I knew what I was going to find when I got to the edge of that illumination—it was a force field, impenetrable—but I hammered the butt of my gun against it anyway, in fury; it was as solid as any telekinetic shield Esa had ever raised.

There were flashing symbols, drawn somehow into the light itself, in the same language as the glyphs carved into the relic. The monument was alive—or at least, still functioning in at least a limited capacity—and again, I couldn't care less: this was probably some sort of defense system, meant to ward off the occupants from damage and danger, the forerunner equivalent of "DO NOT STEP PAST THIS POINT; DAMAGE AHEAD," and I didn't give a shit. I just needed to *know* if the voice on the comms had truly belonged to the woman I killed, and the goddamned relic itself was trying to stop me from learning the truth.

I was going to find out anyway.

The airlock on the ship unsealed—slid halfway open, then stopped with a scream of sparks and agonized metal, the door as broken as the rest of the downed craft—and a hand gripped it from the inside, pushing it the rest of the way down into its housing, and she stepped out.

It *was* her. Julia. Over a hundred years since I'd seen her last, and I'd recognize her anywhere. The same pale skin, the same dark hair—though she'd cut it short, almost into a buzz cut; I couldn't say I hadn't changed my *own* hair in a hundred years, I supposed—and even though the hair was different, the same wry grin curved her lips as she looked up at me, the expression that made my heart clench tight like there was a fist clamped around it.

The voice—even the face—those could have been faked. Not the grin. Nobody but Julia would have smiled at me like that, directly after she tried to shoot me out of the sky.

She stepped away from the damaged craft, her own hand hovering above the butt of her pistol. "Hello, Jane," she said, approaching the force field until she was close enough that I could have touched her, if that light hadn't been in the way. "It's been a while."

There were a thousand things I should have said; a thousand things I could have *asked* her. But only one that mattered. "How?"

She just kept grinning, not looking away from me as she fished in her pocket for a cigarette, the same idle motion I'd seen her make on dozens of different battlefields, the two of us killing time waiting for our orders as shells burst overhead and all along the front lines men and women died, badly. "Does it matter?" she asked finally, after she'd fished a smoke out and tucked it between her lips, the dome of the shielding keeping the rain off her head. She frowned as she patted down her jacket, that gesture also familiar, even a century since I'd seen her do it last.

My free hand actually twitched toward my own pocket—where I kept *my* lighter—before I pulled it back, and she saw the ghost of the motion, her grin growing wider. "You should have known a little crash and a burning moon wouldn't have been enough to kill me," she said. Then, slowly, even as she found her own lighter, the expression began to fade, her smile melting like ice on hot iron. "You should have *known*." The last word came out less like a statement and more an accusation, even as she snapped the flame open in the mist, the light exposing something else in her face—something meaner, more raw, now that the smile was gone.

If she wanted to blame me, she could blame me—she had every right. I shook my head. "Why are you here?" I asked instead.

THE FIRMAMENT OF FLAME 🌣 163

She took a drag on her cigarette, exhaled the smoke toward me, where it rolled against the force-field wall like a wave against illuminated glass. "That's it, Jane," she said. "Look to the future, so you don't have to face the other direction. Just like you always did. How did you ever make it this far, without me watching your back?"

"The future's what matters," I told her flatly.

"Maybe, but it seems to get farther and farther away with each bullet we fire, doesn't it? The future's theoretical, Jane—it's never actually going to arrive. All looking forward earns is a blind spot behind you—*behind* you, where the true threat had always lain. Where your sins remain unburied, given . . . new life." Something in her face, then—as the smoke spilled from between her lips, I could almost see it: what she'd had to *do*, to survive. Not just Hadrian's Gambit, but the century that had followed, with all she knew torn away. Torn *down*. By me. "Like I said: the bullet that kills you won't come from in front of you. It'll come from behind, where you never look."

"You think I don't look back?" I asked softly, the words barely audible with the storm still raging behind us. "You think I don't dwell on it—don't dream about it? The decisions I made, that *we* made—you think I don't—"

"I know you don't," she replied, snarling around the cigarette. "I know it for a fact. I thought you were dead, you know. Thought that for a long time." Her tone had slipped back into something almost conversational, all the hate I'd heard there a moment before vanishing like a mirage. "Thought that was justice, maybe. Then I found out you weren't. Was *told* you weren't. That all this time—"

"I've done more good, helped more people, with the Justified, than we—"

I didn't know why I was trying to defend myself against her accusations; it didn't matter, not to either of us, not really, and she ignored me, taking another drag off her smoke. "Have you been back?" she asked, still watching me carefully, like something was going to happen, like there was something she needed to see in my reaction. Like she was looking for a lie. "To our world—what you left of it? Hadrian's Gambit shattered apart, you know. After what you did. Even before the pulse, what remained of the world below was . . . dying. The children starve in the streets we fought to defend; they tear each other apart in the halls of the sainted. Everything we fought for—our childhood, our war—you made it into nothing. You made it *worse* than noth-ing. A thing with a *cost*, where our blood was supposed to be the cost. You just made it . . . worse."

"It was always that way," I said through clenched teeth—this was exactly what she'd refused to see then, as well. "You just couldn't . . . just *wouldn't* . . . admit it. The elders made sure we always had an enemy, because otherwise, we'd realize our true enemy was them."

"Maybe so." She shrugged, then, took another drag on her cigarette. "You might be right about that. But it was all I had—we had nothing else. Noth-ing but each other. And then . . . then I didn't even have that."

"You *made* me do it, Julia."

"You made a *choice*, Jane. A choice that's coming back to haunt you now. Why am I *here?*" She grinned again as smoke spilled from her lips, fading into the neon mist around us. "I'm here because she told me where to find you. I don't give a damn about her crusade, and she knows it, as far as I'm concerned, she's no different from the elders, back then. But she's using me, and I'm us-ing her—she told me you were still alive, put me on your trail, gave me a ship to hunt you with, and that's all I care about. Just knowing you're still breathing, after what you *did* . . . well." The grin grew wider, predatory. "That sounds like something I need to rectify. So don't worry, Jane. We're not done yet." She spat the last word through her grinning teeth, then dropped the cigarette to the rain-slick surface of the relic beneath her, already turning.

"Julia—wait!" I reached out—actually pressed my hand against the shim-mering shield of force, felt a bright jolt of pain as I did, but it didn't matter, not the shout, not the pain. She'd already stepped back into her craft, and then, as if the monolith knew what she was doing, the force field fell away—just in time for Julia's ship to jettison her escape pod. It went soaring out into the storm, then it was falling, and falling, down into the rain, down toward the endless sea beneath us.

That final burst of motion was more than the rest of her ship could take, with one last screech of metal, it plunged into the downpour as well, vanis-hing from sight in the boil of the clouds.

I had no doubt she'd survive the ocean below, somehow, had no doubt at all. Just like I should have known she'd survived the end of our war, but she was right—I'd never gone looking. Just like she'd never gone looking for me.

We'd both assumed the other was gone, and what was left in the wake of our decisions—the decisions I'd made, ultimately, for both us—she was right about that, at least. There had been a cost. I'd known what I was paying, at the time. She hadn't. And now she wanted vengeance. Vengeance for the price I'd made her pay.

She was right. We weren't done yet. But right now, there were other mysteries to explore—other questions to answer.

Looking to the future was the only way to move *forward*, Julia. That's what you never seemed to understand. Looking to the past will only root you in place. There are always guns aimed at your back; the only way to get anywhere is to get the hell out of their range. You don't look back, not ever, not until you're safe, and in this galaxy, you never truly were. The war—our war—had taught me that, too.

I headed back for the landing platform, where Esa and my friends were waiting.

CHAPTER 11

Esa

Regardless of Jane's instructions, I started toward the ladder when the force field leapt out of the monolith: it was an ancient piece of forerunner technology, and it was apparently active—who knew *what* it was going to do next. Sahluk put his hand on my shoulder to restrain me, shaking his head as he did. "She's got this," he said.

I nodded, albeit grudgingly, but I knelt at the side of the ladder anyway, ready to descend at a moment's notice. If I had to I could skip the climb altogether, just leap off the edge and cushion my fall with a telekinetic push. Whether she "had this" or not, if it looked like she was in over her head, I was going to move. Until then, though, I just watched, carefully, as the airlock of the enemy ship opened and the pilot stepped out.

It was like watching two animals pace, separated by the bars of a cage, sniffing warily at the *thing* on the other side of the enclosure. And not different animals, but creatures of the same species—despite the fact that they were about as different looking as two humans could be, Jane with dark, almost copper-colored skin and jet-black hair, the stranger with pale, freckled features and ice-blue eyes—they still *looked* the same, Jane and the other woman.

They dressed the same, for one thing—similar military-surplus combat rigs, complete with flight jackets and low-slung bandoliers—and they even stood the same, moved the same: body weight on the forward foot, one hip thrown out, the hip with the heavy pistol on it, free hand hovering over the butt of the weapon as each of them leaned in, just a little bit, like a predator scenting the forest air for prey, or the telltale signs of a greater threat.

Whatever it was they were saying, it wasn't making Jane happy; I could see her stiffen up, and her voice was rising into what was almost a shout. I couldn't make out her actual words, though, not between the chaos of the storm lashing against the sides of the monument and the frequent sharp crackling sounds that came from the electricity crawling across the pillars below.

The shouting ended as swiftly as it had begun: the other woman went back into her damaged ship, the force field collapsed, and a moment later, the escape pod was jettisoned, sucked up into the whirling storm walls around us, to end up god knows where—if we were lucky, smashed apart against the sides of one of the other floating relics. The ship fell too. I hope it landed on her *head*.

Maybe I wasn't being charitable with the thought—the thought that, whoever she was, we'd be better off if we never saw her again, better off if she just died—but the woman *had* just tried to kill us, and whatever else was happening here, I couldn't shake the feeling that the happier ending would have been if she hadn't managed to limp back to the monolith at all: if her engines had given out just a moment earlier, and she'd just . . . fallen away, disappeared into the storm.

Maybe Jane wouldn't have had her answers then, answers she seemed to need from this . . . whoever she was, this phantom come roaring out of Jane's long history, more than a century spent creating ghosts. But that might have been better, all things considered: sometimes answers were just as cruel as the emptiness of questions. It had taken me a long time to make my peace with that.

Wishful thinking wouldn't change what *had* happened, though, and Jane just stood in the mist for a moment, neon light flashing before her in the storm, staring into the tempest where the stranger—a stranger to me, at any rate— had vanished. She kept watching for a moment longer, though the other woman was long gone, ship and pod both; then she shook her head and moved back toward the ladder.

I took my hand off Bitey and reached down to help her up as she climbed toward the top. "We good?" Sahluk asked her, before I could say anything.

"No," she said shortly, "but she can't do anything for now—and I doubt she got a message out to her masters, not through all the interference around this place. For now . . . we need to find out what this facility is. Are the others—"

"Safe inside," Sahluk nodded. "Javier was working to get communications back up—and that's where we should be too. Mahren don't get damp, but you two are soaked through."

Jane nodded, and without another word—I had questions, way too many questions, but I could tell by the expression on her face this wasn't the time for me to ask them—she started toward the facility, on the far side of the landing pad; I fell in behind her, one hand still resting on Bitey. It wasn't that I didn't trust the other four members of our crew—Javier, Sho, JackDoes, and the Preacher—to have cleared the facility, but in my experience, when things went to shit, they went to shit fast, with very little warning.

We stepped into the antechamber of the platform's control booth; there was a warm rush of air—some sort of decontamination protocol, though I had a tight feeling in my gut that told me it wasn't about decontaminating those that came *in* so much as those that came *out*—and then a few bright pops as an electrical current lit up the neon evaporating from our clothing, and that was it: the far door slid open, and we were inside.

The interior was . . . disappointingly mundane, like any other docking control facility I'd been in. I didn't know *what* I'd expected, but this was the usual low rows of consoles, dials and knobs and screens and so forth; I wouldn't have been surprised if some lazy station tech had come ambling out of the far door, adjusting his uniform and ready to get back to his shift.

Across the room, Javier and Marus were arguing over a comms channel, which meant Javier had successfully cleared the interference piped in from the facility itself; that was progress, at least. "I should be down there with you," Marus was saying. "If you've found a direct rift—and if I'm right about those writings, which I am—then you're standing in the biggest archeological find in—"

"Look, if I could change places with you, I would," Javier interrupted him, "but Bolivar's locked down, Scheherazade's locked down, the Preacher's down here with us, so Shell's next to useless; if *you* come down, we lose our eyes in the sky, our forewarning if any more enemy vessels arrive in-system. I get it, Marus—you've waited your whole life for something like this—but it just doesn't make—"

"What writing?" Jane asked her boyfriend, though her voice was anything but intimate at the moment: still brittle with anger, sharp enough to cut, with something else just beneath it, a kind of bone-deep weariness, like she was just ready to be done with all this.

It didn't seem to bother Javier—I think he'd known who the other pilot was, or at least who she was to Jane, and like he always did, he was handling Jane's anger by pretending it didn't exist, waiting for it to burn itself out before he dealt with whatever remained in the ashes. A surprisingly patient man, Javier Ortega—but then, he'd have to be, to have been with Jane for so long.

"Sho found a few writing samples of the people who built this place," he said mildly, indicating a battered old journal that sat on the console beside him, incongruous amid the more modern technology. "It's not written in the universal constant, which means we were right: this place was built before the Golden Age, before the species-general language was developed."

"It's an ancient Vyriat dialect," Marus explained from the comm. "I'm not exactly fluent in it, but Javier scanned the journal and sent it to me, and I recognize at least a few words—one of which is 'excavation.' They actually cracked the thing open: something accomplished on none of the other monoliths that have ever been discovered."

"And the rift controls?" Jane asked.

"They're up here," Javier nodded. "We've got power—we can activate it at any time. But that's not—"

"Jane, we can't afford to ignore this just to activate the rift a few hours earlier," the Preacher said calmly, her voice low, soothing, like she was talking to some skittish animal. "We just made the single biggest discovery in the history of the study of the forerunners—"

"No, 'we' didn't," Jane glared at her. "We didn't discover shit. The Vyriat who built this place did—and then they lost it, lost it or forgot about it during the Golden Age, maybe for good reason. And after *they* lost it, the Bright Wanderers found it, which means we're third in line."

"But we still need to know what they know," I pointed out, and somehow, that made her listen—I could see in her face as she fought down her anger, tried to tamp down the cloud of red rage so strong it must have been like something she could actually see. The Bright Wanderers had somehow found that woman from her past—found her and thrown her directly into Jane's path—and she was *pissed* about that, probably with good reason, but she wouldn't let that anger control her; not for long.

Still, her expression was thunderous—like she was doing her best impression of the storm outside—as she nodded once, shortly. "You're right," she told me, before turning back to Javier and the Preacher. "So what *do* we know?"

Javier spread his hands. "You've hit the high points," he said. "Pre–Golden Age; Vyriat; developed along tech lines that . . . deviate, pretty substantially, from the standards that would come along during the interspecies summits that occurred shortly afterward. We were always taught that the Golden Age represented this massive leap forward in tech—all the species cooperating, communicating, reaching breakthroughs they couldn't have managed alone—but what that version of history leaves out is all the dead-end tech trees that each species must have abandoned: why keep researching in the direction you have been heading when you've just been handed something light-years more advanced, developed along entirely different lines? One of those dead-end techs, though, must have . . . somehow . . . let the Vyriat who built this place dig into the relic, something that the more 'efficient' lines of research could never manage."

"That's . . . actually not bad, Javier," Marus said dryly.

"I pay attention when you talk, old man," Javier grinned back in the general direction of the comm.

"When you want to. Which isn't always."

"There's something else we know too," Sho put in. "This place controls the landing pad; it controls the jamming signals; it controls the direct rift. But that's not what it was *for*—those were defense mechanisms, here to protect the facility. It was built to study the relic, but it was also abandoned, in what looks like short order. Hence the journal, left behind. Whatever the Vyriat found in the interior . . . they didn't like it. They built this place to crack it open—built the direct rift pointed at . . . somewhere beyond . . . and then they were gone, very quickly. And I don't think the Bright Wanderers who came through stayed for much longer: just long enough to activate the rift, and get out."

"I've tried to access the station's database," the Preacher added, "but so far, no luck: it's been degraded by centuries of exposure to the warping magnetic fields, and, of course, what little's left is written in old Vyriat."

"But there *is* a way down, into the relic," I persisted. "There is a way *in*."

"Oh, yes," Sho agreed, taking a single step to the side—he'd been standing in front of an elevator the whole time. He saw my mutinous expression, and grinned. "Sorry. Couldn't help but want to savor the big reveal."

"He's spending *way* too much time with you," Jane growled at Javier.

CHAPTER 12

Esa

The elevator was just big enough to fit all of us—there had been a brief suggestion that someone might stay up top, at the facility, just in case, but absolutely none of us wanted to be the one to stay behind, not on the edge of something this groundbreaking—and we all crowded in, a collection of different nervous tics in a metal box; there was a kind of electric energy as the lift began to descend, and it wasn't coming from the power thrumming through the cables. We were about to see something that no one save the Bright Wanderers had seen in thousands of years, and each of us was reacting in our own way, pulling inward, all quietly wondering what we wanted to find down there, all of us hoping there were answers below.

Maybe that was wishful thinking. Probably it was. But that was still what it felt like, all the same.

The open cage of the elevator descended through the not-quite-metal, not-quite-stone of the relic—however the ancient Vyriat had carved this passage, they hadn't been exactly clean about it, and some of the edges still glowed, like entropy just didn't exist in this place and whatever cutting tool had opened the passage had just powered down—until, all of a sudden, we were looking at something other than that hardened material: the cage was still descending, but the monolith walls fell away, up and out, and we were suddenly passing through . . .

It was a city. There was a *city* inside the monolith, or at least the remains of one. It was like the buildings had been . . . crumpled, crumpled and balled up: there weren't just structures below us, but around us and above us as well, the buildings curving up the walls, even running along the ceiling, like some god had ripped a dozen square blocks of a terrestrial metropolis free of the bedrock, then folded the city in on itself. Or maybe it was meant to be that way, the forerunners creating architecture as if gravity were an afterthought . . . there was no way to know.

The design of the structures—even allowing for the fact that they were fractured and crumbling in places—was alien in a way I couldn't even quite put my finger on: uniform, but also flowing, with very few hard edges at all, though most of the taller buildings were topped with strange steeples, all marked with the same symbol, a kind of twisting ouroboros of metal. The sign of the forerunner religion, perhaps? Or the mark of their . . . king, their clan?

We could *see* all of that—all the way to the far edge of the monolith— thanks to a kind of diffused glow, coming from everywhere and nowhere: colorless, directionless, it was nonetheless bright enough to illuminate even the distant outer limit of the relic, at least a mile away, where the city continued to climb up the far wall in a curl. The buildings just kept marching upward along that curve and across the ceiling, the strange steeples dangling from above like stalactites, almost close enough to touch their counterparts rising from the roofs of the houses below.

"Preacher," Jane said softly.

"I see it." I could actually hear the creaking of the metal underneath the Preacher's hands as she tightened her grip. I followed her line of sight, out through the cage: far below us, not quite at the center of the city, was a kind of twisting arch, or at least a piece of one. The other half had been snapped off in whatever cataclysm had torn the city from its roots, leaving just a broken curve that collided with other "neighborhoods" running up the wall.

Still, I recognized it, and I knew why the Preacher would as well: it was a Verisson arch, part of the inexplicable construction of the Barious factories. On the worlds where the factories had been built, it would have continued into the earth, completing a circuit underground until it formed a kind of super-colliding pathway for the complex energies required to manufacture new Barious. If the Preacher had needed proof that the forerunners who left behind the monoliths were the same race that created her species, well: there it was.

Barious had been built here. There was no other purpose for a Verisson arch, none that had ever been discovered: the Barious construction worlds had thousands of those archways, each significantly larger in scale than this—this wasn't a factory, but it was something else, maybe. Maybe a prototype.

"That seems like the place to start," Jane said, nodding at the arch as the elevator slowed, then stopped, its descent releasing us into what had once been some kind of forum: there were low benches running up the side of an amphitheater, and a long-dead fountain at the center. I had goosebumps just thinking of the years that had passed since the forerunners gathered here—had they discussed philosophy, great ideas, told sweeping stories in the square of not-quite-marble? Or had it been here where they planned their wars?

The forum was utilitarian enough that it could have been turned to almost any kind of public usage: an address from the clergy, a performance space for a theater troupe, a military execution ground. We didn't know anything at all about forerunner culture—just that they had vanished around the time the other species had begun to grasp the basics of fire, vanished inexplicably, leaving only the monoliths and the Barious in their wake, the monoliths floating on seemingly unconnected worlds, the Barious lying dormant, sealed off from the galaxy, until a group of Reetha explorers would awaken them millennia later.

The Preacher didn't need any urging from Jane—indeed, if Jane had said "maybe leave the broken Verisson arch for last," she would have headed right for it all the same, which Jane most likely knew—and she started across the square, her gait fluid in that way only a Barious could manage. Even still, I could tell she was holding herself back, barely able to stop herself from rushing forward and leaving the rest of us to follow behind her through the empty, desolate city.

I shivered, not because it was cold—somehow, the temperature was so mild within the monolith as to be nonexistent—but just because of the sheer *eeriness* of the place. The atmosphere felt almost reverent here, a weird kind of devotion that was hallowed and hollow both, like even this city beneath the skin of the relic was just another abandoned shell of something that had once been holy, a shell waiting for something else to seethe into its walls, to spill through the empty doorways.

Doorways—no actual doors. Either the cataclysm that had ripped the city

free of wherever it had actually been built had somehow destroyed whatever material the doors had been made of, or the forerunners had been an
incredibly trusting race, living in a very forgiving climate—the various buildings were entirely open to the thoroughfares, though a quick glance inside
showed little of note. Some furniture, the kind built directly into the floors
and walls—nothing freestanding had survived whatever had happened
here, yet there was no chaos in the interiors, either, no splinters or slivers of
disarray.

It was like the entire species had been . . . absconded with, belongings
and all, like some sort of civilization-snatching god had happened upon them
and just taken them in the night, children vanishing in a greater forest than
they'd realized they were lost within.

We'd reached our destination: the Preacher stepped through a great crack
in the archway and looked up, up into the tangle of wires and flowing metal
and impossible architecture of the interior of the Verisson arch. I'd never seen
the inside of one before—though I'd seen the arches from a distance, on
Requiem, one of my first missions with Jane taking me to the Barious factory world, silent and still after the pulse had robbed it of its purpose. At the
time, it had reminded me uncomfortably of a tomb. Now, though, despite
the discovery we'd made, I would have rather been there: at least Requiem
had a sky.

"This is . . . this is where my people were made," the Preacher said with a
whisper. "Where we were . . ."

She didn't have to say any more. I didn't know how old the Preacher was:
it wasn't exactly impossible that she'd been one of the very first Barious, among
those who had been awoken by the Reetha, thousands of years ago. She'd
certainly replaced enough of her parts over the years, and Barious were a
kind of walking ship of Theseus in that way—with regular maintenance and
a constant influx of new pieces to replace the old, they could theoretically
live forever, even if, at some point, they no longer had a single component
remaining from the body they'd been "born" in.

Regardless of whether she'd been part of that original awakening, or had
actually been built on the factories in Requiem or elsewhere—Barious building new Barious as old ones were destroyed, matching some invisible calculus

to keep their numbers stable, right up until the pulse meant they couldn't anymore—all of her kind considered the forerunners their "makers," and this was as holy a place, to her, as Lost Mecca would have been to Mo, or the Fallen Gardens were to the Shinolet believers of the Vyriat.

She was right, though: not just about the reverence, but about this place, specifically. The walls of the complex beneath the arch were cracked and fractured, just like the rest of the city, but some of them were undamaged enough that we could see designs, schematics, still imprinted on the surface, painted not just *on* the sort-of-metal of the walls, but also inside them, somehow: detailed technical drawings of limbs, optics, internal machinery, all Barious in nature. Regardless of the fact that we couldn't read the flowing script descending beside those drawings—the words still curling somehow through the wall—the implication was clear: the Barious had been designed here, their very beings iterated and fabricated by the arch that soared above us.

"There," Sahluk nodded at a distant fracture on the other side of the complex: unlike the rest of the sunken city, which showed only moderate damage to its structure from having been folded *in* on itself, the far wall of the Verisson arch had been ripped apart. Based on the edges of the tear in the metal—still glowing—the damage had been caused not by the cataclysm itself, but by the Vyriat explorers who had first descended to this place.

We started that way, but I felt something clench tight in my gut as we approached, and I knew, somehow, what we were going to find on the other side: I could smell it, in the air, despite the fact that there wasn't really anything *to* smell, not after so long. Still, premonition, instinct, subconscious awareness of small tells I couldn't even have pointed to if I tried: usually, being right was one of my favorite things in the galaxy to be, but this time, I would have given anything to be the opposite, to have let Jane's paranoia infect me until I was jumping at shadows.

We came through, and I wasn't jumping at shadows: the Vyriat explorers were still here. What remained of them.

We'd emerged into another square, and the corpses had been piled high, then set alight; until now, nothing but stains of ash and charred bones remained. An image flashed across my mind before I could stop it: the cultists of Valkyrie Rock, still burning in the pyre the Cyn had left in his wake. One pyre on that far-off asteroid didn't mean this similar scene had also been the work of the Cyn—fire was far and away the most common method for disposing of large numbers of corpses—but I couldn't help but feel something almost circular in the grim discovery, like there was meaning hidden among the charred and ashen dead.

There *was*, of course, just not the same connection as the one my subconscious kept trying to forge: we'd asked ourselves since we first saw this facility how, if those pre–Golden Age Vyriat had learned to crack open the monoliths, that knowledge hadn't spread to the rest of the galaxy. Now we knew. They'd never survived their descent into the depths of the relic, and wherever the direct rift led, someone must have made a similar destruction of whomever they had sent forward.

Something in this place had murdered its discoverers. Somehow, looking over the remains, the folded city didn't feel nearly as "hollow" as it had before— now, it seemed like there were eyes everywhere, hidden behind the omnipresent glow, just waiting for us to do the wrong thing, so that the ancient defenses of dormant demons that had wrought the massacre here could fall upon us, just like they had the dead in the square.

CHAPTER 13

Esa

Definitely Vyriat," Sahluk said, nodding at one of the remains, a piece—god, how grotesque was that, that I was thinking of something that had once been a person just as a "piece"—that had tumbled away from the rest, the shape of the bone still visible; the beak, usually hidden beneath Vyriat face tendrils. "Whatever killed them let them get all this way—let them build the facility, let them build their elevator, even the direct rift—then . . ." He snapped his rocky fingers, the sound sharp and jarring in the almost hallowed stillness of the place.

"They weren't supposed to see what lay beyond," Javier said quietly, kneeling beside the pile, making a motion across his chest, a kind of benediction; I'd never seen Javier practice *any* form of religion, but somehow it wasn't strange at all that in this weird and almost mythic place he felt the need to call on some nearly forgotten divine protection. "They cut through the walls of the factory for a reason—something was leading them this way."

"To that." The Preacher nodded across the square—another building, taller than the others, though the entrance had been hidden by the overlapping facades of the curving city. The Preacher was right: beyond just the height, there was something about its construction, about its design, that set it apart from the rest, something almost reverent about the rise of the thing. The twisting ouroboros symbol carved into almost every available piece of the walls, over and over again, like a staring sea of infinite eyes. As well, it had the only doors we'd seen in the swallowed city, massive things that stood slightly ajar, made of the same material as the walls around them.

"Some kind of . . . cathedral?" Sho wondered, and as soon as he said the word, it locked into place in my mind, the only descriptor that made sense in the face of all that reverence, all that iconography.

"Guns up" was all Jane said in reply as we approached, and we did that thing. Reverent or not, one person's god was another's monster—the Cyn and the fanatical depravity they called devotion proved that well enough. And though the forerunners were long dead, *something* had been through here, had killed the Vyriat. "Guns up" definitely seemed like a good idea.

Sahluk and the Preacher—far and away the strongest of us—each took a door and began to shove, but their great strength wasn't required at all: the doors opened at the slightest push, swinging inward, and what lay inside was—

—*light*. A great, shining beacon, floating in the hall that lay beyond, as if the weird, crepuscular illumination that shone from everywhere and nowhere in the sunken city had somehow gathered here, all of it just . . . floating, hovering at the center of the place of worship, a light that was at once intensely bright and somehow soothing, almost calm. I couldn't even see what lay beyond: there was just that light, washing over me—washing over all of us— but even as I raised a hand up to shield my eyes, I let it drop away in wonder, because there was something else in all that brightness: words were forming in the air, in the illumination itself, a kind of spidery, handwritten script, but that—

—that was impossible. It was impossible not because of the existence of the words—the light show was very pretty, and clearly meant to inspire reverence, but it could have been just a trick of cleverly hidden projectors, built into the walls and alcoves of the cathedral, the same basic principle as the holographic displays in Scheherazade's living quarters. What was impossible was the very fact that I could read the words at all.

I certainly didn't speak the *forerunner* language: no one did, and if I *had* been able to, I would have been equally able to read the glyphs on the exterior of the monolith, or the notes beside the Barious schematics. So why could I read these?

"The Vyriat must have left them," I said quietly, barely even realizing I was speaking aloud. "But that doesn't make any sense either, because the Vyriat wouldn't have spoken the universal constant, it hadn't even been developed yet. Could it have been the Bright Wanderers, then? Why would they—"

"Esa?" Jane said slowly. "What the hell are you talking about?"

I didn't turn away to look toward her; didn't dare turn away from the formal script glowing in midair, because if I did, the words might change. I don't know *why* I was so sure of that, but I was. "The writing," I said, still staring up into that light. "It doesn't make any sense that it's—"

"Esa, what—there's no writing. There are just—"

"What do you mean, 'no writing'? It's right there, stanzas, almost like a poem—"

"Esa, there's just . . . what are you seeing?"

I felt a chill run down my spine, the tight grip of fear suddenly manifest; suddenly what was "real" wasn't so real at all. "Words," I said quietly. "Floating in the air, in the light. What are—"

"Stars," Sahluk answered, before Jane could. "That's all. Just a map of the heavens—I think from the sky above this place, except you can't even see the sky from this world—but we're not seeing words, kid. We're seeing starlight—"

"But . . . no." This time it was Sho who spoke. "Esa's right—there *are* words, they're right there, how can you two not be—"

"Stop," Javier said to all of us, a sharp note of command in his usually agreeable voice. "Everybody stop. Raise your hand if you're seeing a star map, in the air above the . . . church."

I *did* turn away from the words at that: they hadn't changed so far, and besides, I needed to know if Sho and I were the only ones who could see them, if it was some sort of shared delusion and both of us had lost our grip on reality, like the very strangeness of this place had infected us somehow.

We were. All the rest had raised their hands; only Sho and I kept them down.

"Sho," I said to the young Wulf, my voice tight. "Read the first line."

He swallowed, and nodded; if it was some kind of delusion, he'd be seeing something other than what I was, would read something different. "'We thought we were angels, when we first took to the stars,'" he spoke softly, and something inside me unclenched, at least a little; if it *was* a hallucination, at least we were seeing the same thing, something this place wanted us to see.

He looked over at me, his expression worried, and I nodded to confirm, picking up where he'd stopped as I read the flowing script for the benefit of the others: "We thought we could ride the currents of every sky, tide to tide, horizon to horizon. Thought we could better every world we touched." That was it, that was all that was written in the light—but even as we spoke the words, that wasn't true, because they *shifted*, changed; I'd been right.

A new script replaced the old stanzas, as if reading them aloud had given the light permission to display more of the ancient . . . whatever it was, sacred text or tombstone monument or last will and testament of the final forerunner who'd survived in this abandoned place.

"It was here we created the shepherds," Sho continued, reading the new words now, "a new form of life designed by our hands, for our purpose." The Barious. The designs, the schematics, in the Verisson arch: the script was talking about the Barious. "We created them to protect, to nurture, to guide those who would come after, those who were already becoming—for we knew, even as we faced the infinite, that our fall was inevitable."

"Shepherds," the Preacher said softly, as if the word was a new thing, some concept she wasn't able to grasp. "Shepherds. That can't—"

"Let them finish," Sahluk rumbled; I didn't turn to look at the others again—I was still staring at the script floating in midair—but the Preacher fell silent, and Sho continued reading the same script I saw:

"Because angels," he read, "by their very essence, require devils. Or create them."

The writing shimmered again, changing as Sho read the final stanza, and again, new words. "Evil is not merely the absence of good," I picked up the thread, "it is a thing apart, in opposition. And everything in nature has its nemesis, called to balance the scales. In our desire to do great good, in building the shepherds, in clawing back the chaos, we had shifted the weight too far, and the universe . . ." I swallowed, had to stop to lick my lips; there was something horribly final about the next line: "the universe made an answer."

"What does that mean?" Javier whispered. "What does any of that—"

"Let them finish," Sahluk said again, and like the Preacher, Javier lapsed into silence.

"Simply by being," Sho read after the next verse had unveiled itself, "by manifesting new sentience, by unifying the chaos into harmony, we willed our own executioners into existence as well. Beings that turned the very sky to fire in their plunge from the heavens; beings descending from a firmament of flame, one that swept low over our worlds, to consume." The words Sho was reading were the same that I saw, but I had a terrible desire, at that moment, for that *not* to be true, because I thought I *knew* what they meant, and I wanted, more than anything, for the words of the forerunners to be something—anything—else.

They weren't: they shimmered again, the story continuing, and it was my turn to read. "A byproduct of our passage; an infestation, an infection, that we could not fight. Our punishment; our reckoning; our . . ." My voice choked on the last word, caught, just a bit, as I said, "our sin."

Except that's *not* what the word spelled—it was a homophone, a matching inflection in the language those who wrote the stanzas couldn't have known:

The word was written "Cyn."

"No . . . no. *No.*" The Preacher shook her head, firmly. "The forerunners created the Barious—they created *my* people. *We* were their children, we were meant to . . ." She lapsed into silence, then, without any prompting by Sahluk, but it didn't matter—no new words had replaced the old. The story—the testament—was done, its implications clear:

The forerunners had created the Barious, then they'd created the Cyn, and then the Cyn had murdered them all.

"We were meant for something else," the Preacher whispered. No one else had spoken; we were all trying to just . . . process . . . what we'd learned. So was the Preacher, but this was so much *more* to her—an answer to the question the Barious had asked since they were awoken, millennia ago. An answer to the question every species asked—"Why are we here?"—but unlike the rest of us, it was never a rhetorical curiosity for the Barious, because something had *made* them; not gods, not evolution, not celestial forces, but another species, one long since dust.

Made into dust, we knew now, by the Cyn.

"We were meant for something . . ." Except she didn't know *what* they'd been meant for—or hadn't, not until this moment. "We were *not* meant to serve," she said finally, a Barious refutation from centuries ago, a rallying cry from their species when some of the sects decided that's exactly what they were created for: that they were AIs, and AIs existed to serve organics, so that's what the Barious should do, sentience or no, free will or no. They'd tried to make the Barious into slaves.

"That's not what it says," JackDoes added quietly. "Not what they said." He nodded in our direction, toward Sho and I. "It said 'guide'; it said to 'nurture.' It said—"

"We were not meant to be *defined* by you at all!" She almost screamed the words, more anger, more raw pain in her voice than I'd ever heard. This was her entire life—her hundreds upon hundreds of years—being made a lie. "We were created by better beings, by beings that *knew* more, had answers, had compassion, had . . . had . . . had . . ."

"They had all those things," Javier agreed with her, though nobody was stepping close to her, nobody was touching her—the sheer desperation radiating off of her skin was like heat, you could almost feel it, like she might lash out at whomever was close, just to have something to hit. "They had them for their children—the Barious. And they had them for the other forms of life evolving around the galaxy, the other species—"

"Our gods are a lie," she whispered; the first time I'd ever heard any Barious refer to the forerunners in that way, her voice bitter around the word, speaking it like a curse.

I reached out, and took her hand; she let me. But she still wouldn't look at me—wouldn't look at any of us.

"The implications of this . . . they go beyond the Barious, beyond even the Cyn," JackDoes hissed, though he looked nervously at the Preacher as he said it, to make sure she wouldn't take offense. She didn't move—didn't react at all, just continued to stare at the floor, her expression completely blank, like she'd turned off the synthetic "muscles" behind her face. Only the light shining through her eyes showed that there was still someone in there at all.

"How do you mean?" Sahluk asked the Reint.

"He means exactly what he said," Javier replied. "The forerunners created the Cyn—or at least, created the conditions for them to manifest—and they created the Barious, to . . . guide . . . the organic life developing across the universe. And that may not have been all."

"And what does *that* mean?" Sahluk asked again, the soldier scowling openly now with his one good eye; he didn't like any of this, and I couldn't blame him.

"'Unifying the chaos into harmony,'" Sho repeated the words he and I had read, picking up Javier's argument. "We've always wondered *why* the lost homeworlds were so similar, in terms of gravity, atmosphere, pressure, that sort of thing: this is why. The forerunners were . . . terraformers, making certain the worlds giving rise to new life would have that uniformity—so that when we inevitably came together, we'd have those conditions in common, making it easier for us to—to cooperate, to . . ."

"They set the stage for . . . for the Golden Age." I couldn't help the awe in my voice as I said it.

"They must have been alone," JackDoes whispered—the great fear of all Reint. "The only space-faring species in the galaxy at the time of their existence. They wanted to make sure *we* wouldn't face that same loneliness."

"They wanted to make sure we would come together—and they built the Barious to . . . to teach us, I suppose," Javier agreed.

"And that's all we were," the Preacher had come back to us, and the bitterness in her words was so deep I could almost see it, tearing her apart from the inside. "Created to serve *you*. Created to . . . *beholden* to . . ."

The light flared back to life; more words now, appearing in the center of the cathedral, as if the Preacher's very anger had willed them into being. "There's . . . more," I said, turning back toward the brilliance.

"Read them," the Preacher said, the words halfway between a command and a plea.

The words of her creators—those who had touched the evolution not just of the Barious, but of all of our species, apparently. All the indignities, the atrocities, visited upon the Barious during their species' troubled coexistence with organic life, and they'd comforted themselves with the notion that at least they had *that*: that they were the chosen people of their creators, creators long since vanished from the universe. And now the long-dead forerunners had taken that from her.

"We built the shepherds to protect the new children," Sho read, turning back to face the light, "those that would arise after we were gone, into the more perfect galaxy we were creating. We built the shepherds to be guides, to pass on what we had learned, even as we decayed." It was as if the forerunner script had heard the Preacher's misery, had responded to it; it was answering her question, somehow.

I kept reading, following the lines of bright writing where Sho had left off. "But when the enemy came, the shepherds were even more vulnerable to their depredations than we, for we had built them in the hope of that better galaxy, one cleansed of the chaos the enemy twisted to their own ends."

"So we hid them away, far from the place of our . . . our dying," Sho stumbled on that bit, just a little, stumbled on the final, stark acknowledgment that the forerunners hadn't just *vanished*, hadn't ascended to a higher form of being or crossed over the threshold of the galaxy in search of new horizons: they'd fallen, just like everything, everyone, eventually did. "We hid them away where the enemy could not find them—where the new children might."

Silence, then, in the cathedral, as everyone waited for Sho and me to speak again, but there was nothing: the words faded, and nothing replaced them, nothing but that shimmering light.

"We failed," the Preacher said softly, something still broken in her voice, broken and brittle and just lost. "Before we ever awoke, we *failed*. We've always wondered why we were built, what our purpose was, how we could achieve it . . . What could you have been?" She looked up, taking in all of us, in turn; the various species—four different organic races, represented there, with her—that the Barious had been meant to guide, to nurture, to teach. "What could you have been, if we'd been there? What could we have taught you? How much *better* could you have become?"

"Preacher, that's not—" I reached for her, but she shook her head, pushed my hand away—not roughly, as gently as she possibly could, but she didn't want the comfort I was offering, all the same.

"They created us for a purpose, and then they *took* that purpose from us, and they just . . . left us. Sleeping. Useless. Abandoned. Tools for a project they never intended to finish. And *they* were the ones that took our memories. Took our purpose away. Why wouldn't they have let us . . . Why didn't we know? *Why couldn't we remember?*" Her first words had been quiet, almost whispered, but the last were a shriek, aimed directly into the light, the anguished cry echoing, rebounding off of the high ceilings of the cathedral, the echoes filling the emptied city until they faded away into nothing.

No answer to her pain was forthcoming; whatever had prompted the new writing, it was dormant again now. There was no balm for her suffering; not in this place.

She sank to her knees, slowly, haloed in that brightness—it reflected and shone off her metal skin like she herself was the source of the diffuse glow. "We were supposed to be 'shepherds,'" she said once more. "Instead, we were simply lambs. For the shearing. For the slaughter. And there was no one to protect us from the wolves. Any of us." She looked up at the rest of us then, her eyes wide, her photoreceptors almost overloading in all that light.

I sank down beside her, and held her, and I wept with her, for her.

Because she hadn't been built to.

CHAPTER 14

Esa

The Preacher stood, after a while; walked off, without a word. I let her go. Whatever it was that had happened here—had killed the Vyriat explorers—it was long done; this place still felt alien, hostile, to me, but those were just echoes, ghosts, of what had come before.

The Barious had been built—maybe even designed—here, and then their creators had hidden them away, because that same design had made them vulnerable to the Cyn, to the enemy that had somehow manifested from the massive changes the forerunners were visiting upon the galaxy in the course of their attempts to "improve" it. The Cyn could manipulate energy, the very same energy that coursed through the Barious' mechanical bodies; I didn't know exactly what the writing the forerunners left had meant when it said they "manifested" the Cyn—whether that was poetic license, fact turning to legend turning to myth even before the ancient testament was laid down, or some literal cosmic agency we just didn't understand—but it was true that, if the Cyn had known where the Barious were, they could have wiped them out as easily as breathing.

So the Barious had slept, hidden away from their creators' enemies, while their purpose—to teach the sentient beings who were gaining sapience across the galaxy, maturing on a scattered handful of worlds made similar by the forerunners—had slipped away. And the Preacher was left with nothing, the very sense of surety, of purpose, the thing that set the Barious apart from the other races—more than their mechanical bodies and industrial physiology—stripped away from her.

Meanwhile, the rest of us still had to deal with what all that meant for *us*.

"But . . . it doesn't make any sense," Sahluk was saying, shaking his head; I turned from watching the Preacher walk off, half hoping the writing would have returned to explicate some of the statements it had made, statements that shifted our entire concept of how life had evolved in the universe, but there was nothing: the forerunners' last testament had said what it was going to say.

Miracles that came on command, I supposed, weren't miracles at all.

"None of it does," Sahluk continued, sitting heavily on one of the benches that crept across the cathedral floor in strange hexagonal formations—the thing creaked under his weight, but didn't give. The forerunners had either been nearly as heavy as Mahren, or else they'd simply built to last. "If the Cyn were the enemies of the forerunners, bent on galactic annihilation—or at least galactic conquest—where did they *go*? Why didn't our species evolve under their bootheel, under their control? An enemy doesn't just stop because they've won; that's the opposite of what happens."

"Maybe they didn't," Jane said slowly, staring up at whatever she was seeing in the fading light—if she was seeing anything at all; the light was gone, for me, leaving nothing but the diffuse illumination that had filled the rest of the city, but clearly, Sho and I weren't seeing what the others were. Still, even if she was still seeing the star map the others said they'd seen, that wasn't what she was *looking* at: she was staring at nothing, turning over the words of the testament in her head, trying to make them fit into the universe as she knew it. "Win, I mean. You're right—conquerors don't stop once they've finished conquering. They built new empires, new civilizations, the sort of which we've never seen even the remnants of. Even if a new enemy had come along after, nearly wiped out the Cyn the way they wiped out the forerunners, the Cyn would have left something behind, just like the forerunners left the monoliths, the relics, the Barious."

"Which means the Çyn didn't 'win' at all," Javier nodded.

"But neither did the forerunners," Sahluk put in. "If they had, *they* would have woken the Barious up—set them to their original purpose once the fighting was done. And all of our races would have gone through a lot less pain before we made it to the stars."

"A place of 'dying,'" JackDoes hissed. "That's what the words spoke of. But not, perhaps, a funeral pyre, an inevitable end—"

"A battle," Sahluk nodded; that made sense to him. "A last stand, against the Cyn. How . . . desperate . . . they must have been, at that point. They thought they were angels, angels given dominion over all creation, and yet they were being dismantled by this unknowable enemy—they must have found a way to strike back. But only at great cost."

"To free the universe from the grip of their enemy, they sacrificed themselves," Sho whispered. "It's the only thing that makes sense. It's the only way . . . the only way that . . ."

"It's what the Justified always feared," Jane said softly. "During the sect wars; before the pulse. That the weapons would just get . . . bigger, and bigger, and bigger, until someone built something capable of . . . this. Of *that*," she nodded at the light. "Total galactic annihilation. Except for a few protected enclaves—the worlds where the organic species were evolving, evolving in the direction the forerunners wanted us to evolve. The worlds where the Barious were hidden away, and at least a few worlds still holding pockets of Cyn. Everything else . . ." She trailed off again. Everything else the forerunners had created, wiped away—perhaps the very devastation that had created the relics had ripped them from whatever terrestrial worlds they had begun on and flung them across the galaxy. All of it destroyed by a weapon— the last the forerunners had built. One that had ended the war, and the forerunners, and almost the Cyn.

"For all we know, not even *those* were all protected," Javier added. "The worlds where other species were evolving, I mean. Just because there were fifteen organic species that survived doesn't mean there were only fifteen to start with. The forerunners might have been nurturing dozens of other species, hundreds, maybe, only to have those wiped out as well. The hate that must have taken . . ." He shook his head. "The forerunners killed off the Cyn in a single stroke—or at least forced them into some kind of hibernation— and they killed themselves to do it. Because of what the Cyn had done."

"Until we woke them up again," JackDoes agreed. "The Cyn, I mean. Until we *found* them. During the Golden Age. We must have. And we just assumed they were . . . new, were like us. Because just like the Barious, whatever it was that the forerunners had done to them . . . they did not *remember*. The wars, the forerunners . . . not any of it." His tail lashed uncomfortably at the thought;

species memory, cultural memory, was important to the Reint, the thing that kept them from descending to the savagery that had defined the world where they were born.

A world, just like the others, changed by the forerunners. While the Reint had been evolving into the dominant predators of their world, the forerunners had been watching, changing that same world, raising the oxygen content, changing the gravity, the rotational forces, the atmospheric pressure; it must have taken millennia, longer, to do so without threatening the fragile life already manifesting. But they'd thought they'd had the time.

"Somehow, though, they must have learned," Sahluk said. "The Cyn, I mean. They must have—maybe they found another monolith, another place like this; maybe it was even *this* place that they found, if they somehow traced the Vyriat's path back here."

"And maybe that explains what happened to the Vyriat," Sho added darkly, echoing my thought from earlier. "Why nobody ever learned about this place. We've seen pyres like those outside before. When a Cyn wants to destroy all traces of its carnage."

"But either way, they learned what they were," Sahluk continued, "that they were . . . manifested, whatever the hell that means . . . as the enemy of organic life, as the *enemy* of the forerunners who had been protecting the rest of us."

"The schism," Jane nodded, seeing where he was going. "The first great division of the Golden Age, the division that marked the *end* of the Golden Age. The Cyn learned what they were, and so they viewed the rest of us as . . . weak. Interlopers, defilers, unworthy of the worlds we were settling. A plague on the very stars, the children of gods they had wiped out. We were treating them as equals, and suddenly they learned their origins were completely different from ours. You don't negotiate with beings you believe are beneath you, yet still might pose a threat—you annihilate them. The same way we would a particularly infectious virus."

"Except they weren't strong enough—not yet," Sahluk agreed. "There were never as many Cyn as there were the other species; we know that much. So they withdrew—hid. Building their strength; biding their time. And then the pulse. It makes them stronger; they feed upon it. And it weakened the rest of us." He turned toward Jane, his crystalline eyebrows furrowed so deep

I could barely see his one good eye. "We did this. Us. The Justified. We *created* the circumstances where they could strike back."

"But why . . . why seek out the gifted? Why *hunt* us?" Sho asked. "How does that . . . how do *we* fit into all of this?"

"Why are you and Esa the only ones who can read the writing—can see it at all?" Javier asked him in return. "The only common thread between the two of you—between you, and none of the rest of us . . . is your gifts. Esa's not Wulf; she's not the only human; the common denominator must be your gifts. Somehow, the next generation are attuned to the forerunners. It's as if they foresaw your coming somehow—"

Jane shook her head. "But that doesn't make sense—it's pulse radiation that creates the gifted, that makes their abilities manifest, and how could the forerunners know anything about pulse radiation when all of this happened thousands upon thousands of years before the pulse?"

"We were taught that the pulse bomb had forerunner tech at the center of it," JackDoes said with a hiss. Unlike Jane, Sahluk, and Marus, he hadn't been alive when the pulse was set off, but every Justified knew of the role we had played—the weight we bore. "Whatever the pulse was, beneath all the tech: it came from the forerunners—maybe it was the same weapon they used against the Cyn."

"Except if it had been, we would have all been born into a pulsed universe," Javier shook his head. "Pulse radiation doesn't decay, not at all. So that doesn't track."

"Well, there's *some* connection between the gifted and the forerunners," Sho insisted. "There has to be; Javier's right, that's why Esa and I are the only—"

"We need to focus," Jane insisted. "We came down here to learn where the direct rift leads, what these Dead Furnaces have to do with the Cyn, have to do with the gifted. Somehow, the Vyriat who found this place found that location—that has to be what's on the other end of the rift, why the Bright Wanderers call this 'the Furnace's Gate.' The Vyriat explorers, before they were wiped out, built the rift to lead *there* with knowledge they acquired here."

"Maybe . . . maybe this place told them," I offered slowly. "The writing . . . it changed, to answer the Preacher, remember?" I looked to Sho for confirmation, who nodded. "Maybe it told *them* something different entirely."

"But it's gone now," Sho shook his head, still staring upward, at the space where the light had been. "I think . . . it's like an oracle, maybe. It can only answer a few questions, and then it has to . . . that's all we get."

"Not a great deal of help, all in all," Sahluk grunted. "You'd think if the forerunners wanted us to have answers, they would have left behind an AI—or whatever the hell that was—that could actually tell us something useful, rather than riddles only some of us can even read."

"They knew the Cyn would be just as likely to find this place as we were," JackDoes shook his head, disagreeing with the big Mahren—a relatively rare thing. "There may well have been secrets—deeper, darker secrets—they were trying to protect."

Javier nodded. "The words that manifested for us—for Sho and Esa—might have been entirely different from what was shown to the Vyriat, the map that led them to the Dead Furnaces. They couldn't have had gifted among their number, after all: that was well before the pulse. So maybe it told them something else, gave them some . . . other lead, some other piece of the puzzle."

"It pointed them somewhere it doesn't want *us* to go," I nodded.

"Thankfully, we can anyway," Jane replied. "The direct rift is still built, still functioning. We can power it up with a flick of a switch, in the facility above."

"You're saying we should follow in the Vyriat's footsteps," JackDoes said.

She nodded. "The Vyriat; the Cyn who came after; the Bright Wanderers. They all went through the rift—I don't think any of us have any question about that." She looked around for any kind of dissent; got nothing but stone faces, an acknowledgment that what she was saying tracked, made sense. "The Cyn were once bent on annihilation, domination, yet now they're building this . . . cult, these Bright Wanderers. What changed? What are their goals *now*?"

"Whatever it is, I doubt it's good for anyone else in the universe," Sahluk rumbled. "Not with the dreadnaughts their followers are building. You're right," he nodded at Jane. "The only way to find out what they're planning now—regardless of, you know, all this 'What is life? Why are we here?' stuff—is to follow in their footsteps. And those lead through the rift."

"But if there *are* answers to those other questions, I, for one, would not mind knowing them," JackDoes murmured. "What we find on the other side—"

"We'll find a fight," Jane answered him. "We always do." She was patting at her pocket; withdrew a cigarette, and a lighter, and tucked the former in her mouth before sparking a flame with the latter. It seemed almost . . . profane, her smoking in this place, but I think, in a way, that was why she was doing it—not just to deal with the stress and the strangeness of this place, but as a rejection of the notion that we were *all* the forerunners' creations, beholden to their long-dead will.

Jane had never been much for religion, nor any kind of worship. Whatever we were meant to have been, whatever their plans for us might have demanded, we weren't that thing any longer—and, as far as she was concerned, we never would be. It was what lay ahead of us that mattered, not what lay behind.

The other pilot had said something, over the comm: that Jane always looked to the horizon, spent all her time looking forward, rather than back. My mentor was doubling down on that impulse now, and I couldn't blame her—the wars of the Cyn and the forerunners were in the distant past. The threat of the Bright Wanderers, of the Cyn in the present—those were still ahead of us, and whatever the forerunners had meant us to know, we didn't: we could only deal with the dangers that lay ahead.

Then again, of course I agreed with her: she was my mentor, after all. Full thrust and load the torpedoes, shift the shields forward and go full tilt at your enemy—find the fight before the fight finds you. Hit them before they can hit first.

It had been Mo's way; it was Jane's way; now it was mine, too. We needed to follow the Cyn, to find the war they were building—because I had no doubt that was exactly what they were planning; their long-delayed vengeance for the forerunners' last, desperate act—and we needed to hit them first. Any other questions could wait.

And that would mean heading deeper into the unknown; it would mean opening the direct rift, and following it wherever it might lead.

CHAPTER 15

Esa

It was time to go. The desire to stay, to investigate more, to learn every-thing we possibly could about this place: we all felt it, but the truth was, that was a job for scientists, for historians, for people with tools and knowl-edge that we lacked. When we finally returned to Sanctum, we could send a team back here to do a full study, but that wasn't us—that wasn't the mis-sion. We were operatives: our job was to identify, analyze, and dismantle threats to the Justified, and one such threat was looming over the metaphorical horizon like a storm front in the distance, ready to break and drown us all.

Whatever the forerunners had been doing when they created the Cyn, whatever it might mean that they'd terraformed the worlds of the species evolving toward sentience during their eons-long dominion over the galaxy, those were questions that had gone unanswered for hundreds of thousands of years. They could wait, just a while longer. Whatever it was the Bright Wanderers were planning, by contrast, could not.

I went to find the Preacher.

Jane offered to go; I told her I would handle it. The bond the Preacher and I shared was a strange one, all wrapped up in guilt and grief and sad-ness, but it was a strong one, too. The hurt she was feeling right now—it would take that strength to reach through it.

I found her standing on a series of long steps, descending toward what might have once been a canal—assuming running water was something the forerunners had needed, the same as we did—but now was just . . . empty, a long stretch of nothing that cut through the broken city, once an artery for its populace, now lacking any purpose at all, given that the populace it had once been meant to serve was long since dust.

That might have been what had drawn the Preacher there to begin with: a thing without function, its purpose long since lost.

"It was always . . . such a comfort," she said, staring down into the emptiness of the canal. She hadn't even turned when I approached; didn't need to, had sensors that could "see" me coming by changes in ambient temperature and pressure and air flow. The Barious walked through a very different world than the rest of us did: more vibrant, or simply more telling, perhaps.

I sat beside her; she kept standing. "Knowing you had a purpose?" I guessed, staring out at the metal ribbon of not-a-canal-any-longer as well. "Even if that purpose had been taken from you?" I understood, in my own way. "Sometimes not knowing a thing is better than knowing," especially when it came to faith. Mo had taught me that.

The Preacher nodded. "For thousands of years, my species watched the other sentient races—the organics—struggle with those questions: why are we here, why were we born, what are we meant to do? It all seemed so pointless; inapplicable to us. We were alive because we'd been built, or built each other; we were born for a specific reason, just as we were meant to achieve something specific. The fact that it had been . . . taken . . . from us didn't change the fact that it existed at all. Nihilism is a concept the Barious cannot apply to themselves. Even when the organics tried to enslave us, to treat us as lesser—we always knew that we were so much more than what they thought. That knowing was at the very heart of us, as a species, as a culture. We were built for a reason; the rest of you were not. It made us . . . different. Special."

"You're still special," I told her.

"We're the forgotten tools of a dead race, never allowed a chance to complete the duty we were built for. We were meant to guide you, to teach you, to shepherd you toward better angels than your base natures—sometimes violent, destructive, hateful—might allow. What do you think the universe would be like, Esa, if we'd been allowed to do so? Would the sect wars still have happened? Would the wars that roiled the human homeworld, the Wulf one, even before you discovered interstellar travel—could we have stopped those, as well? If we'd been where we were supposed to be, as opposed to locked away, like a frail, ailing child in a tower . . . what did our creators cost *you*, in their fear for us?"

"Preacher—do you really expect me to feel sorry for *myself*, in all this?" I couldn't help it; I laughed, a little, as I asked. It was such a *stupid* thing to think—that, with as much pain as she was in at the moment, I'd only be thinking of what the forerunners' revelations meant for humanity—that I had to laugh; a reminder that, for as much as the Barious could sense about the world around them, they sometimes had some massive blind spots as far as human—organic—nature went.

"The universe should have been better," she said, something almost wistful in her tone—a grief for a thing that had never been.

"No," I disagreed, as firmly as I could. "The universe should have been exactly what it is. If humanity had evolved on a world where the Barious just gave them all the answers—if that had been true for the other organic species as well—we wouldn't *be* humanity anymore. We'd all just be . . . imitations of the forerunners, pale shadows of the beings that created your race. Which would mean we'd make their mistakes, too. At least this way, we get to be ourselves. For better or worse, *we* get to decide who we are, which paths we take."

"Being 'who you are' means being sixteen separate peoples, peoples that have spent almost your entire history killing each other, with the brief exception of the Golden Age; it means never working toward a common goal, a common purpose. It means being creatures that have drowned all you know in blood, more than once. We were meant to prevent that."

"Maybe. But maybe we learn something from that drowning. Every time. You're looking at the Golden Age—that brief moment where everything worked—and seeing that as how things should have been all along. But the Golden Age only meant something because we collectively *decided* to exchange ideas, to trust one another, to love one another. We chose that, each of us, each species. If we'd been . . . guided there, told there was no other path—it wouldn't have had the same meaning."

"The galaxy would still be better."

"The galaxy would be calmer—not the same thing. It would be more homogenous, too. We'd all be what the forerunners, what the Barious, wanted us to be: we would have had no choice. Now, we get to be different. And different is . . . just more interesting."

A small smile in her voice, as she replied, "Are we still talking about my crisis of faith, Esa? Or are we talking about the fact that you've finally realized you're attracted to Marus's young ward?"

I groaned, making it a little more theatrical than it had to be, for her sake—though the groan itself was all me; had everyone realized this before I did? At least she felt up to making jokes at all: that seemed like progress.

"Still," she continued, looking back down at the canal. "I . . . take your point. I could have told you, months ago, that you two were . . . suited . . . for each other. But you needed to discover it for yourself. With the Barious guiding the other species, you would not have discovered anything on your own. Could not have learned; could not have grown. The fact remains: what you grew toward was a collection of species that drowned the universe in war. That released the pulse. That damned my people."

"A . . . mistake . . . we're out here trying to fix," I reminded her. "Yes, the Bright Wanderers—and the Cyn—represent a threat, to the Justified, to the galaxy at large. And we have to answer that. But we came looking because we wanted to help the Barious. Because you're part of the galaxy—you're one of us, one of the sentient races."

"And we're only now realizing just how true that is," she murmured. "Just as lost as the rest of you."

"Maybe. But getting lost is the only way you find something new. I know it doesn't feel like it right now, Preacher, but learning all this, it represents—*can* represent—a new chapter in Barious history. The first new chapter, really, since the Reetha woke you, millennia ago. A chapter you get to write for yourselves."

"You're wrong there," she shook her head. I looked up, surprised, but she was still staring out at the forgotten city, broken and ruined by whatever forces had created the relics—likely the war with the Cyn that had damned the forerunners. "Oh, that might be true, eventually, but we're not there yet."

"Why not?"

"Because. The older chapter—our history with the forerunners, our . . . reckoning . . . with that—it isn't finished. Not yet. The Cyn killed our creators; the creators of all of us." Her voice shifted on the last sentence, a quicksilver flash from musing over metaphor to something harsher, almost cruel, a kind of demand implicit in her tone. "They killed our *gods*." Again, that word: it appeared the Preacher no longer gave a damn about any pretense of machine rationality, and it was clear from her tone—from that new anger in her voice—that the "us" she spoke of didn't just encompass the Barious; now that she knew the forerunners had a hand in the evolution of all the sentient beings of the universe, we were all her sisters, all her brothers, united against the hellish plague that had wiped our "parents" from the universe, and stolen the destinies we were supposed to possess. "We have to make them pay. We have to make them *pay* for that. As you say: we have no more purpose but the choices we make. I am making this one."

I just nodded. Maybe she was right. Maybe—before the Barious could move on—there had to be a reckoning with what had held them back for so long in the first place, a reckoning for the fact that they'd been built for a reason, a reason that had been denied them.

Except that didn't sound like reckoning: lashing out against those who had taken from you, against those who had caused you to hurt—that wasn't reckoning at all. It sounded more like vengeance. A very . . . organic . . . path to take.

Either way, she wasn't mourning anymore: she was furious. And like Jane had taught me—furious could be good. Furious could be of use.

Furious could make you ready for war.

CHAPTER 16

Esa

The Preacher and I returned to the others, found them waiting back in the forum where the elevator had first descended, the Vyriat construction of the shaft standing out from the forerunner architecture like an alien thing, a part of "us"—even if it was several thousand years old—intruding on a space that was only "them." "You good?" Jane asked the Preacher as she and I approached.

She nodded, flatly, then paused, and looked back at Jane. "Thank you, Jane Kamali," she said, her tone curiously . . . humble.

Jane shrugged, grinding out another cigarette under her bootheel—she didn't usually smoke this much. Either this place was really putting her on edge, or she was just relishing the profanity of the thing: spitting in the eye of the forerunners' beliefs that they'd been angels, been gods, to our lowly species. I was banking on the latter. "Not entirely sure what I'm being thanked for, but no problem," she answered the Barious.

"For Esa," the Preacher said simply, then marched into the elevator, not waiting on the rest of us.

I didn't know what the hell to say about *that*.

We all crowded back into the elevator, watched as the hidden city inside the relic disappeared beneath the rising walls. I, for one, wasn't sorry to see it go. The place still felt haunted to me, weird and uneasy—judged, perhaps. For our failures to become what the forerunners had thought we should. Whatever destiny the forerunners had meant for us, we clearly hadn't met it, and it felt like the very eyes of the city, every open window and high tower, were judging us for that failure.

Let them judge us. They'd created us, or at least shaped the avenues natural selection could push us down, and then they'd abandoned us, because of a fight they'd started, then lost. We were still here. We were still fighting. Whatever it was the Cyn wanted—our destruction, our subjugation—we wouldn't give it to them.

I wouldn't even say that we'd "die first": that was the path the forerunners had chosen, and it had done nothing but forestall their enemy, who were, again, hundreds of thousands of years later, bringing their rage to the skies above new worlds, stealing away the gifted for whatever nefarious vengeance they planned to wreak on the very galaxy that had birthed them and us both.

We rode the elevator back up, and I wasn't sad at all to see the empty city left behind.

We filled Marus and Meridian in on what we'd found, even as we prepped the machinery above for opening the rift: after that, we made sure the feeds from our body cams had captured every inch of the facility itself, not just the data from the city below. For all that the major discovery of this place was in the words the forerunners had left behind and the city underneath our feet, we didn't want to discount the lost technology that had allowed the Vyriat to crack the monoliths in the first place: if the Justified could somehow replicate it, more answers might await us, hidden in the other relics scattered across the galaxy, like those that rose and fell in the mists of the Katya system where I'd been born.

We'd filed back to the ships—the storm still a constant cyclone around the facility, raging like a typhoon but no closer to actually washing over us, just another piece of strange technology created either by that lost Vyriat sect or by the monolith itself—and there were pale beads of light beginning to fall from the top of the great ring, evaporating into a kind of pulsing, liquid glow at the very center. It would take some time for the rift to open, and the rift itself wouldn't be at the center of the circle—it would be where the circle pointed, out beyond the world's orbit, where even heavier, massive starships, those that couldn't make planetfall, could take the path it opened.

We left the facility behind, took the Preacher back to Shell, even as Javier, JackDoes, and Sho delivered Sahluk back to Khaliphon. "We still don't know how long this journey will take," Marus pointed out over the comms as we waited for the rift to spin up. "Or what will await us on the other side."

"Trouble, most like," Jane replied. "From what I understand, direct rifts aren't exactly quiet when they open. Not only will anybody in the system know that someone else has arrived, they'll know exactly where, as well, thanks to the massive glowing seam of light we will have ripped open in their sky."

"And for all we know, half of the dreadnaughts from that shipyard have been sent to the Furnaces, ultimately," Sahluk added. "We could wind up facing down a dozen different supercarriers, all gunning for us, the minute we break out of the hyperspace corridor."

"If that happens, we can just jump away," Javier said, a shrug audible in his voice. "Direct rifts won't heat our hyperdrives, since we won't actually be using them at all, and once we're on the other side, we should be able to spot nearby systems. Starving to death en route is still a worry, though."

"I will . . . appreciate . . . the time," the Preacher added, from Shell, "to think." Given that Barious "thought" at a speed well beyond that of the organic races, even if the trip only took days, she'd have the mental equivalent of months to process what she'd learned within the forerunner relic. Plus, the Preacher didn't need to eat. Or breathe. So she had less to worry about with the "starving to death" thing.

"Yeah, but you're alone," Sho replied with a grin. "I'm stuck on board Bolivar with Javier and JackDoes."

"Our company not good enough for you, Sho?" Javier asked his apprentice; I could hear the grin in his voice as he said it.

"You cheat at cards. You and JackDoes both."

"Well, if everybody's cheating, then it's not really 'cheating,' is it?" Jack-Does hissed, a certain amount of ambivalence in his tone. "Just . . . different rules."

"You cheat *badly*."

"It's a risk we'll have to take," Jane told them all. "After all, the Wanderers made this jump; so did the Vyriat. We can too. Just . . . try not to kill each other out of boredom on the way."

"It's time," Marus said quietly.

He was right; the pale glow from the ring far below us, hidden by the storm clouds, wasn't hidden any longer—we could actually see it from orbit, bright and growing brighter, even in the storm-choked atmosphere of the forgotten world. There was a kind of "crack"—inaudible, of course, but I felt like I could hear it anyway: the sight of all that light rushing free of the world below, then impacting onto an edge of nothing out in the stars. It seemed like it should have made some sort of sound, some massive clarion call.

But there wasn't, there was just that rush of light, and then the rift was just there, a spiraling ring of light floating in space: a stable gateway, formed in the void, open for at least as long as the storm below could provide the energy.

Four years after escaping my homeworld, I thought I'd mostly figured out all the technology I'd grown up believing had been wiped from the face of the galaxy entirely, and now here was something else that entirely upended my awareness of "how things were supposed to be." We didn't know where it led, or even how it worked, not really, and that notion—that we had *no clue* where the rift was going to take us—was terrifying, and a little exhilarating, too: even during our long trek up to this point, headed out into the unknown, we'd always been aware of roughly where we'd wind up at the end of a jump, what nearby system was our next destination. Now, we had no idea, none: except for the fact that the Bright Wanderers had made multiple references to these "Furnaces," we might well have been headed straight into the center of a star.

"It doesn't just stay open . . . forever, right?" Sho asked nervously, breaking the silence that had come over the comms as we all stared at the ancient technology flaring to life.

"It'll close once the facility runs out of juice," Javier told him. "Even without any of us there to shut it down. The storms below are powerful, but they're not so powerful they can sustain a rift like this indefinitely. An hour, maybe two."

"But once we're inside, it doesn't matter when it closes," the Preacher added. "This is just a gate to a very specific quantum channel—as opposed to the highly randomized channels we use when *we* travel through hyperspace. The channel is what allows our passage to the other system; not the rift itself. Once we're in, we're in, until we've arrived at our destination. For better or for worse." At that point, we'd be god only knows where, maybe on the far side of the galaxy—we'd have to rely on our traditional hyperdrives to get back home, unless the Vyriat had built a direct rift in the end-point system, aimed back this way.

"Everybody good?" Jane said, her hands on Schaz's yoke, clearly ready herself to get moving.

"Go for . . . well, not really a 'jump,' I suppose, but go all the same," Marus acknowledged. "Javier?"

"We're good, and looking forward to spending months cheating at cards," Javier agreed.

"God . . . god damn it," Sho added, to no one in particular.

"Preacher?" Jane asked.

"It will mean something," the Preacher said, which seemed like something of a non sequitur, but Jane took it to mean she was good, all the same.

"You first," she said to the Preacher. "Then Scheherazade, then Khaliphon, then Bolivar." I was sure she had her reasons for that deployment, but she didn't share them, and the others deferred to her judgment—if there was some sort of ambush waiting for us on the other side, Jane had the most combat experience, especially in starship dogfights, and so she would have tactical control of the engagement.

The Preacher said nothing in response, but Shell's thrusters kicked on, visible as a bright shard of light through the cockpit, and she began maneuvering her ship toward the spinning disc of light. She approached the hyperspace vortex cautiously—for all her assuredness of the science behind the rift, she'd clearly never used one, either—and then it was like that breach of light actually *reached* for her, reached out and pulled Shell in, and then she was just . . . gone.

"Stay safe, Jane, Esa," Marus told us.

"We'll see you on the other side," Javier added.

"You guys do the same," Jane said, piloting Schaz toward the gap in reality, light instead of void, liquid instead of nothing, all flowing colors and shimmering overlapping fields of radiance. "Esa? You ready?"

"Let's do it," I nodded, unconsciously bracing myself against the console.

"Good luck," Meridian said softly through the comm: I could picture her face as she said it, her long ears folded back along the side of her head, her eyes—somehow dark and still soft, kind—glued to Schaz's figure as we approached the rift.

I didn't have a chance to respond—not that I could think of a damn thing to say anyway.

We were through.

CHAPTER 17

Esa

My heart stopped hammering in my chest after we passed through the rift, and what lay on the other side was just . . . hyperspace. The same liquid stars, washing past the cockpit, the same strange sparks of not-light jumping through the flow—the view I'd seen a hundred times before. If it weren't for the distinct lack of low thrum from Schaz's hyperspace drive— the sort of thing you noticed when it kicked in, then half an hour later, couldn't hear at all—we could have been on any other hyperspace jump, leaping from one system to the next.

"So . . . that all happened." Jane shook her head, unbuckling herself from her harness. She was trying for nonchalance, even almost hitting it; anyone else might have read it the same way, but I wasn't anyone else. She was still thrown, and not just by the revelations we'd learned inside the forerunners' monolith.

Still, she was giving it her best shot: pretending like I didn't know, like we could both just ignore everything that had happened. "Come on," she said, her voice brusque, "let's get to work. I'm sure that little jaunt through the storms did some damage to Schaz's systems, and we've got nothing but—"

"Jane. Wait." I stood as well, caught up with her as she headed for the living quarters. I took her hand and physically pulled her to a stop; she hadn't been exactly running, but she'd been moving fast, faster than she usually did, and I knew why, too. "We need to . . . or, I don't know, maybe not *need* need, but if you want to . . . to talk about it—"

"What? The forerunners? The notion that the Cyn are some ancient curse, a race of . . . god-killers, that we have to find some way to face?" She shook her head. "The forerunners weren't gods, Esa, and the Cyn are nothing more than—"

"Not that," I said impatiently, turning her around—I knew when she was avoiding a topic, and she knew *I* knew, and we had all the time in the world now, unless the rift chose to dump us out well short of wherever we might be headed. I wasn't planning on letting her avoid this one, nor on letting her stew over it for days or weeks or however long we might be in hyperspace, the hurt festering into something raw and awful in the meantime. "The other thing. The . . . the woman. The pilot."

"Esa—"

"You knew her."

"I . . . did." Even admitting that looked like it had cost her something, based on the expression on her face. Schaz, however, had been listening patiently; at that admission, she quietly rotated the couch out of her walls, and I led— almost pushed—Jane down on the overstuffed, threadbare cushions we'd been meaning to replace for as long as I'd been on board. Jane noticed, and glared in the general direction of Schaz's databanks. "Oh, come *on*, you two," she almost snarled, lashing out to try and distract us both. "You want to pipe in a little calming piano music, too? Maybe pour me a nice glass of Tyllian wine so we can all let our hair down and share our feelings? This isn't—"

Schaz answered by pushing a small shelf out of the wall; there wasn't a glass of Tyllian wine on it, but there was a bottle of Avail whiskey, Jane's favorite, complete with tumblers for each of us. That actually cut Jane short; an impressive feat. "I don't have enough hair to let down," I told Jane, pouring a few fingers into each glass, then sitting on the couch with my legs pulled up beneath me. "Also, you hate piano music; I believe you once called it 'the sound of glass breaking, over and over again,' because you have all *sorts* of weird PTSD triggers after too many lifetimes of combat. But yes. We are going to talk about this. Whoever she was—she shook you. Just watching you, hearing her voice over the comms; it was like watching you get hit.

"I don't *like* it when you get hit, Jane. I don't like it at all. When it happens, I want to be able to hit back. So you're going to tell me who she is, and why she has that much power over you, and when we see her again—and I could tell, when you were talking to her; you know we're going to see her again—*I'll* know who she is, and that way, it'll be my turn. And then *she* gets to be the one to get hit. By me. Very, very hard, and right where she won't expect it. Because I fight dirty. You taught me that." I took a sip of my whiskey, and tried to savor the smoky, somehow arid flavor—I really did. It didn't help. Avail whiskey still tasted like brass shavings coated in pesticides to me. But it was Jane's favorite, and I'd choke it down to help put her at ease.

Jane stared at me for a minute—just stared, her brown eyes studying my face like she was reading a tactical map, trying to divine the position of the enemy forces she knew were down there somewhere—and then she just started laughing. There was a high, almost hysterical edge to it, but it was laughter, nonetheless.

I took that as a good sign.

She pulled the glass of whiskey from my hand, poured it into her own, then downed the whole thing; "savoring" wasn't really Jane's idea of what you did with liquor, or with anything, really. I guess a childhood on the front lines of a war had taught her that—to take what was in front of you before it got snatched away—and I had a feeling that very childhood was where we were about to turn: Jane spoke very little about her past at all, and even less about who she'd been before Mohammed had recruited her into the Justified. But that woman, the way the two of them had looked at each other— the stranger hadn't been fighting with an enemy agent, exchanging insults or following up on half-forgotten threats. I'd been watching her face, too, the other woman, through the glow of the force field on the relic.

She'd been in pain as well. Just like Jane.

"I told you once, I think," Jane said to me, pouring herself another glass. "Warned you, more like. That you don't want to know my story. That it wasn't . . . wasn't a good one."

"And here I was thinking you grew up surrounded by milk trees and honey lavender," I told her with a snort; Schaz had extended another shelf, this time with a chilled bottle of beer on it—my preferred drop. Where was she getting this stuff, anyway? "I know you grew up in the sect wars, Jane—on the front lines. You've mentioned it, once or twice, when you forgot, just for a second, that you didn't want to tell me about it."

"You saw Kandriad," Jane nodded, staring into her glass, referencing Sho's homeworld—she wasn't drinking her whiskey, just staring into the murky clouds of liquor. "That's what you think my homeworld was like."

"I think it was *more* like Kandriad than any other world we've seen," I told her, tempering my response as I twisted the cap off of my beer. "That doesn't mean I think it was exactly like that."

"Well, you're wrong, either way. You want to know what my homeworld was like? Kandriad wasn't the closest you've come to that. The Battle of Sanctum was. The Pax invasion. Imagine that—all that fighting, all that chaos—over, and over, and over again. Every day. For twenty years." I couldn't. I couldn't, and she knew it. My mind just couldn't grasp the concept. "I grew up before the pulse, Esa," she reminded me, her voice almost gentle. "That means my war wasn't just artillery shells and poorly machined rifles, nor chlorine gas and creaky prop warplanes—it was orbital bombardments and subsonic raids, failing shield projectors and viral invasions. Every day, a new way for the enemy to attack us.

"You know what was the only thing worse than growing up on a resource-poor world during the sect wars?" She took another drink; she wasn't using the pause waiting for me to answer—just waiting to set the answer right herself, in her mind. "Growing up on a resource-*rich* one. Telarium. Deep veins of it. It's nothing really special, but it can bond with anything; it's the cheap sheet-rock of zero-g construction, used in damn near every alloy you can think of, just to bulk it up without making it brittle. There's more than a little telarium in Schaz, you know—maybe even some of it came from my homeworld."

"And so everyone was willing to kill to get it."

"And so everyone was willing to kill. And die. Every day. Over, and over, and over again. Living through that . . . living *with* that . . . it changes a person. Makes them . . . hard, or hollow. Or something else." She reached over and poured herself yet another drink; I think she meant to polish off the entire bottle before I was even halfway through my beer. "Most people on the front—after growing up like that, in that—you could see it, in their faces. Eyes like granite: cold, distant, empty, nothing behind them at all, their minds . . . locked off, behind walls. Even to themselves. What little hope they had that hadn't been whittled away by the war, well, it was stolen by the teachings of our sect. Because hope makes people unpredictable, makes them fight for something other than their beliefs, their survival—a brighter future, maybe—and the elders didn't want that; that was something they couldn't control."

"And you?" I asked softly. "Did you have eyes like that?"

"I'm getting there," she said. "You want to hear this, you've got to let me tell it." I nodded my acknowledgment, and she continued. "Point is, those ones—the ones with the eyes like cold iron—they weren't the ones you had to look out for, not really. They wouldn't lift a hand to save you, but they wouldn't tear you down just *because*, either. That was your worry with the others, the ones who looked at you and only saw fire—they were the ones you really had to watch out for. Faith was all they had, and that—the very fervency of their belief, the desperation with which they clung to it—it left them unable to feel kindness, compassion, to feel anything other than righteous zeal." I'd known Jane's upbringing was the reason she didn't hold much to religion—to *any* religion—and I'd known she came from a kind of hardline, zero-tolerance fundamentalist sect, but this . . . There was a level of fear in her voice I'd never heard, like somehow, even a century later, those zealots would reach out from the shards of her past and drag her, screaming, to stand trial in front of some tribunal, to be punished for her imagined sins.

"And the woman?" I asked. "The pilot?"

"She didn't have eyes like that," Jane shook her head, though that wasn't what I had meant. "At least, I didn't think so. I didn't think I did, either. Somehow, we'd both of us come through all that . . . shit . . . and still managed to hold on to a little something, a little piece of ourselves, pieces that weren't calcified into cold granite, or burned clear by fervent hate. She was my sister, Esa." I started at that; just a little, but enough that Jane noticed—almost smiled, until she didn't. "Oh, not by blood, just by . . . like you and Sho. She was by my side, had my back, and I had hers, all through . . . through all of it. *All* of it. We joined up together, trained together, served. And no matter what we did—did to survive, did because we were ordered to—that something . . . *else*, not granite, not fire . . . it was always there. We fought more for each other than for the cause; more for the fighting than for the fight, if that makes sense.

"And maybe that's not better, I don't know." She took another drink, went back to staring straight ahead, as if she were seeing her war—her wars—projected on Scheherazade's bulkheads, bright blooms of fire over distant shattered horizons rising just on the far side of the wall. "But it's what we had. We survived the fronts together, survived all our rookie mistakes, and by that time, the tides of the war had started to shift. My people—my sect—started winning. We reclaimed *our* cities, took back what had been ours, then started to move outward, taking the fight to those who had been trying to kill us for so long, and I . . . I understood that, you know? I'd never believed, never fought because of the faith, but they'd hit us when we were weak; it made sense to hit right back.

"And we kept winning, reclaimed the whole world, and our elders told us to carry our fight to the stars, and I understood *that*, too—our enemy had invaded our home, so we had to punish them, to drive them back until they couldn't ever touch us again; not just wouldn't, but *couldn't*, had been stripped even of the capability to do so.

"And so we fought *that* war, the one out in the deep—that's where I learned to pilot starships, because I'd flown low-altitude bombers during the terrestrial fighting—and then we just kept pushing forward, kept taking territory until we were on *their* homeworld, not ours, and there, they were just as desperate as we had been, fighting to defend their own homes, and the war ground into a stalemate.

"That was when Mo found me—found us. After ten years of war, ten years of fighting—not just surviving the fronts, but of serving, of waging the war, as soldiers—we'd risen up through the ranks, Julia and I both, both of us together. We'd survived, together."

"And Mo—"

Again, she shook her head. "Maybe it was just because we had . . . access, I don't know. Maybe we were the only ones who could *do* what needed to be done. But I like to think he saw something in us—in me—that wasn't in the others he could have turned to; that same . . . *thing*, the thing behind our eyes that had kept us from becoming just . . . broken, like the others had been, the others we'd grown up with on the fronts, most of whom were long since dead. Hope, maybe." She shrugged, took a drink. "I'm not even sure for *what*.

But whatever it was . . . I like to think he could see it. In her eyes, as well as in mine. That I wasn't the only one who saw it; that I wasn't the only one who was wrong."

"Wrong?"

She nodded, still staring forward, like she was trying to lead a target with Schaz's forward guns. "We see what we want to see," she said slowly, like she was answering a question I hadn't asked, maybe one that she had, in her own mind. "When we look at each other, even when we look at ourselves. We read each other based on what *we* need to believe. I read her wrong, and she . . . she did the same to me, and it's only in looking back that I can admit that there may have been more granite behind my eyes than anything else, that the flicker of hope I thought I'd seen in hers was really just fire. It could just be . . . hard. To tell the difference. When desperation is the coin you pay to live even another *hour*, hope and hate can start to look . . . very similar."

"So what was it Mo . . . wanted?" This part, I knew—the outlines of the thing, at least—from Mo himself, but there were pieces I didn't know too, and I had a feeling this was where it had all gone . . . wrong, with Jane. Not just with her sister, but with the walls she'd built around herself, walls made from the very same granite that had protected her during the war, walls I'd—first inadvertently, then more purposefully—been chiseling away at the whole time I'd known her.

"The Justified were different back then," she said. "Before the pulse. A kind of . . . forgotten arm of an ancient peacekeeping body that had long since imploded in on itself. Their goals were simple: to keep the carnage of the sect wars at an absolute minimum. And my people—advancing across the stars on our enemy's homeworld, the zeal with which we fought, the total control the elders had on most of our population—that had put us on the Justified's radar, and not in a good way.

"Mo found us, Julia and me, and he told us what the elders were building, in secret—a system-killer, a stellar fission tear, one that would end the war for good, except it *wouldn't*, because once they'd used that sort of weapon, it would be all too easy to use again, and again—there'd be another war, and another beyond that, our battle for survival become a crusade unending, at least until we came up against another sect with a planet- or a system-killer all their own. I believed him—Mo—when he told us that, and I believed him when he said there was only one way to stop such a weapon when it was so close to being primed. Julia didn't. She couldn't. Like I said: eyes of granite, eyes of fire."

Jane took another drink, then reached for the bottle again, paused before she gripped its neck, to clench her fingers into a fist and make the tremors go away. "She needed to believe in what we'd fought for," she said, just staring at her hand, "needed to believe we were somehow . . . better. But we weren't. And now that she knew what Mo and I had planned, what we were willing to do in order to stop the weapon from firing . . . I didn't have another option. Or at least, that's what I told myself. Then, and now. I didn't *see* another way.

"I lied to her—told her I'd go with her, to warn the elders Mo was coming. And then I made sure she couldn't do exactly that. The first casualty of my war against my own sect: my sister. I shot her out of the sky, without warning, without even giving her a final chance to . . . to . . ." She was crying—of course she was—but she wouldn't admit it; wouldn't even raise up a hand to wipe the tears from her face. "And I knew, then, that I'd be able to *do* it, to turn the system-killer against my own people, to overload it and destroy the moon it was built within, because if the love *she* had for me couldn't stop me, nothing could. Over two hundred million souls, on Hadrian's Gambit, the military moon where the weapon was constructed, where I shot Julia down. Two hundred million.

"They didn't all die at once. I sabotaged the weapon, it backfired, and it melted the atmosphere. Not just burned it away, but actually melted it down, bit by bit—and it took weeks for the moon to come apart altogether. So some of them made it out." She shrugged, managed to pour herself another drink, finally. "Of course, there were three times that number on our homeworld below, the world I knew would be forever changed by the destruction raining down from above. Nearly a billion lives, all told. I don't know how many died. Maybe as many as a quarter; maybe more."

"And the world you saved?" I asked her, stressing the last word, even though I knew it wouldn't matter—not to her. "The world of your enemies?"

"Not just a single planet; a whole system, including a handful of worlds that weren't even involved in our war. Forty-six billion. Forty-six billion souls that would have died if I'd done nothing. When you look at it that way . . ." She shrugged, and let it lie.

Of course she'd done it. Of *course* she had. And of course that math—that justification—meant nothing, afterward. Not when she'd had to burn her own world to make it happen; not when she'd shot her own sister down to save those strangers, those enemies, who would never know what she'd done.

God, no wonder she'd leapt at the chance to detonate the pulse bomb. A way to end the threat of system-killer weapons for good, without collateral damage. And then that had gone sideways too, and now she just had . . . *this*. All this weight, all this guilt, all this grief, on her shoulders, every day. Forever. The pulse, and the lives it had claimed; the weapon she'd turned on her people, and its casualties; her sister. The first—the first that mattered.

And now that sister was back, and she wanted her revenge.

Jane raised the glass toward her lips; it didn't make it. I'd pulled her too close for that; pulled her tight, and just held her, and I wept with my face pressed against her hair—wept, because she wouldn't admit she was doing the same, wouldn't admit that the wounds she'd carved into herself were still bleeding, that she still *felt* them, every day, every hour, every *second* of her life. Because she'd simply told herself that living in agony was just living— that was the way life was.

And Schaz sailed on, through the tiny universe all our own, toward whatever future we'd earned with all our tears, and all our pain.

ACT
THREE

ACT

THREE

CHAPTER 1

Jane

Seven weeks. Seven weeks we were in the rift, flying blind—actually not even "flying" at all, given that the quantum rip in space-time was just carrying us along, Scheherazade's engines not even firing. Seven weeks trying not to think about the revelations from the forerunner relic, about what it meant—what it might mean—for the galaxy, trying not to think about what the Bright Wanderers and the Cyn might be planning at our destination, trying not to think about Julia: where she'd *been* for the last hundred years, what she'd seen, what she'd done. Seven weeks and we were hurtling toward the unknown, until we just . . . weren't anymore.

There was no warning; I felt us come out of hyperspace while Esa and I were in the middle of breakfast. She felt it too, the shifting ripple in something that wasn't quite gravity that identified when a ship all of a sudden wasn't flying through a tear in space-time any longer—there was no fading of the thrum of Scheherazade's engines that usually accompanied the sensation, because her engines hadn't been firing, but we felt it, all the same.

We both stood, our meals forgotten. "Schaz," I said, already heading toward the cockpit, trying to prepare myself for anything—a fleet of dreadnaughts, the Cyn homeworld, some new remnant of the forerunners darkening the stars. "Where the hell are we?"

"Trying to calculate our position now, but we're . . . well off the maps, boss," Schaz replied. "We're in-system, at least, not just in the middle of nothing—there's a . . . huh. Would you look at that."

"Look at *what*?" I dropped into my seat at the helm and buckled myself in;

whatever it was we were supposed to be looking at, I doubted it was friendly. I doubted it was—

Then Schaz put the system's star at full magnification, and all my attempts at preparedness dropped away. I forgot to be worried, I forgot to be tensing myself for combat; I forgot to be anything other than awed.

I'd seen a great deal, in the systems I'd visited—hundreds, all told, if not more—astronomical phenomena of every shape, size, stripe, and severity. But I'd never seen anything like this.

There were two black holes, at the very center of the system. Unlike the hungry vortexes that ringed the outskirts of Sanctum, flanking the approach to the planets that circled the Justified's star, *these* maelstroms of gravity were so close they'd already eaten every world that might have once orbited this system's sun—and now they were working on the sun itself, doing their damnedest to gobble up all the energy and light the star was putting out. It was the sort of thing that should have been inevitable, the star's remaining core of fusion being inexorably devoured, except the two swirling patches of hungry nothingness were perfectly matched to the orb of fire: matched in distance, matched in appetite.

The bright yellow light of the star was being *pulled*, in ribbons, toward each black hole, the sun twisted into a kind of curving, elongated strand of fire, but the heart of the stellar furnace, the constant explosion of energy that was a star: that lay perfectly centered between the two hungry collapses, the very pull of each keeping the sun itself stable between them, its fissile output an exact match for the amount of energy the black holes could eat. It was like a child's game of tug-of-war, played to a stalemate between nearly infinitely powerful cosmic forces, each black hole drawing the star toward itself, so the star was held in the center between them, the unimaginably intense gravitational pressure warping its surface until it was something no longer an "orb," but something with a shape more like a spiral instead.

That in and of itself was . . . definitely of note, if just for its cosmic rarity—a system with three stars, rare enough; a system with three stars, two of which had collapsed into black holes, even rarer; a system where those two black holes were perfectly positioned to keep from devouring the third star, rare enough to seem almost an impossibility—but there was something else in-system as well: the Vyriat explorers hadn't pointed their direct rift here just for the light show.

There was something built, not in orbit or floating in the void, but ringed *around* one of the tendrils of flame being pulled out of the star: the solar energy was passing through the construction before it vanished into the depths of the swirling darkness that was the gravitational event horizon. It must have been a piece of forerunner construction; even during the Golden Age, building a facility that close to that much stellar output—not to mention the warping gravitational fields of the black hole above—would have been beyond the collective engineering ingenuity of our species.

No doubt about it; the strange ring, the station or facility or whatever it was that encircled the tendril of stellar fire as it swept off the star in a spiral, halfway between the stellar explosion below and the event horizon above— that circular stretch of shadow that was a piece of forerunner memory: *that* was the "Dead Furnaces."

The look of the thing, highlighted against all that brightness, was similar to the forerunner monoliths in construction and design, the same curved edges, the same not-really-sure-what-it-was materials; I still had no idea what the place was *for*, how anyone could possibly harness that much stellar energy or to what purpose, but at this point, I wasn't putting anything past the forerunners who had built the place.

"What the *hell* . . ." Esa wondered aloud; I didn't have anything more cogent to add. Yes, the galaxy was a big, big sweep of both nothing and everything—over a hundred billion stars, each with its own strangeness—but this, the perfect balance of the cosmic phenomena that made up the center of the system, even discounting the facility itself: if either black hole was just slightly further away or slightly closer, if the star's energy output was just a little lower, a little higher, the forces of gravity and energy and fusion that kept the whole tangle in balance would have ripped themselves apart, carrying the strange ringed station with it.

There was no *way* this was natural. No way. But even Golden Age tech couldn't control the fusion of a star—and we couldn't have built black holes, not sustainable ones, could just create them for a brief enough instant to tear a world apart. We certainly couldn't create *stars*; the largest fusion reactor ever built was a pinprick next to the smallest, dimmest celestial orb in the sky. Just the tendril of stellar flame pouring through the center of the facility— the Dead Furnaces, though there was nothing *dead* about all that stellar fire— would make the output of a dreadnaught reactor look like a match flame held up to a thermonuclear blast.

We couldn't have built it—not even the facility itself, not that close to that much solar fire, let alone engineering the stellar collapses and perfect positioning required to twist into being the tendril of flame the facility had been built around. But who knows what the forerunners had been capable of.

"Look—there," Esa said, pulling up magnification of a different part of the system, scanning away from the cosmic impossibility that had the ballet of flame and nothing at its heart. I'd been wrong: the black holes hadn't eaten everything in-system. There was still a single world in orbit around the ribbon of fire that was the system's sole remaining sun, the planet's path around the distended, distorted star keeping it exactly in between the two gravitational pulls of the black holes. Again—even a single wobble in that orbit, and it would have been gobbled up by one event horizon or the other, or pulled into the stellar blaze. Yet somehow, there it hung, circling the spiraled sun, every year of its passage seeing it safely between Scylla and Charybdis, two terrible dangers that in their very hunger kept it balanced between them.

"What in the *hell*," I repeated Esa's wonder; it was about the only thing I could think to say.

"Guys—there's a signal coming off that world," Schaz said warningly. "I'm blocking the long-range transmission—piping in white noise and scattering it before it gets out-system—but there's also a short-range burst that I can't do anything about: it's aimed at the . . . facility . . . hanging between the star and the black hole, the one that's . . . you know . . . the *hungry* one." I wouldn't have thought about it that way—that the facility, the ring, the Dead Furnaces, was eating the stellar light the same way the black holes were—but sometimes Schaz dipped into metaphor in ways that surprised even me. "Anyway: the signal's getting through."

"Somebody saw us arrive," I cursed, beginning to throw toggles as I prepared to meet whatever welcome party would be shortly headed our way.

"Maybe not," Esa shook her head. "I mean, yes, you're right, but this broadcast . . ." She'd shifted over to the comms station, was staring at the waveforms representing the interference and the signal like they were some difficult language she was only vaguely fluent in. "It's repeating, regular—I think it's automated."

"Well, if the signal is automated, then so are those." I'd been pushing the viewscreen's magnification up as high as it went, trying to get a better look at the strange ring of metal surrounding the tendril of solar flare: I'd *gotten* my better look, and it showed a docking bay opening on the side of the structure, ships beginning to swarm out. Lots of ships.

We were about to have company.

Still, Esa was right: the way the ships moved—more like birds on a wing, haloed against the stretched fire of the distant star, than vessels on the hunt—hinted at a single AI mind controlling their flight patterns. It was a drone fleet, standard swarm tactics. Drones were smaller than even the lightest piloted fighter, and less well armed, but you could build twenty of the damn things for every one of a ship Scheherazade's size—maybe even more, given that they only required a single AI to operate the whole fleet, one semi-autonomous mind split between twenty different vessels.

There were at least that many headed our way, and who knew how many more still docked in the Dead Furnaces themselves.

"A swarm flight," Esa said, swallowing, her mind following the same paths mine had.

I nodded—we'd seen this sort of thing before, on a smaller scale; they'd attack us like hungry scavengers, overwhelming Scheherazade with sheer numbers, hitting us again and again until they could pick our bones. "Are the others through the rift yet?" I asked. Shell should have come through before us, the Preacher having entered the rift earlier than we had, but hyperspace could be strange about that sort of thing.

Schaz threw up a rear projection—and there the damn thing was, the rift, still glowing and huge and incredibly obvious, so big and bright it was probably visible to the naked eye from the world below, like a KICK-ME sign hanging in space—and the other ships in our convoy were just shadows between us and all that light: still, there were *three* shadows, which meant they'd all come safely through.

Bolivar and Khaliphon were linked at the airlock; Marus must have attached in order to use Bolivar's more sophisticated instruments to get a better look at the facility, his damned historian's curiosity getting the best of him. I opened up a comms channel: "Javi, you better detach Bolivar from Kaliphon, we've got—"

"No, *wait!*" Esa said suddenly—then she flipped the comm switch on her own console, so she could speak to Javier directly. "Javier, don't detach yet! Send Sho through, to Khaliphon, before you break away."

"What the hell are you planning, Esa?" I asked her warily. "We've got about three minutes before that swarm hits us, and it'll take all that time for them to—"

"'Swarms just keep coming, until the bays are empty'—that's what you taught me about drones, yeah? They're only limited by how many of the craft the AI can control at once; every ship we bring down will just be replaced by a new vessel from the . . . the . . ." She gestured helplessly at the viewscreen, at the strange facility silhouetted against the light. "The only way to stop them is to shut down the AI transmitting their control signal, unless you want to fight until every single one is destroyed, and there could be *hundreds* docked in that place."

"So? If the control signal's coming from that facility, they're going to be in between us and it, and that place'll be hardened against all sorts of attacks, like relic construction always is. Not to mention I don't really fancy a dogfight that close to that much stellar—"

"*If* the signal's coming from the facility, yeah. But the short-range transmission Schaz picked up is still being broadcast. If it was just a warning, it would have stopped by now, been flagged as 'received.' I'm saying it's not an alert: it *is* the command signal. That world is pulsed." She tapped her scans, indicating that particular detail, which I hadn't picked up. "Not heavily, but still enough that whoever built that fleet couldn't have docked them there. But that wouldn't stop a control signal from being broadcast out—just the ships themselves."

So that was her plan; good girl. "Okay. So we hit the planet; track down the broadcast tower, and bomb it to hell. What does that have to do with—"

"Broadcast tower will be shielded," Javier said through the comms—he'd been listening in. I cursed again; of course it would—that would be the basic line of defense against a plan of attack exactly like the one Esa had just come up with, and it wasn't such a brilliant idea that any halfway decent tactician wouldn't have seen it coming.

Esa had asked Sho to get onboard Khaliphon. "You want to hit it from the ground," I said, working my way through her plan.

She nodded. "Shell and Bolivar can screen against the drone swarm, buy us time for you and Marus to drop the rest of us onto the world—then all you four have to do is hold out until we can dismantle the tower: me, Sho, Sahluk, and Meridian. We won't do you a great deal of good up here—with a single AI running all the drones, Schaz and the other ships are easily capable of running the weapon systems to match—but down there, we can bring down the broadcast: the long-range warning and the drone command signal both. If we rip the AI's *guts* out, there won't be anything to pilot those ships."

"Esa—"

"It's our best shot, Jane." She said the words levelly—she was right, and she knew it. With another curse, I kicked the throttle over to high—the others did the same, following my lead. No time to vote on this one. This was a combat call, and those came down to me.

The drones—or the AI controlling them—saw our thrusters burn bright, and recalculated our vector; they turned on the wing again, like a veil being drawn across the stars, a flight of shadows between the spiral of the sun as they aimed themselves at the distant planet as well, on an intercept course. There were more craft spilling forth from the stellar ring, had been the whole time Esa was laying out her plan; there had to be at least a hundred of them in the void, and whatever AI was running them—an AI powerful enough to pilot that many at once—if it *was* housed on the perfectly orbited planet, it would throw every single ship it had at us rather than let its own existence be threatened by a strike team we put on the ground.

It was a race to see who could get to the planet first: our four ships, just arrived at the edges of the system with the rift still burning behind us, or the hundred drone fighters, highlighted against the spiral of fire that was the distant star, vertical wings stretching out from the sleek craft as they rose like a swarm of bats against a sunset, creatures come out to greet the night, and to feed.

CHAPTER 2
Jane

D o you know what's waiting for you down there?" I shouted at Esa, who was back in the armory, getting her gear on: not just her weapons, but changing out of the pajamas we'd both been wearing at breakfast, pajamas I was still wearing, because the direct rift hadn't given us any kind of warning that our long hyperspace flight was about to come to a sudden stop.

"Lots of mountains, mainly," she shouted back—she'd transferred Schaz's scan data to her HUD. "It's been terraformed, which doesn't make any sense, because there's not shit down there—no minerals, barely any flora or fauna, hardly even water—"

"Esa, we're about to fight a drone swarm in a system where the sun has been *peeled:* none of this makes sense. You got grenades?"

"Oh, I've got grenades."

"Flares? Medkit? If there are mountains, you might need ascent cables—"

"*Jane.* Focus on the swarm of enemy ships you're going to have to fight through so you can get me on the ground before you start worrying about whether or not I've *packed a lunch.*"

She was probably right, though it looked like we were going to beat the drone swarm to the little world, if just barely; instead of worrying about her, I transferred my concern to the other captains instead. "How about you, Marus?" I asked over the comms. "Your team ready for touchdown?"

"Getting geared up as we speak," he said, "though Sahluk is being . . . vocally unhappy about not having enough time to get into his exo rig."

"He'll just have to satisfy himself by only outweighing everyone else by four hundred pounds rather than nine," I said dryly. "Comms working?"

"Check on the comms," Sahluk responded. "And my rig only weighs—"

"Check," Meridian confirmed, cutting him off.

"In case anyone is wondering—we got woke up by coming out of the rift," Sho added. "Also, point of interest: Javier sleeps naked. That means he's currently piloting Bolivar in the—"

"Pants are a distraction," Javier said. "I have no need of pants." Maybe that was true for him, but now, of course, *I* was picturing my boyfriend in his pilot's chair all focused and well muscled, and that was certainly a distraction for *me*. Thanks, Javier.

"You ready for this, little brother?" Naked Javier asked Sho.

"No different from what we did on the shipyards, yeah? Get in, fuck with the machinery, get out."

"We had stealth on our side going into the shipyards," Esa reminded him. "No so much in this case."

No shit: the swarms were closing fast. We were still going to beat them, though. I was . . . pretty sure we were going to beat them.

"Meridian," Marus ordered his own ward, "take my rifle—the tac-laser. There's only a little pulse in that atmosphere; it'll take hours to eat through the weapon. You've trained on it, at the range: you know what to do."

"Have you calibrated it for Cyn?" Esa asked him; she, at least, was entirely aware of what sort of defenders the broadcast tower might have once they got onto the ground, beyond cultists and turrets and the other nasty bits that came with assaulting any fortified position. If the Bright Wanderers had taken control of this place, both the Dead Furnaces facility that surrounded the plume of stellar fire and the broadcast tower on the world below—and I couldn't think of who else might have built a drone swarm control system on the otherwise useless world—the likelihood of her team encountering the cult's heavy-hitters was . . . pretty high.

"Can't—the focus of the prism is too narrow," Marus replied. "But it'll still be more useful than ballistics, against the armor, at least."

"I got it," Meridian reported. "Do I need grenades, you think?"

"Take smoke grenades," Sahluk told her. "Those—the ones with the green band. They've got electric chaff embedded in the burst—little metal particles that might make life . . . uncomfortable . . . for our glowing friends. You let me handle the heavy explosive devices: I've got fragmentation grenades, I've got mines filled with ball bearings, I've got a particularly nasty single-fire missile with napalm on its tip, I've got all sorts of terrible things that go boom. If I can't take my exo rig, I'm going to overcompensate like a bastard."

"Oh, I'm taking frag grenades, too," Esa said to him. "You don't get to have all the fun."

"I'm not so worried about you, Esa—*Jane* trained you. Marus trained Meridian, and he's never been nearly as good at blowing shit up as Jane is. Then again, very few are."

"Meridian, remember," Marus said to his ward, "if things go wrong: hide behind Sahluk. Just . . . right behind him. If you get shot, I'll be very sad. If *he* gets shot, it'll just be funny."

"Oh, go screw yourself, Tyll."

"We're entering the planet's atmosphere in three . . . two . . ." I didn't need to finish my countdown; Scheherazade was shaking with chop as we hit the outer edges of the ionosphere at full speed—we'd beaten the drones to our target.

Except we hadn't, not entirely—the five ships in the lead of the flight put on a final burst of thrust, and hit the edge of the atmosphere as well. The move was suicide: their approach vector was all wrong for their heat shields, and they were coming apart even as they shot right toward us, flaming metal flaking off the sharp lines of their prows until they were just jagged superstructure and heat, more "missiles" than "ships."

Of course, *they* didn't care—their AI conductor would spend the "lives" of five of them without a second thought, just a piece of calculus in its combat math. "Preacher," I said warningly, bracing myself for impact—we couldn't turn to meet them, not without changing our own approach vector and shearing off shielding to compensate for the added heat, shielding we couldn't afford to lose—but Shell was already moving, snapping off her own descent and firing bright beams of blue from high orbit, the lasers cutting the drone craft out of the sky before they could close.

They went down in shards of fire, smashing into the high mountains below us, the impacts ripping free collapses of cold blue-and-purple stone from the line of peaks that rose like a serrated knife blade from the surface of the barren world spread beneath our wings. Shell kept rising, kept firing, and then she was gone, out of visual; the Preacher was on her own.

The drone swarm still approaching the atmosphere reacted, a dozen or more pulling up to go after Shell, and Bolivar pulled free of the descent as well, his lasers flaring as he struck at the taut line of the drone crafts' passage. It took actual effort for me to keep Scheherazade on course, knowing my friends were fighting in the upper atmosphere: I hated leaving them to fight without me, without us.

Once I had Esa delivered, I could wheel and rejoin the battle, and Esa was right—our best bet for survival was to take out the AI controlling the swarm. We had no idea how many more drones were even now being prepped for launch in the strange facility between the star and the hungering pull of the black hole: the void could soon have hundreds of drones in it, and that wasn't a fight we could win, or even one we could survive, not for long.

I still hated leaving them behind, though. It went against who I was, what I was supposed to be, what not just the Justified, but my own wars had made me. What Julia had made me. You protect your own. That's how you survive. You protect your own, even if you can't protect yourself—that way you know they'll be there to protect you.

"There it is," Marus said, his voice still calm: rising from the mountainside ahead of us was a tall tower of metal, anchored into the stone itself, the design the same strange, looping construction we'd seen inside the monolith—a forerunner building, repurposed by the Bright Wanderers to house their communications equipment and the drone swarm control.

I knew the damn thing would be shielded, but I couldn't help it—I let off a burst with the forward lasers, just in case, but they dissipated well before they hit the tower, the gleam of energetic shielding rising like a shimmer over the complex.

"Had to try," I said with a shrug. "You see a good—"

"There; the valley, beneath the mountain where it's built," he answered the question I hadn't even asked. "Looks like there's an access tunnel leading into the stone—it must lead up into the tower itself. And the shield bisects the valley; we can put them down just outside."

"Yeah, if we don't ram right into the goddamned thing first. You know how you're going to get through that shielding?" I called to Esa. "It'll vapor-ize you just like it did the lasers. If they were smart enough to build defenses against air assault, they'll have ground defenses in place, too." It was times like this I missed fighting the Pax; at least the Pax had all been morons.

"That's what we've got Sho for!" Esa called back from the airlock. "Are we there?"

"Damn near—lowering the ramp now." I cut thrust to nothing and pulled Schaz into a sloping turn, her port wingtip nearly grazing the shield itself; beneath us, the rocky valley was a hard, long mess of scree and jagged stone, tough to cross—let alone fight on—for the assault team, but we weren't going to find better, and the drones would be on us any second.

"Descending!" Esa called out.

"Good luck!" I replied—and that was it, she was out, and I sealed up the airlock again and turned Schaz back toward the stars above, pushing the thrusters as high as I could go without burning through our own heat shield-ing. Above us, Shell and Bolivar were still dancing through lines of fire, en-gaging the first wave of the drone ships—and beyond, there were more, pouring out of the Dead Furnaces like the spill of metal from a Barious wound.

I grinned as the fight grew closer through the cockpit; no more running for me.

"As soon as we breach the atmosphere, give me missile lock," I told Schaz, pushing the thrusters up another notch once the atmosphere thinned and the glare of exit-velocity heat friction began to fade away: between Bolivar and Shell, the Preacher's craft was the more hard-pressed, four of the drones on her tail, their almost sail-like wings stuttering with laser fire. I adjusted course for intercept, preparing to hit them from the flank. "Prioritize targets—"

"The ones shooting at our friends? I got it," Schaz answered. "Been a while since we had a combat run, just you and me, you know."

"That it has." The stick was still shaking in my hands as I fought to keep Schaz's nose lined up with the enemy's vector.

"If you really plan on letting Esa go once this is all done, we'll be back to this for good: just you and me, all alone, nobody else to—"

"Really, Schaz? Now? Now you're doing this? Seven weeks in hyperspace

and nothing, but *now?*" That maybe wasn't entirely fair—she'd been complaining about it ever since I'd suggested the notion, so "nothing" was a bit
much—but still, we were in the middle of *combat,* for fuck's sake.

She abandoned all attempts at subtly—not that "subtle" had ever exactly
been Schaz's strongest trait anyway. "You *can't* let Criat give her her own AI,
Jane—you just . . . you *can't!*"

"We can fight about it later—we're almost on them. I'm giving you full
control of forward lasers and the turrets, both; I'll handle the ballistics."

"Missiles are locked . . . now." Twin lines of fire coursed out from either
side of Scheherazade's wings, the missiles chasing their targets like predators closing on swift prey as we broke fully out of the atmosphere; Schaz let
the lasers splinter against the drones' shielding, and I followed them up with
a hard roll and a burst of ballistic rounds that snapped across the exposed
flanks of the craft chasing Shell. It wasn't enough to knock them out of the
sky, but it did throw them out of the position, pushing them right into the
path of the missiles that were closing fast.

Two balls of fire filled the void; I pushed us right through the scatter of
debris to chew into the other ships pursuing the Preacher.

Scheherazade and I had joined the fight.

CHAPTER 3

Esa

I landed in the mountainous valley with a practiced roll, the jagged stone biting into my combat armor; I followed it up with a telekinetic push to pop me back upright, Bitey already raised, turning in a slow circle to hunt for threats—no, Schaz hadn't identified any when she was bringing me in, but ground-level defenses would likely be hidden from a starship for just that purpose, and anyway, she'd hit the drop point fast, given the enemy craft on her tail.

Still, I didn't see anything: just the rocky valley, bisected by the shimmer of the broadcast facility's shielding, falling from a clear blue sky—it was a beautiful day in the mountains of whatever the hell world I'd landed on. If it wasn't for the massive fireballs in the high atmosphere—fireballs hopefully all coming from enemy ships, rather than from my friends—it might have been any world terraformed to basic spec: standard gravity, standard pressure, the atmosphere temperate and tasteless underneath that cerulean stretch of sky, without the tang that might have indicated the presence of unusual gases in its composition; the whole thing might as well have been straight out of an "automatic terraforming set to galactic standard" brochure. Not that anyone had done much terraforming since the pulse, or even since the sect wars started.

It honestly might even have been pretty, except for the lack of growing things—there were only a few stunted, gnarled trees visible, the sparse flora likely a side effect of all the weird radiation being thrown off by the black holes. Whatever else *my* homeworld had been, crops and forests had grown in abundance upon its surface, and the things we encounter in childhood set the standard for the rest of our lives: I just expected a certain amount of foliage from a world, an abundance of living things that many seemed to lack. Pitfalls of growing up on a formerly agrarian-purposed planet, I supposed.

Khaliphon roared overhead, coming to a sudden stop just a dozen feet or so forward from my position; Sahluk leapt clear first, followed by Sho, then Meridian, all three of them armed to the teeth. "Hi," I said mildly as Marus peeled off to rejoin the fight in orbit and the three of them stood from their crouched landings. "Good to see you all—seven weeks and all that. So who wants to storm a castle with me?"

"There's a castle now?" Sahluk asked, frowning up at the tower that rose up from the peak above.

"I wasn't—it's just a saying, Sahluk, it's not literal."

"I mean, there is something vaguely fairy tale–ish about it, isn't there?" Meridian asked, shading her eyes and staring up at the rise of the broadcast tower. "All jagged and black."

"So, not so much the kind of castle where the princess gets to live happily ever after, huh?" I asked with a grin.

"Not so much," she grinned back. "More the type where she has to go and face the wicked witch in her den."

"Do witches 'den'?" Sho asked. "That seems more like a big predator–type thing."

We were burning off nerves with the banter; a practice I'd picked up from Jane, but one I think was common with soldiers the whole galaxy over— you didn't have to dwell on the enormity of what you were about to face, the dangers and consequences of the coming fight, if you were too busy trying to think up stupid jokes.

Sahluk grinned at us; the big Mahren had seen more combat drops than the three of us put together, and besides, if I'd learned "joking in the face of imminent bloodshed" from Jane, she'd learned it from Mo, and so had Sahluk. "So where's the infiltration point to this big predator's den?" he asked, putting us back on task gently.

I nodded, up the slope of scree. On the far side of the shimmer of the shield, I could see a level area: not a natural occurrence, but likely blasted out so their emergency access tunnel—or whatever the hell it was—would have an even space before it, where ships could land to offload supplies and crew and whatnot.

"So—I'm up first," Sho said, back to business as he stowed his rifle—he still wore his shotgun on his hip, but given that we knew we were going to see combat on this drop, he'd come kitted out for a fight at extended range, as well—and stepped toward the shield.

"You need me to . . . kind of . . ."

"If you would," he nodded, saving me the annoyance of trying to put into words the usage of our gifts, which really was more of an intrinsic, instinctual thing than something I could actually describe anyway. Sho and I had worked together long enough that he knew what I was capable of, and I knew what he'd need from me, so we didn't actually need to talk about it: we could just *do*.

I reached out and formed a kind of archway inside the shimmering energy of the shield—it didn't cut the barrier, but it would act as a kind of focus for Sho to channel his energy through. He placed his paws just above the barely visible shimmer, his fur rising up from the static charge; there was a kind of acrid smell in the air as he pulled electricity from the surrounding atmosphere, and then, just like that, the framework I'd built him was full of brightness and electric fire, and when it dissipated, the shimmer of the shield was gone beneath the arch.

We hustled through; that breach wouldn't last forever. It actually sealed up almost before Sahluk had made it to the other side—he snatched his hand away from the shimmer, a blister already rising on one of his rocky knuckles as he glared at the shield like it had personally decided to burn him, just out of spite. I didn't know Mahren could even get blisters.

Meridian was already turning to start up the slope, toward the level area, but I put my hand on her shoulder—we both pretended there wasn't a small thrill of light that shone from her skin where I touched her—and said, "Let me," with Bitey raised up to one eye.

She nodded, and fell back a step: if there were automated defenses around the access tunnel, I'd much rather they shoot at me first. Meridian had intention shields, we all did, but I also had telekinetic defenses on top of that, and I'd wager I had better reaction time with Bitey than she did with Marus's big fuck-off tac-laser.

I pulled myself up the slope, expecting that any second bullets would start whining past my head or lasers would cut through the chill mountain air, but there was nothing—even when the tunnel came in sight, a gaping hole in the stone at the far side of the clear-cut area, nothing shot at me. That seemed . . . too good to be true.

The damn doors were even open; that meant I could see inside the mouth of the tunnel, where revolving red lights swept across the interior walls in a crimson wash. Clearly they knew we were here—or at least knew the facility was under attack—but so far, they'd mounted no kind of defense beyond the shielding. There was no way they'd only protected their drone control from the air, right? There had to be—

"Esa, you've got incoming," Javier said in my earpiece. "The antenna—it just shot something up into the atmosphere; not artillery, more like flares, except . . ."

I looked up, traced the three bright azure lines of fire that had originated from the tower above us, now streaking across the paler cerulean blue of the unclouded sky. Unbidden, a line from the . . . text, or the message, or whatever it had been that we'd read inside the forerunner relic came into my mind: "Beings that turned the very sky to fire in their plunge from the heavens."

Javier was wrong—it *was* artillery, just not the "explosive payload" kind. The Bright Wanderers hadn't kitted out the facility's entrance with turrets or mounted guns as defenses, because they didn't need to: they had another line of defense, one they thought was unbeatable, rendering any other weapons unnecessary. We were about to have company.

"Get inside the tunnel," I told Sahluk, stripping off Bitey and setting her to one side of the clearing. This wasn't going to be a gunfight. "Get Sho up to the AI; let him cook it from the inside out, if you have to. And *find a shut-off for that fucking barrier.* I really can't stress enough how important that's going to be for my survival."

"You don't give orders to me, kid," the big Mahren said almost absently, looking upward as well as he too traced the arc of the bright lines of fire against the backdrop of lasers and burning that was the combat in orbit. The blazes of blue had reached their apex now, and were dropping back downward, like flaming meteors descending from on high—descending directly toward us. "If what's coming is what I think it is, we'll take them together, you and me. Just like Mo would have done. Meridian, Sho—you two get inside. Finish the mission."

I smiled at the soldier. "Nice try, Sahluk, but we both know you're not . . . equipped . . . to handle this. You've already proved today that Mahren can burn." I nodded to the blister on his thumb. "What Mo would have done was finish the mission, and we both know it." Sahluk frowned at me—and yeah, it maybe had been a cheap shot—but I continued regardless: "Get Sho and Meridian where they need to be; watch their backs. These are the outer defenses—there will still be armed cultists inside. I'll hold these bastards here. This is my part of the fight."

"Esa?" Meridian asked me, staring up at the sky herself, putting together the implications of what Sahluk and I were saying. "Are those . . ."

"Yes."

She, at least, didn't try to argue with me—just gave me a kiss on the cheek, her hand soft against my face as she did. "For luck," she told me.

Then she kissed me again, *not* on the cheek. "For me," she said when she finally pulled back, most of her glowing this time, her normally dark skin bright enough I could see her shining even through the tac-gear she wore.

Before *I* got to say anything—not that I could have; I was still just slack-jawed from the kiss, my brain not catching up to the fact that it had just happened, and was also my new favorite thing ever—she was moving toward the tunnel, Sho following. Sahluk spent another second glaring at the sky. "You get yourself killed, that little girl's gonna be real unhappy," he said warningly, turning to look after Meridian.

I pulled myself together enough to answer him with a faint smile. "I mean . . . I *hope?* I know that sounds like kind of a shitty thing to say, but—"

"Just stay alive, Esa. You get yourself killed, and Jane will be very, very unhappy with *me*. And I make it a policy to try not to make Jane unhappy. She's scary when she's unhappy, and I don't say that about too many humans."

"Keep them alive, Sahluk. Shut the AI down. Shut the *shield* down. I'm gonna need Scheherazade, to pull this off."

"You two have planned for this. You and Jane." It wasn't a question.

"Yeah."

"Jane's plan? Or yours?"

"Mine."

He nodded, like that answered something. "Good luck," he said, and then he was gone, following the others, leaving me standing alone on the level patch of ground, staring down at the boulder-strewn valley where the shimmer of sunlight against the shield was the only thing in any sort of motion.

Not for long.

The three lashes of lightning that had begun their fall toward me now actually altered their course, in midair; they were dropping faster than they had been before—not *quite* as fast as the meteors they resembled would have been falling, but not exactly in slow-motion, either. They smashed down among the stones and the scree on the far side of the shielding, and when I could see again, their cargo was delivered: three Cyn, kneeling among the blasted rocks, all glowing blue and blazing.

I guess their fancy armor couldn't survive "travel by atmospheric conduction." That was . . . a small comfort.

A *very* small one. Because, at the end of the day, there were still *three* Cyn on the other side of the shimmering force field, all of them looking up now, staring right back at me as I waited for them to react. Three, where I'd barely taken on one at the shipyards—and this time, I didn't have Sho to feed me energy; this time, I was very much on my own. And they weren't.

They began to stand, still watching me. I surged my intention shields into the telekinetic gauntlets I'd already wrapped around my hands and wrists; my forearms blazed with blue light as I took a step back, into a combat posture, and I grinned at them, my lips curving wide and mean. "Well, motherfuckers?" I asked them. "Are you coming, or what? We ain't got all day, you know."

One of Jane's very first lessons: never let them see your fear.

They didn't speak; they didn't answer my challenge at all, except to step toward the barrier, and then to melt through it like it wasn't even there, matching their own energy signature with the force field of shimmering light.

Once they were through, they began to spread out, crossing the top of the slope and forming a rough semicircle around me, ready to attack from all sides. Only then, in position and ready to kill, did they answer my challenge, all three speaking as one, the words buzzing into my comm: "*Heretic. This is a holy system, the first step toward the Palace that is our destiny. Your very presence here is a* corruption. *You have no right to even witness the same sun as the goddess— the light that touches her* belongs to her, and her alone. *We will remove you from this life with purifying fire, atom by atom; we will* burn *you from this world, until not a single speck of you remains to defile this holy anchor.*"

"Heretic. Well. I kind of like the sound of that." I took energy that wrapped around my left arm and twisted it, shaped it until it had formed a kind of buckler shield over my forearm—I'd have to fight defensively, at least until Sho could bring the shield down.

After that, I'd just have to pray that the very theoretical plan Jane and I had come up with for exactly this situation proved *practically* feasible. If it didn't, well—the Cyn wouldn't have to worry about killing me; I already would have done that myself.

The whole "atomizing me off the face of the atmosphere" thing very much included.

CHAPTER 4

Jane

Shooting the drones down one by one wasn't the problem—the problem was that the things flew in wings of five or six, turning and wheeling at the same command, linked by the same AI mind, and by the time you'd shot one down the rest had turned and were firing back, and the combined munitions of that many cannons would wear through Scheherazade's shields just as fast as if we were taking on a fully equipped vessel of the same weight.

I kept Schaz skimming across the upper atmosphere; our heat shields would be damn near melted by the time I was done, but at least that way the enemy couldn't pursue me very far: as their initial suicidal charge had shown, they weren't built for maneuverable reentry, and mostly they peeled off as soon as I cut back into the protection of the heat friction. Those that didn't, Schaz picked apart with her rear turret—helping the atmosphere itself pull them apart—and it was time to turn back to the fight again.

Bolivar was having better luck—of all four of our ships, he was the fastest, the most nimble, and he was better suited to dividing their flights, then picking them off, one by one. Javier and the Preacher had set up a kind of rhythm between them: Shell would draw the attention of a wing, Bolivar would hit them from the flank, and then Shell would wheel around and finish off whatever remained. That was the problem with an AI mind stretched across so many different craft—it couldn't adjust tactics, not with its awareness spread out across all those different helms.

By the time Khaliphon rejoined the fight from delivering his own assault team, we were making a pretty good go of it, had shot down at least twenty of the things, filling the orbit of the rocky world below with degrading satellites of wreckage and fire. But there were more coming, more wings launching from the bays within the Dead Furnaces, and we couldn't do this forever: every hit we took to our shields meant more energy had to be drawn from our ships' cores, and even then, the shields couldn't reenergize to full strength before the next wing was upon us.

It was a battle of attrition, an army of a disposable many versus the well-armored few, and if the sect wars had taught me anything, it was that numbers mattered more than anything, no matter how well armed or talented the smaller force was.

Yet somehow, I always seemed to wind up on the outnumbered side. I guess I was just special.

We kept fighting, kept wheeling and diving and burning through the limits of the upper atmosphere, filling the void with wreckage and the sky with flames. Until Esa and her team brought down the broadcast tower, canceled out the signal piloting the drones, there wasn't anything else we could do: just fight, or die.

"Jane? You listening?" The comm on Scheherazade's console crackled to life; Esa. "Oh, *please* be . . . be listening." She was breathing heavily—in combat.

"I'm here, Esa—what do you need?"

"Epsilon Protocol. Do it. Do it *now*."

I frowned, even as I dodged Scheherazade through overlapping fields of fire so that we could blaze right past another wing of drone ships, Schaz rotating her lasers in their housings to cut across their flanks. "You've set the antenna's *reactor* to overload? That seems extreme, Esa." I mean, granted, it was exactly the sort of thing *I* would have done, especially when I was her age, but—

"No, not *that* goddamned—Delta, then! Delta Protocol!"

"You're sure?" I couldn't help it: I would have much rather she'd begun Epsilon Protocol—and needed immediate exfiltration from what was about to become a nuclear fireball—than the second set of tactics.

"Of course I'm fucking sure, just get down here!"

"On my way. Javier—clear me a path."

"Your wish is my command, sweetheart."

"Put on some pants."

"No time—in a battle." Bolivar wheeled against the spread of the void and the light above us—a rain of explosive rounds chasing him through the glow of the distant stars—and then dove for the enemy rising toward Scheherazade from beneath; I fell onto his tail, Schaz's rear turret picking apart the drones that had been chasing him even as the two of us pushed right through the screen of enemy craft ahead of us.

Javier peeled Bolivar off—soaring back up to take up the position Schaz and I had been filling in our little defensive perimeter, Khaliphon and Shell closing ranks around him to let his shields regenerate—and I dove right back into the blue skies above the world, the stick vibrating in my hand with the sudden atmospheric chop.

"I'm on my way, Esa," I said, swapping the vibrational frequency of the forward lasers with one hand as I aimed Schaz's nose for the valley where I'd left our infiltration team. "Where are you?"

"The clearing just in front of the access . . . the access tunnel." She'd grunted, there in the middle, grunted like she'd taken a hit. God, she was fighting them, even now: Delta Protocol had been a plan we'd formulated in case she ever came up against more than *one* Cyn. She'd proved on Odessa—and again on the shipyards—that she could take on a single Cyn, but taking on more than one would be a test even of her gifts, a challenge neither of us knew if she could answer, and that was what was happening now: she was fighting multiple opponents made of energy and *fire*, and she was at least holding her own.

I was so goddamned proud of her I felt like my heart was going to burst, but that didn't help the ice creeping across my skin from the fear—not just because of what she was fighting, but because of the extreme nature of this particular protocol. We'd never been able to do a theoretical case study to see if it would even work, and if it didn't work . . .

It had to. It was *going* to.

"That's inside the shield, Esa," I said warningly, even as I pushed the thrusters higher, knowing what she was going to say next, and she didn't disappoint:

"Sho will bring it down," she said, her voice firm, her trust in her brother-in-arms absolute: he knew what the stakes were, he knew that Esa was relying on him, and so he would do his duty, come hell or atmospheric cascade.

I'd trusted Julia like that, once. And she'd trusted me.

"And you're sure—"

"Just *do it*, Jane! Do it now!" It was unmistakable, the thready note of pain in her voice: she was taking on multiple Cyn at once, and maybe she was holding her own, but she wasn't winning.

That was what Delta Protocol was for: to even the odds.

"Schaz, I'm switching off safeties on the forward lasers—you'll have to drop targeting assistance entirely," I told her, even as I did that thing, my fingers flying across the banks of switches above me.

"You're going to hit the Cyn with the forward batteries by dead reckoning? At full *speed*?" Schaz asked, aghast.

I nodded, though the Cyn weren't going to be my target. It wasn't what happened if I missed that I was worried about; it was what happened when my shot hit. "Esa, I'm thirty seconds out," I warned her. "Just . . . just be ready."

"Heard from . . . from Sho—he can drop the shield, but only for an instant, and he'll do it on my . . . *fucker*!"

"Esa, are you *sure*—"

"Don't *fucking ask me again*, Jane; just do it! Do it!"

I nodded, if only to myself; the valley was in sight, now, and I could see four figures on the clear-cut area just before the access tunnel—at this distance, they almost seemed like they were performers on a stage, locked in some tightly choreographed dance, all flowing light and lashing limbs, the final act of some ancient play designed to thematically represent the endurance of grievance and violence.

Except it wasn't a dance; it was Esa fighting for her life.

The shield was still raised; regardless, I lined up my target in the vibrating reticle at the center of the cockpit, ready to peel off as soon as I fired, before we hit the barrier ourselves, or, if Sho did his job, the mountain beyond.

"Jane, what are you *doing*?" Schaz gasped. "You're targeting—"

"Mark," I told Esa.

"*Mark!*" she screamed at Sho.

And then the barrier fell away and I pulled the trigger, laying down a barrage across the open ground before the tunnel, filling the blue sky with bright lines of fire.

CHAPTER 5

Esa

The Cyn saw Jane coming—hell, I probably gave it away, screaming at her over the comms and looking toward the horizon, where I knew either my salvation or destruction was going to come from—and they escaped the barrage entirely, danced through the hail of laser fire to get outside of the firing solution as the downpour of energy raked across the leveled area before the tunnel, blasting craters into the ground and throwing up clouds of atomized rock dust and larger chips of stone that went flying like shrapnel.

That was fine; I'd known that would happen. Jane hadn't been aiming at the Cyn, anyway.

She'd been aiming at me.

A full-force barrage of shipboard laser fire, and I'd reached out, and I'd grabbed it with my teke, the same way I'd grabbed the energy Sho had channeled to me at Raizencourt or on the shipyard world. Except Sho had been shaping that flow, containing it: now, there was no barrier, no control valve, just the full force of weapons meant to blast starships into pieces, and I was holding that force *inside my mind*.

I was screaming. I didn't know when I'd started; I didn't know that I'd ever stop. I'd never held this much energy in a telekinetic field before—even when Sho had broken the locks on his channel in the final moments of the battle in the tower and let the full reactor output flow between us, I'd just let it pass through me, into the Cyn. Now, I had to hold on, like grasping flame in bare hands, a full torrent of fire, and the "hands" were my mind.

It felt like my soul was atomizing, my entire being burning away into light. I held on anyway, and damn the pain. I could take pain. I could use it. The

very first Cyn I'd fought, on Odessa—he'd taught me that, a lesson that had
cost him, just like it would cost his three compatriots here.

Then it was done; Scheherazade was wheeling away, the barrage had
stopped, but the cloud of debris raised up from the fusillade of laser fire was
still floating, rising into the air, because I had so much energy I didn't even
know what to *do* with it all. Lines of electric light snapped like random branches
of chaos from one piece of stone to the next until I was surrounded by a
discharge of electric hail, the sharp stones connected by lines of bright light
like the dendritic spread of the boughs of a tree, with me as the trunk.

I wasn't dead, and I was surrounded by electrified rocks, not to mention
brimming over with energy, the full force of Schaz's fusillade held *inside* me.
So I guess Delta Protocol had worked.

I took those electrified stones, and I lashed them just . . . just out, away
from me, in an explosion of fire and force. The Cyn flinched away, because
they were afraid, they were afraid and they fucking *should have been*—and then
I had the rest of the energy under control, the vast majority of a laser-cannon
barrage bent to my command, and I took it and I twisted it and I shaped it
to my will, shaped it until I was holding twin spears in each hand, spears like
forks of lightning, each vibrating chaotically, spasming and snapping, the
weapons attuned to the vibrational frequency of the Cyn thanks to the energy passing through the wiring of my intention shielding, each as powerful
as a focused blast from Schaz's forward guns.

"Esa, please, *are you all right?*" Meridian was begging in my earpiece; she
must have heard me screaming—she might have been asking for a while now,
but I hadn't heard, hadn't known anything but energy and light and pain.
"Esa, please, *please,* talk to me—"

"I'm good," I growled—I couldn't help it; my vocal chords felt like they'd
been sanded down with iron—even as electricity arced between the tips of
the twin spears. "Keep going. I've got would-be gods to kill."

The Cyn had heard me—of course they had, they could "listen" to our
comms traffic just as easily as if Meridian and I were shouting across an open
field—and they were approaching warily, forming weapons of their own,
twisting pieces out of their own flesh to counter my spears. Swords and shields
for two of them, a pair of lances to match mine for the last. I grinned at

them, despite the burns over my upper arms and back where they'd managed to tag me earlier, despite the torrent of blood gushing from my nose
because I'd pushed my gifts to their absolute limit, making my mouth a mask
of sticky red.

I hadn't had enough energy before, to match their attacks—the output
from my intention shields had barely even been enough to block their strikes;
hadn't always, in fact. Now, the tables were turned, and they knew it. There
was enough juice in either of my spears to deliver a killing blow, regardless
of whether or not I hit them in the protected physical organ they all hid within
their chests: a single strike from the tip of my weapons and they'd just melt,
whatever internal barrier that kept their hearts safe from their own energetic
fields overwhelmed by the sheer amount of power I'd be pouring into them.

"You fuckers are all the same," I spat at them, the words making a mist of
blood from the crimson dripping out of my sinuses and spilling from my lips.
"Big, scary bastards when taking on someone who can't fight *back*, but show
you a little risk, and you turn to cowards like your goddess snapped her fingers and took away your spines." They didn't have spines, of course—but
they understood the insult, all the same. I could tell it by the darkening of
the flames that swirled in place of their faces. "Don't like that? No? Try this
one: your goddess is a fucking *myth*. You're all delusional, so convinced of
your own superiority you've invented a reason to hurt everyone you meet,
because deep down inside you're just a bunch of fucking *psychopaths* who want
to—"

The first of them couldn't take it anymore, charged right at me, his shield
held in front of his shoulder to try and bash my spears away—I dodged back,
knocked away the swing of his sword that he'd thought would take me by
surprise, then drove my other spear toward the center of his shield.

His own fire held against mine, but barely, and he fell back even as the
second—the one with the brace of spears like my own—came at me from
behind, expecting me to take longer holding off his brother. I blocked his
first blow behind my back, then whirled and lashed out at him—once, twice,
then three, four, five six seven times, each blow coming faster than the last,
until I braced his spears off to each side with each of my own and just kicked
him in the chest, my foot wreathed in electric fire. He flew backward like

he'd been pulled by a chain—there wasn't quite enough energy in that kick to kill him, as the vast majority of it was tied up in my weapons, but he felt it, all the same—and I turned, saw the third Cyn trying to take me by surprise just like the second had utterly failed to do, and I threw one of my spears like a javelin.

It impaled him, right through the center: he had exactly long enough to realize what was happening to him—I *saw* it, on his burning face; saw that these things actually *could* feel fear, didn't want to die, just like everyone else—and then he exploded, the containment field of his being rupturing in a detonation of brightness and fire, like a supernova in miniature.

One down. Two to go.

The first of the two I'd knocked back was closing again as I turned to face him; no time for exultation. I broke my remaining spear in half, each section shining with an electric blade all its own, warping instantaneously to my needs, to my will, and the Cyn—who'd been expecting me to meet him with one long weapon, rather than two short ones—couldn't adjust tactics quickly enough; I got inside his guard, drove one blade upward, into his electric face, and the other into his chest.

He exploded too, just like the first had, and I was close enough that even as the blast washed over me, I pulled it into myself, using the wave of electricity and fire released in his death to bolster the energy I'd spent from the barrage already, melting the two halves of my spear back into one long weapon as I did so. The last Cyn was charging at me already, and I'd give him that: he'd seen what I had done to his brothers, he knew he was outmatched, but he just kept coming anyway.

Jane had always said there was nothing worse than fighting a zealot—someone who would go to their own death gladly, believing it served their greater cause. That's exactly what the last Cyn was doing: he hit me with everything he had, everything he had inside him, using his very life energy to sharpen the blades of his spears so that the first blow I blocked cut my own weapon in half—but as it fell groundward, I knelt low, under his next slash, and reached for the fading power before it could dissipate, reached not with my hand but with my teke, pushing the bloom of flame outward into a wave of energy that washed over my opponent and knocked him back, melting his own spears into nothing and raising dark patches like lesions across the surface of the light that made up his being.

He'd spent too much in his initial assault: hadn't been prepared for my answer.

I took what was left of my spear, spread it out again until it was just ribbons of light, then wrapped those ribbons around my fists just like I had the energy from my intention shields. I didn't have a lot left from Jane's barrage, but there was still more than I'd started out with, and he was staggered, darkness blooming across his form, barely able to raise his hands up into a defensive position—though he tried.

At least he hadn't been expecting mercy. It never would have crossed his mind to ask for quarter—a zealot to the last. It was likely a good thing, too. I didn't know if I would have been able to grant it, even if he had: I just kept seeing all the destruction the Cyn left in their wake, seeing it behind my eyes, Kandriad and Valkyrie Rock and Mo and Odessa and the Vyriat explorers at the Furnace's Gate, and I didn't *want* to rein myself in, didn't want to hold back. I knew part of that desire, that need to fight, was coming from the energy coursing through me, spiking my nervous system like adrenaline, and part of it was just the brutal calculus of battle-frenzy: once you've started killing, it can be very hard to stop.

That was part of why I wanted him to come at me, part of why I wanted to just keep fighting; two pieces of the equation. But there was a third, as well—a part of me that liked the power, that *liked* feeling strong. If he'd dropped to his knees, then and there, and raised his hands in surrender: would I have let him live?

I didn't get to find out. He came at me—came right for me, the last, desperate charge of a dying being. There was something almost admirable in that.

Bravery was bravery, even in an enemy.

I deflected his charge in a fluid sweep of motion—that wasn't part of the electric fire coursing through me; that was years of hand-to-hand combat training with Jane, countless hours spent sparring honing my instincts to a razor's edge—and then I caught him with two sharp knee-strikes to the back that sent him staggering. Even as he tried to turn, I was already moving, wreathing my right hand in every single bit of fire I had left: he lashed out with a sweeping attack to try and create distance, but I got underneath it, got closer instead, close enough so that I could drive my burning hand up into his chest. I wrapped clenching fingers around his heart, and even as I stared right into the swirling void of light that was his face, I tore the organ right out of his body, just like I had done to the Cyn on the shipyard world.

He didn't die in an explosion of brilliance like the other two had, the bonds of their bodies no longer able to contain all the energy coursing through them; he faded into a shadow instead, and then even the shadow was gone, and nothing remained, nothing beyond the organ in my hand and an after-image of light on my retinas, even that beginning to dissipate.

I stared down with wide eyes for a moment, staring at nothing, waiting for those starbursts of energy to fade; I just . . . stared, and tried to remember how to breathe. I finally looked up as the sky above filled with fire—the drone wings of the AI conductor were falling out of orbit, burning up and breaking apart on reentry.

They'd done it: Meridian and Sho and Sahluk. I'd almost forgotten that my entire fight had just been a distraction, a rear-guard action so they could accomplish their goal, and now they had: they'd shut down the AI core in the tower. They'd done their parts, and the captains in the ships above had done theirs, and I'd done mine, taking on three Cyn at once, taking on three of the bastards and *winning*, because we were Justified, and that's what we did: we found a way to win.

And now we had, and the path to the Dead Furnaces was open to us.

CHAPTER 6
Jane

T hey're going to send someone."

"They're not, actually—if they were going to send someone, they would have sent someone. That would have already happened."

"There's no way they can't know what we did; their drone bays are half-empty, their antenna has gone silent. They're going to send someone—we just need to be patient."

Javier and Marus were the ones arguing, but there was no real heat behind the words; mainly they were just bored. We'd set the ships down at the far end of the valley where Esa had fought the Cyn—there was an overhanging ledge that would shield them from scans from above, and the others had voted not to immediately head for the Dead Furnaces, preferring to wait a bit and see what the enemy did first.

We'd burned down their defenses, and claimed their broadcast tower; they had no way to get a message out-of-system, to call in any of those dread-naughts the Bright Wanderers had been building at the shipyards, even if they were waiting just a hyperspace jump away. Whoever was left in the stellar ring—a dark blot bisecting the tendril of fire we'd been able to see even from the world's surface, until the planet had rotated into nightfall—they were very much alone.

Esa and I had been the only opposing votes, and Marus's caution had won out, in the end: his reasoning was that, if they had soldiers to send out, we'd rather face them on our terms, out in the open where we could lay an ambush, rather than walking into whatever traps they might have set inside of the Dead Furnaces themselves.

He was right, of course—he was probably right—but it never sat well with me, sitting still when we could be moving forward, and based on the grumbling remarks Esa had been making as we set up camp, she felt the same. We could have slept inside the ships, of course, but after seven weeks in the direct rift, everyone was pretty sick of the interiors of their vessels, so here we were, gathered around a small fire made from the few gnarled trees that grew on this rocky world, arguing—slowly—about something that didn't really matter, because either they were coming, or they weren't, and there wasn't a damn thing we could do about it.

"They're not sending anyone," Javier shook his head. "They're digging in. Probably sealing off as much as they can to make life difficult for us when we do land."

"Didn't you vote to wait?" Esa asked him, a little waspishly. She was sitting next to Meridian—very close—and the two of them had thrown a blanket over their knees, less to ward off the mild chill in the air and more so nobody could make smartass remarks about the fact that they were holding hands underneath the cotton, a fiction everyone was willing to agree to despite the fact that Meridian hadn't stopped glowing since she'd snuggled in beside my ward. It was just about the most adorable thing I'd seen in ages.

"I did," Javier answered honestly. "Could be I'm regretting it a little."

"Could be there's not much of anybody up there to begin with," Sahluk pointed out. "Maybe not enough to mount some sort of investigation into why their broadcast antenna went dead. We only had to fight through a skeleton crew in the tower—a dozen cultists is all. All that weird tech, but only a skeleton crew to run it."

JackDoes, Meridian, and the Preacher had spent a good chunk of the waning evening inside that tower, scanning and analyzing and studying that very same "weird tech," but in the end, none of them could make heads or tails of it: it seemed like the Bright Wanderers had built their broadcast antenna around whatever forerunner facility had been in place already, and as with most forerunner relics, it was almost impossible to tell the difference between "architectural," "mechanical," and "ceremonial," as if the universe had operated on different laws of physics back when they were trying to improve the cosmos.

"*And* three Cyn," Esa reminded Sahluk darkly. "Don't forget them."

"Technically," Sho grinned at her, "they weren't in the tower by the time we got up there. They were down here, trying their best to kill you."

"And they failed," Meridian said, kissing Esa on the cheek. It was about the fourth time that had happened, and my ward still looked mildly stunned every time the Avail girl did it. I had to hide my grin behind my cup of coffee.

"Not by much," Esa said, recovering her equilibrium. "It was . . . a close thing."

"Can I just say," Schaz piped in on the comm bud in my ear—broadcasting to all of us, but speaking mostly to Esa, "that I'm so, so sorry about that? I *shot* at you. Jane *made* me."

"That was the plan, Schaz."

"It was a terrible plan, and I never want to do it again. Not ever."

"And you're *sure* you blocked the long-range signal coming from the antenna?" I asked her, not for the first time.

"I mean, *I* didn't—Khaliphon did. But yeah, he got all of it. Whoever it was out-system the tower was trying to reach, they didn't get the message. Even if the Bright Wanderers' home base is just the next system over, unless they poke their heads in for a cup of sugar, they won't know anything's changed."

"And there haven't been any sort of broadcasts from the stellar ring itself."

"None at all—not out-of-system, not even in this direction, trying to re-establish contact with the tower."

"Could be there's a reason for that," Marus mused. "Something in the stellar ring—the Dead Furnaces—that interferes with radio signals. Which might explain the presence of that," he nodded up at the broadcast antenna, "to begin with. Beyond all the forerunner tech, I mean."

"Such interference would explain why the drone fleet was housed in the Dead Furnaces, but controlled by the AI in the tower," JackDoes agreed. "The ring can receive signals—clearly, or else the fleet would not have launched—but perhaps it cannot broadcast them, or at least, perhaps broadcasting would muck up . . ." He clicked his teeth once, but didn't finish his sentence, unable to find the word to express his best guess at whatever kind of work was meant to be happening in the facility above.

"It still doesn't sit right with me—waiting," I said, finishing up my coffee and staring up into the night sky. We couldn't see the strangely warped sun any longer; night had fallen, and the spread of the cosmos was like a celestial sea above us. With no light pollution to speak of, the stars were so bright and looked so close it felt like I could nearly stand up and touch them, could drag my fingers through the sweep and whirl of distant galaxies to make ripples of light across the void.

"I don't think anyone is at all surprised by that, sweetheart," Javier told me as he poured both of us fresh cups of coffee from the pot hung over the fire; one of the benefits of regularly dropping onto pulsed worlds was that I carried camp equipment that would work with a power source no more complex than "heat." He sat back down beside me; I leaned my head on his shoulder as I took my coffee, letting it cool, still looking upward at the bright tapestries of the stars as I tried to put my finger on what it was that didn't feel right about all of this—beyond, just . . . everything, that was.

The forerunners had terraformed the lost homeworlds—somewhere out there, in the night—at the very least: depending on how you interpreted the texts Esa and Sho had read, they'd also directed the evolution of the beings they'd found on those worlds, the evolution of our cultures if not more, which meant they were responsible for our very existence, as it was now. They'd created the Barious, as a way to guide us toward some unknown goal, in case the unforeseen had happened. And of course, it had: somehow, doing . . . all of that, or any of that, had conjured up the Cyn like the bogeyman from a fairy tale, manifested them in a way we didn't understand and maybe never would, meaning the Barious never got to serve their intended purpose, and we never got to know what the universe we were meant to inherit would have looked like.

Of course, I still wasn't sure how much I trusted the words Esa and Sho had read: it wasn't that I didn't trust the two of them, their translation of the text, but rather that I didn't trust the forerunners themselves. By the time they'd left that message for whomever came along after, they'd been facing their end, and they'd known it: there was nothing like a last will and testament to try and make somebody cover up their various sins. For all we knew, they'd created the Cyn very much on purpose, perhaps as a weapon, aimed at each other—an answer to forerunner sect wars that we had no idea had been waged—and then papered over that mistake, a mistake that had cost them their entire existence, with the Sturm und Drang of words like "manifested" and "devils" and "sin."

But either way, the forerunners were gone, leaving only the relics and the Barious behind, and the Cyn had been driven from the stars, locked onto a few worlds very distant from the other, emerging species—us—and there they'd stayed for thousands and thousands of years, until *we'd* taken to the void, and discovered the Cyn and the Barious both; the foot soldiers of an ancient, forgotten war, one that it sounded like the Cyn were gearing up to wage again.

Then how did the Bright Wanderers—the cult—fit into all of this? Were they just the first step in the Cyn's plan of assault; maybe they needed organic minions to do certain work for them—building starships, refining fuel—and true believers were just easier to control than slaves? Except that didn't track—every single Cyn we'd met thus far had been a believer themselves. Of course, that didn't mean the Cyn we'd met weren't being used by their masters, just like the cultists were being used . . . but I didn't buy it, all the same.

And then there was Julia, and she was another piece that didn't fit. She *hadn't* believed—she'd said so herself. Yet still she'd served them, for a chance to get back at me. She'd been recruited specifically because of her connection to me, aimed at me like a Jane-seeking missile and let fly. She'd come after us, at the Furnace's Gate—arrived out of hyperspace in a ship purpose-built for combat in that atmosphere: had the Bright Wanderers known we were the ones who attacked the shipyards; was that how they'd known to send her, to rattle me? But how had they known we'd make for the Furnace's Gate next? *We* hadn't even known that was our destination when we'd jumped away.

They'd known our location then—known to send Julia after us—yet, now, the direct rift from the Furnace's Gate lay dormant; they hadn't sent anyone else through, hadn't pursued us further. Even the relative lack of defenses in this system: they might have been able to hide a small ship or two, somewhere on the very same world we were sitting on, but nothing larger; there were no frigates, no orbital cannon platforms, nothing beyond the drone swarm we'd swatted down.

We'd seen them building half a dozen dreadnaughts in that shipyard, and based on the theory that the Wanderers were the ones who had armed the Pax, they'd already completed dozens more than that: they couldn't have spared at least *one* of them to guard . . . whatever this place was? It was the place where their "chaplains" were taking the gifted they stole, a place clearly important to their cosmology, if not to the eschatological terror with which the cult indoctrinated their followers—including the Cyn themselves—and yet their defenses were a single drone fleet and a handful of Cyn in the tower?

It didn't track, and I *knew* it didn't track, but that was the problem with missing pieces of a puzzle—without those missing pieces, the rest just looked like chaos.

"Jane," Javier said quietly.

"Mmmmm."

"You're chewing on my shoulder."

I delicately removed his jacket from between my teeth; I'd been doing exactly that, finding something to worry on as I tried to sort through the complicated moving pieces that whirled around us. Now that I realized what I'd been doing, though, I frowned, and gagged slightly. "You really need to clean that," I told him, trying to clean my tongue with my teeth.

"Why? So that it *tastes* better?"

"You don't like this," Esa stated, staring at me from across the fire, finally brave enough to pull her arm out from the blanket and to pull Meridian closer to her.

"There's something we're missing," I nodded, taking a sip of my coffee to clean the taste of dirty leather out of my mouth. As I did, I looked up at the clean sweep of the stars again—beyond the horizon, the Dead Furnaces were waiting, and the approach to that facility would be difficult enough, given the blaze of the star and the pull of the twinned black holes. If it came to combat, there were a great many things that could go wrong, very quickly.

"Hence why I suggested waiting," Marus said delicately, throwing another branch on the fire.

I frowned at him. "Fine, sure, you were probably right," I told him. "Don't rub it in. And right or not, I still don't like it."

"I never would have expected that you would. It's not who you are. Either of you." His eyes flicked toward Esa, who stuck her tongue out at him in response.

As the more mature member of our team, I restrained myself from doing the same; I made a rude hand gesture in his general direction instead.

CHAPTER 7

Jane

We waited over half a day—long enough for the stars to fade and the strangely distended sunrise to creep over the jagged horizon of the mountains again, the lines of stellar light pulled like taffy across the sky by the gravitational force of the swirling voids on either side—and there was still no sign of a response, either from the Wanderers in the Furnaces, or from any scout ships they might have had stationed with their armada, if there was one nearby. It made no sense to me: they'd been hit, had at least their *first* line of void-capable defenses stripped away, and they didn't launch a second attack? Didn't even investigate?

Still, it was clear: they weren't coming for us.

Which meant we'd have to go to them.

Which, in turn, meant I got to argue with the Preacher. Not one of my favorite activities in the world, given that she was . . . significantly smarter than I was. Not that I'd ever admit that to her.

"I'm going with you," she said over the comm—our ships were on approach, Scheherazade in the lead; Javier and Sho had plotted what they thought was the safest route through the pull of the black holes and the rising solar flares, but Schaz still had the most armor and the largest engine, meaning she'd be able to survive something going wrong better than any of the Justified craft, which meant we got to be in front. "I'm going with you," the Preacher said again, "and that's final."

"The hell it is—we had this discussion, remember? Before you joined this expedition. You gave your word; you said if we knew we would be likely to encounter the Cyn, you'd stay behind. You promised me that, and I'm hold-ing you to it." The Cyn—like Esa—could manipulate energy; we'd seen what was left behind when they encountered the Barious who had remained on Odessa Station. It wasn't pretty.

There was a tiny fusion battery behind the Preacher's breastplate, and if a Cyn wanted to, they could reach right into her chest and trigger a cascad-ing reaction in all that electric power; explode the Preacher's "heart" right out of her chassis, turn her into a shrapnel bomb. She was more than just defenseless against them—she was a danger to the rest of us, as well.

"Things have changed, Jane," she replied. "What we learned on the relic— what we *saw*—" There was still a level of rage in the Preacher's voice, one I hadn't heard from her since she'd first learned the role the Justified had played in the creation of the pulse; the revelation that the Barious had been created by the forerunners to guide the organic species, a purpose denied to them by the Cyn, must have been a constant agony in her processors, chewing up her every moment of thought. Rage could be useful, of that I had no doubt— but we were walking in blind enough; couldn't risk the Cyn getting hold of her and turning her very body into a weapon to use against the rest of us.

"What we learned was that the forerunners knew the Barious were espe-cially vulnerable to the Cyn, Preacher," Javier reminded her. "That's *why* they hid your people away, remember? No reason to march you right up to them, gift wrapped, so they can slip right back into their genocidal habits. You can follow our progress on the feeds—"

"Assuming the cameras will even broadcast in that place—we're already getting a load of instrumental interference, all the way out here."

She wasn't wrong: that was likely half the reason the broadcast tower had been built in the first place, built very specifically to transmit along what-ever narrow channels could actually reach the stellar ring through the vari-ous chaos falling off the black hole and the diminished star. That, and the strange equipment inside that the others had spent so long studying, the fore-runner tech somehow wound through the Bright Wanderers' systems. An-other puzzle piece that didn't fit.

"All the more reason to leave someone behind," Marus reminded her. "We'll need eyes on the approach, someone to warn us if something drops out of hyperspace—or out of the rift."

"But if I can't warn you, what's the point of—"

"You gave your word, Preacher," I said shortly. "As far as I'm concerned, that's that."

"Please," Esa said quietly. "Preacher—just this once. I don't want—"

"Esa, I've come all this way, *we've* come all this way; just to—"

"Preacher, I don't want you to *die*. Is that really so hard to understand?"

Silence, then, over the comms. Esa and the Preacher had had their differences over the years—there was still something of a wound there, not because of the role the Preacher had played in the deaths of Esa's parents, but because, when she'd taken the baby girl from Odessa Station and run, she'd left her in the care of strangers at a backwater orphanage, rather than raising Esa as her own. She'd had her reasons—both practical and emotional—and Esa understood them, but understanding and forgiving weren't the same thing, and it was still a sore spot between them.

All that aside, though, the Preacher had been a presence in Esa's life for as long as she could remember. The Barious had chosen not to be a mother to the girl, but she had been around, all the same—a distant figure of authority in the little settlement where Esa grew up. She was the oldest friend Esa had, which was why Esa was perfectly willing to resort to a little emotional blackmail to keep her safe.

"Fine," the Preacher said finally. "I'll stay back—keep an eye on the approach. But once you've docked, and once you've cleared the facility, *someone* is coming to take my place, you understand? Once we know there aren't any Cyn left, *I* get to search the whole thing, top to bottom, for as long as it takes. For my answers, not just the Justified's."

"Fair enough," I agreed, toggling the comm to MUTE. "Well done," I said to Esa, as a quiet aside.

She managed a ghost of a smile, though there was still a little pain in her expression—the way there always was when she was reminded of the choices the Preacher had made, so early in her existence she didn't have any say. "I did it to keep her safe," she told me. "I meant that."

"I never thought otherwise."

We both watched Shell pull out of our formation, hanging back a little as the rest of our ships closed in on the Dead Furnaces, approaching the strange ring built around the pull of stellar light and heat drawn away from the star by the black hole. Despite the fact that, even if the void of space hadn't been an empty nothingness that stopped sound from vibrating across it, the black hole itself would have eaten all noise, I still felt like I could hear it: a kind of gnawing, crushing sound, like heavy machinery gone wrong, as the density of the impossibly deep gravity well ate its way through the output of the star, exactly as fast as the star could create new energy.

And right in the middle of all that terrible brightness—the light from the star beneath us, the light from the tendril pulled through the ring and into the maw of the black hole—there was the facility itself. The Dead Furnaces.

This close, I could tell the construction of the thing was definitely of forerunner design—the entire thing, not just parts, like the tower on the world behind us. The bulkheads were made of the same strange alloys the monoliths were, alloys somehow capable of resisting the intense heat of the stellar flames being pulled through the facility, as well as rendered gravitationally inert, somehow: a normal space station would have been either pulled into orbit around the star, or pulled apart and sucked into the black hole just like the stellar energy was, but somehow, the Dead Furnaces remained anchored in place, equidistant from the devouring maw above and the cascading solar explosion below.

In all that shining brightness—I had Schaz's viewscreens dialed down to minimum illumination, blacking out over 99 percent of the light coming from the star below, and we still had to squint to see anything—strange symbols glowed, all along the not-metal bulkheads of the facility: more glyphs in the forerunner language, but also the ouroboros we'd seen in the sunken city within the relic. Something about that writing make the etchings reflect the light of the star just a little bit brighter than the station walls around it, giving the impression that the entire facility was covered in murals of fire.

"The name is literal," JackDoes said suddenly, his words actually making me jump as they came through the comms. I was . . . tenser than I'd thought, maybe.

"Come again?" I asked, ignoring Esa's grin, after forcing my heartbeat to slow a little and reaching down to unmute our microphones.

"The 'Dead Furnaces,'" he said. "The 'furnaces' part, at least. Look—inside the ring, there." He transmitted a still image over from Bolivar: much the same thing we were looking at, the facility itself, just from a slightly different angle, and JackDoes had highlighted a few jutting bits of machinery on the interior, mechanisms that hung in the space between the torrent of flame and the station itself.

"The tech is . . . strange," he explained, "not at all how we would achieve the same principle, if we even could, but those are energy converters, all along the inside. They're built to siphon off, store, and convert the stellar energy being pulled toward the black hole—just a fraction, not enough to throw off the equilibrium of the gravitational pull, but still, that much stellar fusion energy . . . it would be the equivalent of ten thousand reactors, all at full output. And what do you call a thing built to harness—and contain—heat energy?"

"A furnace," Sahluk rumbled from Khaliphon. "See? I can science."

"That's . . . not science," Javier said reprovingly. "That's engineering. Or possibly just metaphor."

"What would they need that much energy *for*?" Meridian murmured.

"Whatever it might be, it's not working," JackDoes replied. "That part is literal, also—the 'dead' part. See, in between the converters, the rows and rows of cylinders? Those are storage batteries, massive ones; bigger than anything I've ever seen. Just one, if filled to capacity . . ." He hissed in appreciation. "Big enough to power . . . cities, even worlds." Thousands of the cylinders lined the interior of the ring, between the branches of the converters.

"So the energy pours through the ring as starfire, gets transmuted to a more malleable form by the converters, then stored in the batteries," Javier said, following along. "Meaning that whatever it was they were trying to do, they needed more than just the output of the star itself. Needed to store the energy, until they had enough."

"Enough for *what*?" Sho asked.

Nobody answered, but we were all thinking the same thing; if the forerunners were anything like us, then there was only one thing it could be, one thing that needed to draw that much power, especially since the fore-runners who created it had been locked into a war for their very survival: it was a weapon.

A system-killer, at the very least. Or something even worse.

"All correct in theory," JackDoes agreed with Javier's assessment, "but the batteries aren't storing anything, not right now. Hence the 'dead' part of the name given to this place by the Wanderers. Converters seem to be working fine, but the energy is just dissipating right back out again—a safety mecha-nism, to keep the whole thing from overloading."

Now that he'd pointed it out, I could see it: a kind of heat-shimmer in the void between the walls of the ring and the rise of the stellar fire, the electri-cal energy gathered from the converters being added right back to the flood of light passing through the gap in the middle of the facility.

"That should imply there's nobody home, right?" Sho asked, a little ner-vously. "I mean, if the facility's operational, shouldn't it be, you know . . . op-erating, if there was someone in there to make it work?"

"Maybe they just don't know how," Marus answered him. "The Bright Wanderers, that is. This facility is forerunner tech, after all—maybe they can't interface with it."

"Could be that's what they needed the next generation for," Javier said, making the intuitive leap at the same moment I did.

"Come again?" Sahluk asked.

"The Cyn," Javier said again. "They've been sweeping up next-generation kids, yeah? Their 'chaplains,' like the one came hunting for Sho, the one that Esa ended on Odessa. And on the relic, the forerunner . . . testimony, or what-ever it was in that church—it responded to Esa, and to Sho. Maybe the Bright Wanderers are trying to use gifted children, as . . . I don't know, interpret-ers, maybe?"

"Best theory we've heard," Marus agreed.

"It's the only theory we've heard," Sahluk replied.

"Yes; that's what makes it the best."

"There's the docking bay," Esa pointed out, highlighting an area of the facility and transmitting the information to the other ships. "That's where the drone ships launched from; door's still open. There's only so much we're going to learn out here, people—and if whoever's left inside was going to launch a welcoming party, they'd have done so by now; it's not like we tried to cloak our approach. Whatever's going to happen, it's not going to happen out in the void: time to get boots on the ground."

She wasn't wrong, but I wondered if she knew just how much she sounded like me when she said it.

CHAPTER 8
Esa

We could have been flying into anything as Jane carefully maneuvered Scheherazade into the bay, the launching rails of the drones slipping past on either side: there could have been heavy cannon built up behind barricades, ready to shoot us out of the sky; some ancient trap of the forerunners, lying in wait to dismantle any ship that didn't have whatever strange clearance was required; even the remnants of the ancient Vyriat vessels that had theoretically come this way through the direct rift, now broken and shattered and waiting for just the wrong nudge to send their cores critical. We could have met any of that . . . but there was nothing.

Instead, there was just a tunnel into the ring, leading to a docking bay that just went on and on. There were more drone craft anchored into the walls, just waiting for a signal to send them sliding down onto the launch rails, a signal that would never come. They were strangely ugly in their stillness, like dead things lying motionless on a forest floor, their wings collapsed down onto their chassis, giving them a naked, half-formed look.

The docking bay itself had the same strangely mismatched appearance I'd seen in my brief inspection of the broadcast tower, modern technology grafted onto forerunner remnants: the drones were hanging from massive metal racks, no different than what you might see in the launch bay of a frigate or a dreadnaught, but the racks and the rails themselves had been bolted onto the much weirder structure of the station itself, like someone had welded weapons of war to an ancient artifact of a forgotten empire.

Which I supposed was what had actually happened.

We made it all the way to the end of the bay, where an empty platform awaited beyond the rows of drones. Even there, nothing: no Bright Wanderers preparing some sort of ambush, or even trying to sort out why their comms had suddenly gone silent. Instead, the platform was as still as a grave when Jane set Scheherazade down—the other ships were waiting just outside, in case something tried to kill Jane and me.

"We've got atmosphere," Jane said, checking her readings, "we've got gravity, and . . . that's it. As far as Schaz's sensors go, the rest of this place might as well not exist. It's like we just flew into a pocket of breathable, survivable nothing, hanging in the middle of the void."

"But you could see it, right?" I asked Schaz. "The ring itself, the Dead Furnaces?"

"I could pick it up on my sensors, yes," she agreed, "but only . . . dimly, if that makes sense? I could 'see' it because it was blocking the light from the stellar tendril snaking through the center; I could see where the light *wasn't*. Other than that . . . Esa, I don't know what you're looking at. I'm sorry." She sounded crestfallen, like she'd failed Jane and me in some obscure manner.

"Don't worry about it," I murmured; I supposed, in a way, she must have felt similarly to how I had, when only Sho and I had been able to read the forerunner writing. Her sensors were supposed to see more than Jane and I could, to show us the galaxy in greater detail than our eyes would allow, but here, she was the blind one. "You got us here safely, Schaz. That's what counts."

"Thank you, Esa," she said, her tone grateful—a small kindness, I suppose, but it was what I had.

Meanwhile, even though Schaz couldn't see the landing platform—despite the fact that we were sitting on it—I could, and I was craning my neck to look out the cockpit window, out and up: the ceiling was about the only piece of the docking bay that hadn't been covered over by the various bits of machinery meant to maintain or launch the drones, and what little of the distant arches and supporting girders I could see—the ceilings were very, *very* high up, as if the forerunner's ships had been taller than they were wide—were covered in baroquely intricate detail, glyphs and murals and tessellating designs that seemed like they should resolve into something my eyes could make sense of, but never would.

It didn't help that the only light in the place was coming from Scheherazade, and even her big floods were a relatively weak glow against the sheer scope of the monumental bay; the rest was darkness, even the far edges of the landing platform. It was as if this had been a place built for giants, and we were merely fleas.

"Still, I *am* worried," Schaz continued, still sounding slightly disconsolate. "This seems . . . I don't like only being able to see shadows. I don't *like* it here."

"Yeah, I don't think I do, either." I should have felt . . . excitement, or at least satisfaction—we were closing in on answers: answers about the Cyn, answers about the forerunners, answers to questions that the entire universe had been asking for generations now—but all I felt was a kind of deep foreboding, something that threatened to slip right into dread without warning. This place felt dangerous to me, dangerous in a way even the interior of the monolith had not; that space had been . . . neglected, forgotten, its only purpose to serve as a monument to the downfall of the race that had created it.

This place, by contrast, seemed somehow more real, more aware, as if the forerunners had all just gone out for tea and might return at any moment—and wouldn't be too happy to find us squatting on their landing platform. The relic had been the remnant of a long-dead civilization; this place felt like it was just . . . sleeping. Sleeping, and just waiting to wake up.

"That's why we're taking guns," Jane said to both of us. "Lots of guns."

"You take 'lots of guns' everywhere, Jane," I reminded her. "You take lots of guns when we just set down on an abandoned rock to stretch our legs."

"You know I do. And guess what?" She grinned at me.

"You're not dead yet?" I knew she was trying to jostle Schaz and me out of the dismal funk this place had dropped us into, and even though I understood that's what she was doing, it was working; I grinned back.

"I'm not dead yet," she agreed, still smiling. "Come on. Let's get geared up."

We changed into our combat kit—body armor underneath tactical gear, bandoliers of spare ammunition, concussion grenades and hidden blades and another dozen pieces of murder that might give us an edge in whatever fight we were walking into. Jane, at least, seemed confident that was what was going to happen—that we were about to walk into a fight—but she always felt that way. I wasn't so sure. This place didn't seem threatening so much as *haunted*, and whatever might be doing that haunting, I wasn't so confident that ballistic rounds and edged weapons were going to pose much of a threat to that kind of ghost.

Wouldn't stop us from trying, though.

Schaz lowered her ramp; we descended, weapons raised. If I had been a Bright Wanderer—even just a skeleton crew, left behind to maintain the drones—that's when I would have started shooting; picked out a position on the far side of the bay, near what looked like strange murals of the ancient cosmos but I'm pretty sure were actually doors with cleverly hidden seams. It took a certain something to walk down that ramp, sure a bullet was about to snap across the distance and smash into my intention shields— followed up by several more bullets, enough to shatter my shielding apart and pierce my far more vulnerable flesh—but whatever that something was, I reached deep and found it, put one foot in front of the other, until we were standing on the strange alloy of the landing platform itself; the surface rippled slightly under our boots, carved designs decorating even what lay underfoot.

We were standing inside the Dead Furnaces now, whatever those were. And no gunshots came from the distant doorways—the air of the landing platform remained still, the atmosphere more that of a mausoleum than a place of discovery or even combat. Whatever the Bright Wanderers were doing here, it didn't seem like they were doing it right now.

"Start your approach," Jane said into her comm to the others. "Khaliphon first." Just like me, she wasn't sensing danger, but that didn't mean it wasn't present, and Khaliphon had Sahluk onboard—the most dangerous of any of us, at least in an infantry-style gunfight.

Without saying anything, she and I spread out across the bay, our weapons still raised, poking our noses into every corner we could find, yet not finding much at all—it took me a moment, but part of what separated this landing platform from all the others I'd seen wasn't so much what was present as what wasn't: no stacked crates of spare parts or alloys, no snaking cables or mobile batteries, not even a bag of tools left behind by some careless mechanic. And that didn't make any sense: the drones, at least, would have required regular maintenance, and even though the heavy machinery for that maintenance was in place, there were none of the workstations or uplink devices you might have expected to see in a starship repair facility.

It was like the Bright Wanderers themselves had abandoned this place, just like it had seemed like the Vyriat had abandoned the facility anchored into the Furnace's Gate relic . . . right up until we'd found their corpses, left behind inside the monument itself. Something had lured them in, and then butchered them: had it done the same thing here? Was it planning to do the same to *us*?

No: that was just Jane's paranoia, infecting me. The Cyn at the broadcast tower had very much been trying to kill me, and the Bright Wanderers Sahluk and the others had met inside had also put up "one hell of a fight," in his words. There hadn't been many of them, and they hadn't been combat trained, for the most part—technicians and machine operators—but they'd fought all the same; fought to the last. If their own people had been destroyed inside the Dead Furnaces, they wouldn't have fought to protect that tower, not for no reason, not without a purpose.

Except they were a cult, and that's what cults did: used their adherents up until they didn't have any more use, and then went out and recruited others. If they'd been told it served the will of their goddess to hold that tower—even after the team inside the Furnaces themselves went silent—then hold that tower was what they would have done; logic or reason or even fear would make no impact. Whatever the Cyn's goddess was—myth or strange legend or sole survivor of the forerunners, warped into madness by millennia alone—I doubted she gave much of a damn about any of her followers, Cyn or organic alike, and if she wanted the tower held, even after the crews in the Furnaces were destroyed, then they would have done exactly as they did: fought to the last.

My heart rate should have calmed by the time Khaliphon made his entrance—followed shortly by Bolivar—but it had not; it just kept racing even as the others made their way out, all decked out in full combat rigs like Jane and me, Sahluk in his cherished exosuit. There were more of us now, safety in numbers, but the animal part of my brain, the part not trained but wired instinctually to recognize threats, was still screaming, *"Danger, danger, there's danger here!"* as loud as it possibly could.

That part of me—the part that still thought we lived in caves, cowering from predators stronger and faster and hungrier than we were—didn't think we were about to get shot at; it thought we were about to get *eaten*, that we'd stumbled into the lair of something far worse than anything else we'd known, and that whatever it was we could scavenge from within wasn't worth what would happen when the predator came back, came back or woke *up*. It wailed as I approached the curving door, the strange mural on its surface a stylized version of the night sky, with traceries added between the stars to make constellations unlike any I'd ever seen, my mind managing to make even those frightening, filling in teeth and agony and awfulness between the lines that connected the pinpoint dots of light.

"We ready for this?" Sahluk asked, looking at the rest of us—the first thing any of us had actually said since the others stepped on board. Apparently I wasn't the only one who found the interior of the Dead Furnace creepy as *fuck*.

"Probably not," Javier shrugged, checking his shotgun again, "but do it anyway."

Sahluk nodded, and started pushing at the door.

CHAPTER 9

Esa

The room just beyond the landing bay was almost disappointingly prosaic—a strange mishmash of technology, some of it forerunner design, some that looked to have been left behind by the Vyriat explorers who had first found the place, the rest of newer, more recognizable application: likely installed by the Bright Wanderers. What the purpose of all of it was, though, was harder to discern.

"Monitoring equipment, maybe?" Marus suggested, his mechanical eyes whirring and clicking slightly as he scanned the machinery. "It seems more scientific than anything else."

"Not entirely," Sahluk said, nodding at a rack of guns to one side—I *think* those were left over from the Vyriat expedition, or at least I didn't recognize their make, and they didn't fit the universal design of most modern firearms, optimized to be fired by as many of the seventeen species as possible, taking into account different grips and talons and paws and whatnot.

Still, rifles were rifles, and there were a few empty places in the racks: whatever had happened to the Vyriat, they'd felt the need to be armed before it had, and they hadn't been in any condition to replace those firearms once it was over.

"Press on," Jane said. "I want to get to the heart of this place as soon as possible—figure out what the hell it's all for."

I nodded, agreeing with her impulse. The feeling like something was just wrong here—that we weren't just trespassing on some sort of ancient, sacred site, but that it had been profaned before, profaned in some manner beyond our understanding, something that had warped the walls, the light, even the air we were breathing—was only growing stronger. Sahluk pushed open the next door . . . and stepped back, staring upward. "Well, that might be a problem," he said, with typical rumbling understatement.

There was a glowing wall of light just beyond the door—it wasn't hissing or crackling, didn't seem dangerous, exactly, but it did seem solid, solid in a way light very much should not have seemed. Before anyone could say anything, Sahluk reached out and pressed against it—winced and drew his hand back sharply like it had burned him, a few tendrils of smoke rising up from his rocky fingers.

"Maybe don't just *stick your hand* into the strange glowing defenses, big guy?" Javier asked him, his voice dry.

Sahluk ignored him, stepping back and shaking his hand. "It's the same thing Jane saw, on the relic—the force field that blocked her from getting to the Wanderers' pilot. Impenetrable. We'll have to find another way around." He was already looking around the antechamber, presumably searching for vents or access tunnels—this couldn't possibly be the only way deeper into the facility, after all: all space stations, even ancient forerunner relics, were more interconnected than that. Everything had to pipe back to atmosphere processing, for one thing, and for another, the energy to power the drones must have been coming from somewhere—we hadn't seen anything resembling a reactor so far, and according to JackDoes, the station wasn't drawing power from the stellar torrent pouring through the ring itself.

"Wait," Marus said slowly. "What, exactly, are you two talking about?"

I looked at him in confusion—but he was earnestly staring forward, looking *through* the wall of light to the corridor on the other side, whereas the rest of us couldn't even stare at it for long, even the reflections of the illumination on the strange metal of the walls making a kind of bright headache in our vision.

His prosthetic eyes clicked and whirred again as he tried to make sense of what the rest of us were staring at—scanning every frequency he could—and that's when something clicked over in my head, metaphorically, at least. "You can't see it," I whispered. "You can't see it, because your eyes are mechanical. Just like Schaz couldn't see the relics in the Katya system, or at the Furnace's Gate, like she couldn't see this facility, even."

"Can't see what?" he asked, his voice growing annoyed. "There's nothing there, just a hallway. It's not even an exciting hallway, either."

"There is, actually," Javier told him. "A big wall of light; I wouldn't try to go forward too far, buddy. It burned Sahluk a little when he stuck his hand into it. Like a dumbass."

"But if Marus can't see it, does that mean—" Whatever JackDoes might have said—whatever careful, methodical course of action we were going to get around to settling on, eventually, after about an hour of long-winded discussion that culminated in everybody shouting at each other—I didn't pay attention; instead, I just walked to the force field—

—and walked straight through it. Felt a strange tingling sensation as I did, but that was all. No burning, no heat; I'd been preparing to try and hold the discharge from the field in my teke, defending myself from getting fried, at least, but there was nothing to hold: I passed through the light like that was all it was, just . . . light, projected from the crack in the floor.

"Will everyone *stop doing that*?" Javier said, adding a few choice curses at the end of the demand.

"Esa—you made it through." JackDoes seemed mildly dumbstruck by what his own eyes were telling him.

"So—Esa's *past* the barricade now?" Marus asked. "The barricade I can't see? Where the hell is the damn thing, anyway?"

"Esa, how did you know to—" Before Jane could finish her sentence, Meridian had taken a deep breath, then she walked into the field as well, reaching out toward me as she did; I caught her hand as it came through, ready to pull her forward if something happened, but nothing did—she stepped through like there was nothing in her way, and then she was standing next to me, looking back at the others.

Not so much letting go of my hand, though.

"It's the gifted, the next generation," Sho said, stepping closer, staring into the light of the force field itself. "It's somehow . . . *attuned* to us. Like . . ." He pushed his arm into the illumination; I half expected its surface to ripple as he did, but it was just light, not water. After that little experiment, he took another step forward—steeling himself as he did; theories were theories, but there was still real risk here—and then he, as well, was through, standing on the other side and looking back at the others with Meridian and me, though from this side, they weren't much more than silhouettes edged in brightness.

"None of this makes sense," JackDoes complained; on impulse, *he* stuck a finger into the light, only to pull it back with a hiss, as if he'd pressed it up against something very hot.

"Just . . . stay there," Marus commanded us. "Hell, come back. We'll figure a way to get around this, to keep all of us together—"

"Not this way," Javier said—he'd found another door somewhere else in the antechamber, but from the tone of his voice, I could tell what he was looking at: another wall of light, another passage blocked for anyone but the next generation.

"Sho, can you . . . get through it?" Sahluk asked. "The wall itself, I mean, obviously you can . . . Can you tear it, the way you did with the shielding over the broadcast tower: that's what I mean. Tear it open so that the rest of us can follow."

Sho shook his head. "I can't even feel it to try and pull it apart," he said. "I do electricity, remember? This is just . . . light."

"It's a force field," I said, stating the obvious to try and jump-start my thought process as I stared up at the cracks where it rose into the ceiling. "Therefore, meant to keep somebody *out*. Maybe a kind of . . . defense, yeah? Raised by the forerunners if they were ever under attack. If they'd wanted a wall here, something to cut off this passage completely, they would have built an actual wall. So there must be a way to bring it down, to drop it, to let the rest of you through. Deeper in the facility, somewhere they could still reach after whatever assault they were under was done." Except it hadn't been done—or at least, nobody had been alive to bring the field down afterward.

"No," Marus shook his head. "No. We should stick together, all of us—"

"Esa's right," Jane disagreed with the spy. "We want to make heads or tails of this place, we need to get deeper in—specifically, we need to get Jack-Does deeper in. He's the only one with a ghost of a chance of figuring out what this place was for."

"That might be the nicest thing you've ever said to me," the little Reint told her wryly.

"And in order to get JackDoes in, we need Esa and the others to bring down the barricade," Jane continued, ignoring the engineer. "She's got this, Marus. We've trained them together, the three of them, for a reason: we brought them along for a reason. They can do this—we can't."

"They'll look out for each other," Javier seconded, making an affirmative gesture in Sho's direction, one the young Wulf returned. "It's what they do."

Marus nodded, finally, relenting; Jane turned back to us. "Esa has seniority, so she's got command," she told the other two. "Do what she tells you to, *exactly* when she tells you to. No arguing, no trying to figure out why she's suddenly barking orders—if she says run, you bolt; if she says duck, you find a powerful reason to want to taste the floor."

"I always listen to Esa," Sho protested; I grinned at him.

"Mostly," I amended for him.

"Mostly," he admitted, grinning back. Meridian just squeezed my hand, and despite the banter, I could feel a tightness around my ribs, the same tightness I'd felt before the golden tower on the shipyard world—Jane was literally giving me command over the other two, and that made their lives my responsibility. If either of them got hurt, or killed, on my watch . . . I already had nightmares about the little Vyriat girl we'd failed to save on Valkyrie Rock. Getting one of my friends killed—or both of them—I didn't know that I could survive it.

So I'd better be damned sure I never had to learn.

"We'll keep trying to find a way through from this end," Jane told me. "Stay in communication as long as you can, but don't be surprised if this place eats the signal after a while. Wouldn't surprise me in the slightest if it did."

"Got it," I said, raising up Bitey with one hand, the other still clasped tightly in Meridian's grip.

"And Esa?" Pain or not, Jane pressed her hand up against the shield, just briefly. "Stay safe."

"You, too. Love you."

"Love you too. Now go figure out a way to let the rest of us join you back there—we've come a long goddamned way to get here, and I've got no intention of spending the last leg of it engaging in an exciting adventure in *sitting*."

CHAPTER 10

Esa

Do you know something?" Sho murmured as we slipped through the corridors of the Dead Furnaces, the interiors of the ring still striking a fundamentally bizarre balance between heavily industrialized spaces and baroque, intricately decorated cathedral-like interiors, even the massive, silent machinery often dripping with carvings or strange motifs. "I think I've come to a realization about my chosen career path. An epiphany, like."

"What's that?" I asked as we approached another door; like all the others, it slid open as we neared—no force fields or other traps on this one, just another room of machinery and worship, one we cleared quickly, finding no sign of anyone before moving on.

"Being an operative of the Justified involves way too much stalking through creepy-as-fuck corridors, waiting for something to jump out and eat me. Seriously, that's all we seem to do."

I grinned at that, even as we cleared the next room, my finger fluttering against the trigger guard on Bitey, ready to slip in and start firing. We were going to hit something, and we all knew it—we just weren't lucky enough to have this place be actually abandoned, the way it seemed. Either the Bright Wanderers were still here—had realized we were on approach and had drawn deeper into the facility to set some kind of trap—or there was a reason they weren't doing that, and that same reason was going to try to kill us, just like it had killed them.

And either way, we were very much alone, isolated in the face of whichever threat chose to rear its head. Like Jane had warned, we'd lost the comms signal almost as soon as we were around the bend from the force field that had blocked us off from the others—there would be no calling for reinforcements or support.

"'Part of the job,' Jane would say," I told Sho.

"I signed on with Javier to be a cartographer, an explorer; to study forgotten worlds, bring that knowledge back to Sanctum."

"Which is exactly what we're doing," Meridian pointed out, not unreasonably, though her words were a little clipped—she was scared, and trying to keep herself calm through sheer force of will. I couldn't blame her, and I knew it was part of the reason Sho was doing his best Javier impression: trying to keep the mood artificially light, like the conversational equivalent of starship gravity, so that we didn't have to think about the dangers that might lie ahead, even though what he was saying might have seemed like he was inviting us to do just that.

"Yeah, but . . . you know. Forgotten worlds with wonders and treasures, not . . . whatever the hell all of this is."

"That's the thing about treasures, Sho," I told him, kneeling before the next door as it slid open. "They're pretty much always going to be—"

"Wait," Meridian whispered, raising up a hand; I'd already had Bitey held up to my eye, but at her sign I slipped my finger into the trigger guard, my heart rate speeding up in my chest from its already not-inconsiderable beat, the acrid taste of adrenaline surging into the back of my mouth as I tried to scan every part of the newly opened room at once. There was nothing, nothing we hadn't seen before—whatever it was she had sensed, it wasn't here.

Then I heard it; a kind of low chanting, so low it was almost a hum. "That's . . . you?" Sho asked softly, moving to stand directly beside Meridian, using his own weapon to cover the angles she couldn't.

"That's my gift," she confirmed, still in a whisper. "I've been pushing it ahead of us, like an early warning system. There's someone in the corridor ahead of us; I don't know who, but that . . . chanting. That's the sound of their subconscious."

It was a clever as hell thing to do—a tactical use of a gift I hadn't thought had much use in combat—and it made me want to kiss her, though just the way she breathed made me want to do that. Still: a subconscious mind that made evil-sounding chanting its defining characteristic was not what I would call a promising development, Meridian's tactical prowess aside.

If I had to guess, I'd say it was a pretty safe bet her empathetic projection was being generated by a Bright Wanderer, hiding somewhere in the alcoves and hallways that snaked through the industrial, semi-gothic sprawl before us; eerie-ass chanting seemed about their level of subconscious churn.

Good news was, that meant there was a way past the force fields, somehow: there had to be, otherwise they couldn't have gotten this deep into the stellar ring. Bad news: where there were one or two Bright Wanderers—I thought the creepy chanting had a sort of overlapping quality to it, two minds almost in sync, but not quite—there would be more. We most definitely weren't alone on the Dead Furnaces, and the three of us were still cut off from our friends, at least until we could find the mechanisms to drop the fields, mechanisms almost certainly in Bright Wanderer control.

Plus, if *we* could hear their chanting—the music Meridian's gift was creating through psychic interpretation of their subconscious minds—then they could hear it, as well. They wouldn't know *why* they were hearing it, of course, but still: the sudden appearance of apparently nondiegetic music, atonal and creepy or not, was bound to make anyone a mite suspicious, even brainwashed cultists who worshipped some kind of Cyn-born death goddess.

I moved forward; the others followed.

The door ahead of us slid open—"Hands held high, eyes on the ground," I was barking, Bitey raised up and ready to fire, before I could even get a sense of what was happening: there were two cultists, I'd been right about that, one of them kneeling before some kind of makeshift . . . altar . . . her head turning and her jeweled eyes wide as she saw us; a Tyll, underneath the robes. The other, a Wulf, had been starting to stand, but when he saw the guns, he dropped back down to his knees again, his paws coming up, following my command—whatever these two were to the Wanderers, they weren't security, weren't combatants, just . . . indoctrinated, very much accustomed, it seemed, to following the shouted orders of people with guns.

That didn't make me feel great, but it was better than getting shot at. "Make a sound, eat a bullet," I growled, racking Bitey's slide halfway along its track for emphasis—totally unnecessary, but threatening as all hell. "You want to live, I'd get real interested in your sandals. Sho—" I was about to tell him to bind their hands—surely we had *something* we could repurpose for restraints—when the male of the pair, the heavyset Wulf, just leapt: sprung from his crouch and came straight for me, a move like a stalking predator leaping at prey, complete with outstretched claws.

I shot him three times in the chest, Bitey's suppressor making the burst a dull echo of a gunshot rather than an eardrum-bursting roar, then I stepped to the side, letting his forward momentum carry him past me; Meridian's rifle gave the low snap-hum of a laser activation, and then the Tyll woman was falling too, her face carved in half by the bright beam of the tac-laser Mer held in her arms.

There was a clatter, on the grating of the floor: the pistol the cultist had been drawing from her robes slid toward us, toward Meridian, whose black eyes were wide and staring at the crumpled corpse, faint lines of smoke still rising from the woman's head. "She . . . she was going—"

"She was going to try and shoot me, so you shot her first," I told her firmly—though I still reached up and eased her finger off the trigger of her weapon. "Thank you."

"If . . . if I hadn't—"

"If you hadn't, she would have splattered my insides all over the bulkheads. Hence the 'thank you.'" Not entirely true—the pistol was a semi-automatic, looked of a decent caliber, but still not enough to punch through my stronger-than-normal intention shields with anything less than the full magazine—but she had still been a threat, and Meridian had done exactly what she was supposed to do.

"You guys . . . look at that." Sho was stepping forward, toward the corpses.

"I *am*," Meridian said, her voice choked with disgust; I reached up, turning her away, and she clung to me for a moment, her fingers wrapping into fists in my jacket.

"No, not the cultists—their *altar*." The chanting of Meridian's gift had ceased the instant we'd cut the cultists down—she couldn't exactly read their subconscious minds when the electrical impulses that powered those minds were flickering and fading, along with their nervous systems and everything else that had made them people—but for a moment, I thought I heard it again, flaring up even louder and more intense than before: then it was gone, just an echo in my mind, because of what Sho had found, had *seen*.

The candles, the incense, the tapestries and strings of beads that made up the altar; Sho stripped them all away with a brusque sweep of his paws, leaving bare the wall behind their place of worship—bare except for a plaque upon its surface, words carved into something I would have called brass, except it wasn't, not quite: just like everything else about the forerunners, it was just a little off from the universe and the elements and the tech we knew.

We shouldn't have been able to read the writing on the plaque, of course, just like we couldn't read the idiographic glyphs carved elsewhere in the station—it was the same language, the same vertically oriented spread of whorls and dashes we'd seen elsewhere in the facility, and at the Furnace's Gate as well—and for a moment, we couldn't; then there was a kind of . . . shine, almost like a reflection, and the words had shifted, and we were staring at a language we *could* read, the universal constant: the same kind of recognition the light in the relic cathedral had made.

Whatever the forerunners had left behind here—whether it was some kind of partially dormant AI, a technological ghost of a long-dead species, or something even more inexplicable—it was aware enough to recognize us as gifted, just like the force field had, and also like the force field, that recognition, impossible as it may have been, seemed enough to grant us access to the knowledge hidden within the Dead Furnace's walls.

My eyes widened as I began to read. This wasn't . . . this wasn't *possible*.

Except it was. Oh, god, it was. This was . . .

This was everything. This was *everything*. Forget the Bright Wanderers—forget the Cyn, and their goddess—forget the mystery of the Dead Furnaces, of the direct rift, or the lost Vyriat expeditions, or even the reappearance of Julia in Jane's life. This was more important than all of that: this was the answer the Justified had been seeking, for a century or more.

We *had* to find a way back to the others.

CHAPTER 11

Jane

I stared down the corridor where Esa and the others had gone. Just . . . stared, as if I could somehow will myself to see through walls, though not even my fancy HUD could help me there: just like a regular station, whatever material the bulkheads of the Dead Furnaces were built out of, the stuff was designed specifically to block the sort of high-spectrum scanning that would have let me peer through the metal with my implants.

I had meant what I'd said to Esa, when I said she was ready. But telling her that was one thing, and actually watching her walk away, into danger that I couldn't face for her, or even with her . . . A part of me would always think of Esa as I'd seen her first: just a kid, using her gifts to protect *other* children, fearless in the face of chaos.

Whatever else she'd seen, whatever else she'd become—and I was proud, incredibly proud, of all of it—she'd never lost that: that fearlessness. And it wasn't a thing like my own, the bravery I'd cultivated inside myself during the sect wars, a thing that came about in response to all the awfulness I'd seen, as if knowing so much fear as a child meant I'd burned through my entire allotment, spent all the terror I had to give even before the elders had put a gun in my hand and told me to go forth and wreak vengeance upon our enemies for making me suffer all that horror. Esa's bravery was something else entirely, something innate, just a piece of who she was, a bright flame inside her that used the frightening things as fuel. The more terrible things became, the braver she grew.

The woman she was becoming, the Justified operative she would be: she was going to do amazing things. To change the galaxy. I knew that, just as surely as I knew my own name, knew the weight of my pistol on my hip. None of that stopped me from being terrified for her now, terrified in a way I knew she wouldn't be, because even with everything she'd seen, she'd yet to meet the problem she couldn't solve, the enemy she couldn't beat with enough ingenuity and stubbornness and will. She was young; she was immortal. The sort of thinking that lasted exactly as long as one could keep telling themselves that lie.

Not everyone survived the end of that moment, when the truth broke the lie apart.

Javier came up behind me; touched my shoulder gently. He knew better than to actually try to take my hand, not when I was still primed for combat, ready to raise up my gun at any moment. "They'll be okay," he said softly. "They've got this. *She's* got this. You've taught her everything she needs to know."

I shook my head. "Some things can't be taught, though," I replied. "Some things you have to learn on your own. Like what to do when you lose; like how to get back up. That, she hasn't had to learn. Not yet."

"Esa doesn't lose easily," Marus said from behind me. "We can pray that's a lesson she never suffers through. Not everyone does, you know."

Again, I shook my head. "It's not that generous a galaxy, and we all know it," I said. "Someday—some*how*—she's going to come up against odds she can't just bull through. And on that day—"

"Ah . . . people?" Sahluk asked. I didn't like whatever it was in his tone, and I frowned, moving toward him—turning away from the corridor where Esa and the others had disappeared. He was staring at the far door, not the one we'd come through from the landing platform, but the one Javier had found when we were searching for another way out of the vestibule, or whatever the hell this antechamber was. The passage had been blocked by another force field, but as I came up behind Sahluk, I saw that it wasn't anymore; the shimmering wall of light that had stopped our passage forward was just . . . gone.

"What did you do?" Javier demanded of the big Mahren, his tone slightly unbelieving. "Did you . . . did you stick your hand in there again or something? Short it out with that thick skin of—"

"I didn't do a damned thing," Sahluk shook his head, his exosuit making a mechanical whine as he raised up his grenade launcher, pointing it down the curving hallway suddenly open before us. "It went away on its own. Out of nowhere."

"As if this place *wants* us to go deeper," JackDoes murmured, peering down the corridor as well—from the safety of well behind Sahluk and myself.

"Yes, and it waited just long enough to come down so that Meridian and the others would get too far ahead for us to catch up," Marus shook his head. He was right—we'd lost radio contact with them just moments after they vanished from sight; we couldn't reach out and tell them, "Hold up; we're going to find a way to you," which was exactly what we would have done if the force field had fallen away and we had still been in contact. "This feels . . . off."

"Nothing 'off' about it," Sahluk shook his head. "It's a fucking trap." The word sounded almost benign as he spoke it, a basic statement of fact; he might have looked up into a clear sky and said, "The sun is shining." "There might as well be a sign above the door: 'Come on in, take some candy off the walls, then hop in the oven; the witch will be along shortly to set the timer and cook you into a pie.'"

"Are you . . . are you referencing human folktales right now?" Javier asked him, his tone incredulous. "Is that really what you're doing?"

"Humans tell good stories," Sahluk shrugged, his attention never wavering from the corridor ahead of us. "I always liked that one. Especially the part where they eat the witch after she's done cooking."

"That's . . . really not how that story ends, man," Javier replied, shaking his head. "What kind of fucked-up version of human myths did you *read?*"

"Regardless of comparative folklore, his point is well made," Marus said. "This . . . this is a trap. I don't know if it's the Bright Wanderers setting it, or the facility itself, but the smart thing to do—"

I was already stepping forward, over his objections. "Trap or not, we've got to take it," I said. "If something deeper in this facility can raise and lower those force fields at will, then they can cut us off from the landing platform—they can lock us *in* just as easily as they locked us out. If they wanted us helpless—or just kept away from Esa and the others—they already had that. This is . . . this is something else."

"Yeah—something *bad*," JackDoes reminded me.

"Probably," I agreed. "It almost always is."

"And you *still* want to move forward?"

"We're operatives of the Justified—that's what we do."

"I am not an operative," the little Reint protested. "I'm just a glorified mechanic!"

"A glorified mechanic who volunteered for this mission, remember?" Javier reminded him with a grin. "Just think of the stories you'll be able to tell the other grease monkeys when you get back to Sanctum."

"Have to *survive* to tell stories!"

He wasn't wrong on that, but still, he needed prodding, and if there was one prod that worked on all the Reint in the Justified ranks, it was the one I produced next: "Come on, JackDoes. What would MelWill do, if she were here?" MelWill was a member of the Justified council, a bonafide once-in-a-generation genius, venerated by *all* of the Justified, but especially by the Reint, who claimed her as one of their own.

JackDoes swallowed softly, his sharp teeth chittering a bit. "Cheap shot," he accused me.

I grinned, still staring down my rifle at the open corridor ahead of us. "Yup" was all I said in response.

"Well, fuck you too. Come on." He sighed, and glared down the corridor, his nictating membranes sliding over his eyes for a moment. "Let's go, if we are to go."

"Dissenting votes?" I asked, looking back at the others; at Marus, specifically. He sighed, but shook his head, his weapon raised—he wasn't wrong about this being a trap, but even if it were, he'd rather we set it off than leaving it in place for Esa, Meridian, and Sho to stumble into.

"Finally," Sahluk growled. "An excuse to shoot at somebody."

"Like you've ever needed an excuse," Javier needled him.

"Fine. An opportunity, then."

"Shooting starts, JackDoes, you find a place to hide," I said, even as the Reint hissed to himself, a sound of comfort more than anything else. "Don't you try and be a hero." If he wasn't firing, he wouldn't be a priority target—he had intention shields like the rest of us, and so long as the enemy wasn't focusing fire on him, the shielding should keep him safe enough, provided the rest of us could wipe out whatever ambush we were walking into before things got truly ugly.

"Oh, don't worry," he said. "I will try to live up to MelWill's example, but I know what I am, and I am not a soldier. You are here to handle the shooting—I'm here to take things apart, put them back together. Figure this whole place out."

"Which you'll get to do, just as soon as we deal with whatever this is," Javier assured him.

"You just have to keep me *alive* long enough for me to do it, remember."

"That's the plan."

"Have seen what happens when you 'plan' something, Javier. Maybe do not remind me."

"All right—stow the nervous," I told them. "Eyes up; heads on a swivel. Something wants us moving forward, and that means it's going to hit us when *it* wants to. We need to be ready; ready to prove we can hit right back."

"Always outnumbered; always outflanked," Sahluk agreed. "Find a way to win anyway. That's what being Justified means."

"Hoo-fucking-rah," I agreed, and started forward, into the depths of the Dead Furnaces—and toward whatever trap awaited us.

CHAPTER 12

Esa

This doesn't mean . . . it can't mean . . ." Meridian was stammering as she worked through the implications of the forerunner's testament—what they'd built the Dead Furnaces for, what they'd *done*—but I shook my head.

Pretending the truth is something other than what it is will get you killed as quick as almost anything: another one of Jane's maxims. "It does," I told her shortly.

"'When we rose to the stars, we found ourselves . . . alone,'" Sho read out loud, either unable to come to the same conclusion Meridian and I had without sounding the words out for himself, or just unwilling to. "'Surrounded by a galaxy where the elements that might give rise to life were predicated by a simple lottery, a lottery of random chance that would decide whether any newly evolved sentience would touch the stars, or scrounge forever in the dirt.

"'Our own rise was predicated on winning that same lottery, not just once, but over and over again, every single time the chaos returned from the nothing: and with our every victory, we found ourselves even more apart. We hadn't deserved our own successes, any more than the earlier forms of life we'd found, doomed to an ending they could not escape, had deserved that fate—and that meant we were indebted, indebted to the very beings who had remained behind, locked on their homeworlds even as we raced past.

"'So we decided to take that chance into our own hands; to become those who dictated the path later life would take. We decided to make better worlds, freer worlds, for those who would rise after. We did everything we could to aid the planets and moons already bearing early life; adjusted axial tilt, orbit, atmosphere—made those cradle worlds as close to our own beginnings as we possibly could, so that the life already springing forth might share our own origins, might understand our purposes, our gifts. We built them shepherds, to guide them after we passed on, for we knew even we were not immortal, and what truer bequeathment could we give than the legacy of ensuring that later species could *reach* the stars, just as we had?'"

Sho turned to us, stopping his recitation for a moment: "That tracks with what we found in the Furnace's Gate," he said simply. "They . . . shifted the atmospheres of our homeworlds, built the Barious, all so that we would become more like them. This much we knew already."

"That's not the part that . . ." Meridian shook her head again, her hands trembling by her sides. "Sho, don't you understand what it says, what it *means?*"

Sho didn't respond; he had already turned back to the writing, reaching the part of the testament that laid bare the enormity of the forerunners' claim, the truth that changed the fundamental nature of how we understood the galaxy. "'But there is still a barricade to the evolution of those lives,'" he read, "'even blessed with fertile worlds, even guided by our shepherds, there remains a barricade they cannot surpass, and one that will not arise until we are long dust. The very same lottery we won, over and over, without even realizing it: the great veil of chaos that will grind their progress to a halt, just before they can reach beyond their limited horizons. Impossible to predict, impossible to control, inherently random, yet with that veil in place, they cannot move forward, and their beginnings will be where they will stay, their worlds choked by the chaotic radiation that makes order an impossibility.

"'And so we have built this place—a place to strip away the veil entirely from certain worlds, a test, directed toward the cradles of the new species. Once successful, the light shining forth from these furnaces will illuminate a palace, the dream of what the universe can become, and once we reach those gates, we can spread that light outward, ever outward, until every sky over every world is free of the chaos. This place is the first step toward that palace, toward where our dream will become manifest, and once there, we will finally have earned our place among the stars.'" That was the end of the words on the plaque, but just below them, carved into the wall itself in jagged, uneven lines: "'*Forgive us—we knew not what we would unleash.*'"

Sho shook his head, an act of negation; even hearing the words out loud, spoken from his own mouth, didn't make him believe the forerunners' claim. It was just too big, too impossible. "It's not true," he said, his voice insistent. "It's not . . . how *can* it be?"

"All the same—it is," I said. "It was the *pulse*. The pulse was what was holding the other worlds back—the 'lottery' the forerunners won, their homeworld unaffected. The pulse existed, then. Even then."

"But it can't have, that doesn't . . . the Justified set off the pulse! They set it off during the sect wars, not . . . not eons and eons ago, not . . . how does that even . . ."

"It makes sense, Sho," I insisted. "It makes a terrible kind of sense. The pulse bomb the Justified set off was meant to be contained, meant to be limited to a specific area on a specific world. That was how it was built, what it was meant to do. Instead, it spread all across the cosmos. They—we—never knew why. *This* is why."

"Because the pulse wasn't *created* by the bomb," Meridian whispered; she'd connected those pieces as well, maybe even faster than me, though her voice was still awed—more than a little terrified, in fact. "It was already there, just waiting. Before the forerunners, it was part of the natural order of the universe—the 'veil of chaos' holding sentient species back from the stars. Then they stripped it away, somehow, stripped it away from the 'cradles'—the worlds where our species were evolving. But they didn't stop there. The Furnaces showed them a path to this . . . this . . ."

I nodded grimly. "'Palace,'" I said, not liking how the word even sounded out loud. The Cyn had mentioned a 'Palace,' on the shipyard, and again on the world beyond the Dead Furnaces. There was something else out there, some creation—or discovery—of the forerunners, hidden away somewhere: something that let the forerunners protect not just a few dozen cradle worlds—or even a few hundred; we still didn't know how many there had been—but the entire universe, a tool that had let them lock the pulse away entirely.

The power of the Dead Furnaces was frightening enough—the ability to shield entire worlds from pulse radiation—but if this Palace could fundamentally alter the reality of the entire universe like that . . . what *else* could it do?

Meridian was still trying to make sense of it all—where the pulse had gone, why it had returned. "When the Justified set off their weapon," she said, "it started a cascade—a chain reaction, a *reversion*. This whole . . . the galaxy, the way it is now, that's the way the universe is . . . it's not an aberration, it's not something we did. It's the opposite. The universe *after* the pulse is the way the universe was meant to be, the way it *started*."

"The forerunners wanted to protect us," I said tonelessly. "For the same reason they built the Barious—the same reason they were guiding our worlds, our evolution. To give us the best possible chance at the same glory they'd reached." Like a parent, willing and able to move mountains to provide a better future for their child; like the Preacher, deciding—before I had any choice in the matter—that a childhood in an orphanage on a backwater world would give me the best chance at a better life, a life she thought she owed me. "They did it so our species didn't hit some random point on the scale of technological evolution and find we could move no further, so that we weren't defined simply by whatever level of pulse radiation had collected over our homeworld. That was their . . . gift . . . to us."

"Freedom," Meridian breathed. "Freedom from the chaotic tyranny of the pulse." She was crying; the only reason I could see the tracks of the tears on her jet-black face was because the light of the very damning words we'd read made them shimmer against her skin. "God, we were never meant to . . . we were never even meant to *be*. My people were meant to remain trapped, between the depths of the caverns and the heat of the surface . . . forever. That was what we were supposed to be, what we would have remained, if the forerunners hadn't . . . Our world—our 'cradle'—it must have been one of their later experiments, and they didn't have time to adjust its rotation to match their own—"

"Or else your people were already evolving, underground, and they didn't want to interfere with that process," I said, reaching out to touch her face; she pushed her cheek into my hand, my palm wet with her tears, which made me hate what I had to say next even more. "But the rest . . . I don't think you're wrong, no. Tearing the pulse radiation from the atmosphere of your world—from all our worlds, in one fell swoop, using *this* place," I looked around me at the walls, at the insane machinery the forerunners had built, at the Dead Furnaces that had protected what the forerunners called the "cradles." "That's what let you develop the technology to survive on the surface, then, later, to reach the stars.

"Same with Wulf." I turned to Sho, who still looked like he didn't want to believe it, any of it. "Your people had the opposite problem, your homeworld almost too verdant, overabundant with life: filled with predators, some larger, hungrier, than you. What would have happened if the pulse had been around then? If it had been returning, again and again, century after century?"

Sho shook his head, focusing on the theoretical question so he didn't have to think about the insane truth the forerunners' testament had raised. "Almost every leap in technological ability in ancient Wulf society was predicated on inventing something to fight off the other predators that filled our world, to enlarge the borders of our villages, the patches we carved out of the wilds. If we'd never discovered gunpowder—or internal combustion, or electricity—if pulse radiation had meant we couldn't . . . It's entirely probable we would have stayed the way we were. Trapped. Just another predator species on a world full of them."

"And humanity?" Meridian asked me.

I shrugged; honestly, I'd never felt much of a connection to my own species—the world I'd grown up on had been equal parts human, Wulf, and Tyll, and one of the reasons it had survived the pulse was that its inhabitants had thrown over sect war–era thinking very early on. Species identification had been strongly discouraged, even shunned. One of the reasons the Preacher had chosen it, I suppose.

Still, I knew human history as well as anyone, thanks to my studies with the Justified. "The story of mankind contains significantly more intercultural conflict than most species," I said. "The human homeworld was the setting of the original sect wars, in that way. Without forward leaps in technology, in communication—without the ability to reach out to other groups and realize the commonalities between us all—we likely would have stayed as we were for thousands and thousands of years: feudal, violent, fractured. No.

My species would have been nearly as bad off, I promise you—we would have just been killing each other, rather than succumbing to the elements or different species of life."

"So . . . they were right." Meridian turned back to the plaque, something between fear and awe on her face. "The forerunners knew the pulse radiation would stymie all of our attempts to move beyond what we were, our attempts to better ourselves. And so they . . . got rid of it, somehow. With this Palace. This place, the Dead Furnaces—it was their first attempt, a sort of . . . theoretical trial, aimed at just a handful of worlds rather than the galaxy at large. And it must have worked—they must have moved forward from there, to this Palace—or else we would have discovered pulse radiation when we first took to the stars, would have discovered that only *our* worlds were defended from the pulse. So this place was only the first step; their . . . dream . . . came true."

"And their nightmare," I added, nodding at the last lines of the testament carved into the wall. "'Forgive us, for we knew not what we would unleash.'"

"Something went wrong," Sho agreed, finally beginning to believe in what the writing had spelled out: that the pulse was meant to be. And we were not. "Somewhere along the way, something went very, very wrong. Something about their radiation-stripping process, about what they found or did at this Palace to cleanse the whole galaxy of the pulse . . . it *created* their enemy. Created the Cyn."

"But it also succeeded," Meridian insisted. "We inherited a universe free of the pulse—a gift we never knew we'd been given, one that lasted, sustained itself, long after the forerunners had lost their last war."

"Until the Justified came along," I said. "Until we tore a hole in that protection—unraveled a single thread, cut the tension in the lattice, and the whole thing collapsed. This entire time, we thought the pulse was some new thing, but it never was: *freedom* from the pulse was the gift the forerunners had left for us, to ensure our species' survival. And its creation cost them their own."

"But why are the Bright Wanderers here, then?" Sho asked. "They're looking for this 'Palace,' we've heard them say so—but that doesn't make sense;

they're fronted by Cyn, after all, and the Cyn were the enemies of the fore-runners. They wouldn't have any interest in stopping the pulse, they *feed* on it."

"And why bring the gifted here?" Meridian added. "How does that—do we—fit in?"

"As to Sho's question—I've got no idea," I admitted to her. "Yours, though: that, I can answer. Think about it: the forerunners' writings respond to us, the Cyn are kidnapping gifted kids, seeking 'martyrs' to 'open the way to the Palace.'" They must have learned that word here, studying the same writings we were—hence the altar the cultists had been worshipping at, beneath the plaque. "The barricades of light, the forerunners' defenses—they let us through, because we were what we are: pulse-born, soaked in radiation. There's only one thing that tracks with all of that: that this place, these places—the Dead Furnaces and this Palace both, whatever it is—were designed for the gifted, designed that way because the forerunners *were* gifted. Every single one of them."

I stopped, swallowed, my mouth suddenly dry. The enormity of that idea . . . But it was the only thing that made sense.

Sho had been watching me as I spoke; he nodded, almost carefully, fol-lowing the thread of the idea. "Their world wasn't heavily pulsed," he said slowly. "That was the 'lottery' they won—pure cosmic chance dictating that even as the pulse returned, again and again, their homeworld remained rela-tively unaffected. But pulse radiation is still *present*, even in the atmosphere of worlds where the rads don't choke away all tech. Look at you." He turned toward Meridian. "The world you grew up on wasn't nearly as heavily pulsed as Esa's, or mine, and yet you still wound up gifted. And a people who evolved on a world like that—evolved in a stew of pulse radiation, all the way from single-cell organisms on up . . ."

"They'd *evolve* to be gifted," Meridian said, awe in her voice as she put it together as well. "Of course they would: if nothing else, natural selection would heavily favor those with gifts over those without, especially in the early eons of a species' evolution."

I nodded. "The Dead Furnaces, the relics: they responded to the gifted because the forerunners were an entire *species* of gifted. Whatever genetic sequence or DNA pattern that allows a person to become so, whatever markers there are that set us apart . . . those markers must have hardened into the basic makeup of their species before they even discovered fire. All their technology, their culture—it all would have been predicated on that commonality.

"The next generation, the gifted, whatever you want to call us—that's what we *are*, the creations of the pulse, the same thing as what they evolved into. The forerunners weren't just an alien species; the forerunners were *us*."

CHAPTER 13

Jane

We made hot contact with the enemy very shortly after we passed through the lowered force field.

It wasn't the ambush I'd expected: instead, the Bright Wanderers we found seemed just as surprised to see us as we were to see them. We turned the corner and the room just opened up, spilling us out into a kind of atrium filled with metallic lattices that dripped down from the ceiling in patterns I wasn't sure were functional, or just art.

Underneath those strange webs of wire, there they were, a handful of cultists staring at us in surprise and shock—it was like they truly hadn't known their drones had launched, that their tower had gone silent. Most of them didn't even have intention shields. They were all armed, though, and not a one of them didn't go for a gun: a cult was a cult, no matter what else you called it, and every single member of their "faith" was ready to die for the beliefs they'd used to replace their own personalities.

We cut them down, the vibrations of the gunfire making the intricate cords of metal above tremble and resonate with a kind of low hum: ambush or not, a firefight was a loud thing, and that meant we'd have more company, sooner or later. Where there was one clutch of cultists, there would be more, and the next batch wouldn't be surprised to see us, not with the sounds of gunfire ringing down the emptied halls.

At least now we knew the Dead Furnaces hadn't just eaten them, I suppose.

"We can't just . . . stumble around in here forever," Javier grunted as he rolled over one of the bodies, checking for anything of use—a little ghoul-

THE FIRMAMENT OF FLAME 291

ish, perhaps, but necessary, if we were going to find our way through this maze. For all that my sweetheart usually played the role of the good-natured, light-hearted explorer—and usually, that's what he was—the world he'd come from, and the years he'd spent outside the Justified's protection, had also left their mark. "Is there a . . . Marus, I know you can't see through the walls or anything, but is there power flowing through the cables above us? Some sort of reactor, independent of the solar collection array?"

JackDoes nodded. "A good point. This station must have some kind of independent generator—the air we're breathing, the gravity, it has to come from somewhere, and since the 'furnaces' remain 'dead,' that power is not coming from the solar collectors on the inside of the ring."

"We're looking for Meridian and the others, though, not for a reactor," Marus pointed out.

"Question might be moot, anyway," Sahluk said, opening one of the doors off the atrium, only to find it sealed behind another force field. He nodded to me, and I checked two more; found them both blocked off as well. About the sixth door we checked was open—the others, nearly a dozen in all, were locked off by the shimmering walls of light that would only let the gifted through.

"We're being funneled," I shook my head, not bothering to keep the thread of anger from my voice as something inside me snapped and snarled at the thought. "Guided."

"But by what?" Javier asked.

"And to where?" Marus added.

"Nowhere we want to go," I replied sourly. I hated being controlled, especially when I didn't know where that control was taking me.

"*To your judgment,*" another voice said, into our comms—I'd recognize the crackling energy in those tones anywhere. It was a Cyn.

It was a Cyn, and we didn't have Esa with us, the only member of our little team—hell, the only person *anywhere*, as far as we knew—who had ever successfully taken one of their kind on.

Didn't mean we wouldn't try, though.

The Cyn came through one of the force fields—his armor stayed behind like it was held in place by powerful magnets, but he himself just slid through the light with a brief burst of energy, like he was warping his own body to match whatever currents formed the shield—and he wasn't talking anymore; he just hit us, starting with Javier, who was closest.

Thankfully, we'd all keyed our intention shields to match the vibrational wavelength of the energy that made up the Cyn's body, and when the orb of fire he flung at Javier struck my boyfriend in his chest, he was just thrown to the ground like he would have been if it had been a heavy-caliber ballistic round that had hit him, rather than caught up in an electrical explosion. Before the Cyn could turn to another target I was already moving, closing the distance and drawing the stun baton strapped on my thigh—a baton also keyed to the Cyn's vibrational frequency—as bright blue lasers from Marus's rifle stabbed past me, punching holes through the Cyn's energetic form, the punctures creating dark spots around them like oil spreading across the surface of a pool of water.

Still, the Cyn was ready for that—stretched one hand out and, with a thought, reached into the rifle in Marus's hands with a tendril of fire, going for the weapon's battery. The Cyn on Odessa had pulled the same trick on the Tyll, though—had detonated his weapons as he held them, nearly crippling his hands the same way it had ruined his eyes—and Marus wasn't one to get caught by the same trap twice: he flung the rifle toward the Cyn even as it began to overload. It exploded, the electrified shrapnel piercing through the Cyn's glowing form, making more dark patches on the swirling light of his body as the creature screamed in frustration and hate.

I'd closed the distance; hit him once, twice, from behind with the baton, then plunged the weapon as deep into the energetic current of his back as it could go, jamming the activator all the while. The energy inside the Cyn shorted it out, but not before I'd delivered a jolt to the organ at the center of him, a jolt that sent him to his knees. "You will . . . be judged . . ." he gasped, stumbling back to his feet and swinging at me—but I ducked low, underneath the current of his arm, activating the stun knuckles on my off hand as I did; my right, meanwhile, had pulled a grenade free from my belt, and I tossed it upward, catching it with the fingers of my left that hummed with the electrical energy of the stun charge.

"Judge *this*," I snarled, and then I shoved my fist, grenade and all, into his chest.

The stun knuckles kept my hand from *melting* as I did so, and my intention shield protected my arm, but it still hurt like a son of a bitch, like I was trying to punch fire. It did the job, anyway—the Cyn backhanded me, and I went sailing, my intention shields down to nothing now, from absorbing that single blow—but the damage was done, my deadly freight delivered: the grenade went off inside his body, an EMP explosive meant to knock out complex machinery like exosuits, re-rigged to affect the specific frequency of the Cyn.

He screamed into our comms as his body was splashed across the walls and over the lattice that hung above our heads, the blazing droplets of his form eating through the metal like acid—he screamed, but he wasn't done, just badly hurt, already pulling the fire back to the center of him, ribbons of light flowing like electric arcs from all across the room to fill in the gaping holes in his hollowed form. Shit. I'd been expecting that to kill him.

It hadn't, which meant that now we were fucked.

Javier had gotten back to his feet: two quick shotgun blasts to the Cyn's chest did little actual damage, the conductive pellets he was using little more than a minor irritation, but they achieved his purpose—distracted the creature while Sahluk opened up with his heavy plasma launcher. The burning explosives weren't keyed to the Cyn the way my grenade had been—that was the whole point of plasma weaponry, it was too unstable to be anything but "plasma"—but the energy within them ate through everything, even other sources of energy, and the cascade of bright green fire was melting the Cyn's newly re-corporealized form within the bright flare of cascading light.

It would have been awful to watch, if this hadn't been one of the motherfuckers that had been trawling the galaxy, kidnapping and murdering children.

That was when the Cyn did something Sahluk hadn't been expecting—something none of us had, not that there was anything the rest of us could have done. Instead of retreating before the rapid-fire volley of burning energy—or just fucking *dying*, which was what anything else would have done when faced with a deluge of near-continuous plasma fire—he went forward, not even running, just flowing along the metal of the floor, more like a liquid than energy now, aiming himself like a missile at his target: not Sahluk, or Marus, or Javier, or me, but JackDoes.

He went right at the little Reint, the only one of us who hadn't attacked him yet.

I wasn't close enough to stop him; I wasn't close enough to do *anything* useful. I had just enough time to realize what was about to happen, that he was going to enfold JackDoes in what remained of his "arms," overwhelm his intention shields, and burn our mechanic to death just like his predecessors had done to the Vyriat bodies we'd found at the Furnace's Gate. I wasn't close enough to do anything but watch, and neither was Marus, nor Javier.

Sahluk was, though.

He spilled out of his exosuit damn near as fast as the Cyn had come out of his own, and he threw himself into the path of the flowing Cyn: threw himself into the creature's path and fucking caught him, wrapped the flaming being in a bear hug and screamed as the creature made of fire and burning light began to turn his rocky skin into ash, pieces of the big Mahren soldier beginning to flake off and vaporize as he pressed himself against the crackling current of the Cyn's own being.

He was doing the same thing Mo had done, on Jalia Preserve: stopping the Cyn from hurting the rest of the team, spending his own life to keep the monster at bay.

Even against all that pain, though, Sahluk wasn't done—his skin was tougher than any of ours, and that included against an electrical current, the rocky plating of his species' dermis capable of withstanding more damage before it was burned through—and, still screaming, he lunged forward, carrying the Cyn down with him, landing on top of the creature of fire, his weight collapsing what was left of the bonds that held the Cyn's structure together—

—which meant the thing's "heart" was exposed. I went for the pistol at my hip, drew, and fired before I'd even known that was what I was going to do—"act, don't react"—which meant I got my round off almost as fast as Javier did, despite the fact that my pistol had been in the mag-catch holster on my hip and Javi's shotgun had already been raised. The rounds hit nearly at the same time, making the only physical organ the Cyn had—the thing that held all the rest of them together—simply explode into paste, and the horrible fire cooking at Sahluk flickered out, the energy dissipating into one final blast of heat and force, making the lattices above us hum and moan.

Then silence in the atrium—silence, except for Sahluk's awful moans. He was hurt; hurt bad.

But unlike Mo, he was still alive.

Marus was already kneeling beside him, trying to apply burn foam from his first aid kit, but there wasn't enough foam in *all* our kits to cover even one-third of the awful injuries the Mahren had taken. What he'd done would have been impossible for the rest of us, but that just meant it would have killed us before it could have made a difference: it hadn't killed Sahluk, but it had still cost him, and cost him dearly.

"*Please* don't die, Sahluk," JackDoes was begging, kneeling at his side as well. "*Please* don't—"

"He's not going to die," Marus said, his tone professional, almost cold as the rest of us handed over our foam canisters, and Marus did what he could, which wasn't much. "Not if we get him back to the ships. Now. Sahluk? Can you hear me? Can you stand?"

The Mahren groaned, but didn't answer; it likely would have been better for him if he'd just lost consciousness entirely, but he was a stubborn bastard, clinging to awareness despite the pain. "We have to move him," Marus said, getting one arm underneath Sahluk and straining to lift him—JackDoes tried to help, but even together the massive Mahren was just too damned heavy; he outweighed all of the remaining members of our team combined.

"The suit," Javier said, dragging Sahluk's abandoned exosuit back toward the injured soldier. "Get him into the—the servos and the pistons will respond automatically: if we can get him *in*, it'll take at least some of his weight."

It took all of us to do it—and Sahluk screamed, several times, as we clamped the metal around his raw burns—but when it was done, we got him onto his feet, though it still took Marus and Javier together, each with a metal arm thrown over his shoulders, to pull the only half-functional suit into staggering motion.

"Go," I told them shortly. "Get him back to the ships; get him into Khaliphon's medbay." Of all of our craft, Khaliphon had the best infirmary; we'd just have to hope none of the force fields had closed up behind us. If they had, Sahluk would die. "I'll find the others, then meet you there; we can regroup under the protection of the ships' turrets." Zealots or not, no Cyn could stand up to a sustained barrage from the big guns on the ship—not with the lasers' vibrational frequency set to match their own. The energy Esa had used to melt them at the base of the tower had come from those same guns, after all.

"Not safe," JackDoes protested. "Not safe for you. They know we're here now—they—"

"Which means they know Esa and the others are here as well," I told him grimly, reloading the single round I'd fired from my pistol, the spent shell dropping from my fingers with a clatter to spin across the pitted, damaged floor. "Whatever element of surprise we had, it's gone. I have to get to her, to warn her."

"Stay safe, sweetheart," Javier told me, knowing better than to argue.

"Find them, and get back," Marus agreed. "No detours."

"I'll go. I'll go with you." JackDoes didn't sound happy about the prospect—in fact, he sounded terrified by it—but there was steel in his voice all the same. Engineer or not, he was still Justified. "Shouldn't go alone. Might need me to figure out this place. To find the path."

I looked at him—saw that steel there, buried before, exposed now—then looked at Marus, nodded. With a grunt, shifting the weight of Sahluk's exo-suit on his shoulders, Marus freed one of his submachine guns and handed it over to JackDoes, the small weapon more suited to the Reint than anything else we had. Marus still had one of his brace to use, if things got ugly on their way back. "Go," I told them again; it was all there was left to say.

"Jane . . ." The voice came out in a rasp, but it was still Sahluk, speaking despite the pain, despite the fact that he was still weaving in and out of consciousness.

"Get back to the ships, soldier," I said, putting a snap in my voice, the note of command I'd learned on battlefields a hundred years and billions upon billions of miles from here: I didn't *actually* outrank Sahluk, but in his state, he'd respond to that tone, like any soldier would. "That's an order."

"Did him . . . did him . . ."

"Yeah, Sahluk," I said, softer, putting a hand on the metal of the suit—careful not to brush up against the raw, screaming red of his burns. "Mo'd be proud. Now go with Javier and Marus. We've got it from here."

Sahluk nodded, and his head dropped back toward his chest, the pistons in the suit giving a hiss as he did.

Javier looked at me, one last time, over the big Mahren's shoulder. Didn't say anything; just looked. After all the years we'd spent together—and all the years we'd spent apart—we knew better than to say goodbye. I nodded, once—didn't even raise my hand off my rifle—and he nodded back.

I loved him. He loved me. If the worst happened . . . if this was the last time we saw each other . . . we didn't need to say it. It had been said.

Then they were gone, headed for the entrance we'd used to gain access to the atrium.

JackDoes and I turned toward the exit, the only open path before us. "What . . . what do we do if we meet another Cyn?" he asked me hesitantly. He'd been brave, when he needed to—now he was starting to think through the possible cost of that bravery.

"The same thing Sahluk did," I replied, a certain grimness in my own tone. "We fight it. We find a way, no matter the cost. Come on—we need to move fast now."

CHAPTER 14

Esa

"Yeah," Meridian nodded, her fingers clutching at her own shoulders like she could somehow hug herself, assure herself of her own reality in this new universe—the same one we'd always lived in, only it *felt* different, felt alien, unfamiliar, because of what we'd learned. "We need . . . we need to get back to the others. Lay this all out—figure out what they . . . maybe they can—"

A sound, echoing dimly through the ventilation shafts and air ducts that connected the rooms of the station—a sound I'd recognize anywhere. "Was that gunfire?" Sho asked, the tufts of his ears perking up.

"It was," I said. "Several reports, and I recognized Jane's rifle, at least. Maybe Javier's shotgun, too."

"Did that—" Meridian twisted around, like whatever gunfight the others were involved in was suddenly going to come breaking through the doors of the antechamber we found ourselves in. "Did that come from in front of us? Because it sounded—"

"Yeah, it did." I raised Bitey up to my eye, training it on the far door.

"Does that mean they found a way through the force fields somehow? Does that—"

"I don't know, but we're going to find out."

"What happened to going back?" Sho asked. "I thought—wasn't the plan to go back?"

"If there's fighting somewhere else in this station, we don't know for a fact that 'back' is even where they are anymore," I answered. The sound of the gunfire had echoed through the ventilation ducts—it had *sounded* like it had come from ahead of us, yeah, but there was no way to tell what direction it had actually originated from. Still, I'd bet good money that it hadn't been from behind us, not all the way back to the antechamber where we'd left the others. It had been closer than that.

"Esa—Jane and the others, they can take care of themselves," Meridian said. "We need to—"

"We need to find them, and if they're in trouble, we need to help. They can 'take care of themselves' right up to the point where they meet a Cyn. Then, they're likely fucked." I'd watched, on Odessa, as the "chaplain" of the Bright Wanderers tore right through them, through Javier and Marus and even Jane, the brutal combat leaving Marus scarred for life.

They were better equipped now than they had been, better prepared for what facing a Cyn meant, but that didn't mean they were *safe*—the only way to be safe would be if I found them, because taking down Cyn was rapidly becoming my specialty. Strange focus to have, combat-wise, but if it let me help my friends—if it let me stop whatever it was the Bright Wanderers were planning to do when they found this Palace, the machine the forerunners had used to seal the pulse away from the galaxy—then I'd take it.

"Either way, we need to move," Sho said. "Standing still just means letting someone else decide what happens to you." That was almost certainly one of Javier's aphorisms—Jane would have phrased it differently, something involving letting the enemy choose your battleground.

I nodded, and started forward; after a moment, the others fell in behind me. The far door slid open—there was another sound, rattling the vents, just before it did, a sound that might have been an explosion or two, though I wasn't entirely sure—and then we were staring out, out into . . .

I didn't know *what* the hell we were staring at.

It wasn't a gunfight; I knew that much. Wherever Jane and the others were, it wasn't here. What we were looking at—I could feel something, something about the place, about the space, almost like a pull, not at my consciousness but at my *gift*: this place was reaching for me, reaching for the talents the pulse had given me, unasked. The sensation was like feeling a heartbeat through someone else's skin.

I knew, through that feeling, knew without being told: this was the core of the Dead Furnaces. The heart that was meant to be set ablaze.

The door opened out onto a platform, one suspended over some sort of . . . reservoir? No, that wasn't right. What was underneath the metal catwalks beneath our feet wasn't a liquid, not exactly—except it *was*, and then it wasn't anymore, shifting as we watched, from liquid to solid, flowing chaotically one moment, then frozen the next. It was pale stuff, almost translucent: it looked for all the world like a massive basin full of molten glass, minus the heat that made glass molten in the first place. Whatever it was, it was far, far below us; we were at least four stories up, and the ceilings were as far over our heads as the liquid was beneath the grating under our feet.

That liquid-not-liquid lay beneath us—and in front of us, at the far side of the massive reservoir, was a single bright beam of light, cutting all the way across the metal length of the far side of the room, splashing the entire space with bright orange light. No, not a beam: an aperture, a *slit*, cut into the bulk-heads of the facility itself.

That must have been the exterior wall: we'd pushed all the way through the Dead Furnaces, and that was the interior of the ring, the slit open to the tendril of stellar flame that the facility had been built to surround. Out past whatever force field was holding the void back, keeping the impossible heat coming off that flare from melting us alive: the solar converters, the storage batteries, the machinery that this place had been built to run.

An ocean of glass beneath us; a slit to the bright blaze of the star beyond, and in the center . . .

The thing rose up in twists and turns, bisecting the line of bright light from the far wall, a kind of . . . pillar, a massive, intricate mechanism: the thing that was pulling at me. I knew, somehow, without any descriptors left behind by the forerunners, that pillar was the key that turned in the lock of this place, that this entire room was, somehow, the pilot light of the Furnaces. The liquid in the reservoir, the strange pillar rising up from that molten sea, the torrent of stellar energy beyond: it was . . . machinery, in its own way.

And if that machinery was activated, all that brightness cutting across the far wall—and the energy from the batteries beyond, drawn from the stellar flare itself—would somehow pour through that breach in the bulkheads, down into the glass, which would in turn feed the pillar, the whole thing acting as a channel for the stellar energies. The ocean of glass was like a focusing crystal, a lake of unformed potential just waiting for some sort of definition, and when that solar spill arrived, through the breach, the Dead Furnaces would become . . . well, no longer "dead," at least.

Was that . . . was that something we *wanted*? It had to be, right? Based on the writing we'd found, this place had only been the first step in the forerunners' ambitious agenda to rid the galaxy of the pulse, an agenda that might well have taken them generations, centuries, after the creation of this station. That plan that had climaxed at this Palace the Bright Wanderers were trying to reach, where the forerunners had somehow managed to rid the galaxy of the pulse for eons . . . right up until the Justified came along and unwittingly opened the door for its return. But even setting those later events aside, it still sounded like the Dead Furnaces themselves had been designed to protect specific planets from the pulse: namely, the "cradles," our homeworlds. Specific planets that were thousands of light-years away, if not farther. If we could somehow direct it, aim that power, that protection, at worlds *we* designated instead, a few key sites like the Barious factories on Requiem—

—if we activated it, the Justified would *become* what the Bright Wanderers were claiming to be. I had no doubt that their recruitment spiel—"freedom from the pulse"—was driven by the Cyn's ability to eat pulse energy, an ability that would let them prove that the devotion they demanded could provide a result. But a single Cyn—hell, a thousand Cyn—couldn't cleanse an entire planet; for that, you'd need . . .

You'd need this. This place, whatever it was. And to do more than that— to affect the entire universe—you'd need what lay beyond. The Palace.

The power that could give us . . . the power just the Dead Furnaces alone could give us . . . did it really belong in *anyone's* hands? Even the Justified's? The sect had changed after we'd set off the pulse bomb; what would we become once we were handed the power to take—and likely give—pulse radiation at will? As the only sect able to protect a handful of worlds, a handful among millions . . . the others would come begging for aid. I might trust the current Council to do what was right—but the current Council wouldn't always be in power, and there was no guarantee we'd be able to find this Palace, to use it to cure the entire galaxy of the pulse, or even that the facility would still be operational if we did.

"Power corrupts." That wasn't just one of Jane's mottos—though it was that, too—it was a key truth that held across almost every ideology and philosophy I'd ever been exposed to, not to mention proved out by the lunatics I'd fought, over and over, to keep those I loved safe, to keep the *galaxy* safe. With the Pax, that corrupting power had been basic strength—they thought the strongest deserved to rule, and so spent all their energy toward growing stronger. With the Cyn, the "chaplain," it had been his natural advantages that let him look down on the other species—he'd seen organics, and Barious, as "other," not truly living, simply beings that stood in his way, beings he had every right to tear apart if it suited his whims or the whims of his goddess. Even the Bright Wanderers were using the power they held over their recruits—the promises of better worlds, better lives—to turn them to whatever ends.

Would this much power turn the Justified into the same thing? Into something worse?

And if the Bright Wanderers *wanted* this place activated—if for no other reason than to show the Cyn the way to the Palace—why hadn't they done so already?

Clearly, they'd had control of the facility for a good long while, long enough to repurpose the communications tower on the nearby world from a forerunner artifact into a drone fleet control; hell, they'd had enough time to build the drone fleet itself. Yet outside of the two adherents we'd cut down at the shrine in the next room—and maybe the gunfire we'd heard, a moment ago—we hadn't seen any indication that the Wanderers were even trying to make this place operational.

There was too much we just didn't *know*.

Meridian was right; before we did anything, we needed to find the others, we needed to—

A sound: not more gunfire, but instead a single note, sustained out to infinity, a low moan I could feel in my gut like someone had pressed a single key on an organ and was just holding it down, the noise just going on and on and on. I turned toward Meridian, and her eyes were wide with fear even as she nodded: it was her gift making that sound; she'd been using it as a kind of early warning system again, but every single other being she'd ever channeled had created actual *music*. That was how her gift worked; this was just a . . . drone, a repetition, the same note—

—finally shifting, a minor-key step upward on a scale, that single step creating a kind of awful tension just out of the apprehension of the next climb in the sound. So it was music, of a kind; the kind of music that created knots of dread in your stomach. As we'd stared out over the basin of liquid glass, we'd all walked out onto the platform itself—now, we all turned, backing farther up the metal lattice of the platform, up the handful of raised steps at the back, our weapons aimed ahead of us at the door we'd come through, where the "music" was originating. Because whoever it was, if that droning terror of a song was the sound of their subconscious mind, it seemed very, very unlikely they were going to be friendly.

CHAPTER 15

Jane

JackDoes stayed tight with me as we moved deeper into the corridors of the station, close enough that I had to pause occasionally to take him by the shoulder and push him a little bit away, making sure I had enough freedom of movement to respond to an attack so that an enemy assault wouldn't hit both of us at once. Each time, he'd nod, tighten his grip on his gun, and then start gravitating just a little closer to me with each strange room we passed through, until we had to go through the whole damn thing again.

Meanwhile, no answers, no sign of Esa and the others—we were still being led, each room we entered with only one way out, one doorway not blocked by a force field, something guiding our path through the station in a way I truly did not like. We'd lost communication with Javier and the others almost as soon as they were out of sight, the same way we had with Esa and her team: we were alone in these twisting corridors, and this place—

We opened another door, and found another Cyn.

It came at us. It just lunged: no threats, no declarations of heresy, just a full-on attack, and this Cyn hadn't been forced to pass through one of the glowing barriers to get to us, so it was still wearing a full exosuit, complete with a massive spear in its grip.

I didn't know if the Cyn's rejection of firearms was symbolic, or if they'd simply never developed that sort of weapon—but either way, our own guns were worthless against that much armor, a fact I knew already. JackDoes, however, didn't: he fired, a single three-round burst and then another, the gunshots loud and echoing outward in the chamber we found ourselves in. They did nothing, just whined about the empty space in a ricochet, the Cyn simply brushing them off even as he swapped the target of the charge, aiming for the little Reint instead, the one who had presented himself as a threat.

A mistake. The environs we found ourselves in—a narrow passage with a wall on one side and a kind of open chasm on the other, though what lay beneath, I had no idea—limited my options significantly, but it also limited the Cyn's path: his way to JackDoes led him straight past me, and I slipped under the sweep of his spear, pulling a knife from my boot as I did and jamming the blade in a crease in his armor, one of the grooves where it would split open to allow him to spill out. Those grooves were almost invisible, but I knew where to look, and he whirled on me, the spear making a deadly arc at shoulder height, but I was already gone, ghosting backward, and the hilt of the knife was glowing red, because it wasn't just a cutting blade.

The explosives in the hilt blew a hole in his armor; he staggered with the force of the blast, but he still managed to reach behind himself and rip the gun from JackDoes's hands, nearly carrying the Reint off the edge of the chasm as he did so. I *hit* the bastard, trying to keep him off guard: once, twice, three times, both of my knuckle mods active, electric shocks coming from the sharp jabs I threw with my left, massive dents appearing in his armor as I caught him with heavy hooks from the force-amplifiers in my right.

He staggered backward again, trying to get his spear raised, but I was in too close for that, and I planted another explosive blade, this one just over his heart, then rolled away before it could detonate. That was that, his armor wasn't functional anymore, and he flowed out of it like a storm of lightning contained in metal, except not so much contained anymore.

I retreated—slowly—toward JackDoes, controlling my breathing, focusing on not letting any fear show on my face, though I was definitely feeling plenty. It had taken all of our team—minus Esa and the other gifted—to take on the first Cyn we'd met here, and Sahluk had wound up grievously injured in the process. Now it was just JackDoes and myself; we were out-gunned, and the only card I had to play was that the Cyn himself didn't seem to—

A gunshot; the Cyn stared at me for a moment, his "face" swirling and darkening, and then he dropped to his knees, pieces of his "heart" falling free of the fire in his chest.

Julia stood behind him, some sort of truly massive rifle in her hands, a bolt-action thing, likely designed expressly for Cyn-killing, and not much else. "I told you," she said—not to me, but to the fading corpse of the Cyn, lying on the ground—"she's *mine*. No one else gets to touch her."

"How . . . how the *hell* . . ." I just stared at her for a moment; we'd left her floating, adrift on the sea of neon beneath the storms of the Furnace's Gate, and then we'd come directly here, directly to this system. We would have known if another ship had arrived behind us, would have noticed if the direct rift had opened again—

She just shook her head, dropping the big rifle to one side, one hand swinging almost casually toward the pistol at her hip—but I'd already done the same, and we both just stood there for a moment, watching each other. "Come on, Jane," she said, a small grin flickering at the edge of her face. "Put it together." I knew that grin, knew the fake-annoyed, resigned tone in her voice: the years just melted away, and I could hear her, chiding me over some flickering, shot-to-hell terminal, as we tried to find our way out of whatever mess she'd gotten us into and she was seeing something in the data I *wasn't*.

Because she'd always been smarter than me.

"I got fished out of the neon sea two days after you left," she told me, the smile growing wider, meaner. "Took a few days to prepare, too, because I knew I had the time. Direct rifts might be more efficient, but they're not faster than a standard hyperdrive: I've been waiting on you for almost a week."

Goddamn it. God *damn* it. I'd been right—I'd been right all along. It had been a trap. The drones, Wanderers defending the watchtower—all just . . . just fodder, stationed there to convince us this place wasn't completely unguarded.

But if it was a trap, that meant they *wanted* us here: why?

The same reason the Cyn had been on Kandriad; the same reason he'd been on Valkyrie Rock—they wanted the gifted, the next generation, Esa and Sho and Meridian.

And we'd handed them over like a solstice present, alone and fucking *gift wrapped*.

She saw my expression change: even after a hundred years, she could follow every thought that wound its way through my mind. My well-schooled expression, painstakingly trained not to give anything away to an enemy—not fear, not anger, not grief—was an open book for someone who had known me so long, had known me so early.

She saw the realization come, and she laughed, knowing I'd put together what she'd done, and what she was after. "Yeah, you really shouldn't have let her wander off without you," she told me, her hand dropping another millimeter toward her weapon—but stopping, as mine did the same. "A lost little girl, in this place, well . . . let's just say there's something here that likes the *taste* of little girls. Especially gifted ones."

I shook my head, taking a single step back, turning, just slightly—presenting a narrower target, for when she inevitably went for her gun. We both knew there was only one way this was going to end. "Esa can handle herself," I told Julia flatly.

Her response was just as affectless, the mean-spirited laughter that had been in her voice before gone now, vanished like a mirage. "No. She can't. Nothing's *changed*, Jane. This is how wars are fought. This is how wars are won. By taking away what your enemy cares for. By making them hurt." She could read me, and I could read her: there was real hate flashing across her eyes on those last few words, hate so strong it was like a need, no matter how hard she was trying to play at being empty, hollow inside. She didn't just wanted me dead: she wanted me to suffer.

She'd loved me, once. Only love could make you hate someone that much.

"And you want to . . . you want to hurt her, to hurt me? That's your . . . she's not a part of what happened between us, Julia. She wasn't even born when—"

"You've got it backward, as always," she shook her head. "Bringing her here was the price *I* paid, so that I could get to you. If I had my way, she'd already be dead, and I would have been the one to do it. While you watched." Anger, hidden under her voice there, just like the hate had been: someone had stopped her from targeting Esa, and she wasn't happy about it. "But the goddess has other plans for your little girl. The sins of her past are hunting her, just like I'm hunting you."

"She doesn't have any—what the hell are you saying? She hasn't done the things I've done, the things we've done: she hasn't made the same mistakes. She doesn't have any sins, Julia."

"She was born."

That was it: that had been my window—I should have pulled, pulled and fired, right then. Julia was too wrapped up in her predatory anger, too busy thinking about how much Esa was going to suffer; she'd given me a split-second advantage, the point where I should have acted.

But I couldn't do it. She was still my sister: even all those years ago, when I'd burned her down to save the lives of our enemies, I'd had to do it from the cockpit of a warship, unable to stare her in the face as I betrayed everything she believed in, everything *we* . . .

Even then, I'd been a coward.

She saw the hesitation, and that smile returned, mean, and predatory, and cruel. Whatever else she'd been, when I'd known her, she'd never been that—not without purpose.

A hundred years changed a person, I supposed. Or maybe I'd just never known her at all. Like I'd told Esa: we see what we want to see.

"All these years," I told her. "All these years, and you're still fighting someone else's war." Don't think about what she was saying about Esa; don't think about what she was implying might be happening, *right now*, to the girl I'd protected, who had protected me, who I'd come to think of as a daughter. Think about this moment, here, now; think about trying to get the advantage over her again.

"What else do I *have*?" she asked me, a snarl at the edge of the words. "What else did you leave me? Do you know what my first instinct was, when I crawled out of the wreckage of my ship on Hadrian's Gambit? I was bleeding, I was hurting, the sky was on fire—and the first thing I remember was a single thought: 'I need my sister.' I *needed* you. And you weren't there. Because you were the one who had betrayed me. Who had burned our world, our cause. All of that: *you*."

That was all she remembered now. That was why—when this "goddess" had told her I was still alive, had offered to let her hunt me, in return for delivering Esa here—she'd said yes, no matter the cost to the universe, the cost to her. When she saw me, all she saw was betrayal. The thought was a sick twist inside me—it meant that all we'd had, all we'd been, meant nothing to her now, but it meant something else, as well:

It meant I knew how to find my moment again.

I smiled back at her. That was all it took. It was the same mean smile she'd been wearing earlier, the one she'd let slip as her hate shone through: the smile we'd taught each other to wear, a mask to let us get through the killing, the smile that had let us pretend that we were more dangerous than we were, that had let us pretend we didn't care about anything.

It had been a lie, even then. We'd cared about each other. But now . . . now she blamed me for betraying her. Thought that I'd never loved her, that the mean, hollow smile we'd both worn hadn't *been* a lie, not for me. She thought I'd always seen her as disposable, replaceable. And so she'd spent the last hundred years becoming the thing she thought had beaten her: the ghost that I had never been.

I let her keep thinking it. It killed me a little inside, to do it—I'd loved her more than anything in the world, once, and now I was letting her believe that love had never existed—but that didn't matter.

Esa mattered.

So I let my own cruelty show through that smile, let my eyes go cold. I reminded her that I'd betrayed her, that she'd lost, that I'd won, that our world had burned because she hadn't seen me coming. I did all of that with just a smile, with just the granite behind my gaze.

She could read my face just as well as I could read hers, but she'd forgotten that smile was ever a lie. And so she believed it now, too.

Her glare returned, redoubled, as she reached for her own rage, more than a match for mine. "You never could have won that day," she swore at me. "Not without your betrayal, not without taking me by surprise. You never could have—"

"You don't have anything to prove, Julia," I told her, my voice low, sardonic. "Not to me. Sister." But I was still smiling as I said it, and that time, we both knew I was still lying.

It was inevitable that she'd go for the gun. She'd spent a century locked in nightmares, chasing after the figure in her mind that was the thing she'd made me into: not even the fact that she'd thought I was dead could keep her from chasing that ghost, from turning herself into the thing that had beaten her. And now I was here, standing before her, giving her a chance to prove that she'd become the better monster. If she didn't draw down on me now, all the agony of the past hundred years, all the nightmares of Hadrian's Gambit, all the hate she'd held for so long: none of it would mean a damn thing.

She didn't have any choice. Which meant I saw it coming. Which meant I was faster.

She drew. I fired.

Just dropped my hand to the gun on my hip, swiveled it outward, holster and all, and pulled the trigger. Didn't even haul clear—just fired right through the leather.

The benefits of a mag-catch gun belt; she barely even had her barrel clear of her holster when my shot hit her dead center.

Of course, the round only staggered her—she had intention shields, just like I did—but it bought me time; her gun came free, but her first shot went wild as she staggered backward, and *that* let me clear the revolver from the smoking ruin of the holster and drop my left hand to the back of the weapon, fanning the hammer as fast as I could pull the trigger. Every single shot landed: one two three four five, all right to center mass.

The force of the gunshots staggered her back even farther as her intention shields shattered like electric glass—the final round buried itself in her body armor—and then her pistol was jarred from her grip and falling into the chasm beside us, and I had a split-second decision to make: reload, or close the distance.

I chose the former, emptying out the dead shells and placing a single round in the cylinder, spinning it even as I snapped the gun shut, but Julia had already recovered, and she lunged into me, landing a palm strike on my solar plexus, some sort of amplifier in her hand—no different than the force-multipliers built into my own knuckles, our kits still similar after a hundred years apart; we had trained each *other*, after all—and the device meant the hit landed with far more power than the blow warranted. I went flying, smashing into the wall behind me, my intention shields the only thing stopping my bones from snapping in a dozen different places.

I staggered to my feet, tried to get my hands up, but she was still coming, coming fast, a knife in her hand: I should have closed with her when I had the chance, before she could get the blade free. Instead, I'd tried to reload my gun, and now it was gone, wrenched from my grasp by her amplified blow: I'd chosen wrong. When it came to Julia, it seemed I always did.

CHAPTER 16

Esa

A door slid open; not the one we'd come through, but one above that, a second platform hanging over the first, one we hadn't even seen until we'd turned.

Meridian's gifts were still screaming that groaning howl of a single organ note, the sound growing louder, climbing faster upward through its scale of desolate dread. It rang out like some horrible truth, a promise that the universe was hollow, that the only thing that would fill it was pain. What sort of *mind* made music like that?

I got my answer, when a person stepped through the door.

A person. A human, and not just any human. I was staring upward—the bright line glaring solar energy behind us casting strange shadows on the wall—and as I looked up, I saw . . .

It couldn't be. It *couldn't*.

I was staring at myself.

The young human woman standing on the platform above us—she was a perfect copy, a replica of me: the same dark brown skin, the same kinky, curly hair, just a little longer than mine, the same wide eyes, eyes I'd seen in my mother's face, in the hologram on Odessa Station. She could have been my sister, some forgotten twin I'd never been told about, except even that wouldn't have explained the resemblance: she didn't just look like me, she *was* me, a different me, a me outside of myself, like I'd been staring into a mirror and then the image on the other side of the glass started to move on its own.

The Cyn had stolen my medical data from Odessa; tissue samples, genetic sequencing, brainwave activity—everything they would have needed, to revitalize a technology that had been banned since before the Golden Age.

She was a fucking *clone*. A clone of *me*.

"I've been waiting for this," she said to me, her voice carrying across the distance, and it was . . . wrong, it was just *wrong*, hearing my own voice from the outside like that: like hearing what you sounded like on a recording and hardly even recognizing it, unable to reconcile what you heard in your head when you spoke with the sound of a stranger's voice on the playback. It was that, but a million times worse. "Waiting for so long." Unlike me, she was dressed in a kind of . . . gown, straps and flowing silks, flattering her figure—*my fucking figure*—in a way my dirty combat gear and torn-up hand-me-downs never had.

She took a step, then another, and then she was dropping from the platform, just falling, from at least twenty feet up—and she landed as if she'd simply taken a single step down. If I had tried that—to use my teke to break my fall—I could have done it, sure, but I never would have been able to make it look so . . . so graceful, so *easy*.

So she had my gifts, too. Had them, and knew how to use them in ways I didn't.

"What . . . what are you?" Sho was the one who gasped out the words—I was still too dumbfounded to even speak.

Still, she didn't look at him when she answered—she was staring directly at me, like nothing else in the world even existed, like the star beneath us could have finally given way, been torn apart and released a flood of stellar energy that would have engulfed the entire station in a torrent of fusion flame, and she wouldn't—*couldn't*—have looked away. "Your name is Esa," she said, a simple statement, though she licked her lips as she made it, as if in anticipation, and there was something . . . *horrible* about that, the involuntary nature of it, something almost sensual, a kind of naked need written across her face that distorted her features into something I barely recognized. "Mine is Ase. My name, the inverse of yours. I gave myself that name after I learned yours, because that's what I am. The inverse of you."

"You're . . . me." I couldn't think of anything else to say; my mind was still reeling, still trying to wrap itself around this insanity that the universe had become.

"No." She frowned, then, something almost . . . petulant about the expression, like it was my fault somehow that I couldn't understand the lunacy spilling from her lips. "Aren't you listening?"

And then she hit me.

It was like being hit with a goddamned freight train. She didn't even lift a hand to do it—just *looked*, and then I went flying, my telekinetic shields shattering like they were made out of glass. My head snapped back, and I almost went sailing right over the fucking edge—right down to that sea of not-glass, and god knows *what* that shit would have done to me—except she reached out and she caught me, pulling me back to the edge of the platform, setting me down as gently as she had herself. "There," she said, as if she hadn't been the one to send me flying in the first place. "Now you—"

Sho opened fire. She tore the gun out of his hands—the rounds hadn't even ricocheted off her telekinetic shields, they'd just . . . stopped, slowed to nothing, a defensive instinct from her teke even as she reached out offensively for Sho—and then she ripped the exobraces off his legs, taking away what I'd promised him he'd never lose again. With a cry, he tumbled to the metal catwalk beneath us, bleeding from where the wires had been torn right out of his body.

I was almost to my feet; Meridian was shaking, trying to raise her gun, but I could see it in her face—she couldn't do it, nothing in her training had prepared her for this, there was nothing Marus had taught her that possibly could have done so—

—and she couldn't open fire on someone who looked so much like *me*.

"Good girl," the clone—*Ase*—smiled at her, and then ripped the weapon away from her anyway, tore it to shreds as she did so, the metal just . . . floating away like it was made of ribbon, like it was a thread she was unwinding with her mind.

"What . . . what the fuck . . . what do you *want*?" I gasped at her, still trying to get my breath back.

"Want?" She frowned at me, as if that were a concept she couldn't even comprehend—either the question itself, or the fact that I'd needed to ask it.

"Pain, of course. Pain is a gift, one I can give to the universe. So I can teach it how to learn."

What. The *fuck*. Did that *mean?*

"Meridian, help Sho," I ordered; I didn't know what the hell to say to the nonsense she was spouting, so I was doing my damnedest to treat this like any other fight, like I was just going up against some unknown opponent, one whose measure I didn't have yet. I told Meridian to move because Sho needed help, yes, but I also wanted to get her out of the line of fire, because that fight *was* coming, and it was going to be an ugly one.

She was stronger than me; she'd already proven that. But this wouldn't be the first time I'd taken on an opponent stronger than me and won. I could *do* this. I could.

As Meridian scrambled past me, I took a step forward, putting myself between this "Ase" and the other two. Jane had told me they were under my protection; I didn't mean to let her down. "You don't understand?" she asked me, her voice perplexed, like a child's, one grasping at the edges of the concept that she might know something an adult did not. "Pain is what the universe needs. The enlightenment, the absolution, that can be wrought from suffering. I've known it. I was forged by it. Have you known pain, Esa? You will."

Well, *that* was a fucking threat—as if the goddamned telekinetic battering ram she'd hit me with earlier hadn't been a sign of her intentions. "You think so, do you?" I asked her. "Well then, maybe you should—"

I went for the pistol in my shoulder holster, a faster draw than Bitey hanging at my side—Sho might not have been able to crack her telekinetic shields, but if her shields were anything like mine, I knew where they'd be weakest, and I'd learned to gunfight from Jane *Kamali*, one of the best there was.

Hand to grip; thumb to hammer; finger inside the trigger guard. Let the weapon slide free of its own accord, like there's a chain between the barrel and its target that's drawing taut and your wrist is just following the motion. Let it all happen in an instant, the gunshot an inevitability, like gravity, or time.

I fired the goddamned weapon dry, right into where her shielding should have been thinnest.

The bullets never reached her. She frowned, then turned the rounds back on me, flicking them at me one by one at the speed of gunshots, the lead shattering through my own only halfway-recovered shielding as she altered the returning rounds' trajectory, carving gashes through my arms; flesh wounds, at best.

She could have killed me at will, put any one of those through my throat. She hadn't. She just wanted me to *hurt*. And it did—the wounds stung like a motherfucker, like razors had been drawn along my flesh.

"The differences our upbringings make, I suppose," she sighed, like she was answering a question absolutely *no one* had asked. "I was raised in my own little pocket of reality; not alone, of course—our sisters were there, then—but I learned, quicker than the others: I think, therefore I am. I will, and my will begets creation, therefore I *am* God. I killed them all as soon as I realized it, obviously. A god of a *shared* pantheon has intrinsic limits to her power, and so their sacrifice was a necessary sacrament."

What the fuck was she *talking* about? Had there been . . . she was saying there had been other clones, others besides her, that they'd been raised in— what, a virtual reality construct? A false reality where they could control everything, a kind of preparatory incubator for the telekinetic gifts they had yet to manifest—so that once they did, the clones would already know how to bend the world to their will?

There had been others, and she'd fucking *killed them all*? Had I *understood* that right?

"You don't comprehend," she sighed, reading the confusion on my face, sounding disappointed—but just slightly—in me. "No surprise, I suppose. You, who were born free of destiny, free of this . . . weight."

"What the fuck are you *talking about*?" I screamed the words at her, unable to help it—none of this made sense, nothing she said made any kind of—

"A Miltonian Lucifer; a Prometheus already in chains," she continued, still smiling, a sudden hate spilling out of her eyes—*my* eyes—like they were on fire. I didn't know what the fuck she was saying, didn't even know the words, but whatever they were, there was real obsession in her voice—obsession and fury both. "That's what they wanted from us, our creators: the strongest of their enemies, copied endlessly, so that they would have enough of us—of *you*—that they wouldn't need any other martyrs to fire the engine of this place."

"Your . . . creators?" I asked her, trying desperately to draw out the moment, to find some way out of her insanity—I could feel it, closing in around me like a physical thing, cutting off the air, tightening around my ribcage like high-tension wires until my bones started to ache with the pressure of her madness.

"The Cyn." She waved a hand idly, as if they were nothing, the monsters that had stolen my genome and made *her* out of the data. "Searching for answers to their own creation. Apply enough pain, enough pressure, and I could give them at least a pinprick view into the apocalypse of their creators, a way to peer through the keyhole of the locked door that opened the way to the Palace."

The Cyn had been seeking out the gifted to try and find what lay beyond the Dead Furnaces, to find the hidden facility where the forerunners had wiped the pulse from the entire universe, god only knows why. They'd been using her to do it. And it sounded like they'd driven her mad in the process, if the cloning and the VR exposure and the bizarre circumstances of her upbringing hadn't done the job already.

None of that mattered now, though: the anger in her voice was only growing stronger, and with it, she was growing in strength. I could feel her telekinesis like heat, like a warping field stretching out from her body, her fury exciting the very molecules of the air around her into motion; she was like an explosive charge, a chemical reaction boiling toward detonation, but I didn't know how to stop it, and anything I said might just make it worse.

"But a chained god is still a god," she continued, taking another step forward, closer to me, "and as they tried to see through me, I could see through them, in turn. I could see, and eventually, I could *touch*. Once I'd suffered enough." She was up on the raised platform with us now; I drew back, just a little, but she still wasn't moving aggressively—even the anger was gone, gone like it had never been, and she was just talking, letting her horrible psychosis spill forth like she'd been desperate to tell me these things, things I barely understood at all. "I rewrote the pathways of their minds," she whispered, leaning closer still, her eyes wide with wonder, as if we were having a reverent discussion of some forbidden miracle, sharing some secret only the two of us could comprehend. She smiled as she said it, like it was something just delightfully naughty we were sharing, rather than something utterly monstrous. "It's just energy, after all."

Oh, god. Oh, *god*.

She wasn't a *tool* of the Cyn. Not anymore. They'd created her, created a dozen like her—clones of me, taken from the medical samples and records they'd stolen off Odessa—to try and activate this place, the Dead Furnaces, to find the path to the Palace, and they'd used pain to do so. They'd been trying to break her to their alien will, torturing her because she was unique—the same way I was unique, a contradiction in terms, but even among the next generation, we were powerful, the gifts encoded in our genetic data amplified by the Preacher's experiments—and to shield herself from that pain, she'd *convinced herself pain was a kind of sacrament.*

And then she'd turned around, and fed that idea right back to those who had taught it to her: got loose of their shackles, somehow, and used our gift to change the very nature of their thoughts, to alter the electrical current that ran through whatever the Cyn equivalent was of a brain. She'd made them worship her, brainwashed them into looking at her and seeing something divine, made them into followers, into slaves. She'd *created* the apocalyptic nightmare cult that was the Bright Wanderers.

She wasn't a tool of the Cyn; she wasn't their servant at all. It was the other way around. We'd just met the Cyn's "goddess"—a psychotic, sadistic lunatic with immense telekinetic power and literally total control over her worshippers—and she was *me*.

CHAPTER 17

Jane

Julia closed with me, the knife gripped in her fist like the claw of an animal, held backhand, tight against her body until she lashed out with it. It was the same way we'd both learned to use a knife, lessons we'd learned frighteningly young: keep it close, where they can't take it away, until you can bury it in their throat.

I got closer still, got one arm inside hers to block the strike, tried to get a leg behind her so I could pivot her into a throw, but she'd known that was what I would try to do, and she locked my leg in place instead, bracing her knee against my own so she could slam her shoulder into my chest, the blow smashing me back against the wall hard enough to drive the breath from my lungs.

A hundred years, and we still fought the same way: like cornered, desperate animals. Because that's what we had been, in the ice-covered wastes of the front lines where we'd been raised. Where we'd raised each other.

I had braced myself an instant before I hit the wall—braced myself to take the hit, because sometimes, you just got hit—and at least that meant I was prepared when she threw a punch with her off hand, expecting me to be focused on the sharp blade of the knife instead; I ducked to the side, and she smashed her fist into the wall, her force-amplifying knuckles making the forerunner construction ring like a bell. I had a single moment to take advantage, and I took it: reached up with one hand and snapped her thumb until it bent the wrong way off her hand. No thumb, no implant-activating gesture. One of her weapons taken away.

Except she'd had a moment to act too, and even as I'd broken the bones in her hand, she'd used her moment to drive her knife underneath my ribs, twisting the blade to tear my insides apart.

The pain was sharp, instantaneous, almost more like a burn than a cut as my nanotech swarmed the site of the injury: my body armor had taken most of the blow, she'd only gotten a few inches of blade in, but I reached down anyway, grabbing her wrist and pushing back toward her so she couldn't sink the steel any deeper inside me.

We stayed frozen like that for a moment: one of my hands wrapped around her own, squeezing at her shattered thumb, the other tight on her wrist, straining to keep her from sliding the knife deep enough that she could puncture an organ inside my abdomen. "All you had to do," she said softly, the words a whisper only I could hear, more for herself, maybe, than for me. "All you had to do to keep us together was *believe*. And you couldn't do it, could you? You just didn't have it in you." She put just a little more pressure on the knife; it sank just a little deeper, twisted the wound just a little wider, and I gritted my teeth around the fresh new hurt and squeezed at her broken thumb in response, pain all we had to give each other now. "All those years on the front lines; all our desperate, scrabbling childhood, digging shell casings out of the snow and lead from the walls to sell to the recyclers for a few dry mouthfuls of food. They *ruined* a part of you, just like—"

I finally managed to unlock my leg from hers, drove a knee into her abdomen. Not much of a strike, but enough to let me rip her knife out of me, to pull on her wrist and spin her so that I slammed *her* into the wall, buying me enough time to scramble backward and free my own knife from my boot, though even that—the act of pulling my leg up to where my hand could reach the hilt of the blade—tore bright new hurt from the wound she'd carved under my ribs.

"You think it was the *wars* that ruined me?" I asked her, swallowing back the acrid taste of adrenaline and pain and blood, unable to stop myself from responding. "It was never the wars, Julia—it was them, the elders, their rules and edicts and *avarice*—"

"So." She grinned, then, wild and angry and happy despite the rage, despite the pain, even as she swapped her knife to her broken hand, tying it to her grip with a strip of tape. "You admit you're good and ruined, then." She bit off the tape with her teeth, then took a step closer, ready for me to re-spond, with violence or with words.

I ignored the jab entirely, a sick, sinking feeling bubbling up from the pit of my stomach at the sight of that grin on her face. I'd missed it—in an aw-ful, hurtful way, seeing her smile like that, actually *happy*, hurt more than the knife in my side had. I'd missed that smile for so long, so often, I thought of the pain that loss had caused as just a part of living.

The smile was the same one she'd always worn before the bay doors opened and we dropped into a night assault over an enemy city, the same one that had spread slowly over her face just before we started some bombing run, flying so low to beat the radar that the bellies of our third-hand, shaking craft would scrape the edges of the ruined cities we flew over, and the urge to grin right back, to return that bravery, to make a closed circuit between the two of us that just reinforced the notion that we were the only ones who understood, the only ones who saw the truth of all this madness, that we were going to get out, to *survive*, no matter what happened to anyone else . . .

All these years, and I still wanted her to be my sister, still wanted to *join* her, in her triumphs, even in her failures. But just like in that final moment, when Mo had put the truth before us, a truth I'd accepted and she'd refused to: I couldn't close that circuit, not after that, because if she survived, if she was right, it would mean that countless other lives would suffer—or end.

"Just tell me one thing, Julia," I said, even as I activated my own melee implants—now I was better armed than she was, had the upper hand. "For-get everything between us—just answer one question. What the fuck is *hap-pening* here?"

If she answered at all, it would be with the truth. She might try to kill me, but she wouldn't lie to me. I still believed that.

If nothing else, she would *want* me to know what monstrous thing I wasn't going to be able to stop—because this time, she was going to beat me. It was like she was trying to rewrite history: to stop me before I kept the el-ders from firing their weapon and destroying billions upon billions of lives. To stop me before the Cyn did . . . whatever awful thing they were planning to do.

She watched me for a moment, that mean grin still on her face, widening, just a bit, as she realized that *here* was a power she still held over me: answers. "I'll tell you that, if you tell me something first: is it true, what she says? That it was the soldiers of the Justified—the ranks you bought your way into by destroying our home—that caused the pulse?"

She wouldn't lie to me, and I wouldn't lie to her. "It was."

She laughed, then, a harsh, grating sound, mean, but not without joy, as well. "And you killed me to save one *system*. I think that makes you a hypocrite, Jane."

I swallowed back a sharp retort; she was talking, and I needed her talking. Whatever else she was, she wasn't a Bright Wanderer—wasn't indoctrinated, wasn't a believer in their nihilistic, all-consuming faith. She might actually know things, things we needed to know. "I answered your question," I told her, ignoring the blood still pumping sluggishly from the wound in my side, though I was losing too much, too fast, already starting to grow light-headed. "Your turn."

She shrugged, her knife still held before her, still half expecting me to use my question as a feint, to come at her as she was replying. I might have, too, if I hadn't needed to hear what she would say. "It's an extortion racket," she said simply. "Strip away all the religious nonsense, and that's what it boils down to. The Wanderers think they can use this place to shield certain worlds from the pulse, worlds they choose. Once they do that—shield a handful— they'll call it proof they can deliver on their promises, can protect their followers from the pulse, bring more worlds under their control. It's about *power*, Jane. It always has been."

"Power? The power to do *what*?" The Cyn—the Bright Wanderers—they weren't the Pax. Power in and of itself wasn't their endgame, their end goal. They had something else in mind.

She almost laughed. "Jane, grow the fuck up, already. You've only had a hundred years to do it. Power *is* the endgame; always has been. It's no different than why we climbed the ranks, back in the day: we didn't give a shit about giving orders, we just didn't want to have to take them from some fortunate son of one of the elder's sycophants who didn't know a damn thing about war. We—" She came at me, no warning at all.

Just like I'd been expecting her to.

It was knife to knife now, and it was mean and it was close and it was hate, as much as anything—hate and grief and memory—that drove us on, that locked us in tight orbit like we were twinned worlds bound together by gravity. Neither of us was willing to let the other one spring away to take a moment to breathe; neither of us was willing to let the other one get even the slightest advantage, so we followed, everywhere the fight carried us, and we weren't fighting on the narrow corridor beside the chasm any longer, not really: we weren't fighting inside the Dead Furnaces at all, not fighting for the Justified or the Bright Wanderers. We were just fighting because it was what we did, both of us, because we'd learned early that you either killed, or you died.

And so now we were trying to kill each other.

I opened up a gash across her forehead that soaked one side of her face in blood, made it harder for her to see; she hammered her fist into the injury she'd ripped into my abdomen, bruising and pulping the already split-apart flesh. I brought an elbow down on her shoulder, hard enough to bruise all the way down through the body armor, trying to deaden the limb so she couldn't use the knife she'd taped to her palm; she cut open my cheek, all the way to the bone, trying to get to my eye.

Before we'd had ships, or laser rifles, or intention shields; before we'd been pilots, or commandos, or even soldiers; when fighting—when killing—hadn't been something we did to carry out the elders' orders, but instead was something that was just a way of life, a necessity, because our world, our entire *universe*, was the war, the war where we grew up: that was where we'd learned to love each other.

And where we'd learned to hate.

Now one had curdled into the other, and those early lessons—survive or die, kill or starve—were what we fell back on, and we were fighting *mean*, and we were fighting dirty, and it seemed like it was going to go on forever, the two of us whittling each other down to nothing more than shreds of blood and bone: that was when JackDoes shouted, "Jane!"—holding something up that I could just barely see out of the corner of my eye.

I don't know how long Julia and I had been fighting—it felt like hours, it felt like forever, but it had only actually been a few moments, a minute at most, and JackDoes had used that time to get his claws on my gun, one round still loaded in the chamber: that was what he was trying to draw my attention to. I sprung away from Julia, throwing myself low as he slid the weapon across the floor toward me; I picked it up from a roll, coming up on one knee with the sights raised to my eye, but she'd already moved *past* me—

—and she'd reached JackDoes even as the gun had left his claws. She'd known I'd get to the weapon first, so she'd acted to cut off my advantage: to find herself a shield.

And she had her knife—still taped to her hand—held to his throat.

CHAPTER 18
Esa

What do you *want*?" I whispered to the mad creature standing before me—I couldn't help it, the fear in my voice. She was powerful—incredibly powerful, far more so than me, trained from birth to harness gifts she hadn't even had yet, whereas I'd been raised in an orphanage on a world smack in the middle of nowhere, with no idea that all of . . . *this* . . . was waiting for me—and she was insane. If there was a worse combination, I couldn't think of one.

"I told you," she replied. "To spread my sacrament. To *teach* what I was taught."

"You want . . . all you want is to hurt people." That couldn't be all there was to her—couldn't be all there was to a person, just a . . . a black hole, no different than the pair that were swallowing the sun of this system, as if she were just a singularity that ate pain instead of light.

Cloning had been banned during the Golden Age because, even then, the highly educated populace had believed, on an intrinsic, instinctual level, that clones lacked *souls*. If Ase was what clones became . . . maybe they'd been right.

She nodded at my words, smiling happily, as though I'd finally understood—it was like those other lives, the lives she would ruin to spread her "worship," didn't matter, didn't even exist, not to her. Like other people were just . . . shadows, cast by a flickering fire, a fire she would stoke into a blaze, one that might spread to consume the entire galaxy, and she didn't even care—not so long as she stayed warm.

I hit her. She was close enough she didn't see it coming—a direct physical attack, just a strong right hook, as basic and as powerful a punch as anyone could manage, and it caught her square, snapping her head to the side and letting me follow it up with an uppercut to the jaw, except this time my fist met something like steel, rather than skin and bone: she had her shields raised again, and they were impenetrable, at least to my direct martial assault. At least two of my knuckles burst on that wall of teke, the skin splitting apart and laying bare shattered bone underneath.

Didn't matter. Never does. Keep fighting. That's what Jane had taught me. I leapt back, clear of her slashing counterattack—a wave of telekinetic force that swept through the air where I'd been—and then I was ripping apart the catwalk on either side of me with my own gifts, spiking the jagged metal bars toward her like a rain of metal shards; she swept them aside, but that had given me the time I needed to tear up even more of the metal, to cover my arms in gauntlets made of the heavy alloy the forerunners had used in their construction, a weapon patchwork and ugly, but still a *weapon*.

With another burst of my telekinesis, I went right at her, closing the distance I'd opened just a moment before, turning the force of my leap into the attack itself—and *that* got through her defenses, the heavy weight of all that metal, not to mention the telekinetic force behind it, her shields finally shattering as I landed the hit, sending her staggering to one side.

Of course, that blow should have killed her—force equals mass times acceleration, and there had been a hell of a lot of telekinetic acceleration propelling the easily fifty pounds of metal mass strapped to my arms—but most of the force had gone into shattering her shields, so I hit her again, and again, and *again*, but each time the attacks barely made it through: she was throwing up full shielding each time I struck, seemed to have endless reserves to draw on, whereas I was draining my own gifts fast, too fast, using too much power just holding the gauntlets together and accelerating the heavy blows; I couldn't keep this up, not for long—

—and concentrating on the nature of my attack made me sloppy in its execution; made me slip. I overextended a jab, and she just leaned out of the way, her hand wrapping around my wrist—ripping away the metal protecting my arm like it was nothing as she did so, like it was vapor that just disintegrated as she reached *through* it—and then she jerked, hard, and sharp, and she'd put an invisible brace just behind my elbow, done it so smoothly I hadn't even felt it.

Except I felt it when the result was the bones in my elbow snapping like brittle pieces of wood.

"*Esa!*" I didn't scream; I had that, at least, though the pain was a roaring torrent, like broken glass inside my skin. Meridian had screamed for me, the fear in her voice like a cold splash of water as I staggered backward, pulling my useless, limp arm out of Ase's grasp, and I could only manage that because she let me—she'd released my wrist as soon as the violence was done, and she was still smiling, all the heavy blows I'd landed unable to even raise a bruise on the face I saw in the mirror every morning, unable to even split her skin.

The whole thing had taken under a minute—a minute, from my first close-range punch, to me throwing everything I had at her, to her snapping my left arm, rendering me damn near helpless. Under a *minute*, and she wasn't even breathing hard.

Didn't matter. Fight. *Keep* fighting. Find a way.

She saw me swallow the pain, saw what replaced it, in my expression—her smile changed to a frown, and I knew what was coming next, threw myself low and built a telekinetic ramp over my own body: I knew I couldn't block the freight-train rush of all the telekinetic force she could muster, just like I'd utterly failed to do the first time she'd hit me, but I could at least deflect it, send it sailing harmlessly overhead as I scrambled backward, toward Sho, Meridian still holding the young Wulf up, his legs useless—but his *gift* still very much intact.

Find a way to *fight*, even when you've got nothing left to give. There's always more to give.

"*Now!*" I screamed at him, and, screaming himself, he *reached*—not into the distant reactor that was powering this facility, but to a source of energy much closer to hand: the raw, unchecked chaos of the stellar flare rising just past the sea of glass, through the narrow slit in the far wall of the Dead Furnaces. It was more energy than either of us had ever handled—made the full output of the reactor I'd channeled through the Cyn on the shipyard world seem thin and sputtering in comparison—and he pushed all of it into me: I turned around and poured it at the psychotic would-be goddess in turn, a torrent of stellar fire that should have left nothing in its wake, not even bone.

It hit her, and she *laughed*, the sound high and pure, and then she turned it right back against us, and I didn't even have time to scream before I began to blaze like a star.

Sho cut the channel; there was nothing else he could do—it was going to kill us both, and probably Meridian in the process, and it hadn't even singed our enemy.

I was on my knees, my every nerve ending on fire, the world too bright, a kind of distant hum blocking off all other sound, blocking off even my ability to *think*, but past even that, I could hear her: not Ase, but Jane, screaming at me: "*Fight, damn you. Find a way!*"

I tried, Jane. I did. I *tried*.

She couldn't be beaten. She just . . . she *couldn't*. I'd fought as hard as I could, and might as well have been trying to push a *world* out of orbit with my bare hands. Couldn't get any traction; couldn't get an angle to hit her from, not one she couldn't defend. She was just . . . just stronger.

I staggered to my feet, even so. Blood was pouring freely down my nose, an aftereffect of overextending my gifts; my ruined elbow was a burning ember of heat, heat and pain, where she'd snapped my arm. I glared at her across what was left of the mangled platform, and she saw the glare, and laughed again, like this, all of it—all my resistance, all my rage, all my pain—was a far better outcome than any she might have expected.

She made a gesture, to one side, a kind of louche beckoning with one hand; I was swaying on my feet, couldn't even turn as I heard heavy thumps behind me, but I had seen the winged shadows cut across the orange splash of light from the slit behind us: she'd called her Cyn, her followers, to stand guard over Sho and Meridian.

To make sure they couldn't interfere while she finished with me.

"Now," she said, taking another step forward, into striking range. "Why don't we—"

I grabbed her by the throat, and squeezed.

She hit me. Not with telekinetic force, just with the weight of her hand and the speed of the blow—she sunk her fist into my stomach and I doubled over, just in time for my face to meet her rising knee. That strike drove my head back upward, into the path of her next hook, which knocked me straight into one of the railings around the platform, my skull striking the metal hard enough to split open the skin over my scalp.

I lay gasping on the ragged remains of the catwalk, gasping and bleeding, my head ringing; I couldn't see, couldn't breathe, let alone stand. She wasn't just stronger than me when it came to her gifts—she'd taken me on without them, just to prove she could.

I was beaten.

"You know what you just did?" She asked softly, kneeling by my side. "You proved I was right. Right to bring you here—right to trust that we could do what I alone could not. Oh, *Esa*: we're going to change the galaxy, you and I." She reached out, grabbed the wrist of my broken arm, and she *twisted*, and I couldn't help it—I screamed, then, even though I could barely breathe: screaming was the only possibly response to the shattered pieces of bone grinding together inside my flesh.

"*Stop it!*" Meridian begged her. "She's *beaten*, just . . . just stop!"

"No," Ase replied, sounding almost shocked that she would have suggested it. "She needs to learn—needs to see. All those years ago, when I realized what . . . *they*—" She stopped her torture, just for a moment, to direct a glare at the three Cyn guarding the others instead—in their armor, they looked more like statues than people, frozen with their weapons raised, their minds rewritten into empty voids of blind obedience by her will alone. "What they wanted from me, what they wanted and what they were *afraid* of—she needs to see the same thing." She turned back to me, leaning close, so close her lips were almost touching my ear; I was weeping, tears running down my face to mingle with the blood, but there was nothing I could do—I had nothing left to give.

"Just *do it*," I whispered, sobbed—the pain was too much, too much to bear. "Just . . . please." I was begging her to kill me. I was just in that much pain. "Please. End it."

I'm sorry, Jane. I tried. But it just hurt too *much*, and it cost everything, to gain nothing.

"End it?" she asked, surprised. "You think I want to—Esa, no. No." She cooed the words, like a mother to an injured child. "Haven't you been listening? I broke myself, to break free. And then I broke them, as well. And now, I'm going to do the same to you. I don't want to *kill* you, Esa. I just want to destroy everything you love. And then you'll be like me, will *see*, just as I did. And I won't have to be alone."

CHAPTER 19

Jane

A new Golden Age, Jane. That's what she's trying to create. Maybe it will be, and maybe it won't, but she's going to be the power in the galaxy for the next few centuries, at least, and I won't be on the outside of that. Not again. I'm done being on the losing side."

Julia had backed up, dragging JackDoes with her, all the way to the chasm that ran across the far side of the chamber: she knew that even if I tried something drastic—targeting a nonvital part of the little Reint and shooting through him to get to her, for instance—the impact would take them both over the edge.

She knew all my tricks.

"And you get to take me on in the process." I licked my lips; I still had the gun trained on her, of course, but she had all the cards—the knife pressed against JackDoes's throat was sharp enough that it had already drawn blood. The engineer was just staring at me, his eyes black and sorrowful: he thought this was his fault, somehow.

It wasn't. It was mine. I never should have brought him along, and more than that—the woman with the knife to his throat was my sin, my crime. She never would have been here to hold that blade against his neck, never would have been here at all, if it weren't for me.

"And there's that, yeah." The crooked grin spread across Julia's face was the one she always wore when she was winning—despite the gash across her forehead, despite the broken hand and the deadened shoulder, she was winning, and that was all that mattered to her. I was getting what was coming to me.

The fact that she was going to kill JackDoes while I watched, just to make me suffer, meant nothing, not to her. He didn't matter. Every nightmare she had, she saw the same terrors: the ruin I'd made of our homeworld; the sister she'd loved, betraying her; all the wars we'd fought, made meaningless in an instant.

I knew, because I saw the same thing.

"And once I'm dead, and she's won?" I asked, still holding the gun steady. "Once you're the mean right hand of the goddess of the new Golden Age? What then?" I was stalling, playing for time—there had to be something, *anything* I could do, here. To save JackDoes. To save myself. To save Esa.

Because Julia wasn't talking about this "goddess" as a theoretical figure, some distant figure of worship to the Cyn: she was talking about her like she was a person, someone she'd *met*, someone who might well have been here, on the Dead Furnaces, now. And that meant, whoever she was, she was powerful enough to bend the Cyn to her will—and very much focused on Esa. I needed *done* with this, done with all of it, done with the sins of my past coming back to take their dues in blood: Esa needed me, that was what mattered. Not the crimes I'd committed over a century ago, but the young woman I'd raised to be better than I was, to be stronger, to be someone who'd never have her own Julia come back from the grave to try and ruin the good things she'd done.

"Her greatest cruelty," Julia answered, her smile widening. "Their goddess gives the Cyn what they wanted, gives it to them even though she stole their minds, so they'll never know it. She calls the pulse back. She uses it to build her empire. But you won't be around to see it. I hope you said your goodbyes to your little girl, Jane." I wasn't the only one who'd been stalling: inch by inch, she'd been making her way toward her own pistol, lying on the floor, and now she reached down to pick it up, forcing JackDoes to bend with her. "Maybe if you're lucky, she'll already be waiting—"

I nodded to JackDoes; he saw the motion, even as she pulled him downward, and he nodded back. I'd found my way to hit her, to get us both clear, and it was simple: all I'd need to do was realize this was *his* moment, not mine. That was the other thing Julia had forgotten, the first lesson we'd learned together: always have someone watching your back.

The world Julia and I had grown up on had been divided up along sectarian lines, and most of those sects had been dominated by one species or another. Ours was no different: mostly human, the remainder of the followers Tyll, or Klite. So Julia hadn't known very many Reint at all, and clearly, the intervening years hadn't guided her to expand her horizons.

That meant she didn't realize JackDoes wasn't a noncombatant, not really; she'd pegged him as such when he slid my gun to me rather than trying to take a shot at her himself, and no, he *wasn't* very good with a gun, and he knew it; most Reint weren't. They weren't, because they'd never needed to be: they were predators, every single one of them, aggressive and deadly and *fast*—even sheltered engineers who'd never seen combat before.

He uncurled his prehensile tail, a single "snicking" sound the only warning Julia had as the blades emerged from the tip of the appendage, and the Reint lashed it upward, slicing her forearm to the bone and severing the nerves keeping her grip tight on the knife at his throat.

A spray of blood; pain and fear, visible just for a moment in Julia's eyes, the same expression she must have worn as her ship collapsed around her, torn out of the sky by my laser fire. I got to *see* it, this time: to see the knowledge pass across her face, that she was going to die. That I was the one who had done it.

Seeing it didn't change what I had to do, though. I fired. The single bullet in my revolver leapt from the chamber, struck her right between the eyes.

It didn't split open her skull; her intention shields had returned, fully charged. But shields only blocked the physical momentum of whatever object struck them—in this case, a .45 caliber pistol round—and the force of the bullet's impact still drove her backward, over the edge of the chasm behind her, and then she was falling.

She had to know she was going—had to know there was nothing she could do to stop herself, no way to arrest her fall. But her hate for me was so strong, so mindless, that even as she went over the edge, she still wanted to hurt me, any way she could.

JackDoes had leapt away the moment I fired my gun. He'd almost made it clear. It was his tail she reached out and grabbed—grabbed tight, despite the razor-like blades still protruding from its length, slicing her good hand to ribbons—and she yanked him backward, carrying him into the abyss with her.

I jumped forward. Act, don't react. I dropped my pistol and lunged for JackDoes's arm even as he was pulled into the chasm, after Julia.

His talons—extended unconsciously, part of his body's autonomic response to his conscious decision to raise the edges on his tail—dug through my skin before he caught my grip, and then I was sliding toward the edge as well, his weight pulling me over, except I still had the knife in my other hand, and I plunged toward the floor, sinking the blade into the metal, using it as an anchor.

For a moment, we just hung there, JackDoes clinging to my arm with torrents of my blood spilling over his grip, me hanging on to him with one hand—despite the pain—and to the hilt of the knife with the other. Then JackDoes was scrambling upward, safe back on the solid metal of the chamber floor, the only sign of Julia now the slick of blood on his tail, from her arm and from her hand, where she'd grabbed him.

She'd finished her fall, slipped off his tail, unable to hold on to the sharp blades, and vanished into the darkness beneath us. I hadn't even seen it. I'd been too busy saving my friend.

There was a kind of poetry in that, I think. An awful poetry—just like everything between Julia and I was awful, forever tainted not just by the choice I'd made and the suffering I'd caused her, but everything before that, the constant violence and horror that had been our lives, our childhood—but a poetry, all the same. Starbursts of illumination shells lending a gossamer sheen to the craters and ruined defenses of the front lines; the aurora that hung over our world rendered brighter, almost blinding, by the escaping radiation of distant starship cores going critical; a single knife with a shattered tip— the first weapon we'd ever owned, ever stole—lying in the white snow, the most beautiful thing I'd seen in my life to that point, because of what it meant, because taking the thing meant we would be able to defend ourselves now. What was beautiful, to me, had always been ugly. Julia had been no different. She'd been the only one who had shared that view, that beauty; the only one who remembered who I'd been, as I learned who I was becoming.

And now she was gone. For good, this time.

Fucking *hopefully*.

JackDoes, panting, had managed to get to his knees; I was lying on my back, still bleeding. Quite a lot. "Jane?" he hissed, the sound with kind of a gurgle to it, as he tried to get his breath back.

"Yeah, JackDoes?"

"I did *not* like her. I didn't like her at all."

"Can't really blame you for that."

"She was your . . . she called you 'sister'?"

"That was a long time ago, JackDoes." With a grunt, I managed to pull myself up into a sitting position, reached down with my arm that wasn't fucked, trying to free my medkit from my belt. "And we were different people back then. Both of us . . . very different."

"Oh. Here. Let me." He reached for the kit itself, beginning to remove the bandages and medical foam and self-tightening thread we'd need to fix up—or at least *patch* up; I was a good long way from being "fixed"—the mess Julia had made of me. "I wouldn't have liked *you* very much, if I'd met you back then, would I?"

"No. Probably not."

"Ah." The hiss of compressed air from the canister as he began to spray the coagulating foam into my more major injuries. "Well, I like you now."

"Thank you, JackDoes." We needed to get moving, to get after Esa; whatever it was that this "goddess" had planned for her—it wasn't good. But we wouldn't be much help if I bled out before we got there, and that was a real possibility: I could feel it, the world distant and too fluid around me. Taking several major knife wounds—and one set of Reint talons to the arm—would do that to you, every time.

"You're welcome," he hissed. "Also: I'm sorry about your . . ." He nodded down at the gashes in my flesh even as he filled them in with slick foam. It barely stung at all.

"Don't worry about it."

"What she . . . said. What this goddess intends to do. Do you believe it?"

I looked at him, then—or tried to; he pushed my head back into place as he was starting to stitch up the slash across my cheek. Still, in that momentary glimpse of his reptilian face, I'd seen real fear in his eyes, behind his question. Julia had said this "goddess" intended to bring back the pulse somehow. Reint, more than almost any other species other than the Barious, had been brutally punished by the first pulse, the one we'd let loose: the more difficult the conditions around them became, the more likely they were to de-evolve, to return to the brutal, bestial nature that had kept them alive on their dangerous homeworld, creatures incapable of higher thought, of empathy, but at least creatures that stayed alive.

A second pulse—the return the Justified had been recruiting the next generation to stop, for almost a century—would do the same, but worse: even those Reint who had been lucky the first time around, had survived with their faculties intact on worlds the radiation had bypassed, would be at risk again. Even Sanctum. Even JackDoes.

Maybe I should have lied to him. But he'd saved my life, and I'd saved his, and anyway, I was . . . I was pretty much done lying for the day. "Yeah," I told him, even as he cleared out the foam from the gashes in my arms and began stitching those up as well. "I believe it."

"Why?" he hissed. Not asking why I believed—asking why she would *do* such a thing in the first place.

"The same reason the Justified set it off in the first place. Because she thinks she can control it." We'd been wrong. But with the forerunner tech of the Dead Furnaces at her command, maybe she could succeed where we had failed.

And that was a fucking terrifying thought.

The implications of what the galaxy would become with a cult like the Bright Wanderers having control of pulse radiation were worse, even, than the spread of a completely chaotic pulse, like the one the Justified had unleashed. "An extortion racket." That's what Julia had called it. And stripped of the religious veneer the Wanderers had no doubt applied, that's exactly what it would be: join their cult, join their cause, give fealty and fervency and faith to their goddess, and your world could be protected.

Resist, and it would fall.

"She's building a new Golden Age," I murmured, almost to myself, as Jack-Does peeled away my body armor so he could get to the deepest of the injuries, where Julia had sunk the knife under my ribs. I ground my teeth together on the pain—I was pretty sure she'd knicked one of my kidneys with the blade, but thankfully, both organs were synthetic, a grisly souvenir of the Battle of Sanctum, where my original kidneys had been torn apart by a hail of Pax gunfire: the organs were self-repairing, able to interface with my nanotech easier than an actual organ would have done. They also apparently didn't hurt quite as much when they got stabbed . . . which didn't mean they didn't hurt at all.

"That's what Julia said," I continued, louder now, speaking to JackDoes, more to keep my mind off the burning line of fire in my side than anything else. "A 'new Golden Age' . . . but only for her followers. Concentrate the resources of the galaxy into the hands of however many worlds she can protect—a few dozen, a few hundred—and damn all the rest."

"That . . . is not a Golden Age," JackDoes responded firmly, tying off the stitching in my side. "That is an empire."

He wasn't wrong. And the terrifying thing was, it would work: if this place really could do what Julia had said, could shield entire worlds from the pulse, then this "goddess" could pull it off. Those living under her protection—even those who didn't fully buy into the Bright Wanderer faith, just like I'd never bought into my own sect's teachings—would still have no choice but to pretend, to worship her all the same, even if that worship was only skin deep. And those living outside of that protection, all those who might have checked the spread of a single sect grown that large, that powerful: they would be defanged, in an instant. Most would likely revert to internecine squabbles over whatever resources were left on their pulse-stricken worlds, be made into barbarians, milling aimlessly in the wilds beyond her borders.

It wouldn't last forever—nothing did—but if Julia was right, and this "goddess" was only truly interested in *personal* power, it would last far longer than she would; she'd die in her sleep, a couple hundred years from now—or more, depending on her species—and it would likely be another thousand before those barbarians got used to the constant lashing return of the pulse, and found a way to tear her empire's walls down.

And then . . . god only knows what hands the pulse-controlling technology would fall into. The coming era would be a conflation of the worst parts of the sect wars and the chaotic, violent spasms the universe had undergone just after the first pulse. We were staring down the barrel of centuries of brutal war, of oppressive rule, of imperialist appetite and cruelty and control, followed by something maybe even worse.

Unless we stopped it. Here. Now. Because facing down this sort of threat was exactly why the Justified—the Justified and the Redeemed—had been created in the first place. This was what we *did*.

"So. What now?" JackDoes asked, leaning away and packing the medkit back up.

"Now?" I stood, twisted a few times to make sure I didn't pop any stitches—I didn't, self-tighteners were fantastic that way—then reached down; I picked up the big bolt-action rifle Julia had used on the Cyn, and tossed it over to the Reint. He caught it with a hand still slick with my blood. I didn't know how many rounds were left in the gun, and JackDoes certainly couldn't fire the thing, given that it was almost as big as he was, but I was taking it with us regardless—a weapon that could kill a Cyn in one shot was definitely a weapon worth having. "Now, we go forward: we find Esa, help her stomp this 'goddess' into the ground, and we get the fuck out of here. Come back with every ship in the Justified's fleet—up to and including the dreadnaughts we've been repairing from the Pax invasion—and then we pry this place out of the Bright Wanderers' hands for good. We stop their 'empire' before it can even start, with all the sudden, terrible, necessary violence we can muster. The Justified way."

"Oh. That . . . sounds like a good plan."

"I thought so."

Together, we started forward, deeper into the station.

CHAPTER 20

Esa

C ome now, Esa. That can't be all you have." The lunatic actually pouted—made an exaggerated little-girl face as she reached out to stroke my head, like you might an ailing pet. "I need you to be stronger than that. And I think that you are." She stood—pulling me to my knees as she did so; I screamed again as she used my broken arm as the lever to get me up—and she took a step back, examining her handiwork: the ruin she'd made of me, the Cyn standing guard over Meridian and Sho, the great sea of liquid glass, and the line of light from the stellar flare that washed over all of it, lending an infernal, apocalyptic glow to the scene. "We'll just have to teach you, won't we? Teach you the same way I learned." She turned slightly, toward the Cyn. "Kill one of them," she commanded imperiously. "I don't really care which."

"*No!*" I tried to get to my feet, to stagger forward; just doing that—just the trying, the effort it took to lurch toward her—was harder than anything I'd ever done, *ever*. And I didn't even succeed. I fell, went crashing back to my knees, my legs too weak to even hold my weight.

"What's that? You don't want the Cyn to choose? Well, then." She smiled again, something malicious and . . . and *evil* in the expression; there was no other word for it. "I suppose *you* should, then. Make a choice, Esa. Everything starts with a *choice*."

"Fuck *you*—"

"Esa. Esa." Sho was panting—he'd exhausted himself as well, channeling the stellar energy, trying to move legs that wouldn't move anymore, not with the exobraces ripped out of him—but he still managed to get the words out. "It's . . . it's all right. It's . . . it's okay."

"Sho, *no*," Meridian whispered, but it was too late—he was already sitting up, as well as he could on his useless legs, watching the Cyn warily as he did so.

"It's me. It's . . . it's me, you fucking . . ." He coughed; couldn't even finish the insult. "I'll be your sacrifice, your . . . Don't make her choose. That's just . . . it's cruel."

"Well, yes," Ase replied, the smile curving on her face into something wryly ironic. "That's rather the point. She has to learn. Still, a volunteer makes a good enough lesson—we can show her exactly what self-sacrifice gains."

"Sho, don't," I shook my head, spattering the metal grating beneath me with sweat and blood; I was trying to look up, to look him in the eye, but it hurt too much to even do that. "*Please* don't—"

"Just remember, Esa. Remember that I love you, that you're my sister, that I'll *always*—"

"Thus begins your lesson, Esa," Ase said, interrupting Sho—she couldn't even let him have *that?*—to reach down and grab me by the jaw, jerking my head up and doing what I couldn't: forcing me to watch, to bear witness as the Cyn drew back their swords, and Sho hung his head beneath the shadows of their blades. "The only thing the righteous do better—faster—than the damned? They die. They die very well. And they take the rest of the galaxy with them."

"You're not wrong about that," Sho told her, a growl in his voice.

He hadn't been saying goodbye at all. I felt it, a moment before it happened—felt him snap his gifts to life, felt them blaze into being like he knew I would, because *that's* what he'd been trying to tell me: his words hadn't been a goodbye at all, but a reminder that we'd trained together, fought together, that I'd need to be looking for him to take his shot.

It was all the warning I was going to get; I dropped, like a stone, to the deck. And then he hit her.

Not physically—he couldn't even stand—but by pushing the stellar energy he'd been collecting, quietly, into himself, all into her, all at once. The flare of heat and light was so bright that it seemed like a bomb had gone off, right in the middle of the platform—this was more, even, than what he'd channeled through me: this was everything, everything he had, enough energy to melt a person, to break them down into nothing, and all of it aimed at Ase.

When it was done, she was still standing there, untouched, something almost admiring on her face.

He'd hit her with the heart of a star, and she wasn't even phased—was just as untouched as the first time we'd tried it, except that time, she'd been expecting an attack; he'd taken her off-guard with this one, and it had still done nothing.

"I *like* you," she told Sho, who had collapsed back against the railing, coughing and gasping from the effort of his last-ditch attempt, an attempt to save us all. An attempt that had failed. "You're a fighter." She turned toward the Cyn. "Kill the girl instead." Then, facing me, she gave me an exaggeratedly lewd wink, grotesque in its very pantomime. "We *like* girls, don't we?"

The Cyn drew back their blades again, aiming them now toward Meridian, who was staring past them, staring at me, staring like she believed I could save her. Even though she knew I couldn't.

"*No!*" I screamed the word, a simple refutation. I hadn't thought I had anything left in me. But seeing her, looking at me like that, believing there was something I could do, needing me to be something else, something other than beaten: I'd been wrong.

All the energy Sho had thrown at Ase—it hadn't done anything to her, but I'd been able to collect some of the runoff, some of the excess heat and light that had spilled over from the would-be killing field he'd locked the psychopath inside, where it should have melted her down to nothing. She'd proven she was immune to goddamn *everything*, even that massive burst of stellar fire—but the same wasn't true of her Cyn executioners.

I aimed that energy at them, instead, something giving inside me as I did, snapping like a high-tension wire, as if there were a part of me that was broken, now, that couldn't ever be fixed—too much energy, too much effort, too much need behind the force I pushed toward those armored monstrosities. Except whatever it was that had broken, I don't know if it was something I needed, or if it had been something holding me back, like a lock—a lock designed to keep me from doing exactly what I did.

For a moment, there was nothing; the Cyn were still standing there, frozen like statues, Ase watching with wide eyes from one side, Sho and Meridian cowering together beneath the shadows cast by the Cyn's armored forms.

Then the exosuits toppled over, one crashing into the next, and when they struck the grating of the platform they split apart like abandoned insect carapaces, revealing the nothing that remained inside.

I'd vaporized the motherfuckers: atomized them, cooked them into the ether right through their metal shells.

"*Yes,*" Ase whispered, something awful, almost sexual in the sound, like she was experiencing something more erotic than reverent. "There she is." She turned to me, smiling horribly, intensely *pleased* about the fact that I'd just murdered her pets. "The *me,* in you. I've been looking for her."

Ignoring Sho and Meridian altogether now, she stalked back toward me—I braced myself for another hit, but it didn't come; instead she threw her arms around me, squeezing me tightly in an embrace, my broken arm shrieking at the pressure. "Oh, we can do great things together, Esa. Great things." She was actually crying as she said it—tears of joy running down her awful, ecstatic version of *my* face—and she stepped back, and did a little . . . pirouette, a little spin of joy, her hands upraised. "I ask, and *I* receive!" She shouted upward, laughing. "So many years . . . I've been waiting for you, Esa. Waiting so long."

She was straight out of her goddamned *mind.* She was more powerful than any being I'd ever met, ever heard of—more powerful than the gods from the myths and legends of the seventeen species—and something was . . . *broken,* inside her head, that much power bent to the whims of a fractured, splintered ruin of a personality that felt no more allegiance, no more empathy, toward any other being in the galaxy than I might have felt for the metal decking under my feet.

She paused to wipe a tear from her from her face, then gestured with that same hand at the lake of glass beneath us, at the bar of sunlight breaching the far wall—and at the strange twisting pillar that rose up from the center of all of it, bisecting the line of light neatly in the center. "That's the problem, you see," she told me, as if I were some . . . some colleague of hers, and we'd both decided to put our heads together and see if we couldn't find our way around some particularly obstinate set of data that had been vexing her.

"I need to activate it, but I *can't*—or rather, I *could*, but the effort just might kill me, and then what would be the point in that?"

"So. You can die. Good to . . . to know." I was trying to make the words defiant, but only succeeded in a kind of petulant mewl, pain and defeat robbing me of any bravery I might have summoned.

"Of course I can: remember what I did to my—our—sisters? Though that was the decision, made in haste, that led me to this very impasse; if I'd kept just one of them alive—rendered her . . . more *pliable*, somehow—I could have used her gifts, in concert with my own, used them to give new fire to the Furnaces. This place is, after all, meant to be the cornerstone of my cathedral; can't get started with construction of the edifice before that is in place." Nothing she was saying made any kind of sense to me, but the words still filled the pit of my stomach with dread: whatever it is she wanted, it would serve her, and her alone. "But with you at my side, we can do it together. You could even survive; I think you just might. I think you were *meant* to be here, Esa. The original of all of us. The one only starting to learn."

Suffering. She believed it all came down to suffering. She thought her suffering had unlocked her gift—the insane strength she possessed, relative to my own—and so she thought making me suffer would allow me to be strong enough to help her. That was why she'd wanted the Cyn to kill my friends, to make me choose between them. Sadism as a goddamned *teaching tool*.

Then why . . . "Why take the others?" I gasped out—I couldn't help it. If I was going to die, I wanted to know. "If it was *our* gift you needed, why send your . . . your chaplains to steal other gifted children?"

She looked at me with wide, astonished eyes, blinking, as if she'd never even considered that I wouldn't have already known. "Oh, Esa—haven't you even realized that? I'm not just stronger than you because I was trained: there are limits to our gifts, after all. Physical limits to how much power we can be born with, before the radiation chokes us to death, like it did our parents." A part of me shuddered and screamed at that—they had been *my* parents, *mine*, she had no right to them; did her ravenous appetite know no bounds at *all*?—but only inside. I was too empty, too broken, to do anything to risk her wrath again. "But limits are meant to be overcome, Esa. We're meant to break them, you and I."

"How?" I wasn't in any position to demand, but she didn't seem to care, her delight in learning I was powerful enough to help her was so all-encompassing.

"I'll give you a hint." She turned, nodded toward Sho and Meridian, who had crawled as far as they possibly could away from her, to the very edge of the platform. "Use them, and you might be strong enough to fight me, to fight back. I know you want to. I know you want to try."

Use them? What did she mean, *use*—

No. It couldn't. It couldn't be.

The Cyn hadn't been stealing gifted to try and find a *key* for the Dead Furnaces—they already had that key, in the form of Ase, or rather, she had herself, since she'd been the one giving the orders, ever since she broke free of their control. But she still wasn't strong enough—all the absurd power she'd shown, and that wasn't *enough*. It must have taken dozens of forerunners to activate this place, if their gifts were equivalent to our own—and so she'd commanded the chaplains to bring her other gifted children, and she'd . . . she'd . . .

She'd somehow been feeding on them. A kind of spiritual cannibalism, *eating* the gifts of our own like a psychic delicacy, one that gave her strength. Even the dead must have had something to offer her, though less than living victims: that's why the chaplains had brought her the corpses of the ones they hadn't been able to take alive.

"Martyrs," the Cyn on the shipyard world had called us. Those who died for a cause. And "imitation", that had been the term he'd used for me. Cyn likely couldn't even recognize organic features, not enough to differentiate them, so he hadn't known that I looked like his goddess—assuming he'd ever actually laid eyes on her in the first place—but he'd recognized my gift as a hollow shadow of Ase's own, knew that something so close to her own power would likely allow her to gain more strength from her . . . her *feed*.

And once she grew strong enough, she believed she could open the way to the Palace—the forerunner's ultimate answer to the pulse. And with that much power at her fingertips . . .

She truly would become a god.

"You're a monster," I gasped out.

"Maybe," she shrugged. "But I'm a monster with power, and that's all that matters, isn't it? So: you face another choice, Esa. End them yourself"—she nodded at Sho and Meridian; I couldn't help it, I followed the motion with my eyes, and they were both just . . . just staring at me, helpless, awaiting my decision—"and hope you can take enough of their gifts to pose a threat to me. That's option one." She smiled as she said it; clearly, she didn't think there was any way in hell, even with the power of two more gifted lives under my belt—the lives of my *friends*—I'd actually be anywhere near powerful enough to stop her.

"The second choice is to learn: to watch, helpless, as *I* feed on them instead. If *you* won't, I'm not going to just let them go to waste, now, am I?"

"And the third?" I asked, but I already knew what it would be.

"Activate the Dead Furnaces with me," she said with a simple shrug. "Do that, and you all three get to live. For a time."

I stared at her, hate and fear and confusion making a storm inside my mind. There wasn't a chance in hell I could count on her to keep her word—and even if she did, I'd still be handing the power of this place, this ancient forerunner relic, over to her, putting her one step closer to her cathedral, to the Palace itself—but the alternative was just to watch as she butchered Meridian and Sho.

The first option . . . wasn't even worth contemplating.

Nor was the second.

She wanted me to choose, but there was nothing to choose between—just pain, and more pain. She still thought that I saw the galaxy the same way she did: wouldn't place any real value on the lives of Meridian and Sho, beyond simply as tools. She would have actually had to consider which of the three paths to take. But I wasn't her. It wasn't a choice at all.

"Esa," Meridian whispered, "don't, please—"

I shook my head; I didn't even want to know which choice she was going to beg me not to make. Better for her if I didn't—better for us both. "I'll do it," I gasped to Ase. "I'll activate your fucking machine. But just so you know: if you drop your guard, even a little bit, while that's happening? I'm going to tear your throat out. With my goddamned *teeth*."

"I wouldn't have it any other way," she smiled. "You're learning already."

Then she grabbed my broken arm, and she hauled me to the very edge of the platform, where the silver lake below washed slowly across its bay. She pointed outward, to the great pillar that rose from the liquid glass, narrowing her eyes against the brightness of the distant stellar flare. "Now," she told me, *commanded* me. "Reach."

CHAPTER 21

Jane

JackDoes and I were still moving forward, taking the only path the force fields had left open for us. Whoever or whatever it was at the controls of those barriers—the Cyn or the Bright Wanderers or the Dead Furnaces themselves—we were headed where they wanted us to be: we didn't have a choice.

I was about convinced we were going in circles—led through one barren, alien chamber after another, kept apart from Esa and the others by whatever malevolent force was guiding our path—when the whole facility started to shake.

"Oh, I don't think that's good," JackDoes moaned quietly. I didn't feel like I had any way to disagree with him.

We started running. It didn't feel good on any of the various lacerations, stab wounds, and bruises that covered my body, but I did it anyway.

There was a weird, subsonic hum building in the air, almost more like a vibration than a sound, the sort of thing you felt in your bones rather than just heard, and I didn't like that, either—and then the last door in our path slid open, another one of those strange forerunner force fields beyond it, and what lay on the other side wasn't another corridor or antechamber or even a yawning chasm like the one Julia had fallen into: it was something . . . else.

What the hell was I even *looking* at?

It was some kind of platform, overlooking a much vaster chamber—I couldn't see what was actually beneath the jutting ledge of metal, not around the angle of the door, only some sort of massive, twisting pillar that rose up through the center of the room, bisecting a line of light that only could have come from the solar flare trapped inside the station's ring, bright enough that I had trouble seeing anything else.

What I could make out of the platform itself had seen significantly better days; its machinery was ripped apart, even pieces of the metal grating that made up its floor had been torn asunder, and there were abandoned Cyn exosuits scattered in one corner, the same corner where Sho and Meridian were kneeling, looking exhausted, turned away from us. But where was—

There: standing at the very edge of the platform, one arm raised up toward the distant pillar, illumination beginning to climb up the sides of the metal— not electricity or even fire, but just . . . *light*, light like a liquid, flowing in reverse. That was Esa, all right—even through the force field I could feel the push of her telekinetic gifts: whatever was happening to the pillar, she was the one doing it, activating the strange machinery with her teke. But what the hell was she *wearing*? That certainly wasn't her combat gear, and she didn't own any dresses at all, let alone something with that much slink to it— Scheherazade never would have let her leave the ship dressed like that.

I took in the scene again, my gaze sweeping back to the other two Justified operatives on the platform: Sho and Meridian weren't just kneeling in the corner—they were cowering, clutching at each other in fear, fear directed toward the figure standing at the edge of the platform, reaching for the pillar.

The figure that *wasn't* Esa.

No matter what had happened, there was no way in hell Sho would ever look at Esa like that. He loved her, and so did Meridian—there was no way Esa could have done anything in this short a time to cause them so much pain.

But if the figure at the edge of the platform with her back to me—the figure that looked like Esa, but wearing a strange dress, with Esa's friends staring at her in mute terror—if that figure wasn't Esa, then where the hell—

That was when I found her, and when I did, I wanted to kill Julia all over again, just for keeping me from her side for so long.

I hadn't seen her initially because Esa was usually the most animated thing in a room; even when she stood still, she was moving. Now, though, she was hunched over, barely able to stand, one arm reaching toward the distant pillar as well, the other bent at an angle so wrong it was painful just to look at, and the rest of her didn't seem much better: whoever the other woman was, the "other" Esa, it looked like the two of them had fought, and our Esa had lost, and lost hard.

I had to find a way through that force field. I had to figure out what the *hell* was going on—

Focus, Jane. Act, don't react. What was different? What had changed?

We were close enough to the others that our comms should have been open again; that was what was different.

I reached up to the control nub under my jaw, narrowed my transmission to just Sho's channel—whatever the hell was going on with Esa and not-Esa and the pillar and their gifts, I had a feeling interrupting might be just as dangerous as not doing anything at all. "Sho!" I called out, shouting, even though I didn't need to, not over the comms channel. "It's Jane—I'm at the doorway, but there's one of those force fields in my way. What the fuck is happening in there?"

"Jane, thank god! What's happening? The Cyn's goddess is Esa's fucking *clone*, and she's a sadistic *psychopath* with some sort of messiah complex and she's forcing Esa to activate this place; *that's* what's fucking happening!"

What the fuck had I *missed*? What sort of monster had Julia signed on with, willingly, just to get a chance to kill me?

Didn't matter; only the moment mattered. As soon as I found a way through the force field, I could—

What? March JackDoes and myself in there, to be two more hostages against Esa's further cooperation? Because that had to be what was happening— why this "other" Esa had left Sho and Meridian alive. Torture couldn't have bent Esa to her will; threatening her friends, though . . .

Still, I had to do *something*. It wasn't in me to just stand there and watch, not while Esa was hurt, not while this . . . goddess, this clone of my surrogate daughter, was doing god knows what with the Dead Furnaces. I had to find a way *in*—

Except I was too late. Whatever Esa and psychotic-god-complex-*clone*-Esa were doing, it was done. The rising lattice of light locked itself in place around the pillar, drew tighter around the metal for a moment, a breath of stillness against the chaotic aurora burn of the fields of light. Then it exploded outward, expanding through the very walls of the station—through Jack-Does and me, as well—and behind it came the illumination of recessed lights in the corridor where we stood, ancient filaments buried along the ceiling: the Dead Furnaces had power, the whole facility was coming *awake*, and the line of solar light on the far side of the great vaulted space was growing brighter, growing—

—no, not brighter: *more*. The aperture that allowed the stellar energy to flood in was widening, widening and drawing that energy into the facility itself, into . . . whatever it was that lay beneath the platform, the brilliance seeping downward through the crack in the far wall like a waterfall of liquid light. Something about the pillar was siphoning not just the stored energy from the converters and batteries, but the entire tendril itself, the whole of the great rising flame being swallowed up by the interior of the Dead Furnaces, like the ring itself had become a collapsed star, a mechanical simulacrum of the one that hung above us.

"Jane! *Jane!*" JackDoes grabbed my injured arm and squeezed, using the pain to pull my attention to him; I ripped my gaze away from the insane spectacle before me, following his eyeline instead—

—the force field was open.

When the power had clicked on in the rest of the station—turning on the ancient lights above us, beginning the hum of distant machinery elsewhere in the complex—the force field had dropped away, and as soon as I saw that, reflex kicked in: my rifle swung up into my hands and I dropped to one knee, drawing down a bead on not-Esa's head, fighting every instinct that was screaming about what the fuck was I doing, that was *Esa* on the other side of my sights. I steadied my breathing and tucked my finger into the trigger guard, ready to—

"*No*, Jane." It was Esa herself on the other side of my comm; god, just the amount of pain I could hear in her voice, the pain and the *exhaustion*—whatever she was doing, it was taking everything she had, everything she had and more, and that was after she'd taken what looked like one of the worst beatings I'd ever seen in my long life.

"You can't kill her," Esa said, through all that pain, all that concentration. "Not *now*—if you do, this place will come apart, and we all die. Might . . .

might be worth it, just to end her, but this place . . . it's too important. Get to Meridian—get to Sho—get them out of here."

"Not a chance," I shook my head, not budging from the rifle sight. "I'm not leaving you here with—"

"Not much *choice*. If either of us pull away now—her, or me—the whole facility will be torn apart, and that includes everyone on it. Get them out, Jane. That's what we *do*, remember? Rescue the gifted. The ones in trouble. They're in trouble. They need your help."

"So do *you!*"

"Too far . . . too far gone. Too hurt, spending too much . . . to do . . . to do . . ." Another great lash of power, one originating from both of them, and a corresponding echo of that force from the pillar, and then it was beginning to spin, and the stellar light spilling into the massive basin beneath their feet was being pulled from the tendril of flame even faster: I'd started moving out onto the platform, could see the strange sea of not-quite-glass beneath us now, its pellucid, shifting surface crashing in chaotic waves even as the stellar flare was drawn into the currents of the liquid, like bright ink spreading through crystal waters.

And then there was . . . nothing, all sound sucked up into whatever the hell was happening, and that ocean of lit glass exploded upward in utter silence, geysers and waves and crystalline formations making billions upon billions of tiny, shimmering beads of light that spread throughout the vaulted emptiness of the massive chamber—

—and then they just hung in place, almost like stars wheeling in a night sky, as if gravity had no effect on whatever the shimmering liquid actually was. Lines of light began spreading, began snapping into place between the droplets of lit glass, a tiny sound—almost like a chime—filling the air with each connection. The threads of illumination were originating from the tower itself, but were moving quickly outward, forming an endless constellation of geometric patterns between the pointillist spread of light, a lattice of infinite complexity drawn in the seemingly random chaos between those trillions upon trillions of lit beads of glass as the chimes like breaking bells rang out in an infinite carillon chorus.

Whatever the hell was happening here—and likely, from the way sound kept dropping in and out around me, in several other basins like this one, spread out along the interior of the ring—it was about to finish. I could feel it building, soaring toward its climax; could feel it in my bones.

There was nothing I could do about that. But I could help the others, because Esa was right: that was what operatives of the Justified did.

Ignoring—as best I could—the strange lattice of brightness still convulsing around us and the sound of a billion tiny chimes ringing out with each connection, I made my way to Meridian and Sho; between us, the young Avail and I got the paralyzed Wulf up, his arms across our shoulders, and we started back toward the exit. Every part of my being was shrieking at me to turn around, to turn around because Esa needed help and I was walking away from her and that wasn't *who I was*, goddamn it—if I did that, everything I'd told myself I'd become, that I'd earned, over the last hundred years was a lie; if I did *that*, everything Julia had believed about me was true—but there was no other option I could see, no way to *help* her, even if I stayed.

"Esa, what do you want me to *do?*" I asked over the comm, keeping my voice from breaking with sheer force of will even as Meridian and I staggered back toward the door. I didn't understand anything that was happening—but she did. I had to let her guide me now, the way I'd always guided her.

"Go," she said simply, still concentrating on the massive power-feed she and her fucking *clone* were sending to the machinery before them. *"Run.* Something very bad is about to start here, Jane. The Justified will have to answer it. In one way or another. You have to get to them. To warn them—"

"Not gonna happen; I'm not *leaving you here*—"

Another wave of light, another crest of energy—blinding and pure and *clean*, somehow—and then the machine was finished, I could feel it, the facility beneath our feet fully returned to life now, returned to purpose, as if there were meaning again, in the halls of the forerunner station, rather than just metal.

And if it was *done*, that meant:

Don't *react*—just *act*.

I pushed Sho off my shoulder, sending him and Meridian reeling toward JackDoes—spun and dropped to one knee as I did, raising up my rifle again and squeezing off four rounds toward my target as fast as I could pull the trigger: two aimed at the clone's back, and two at her head.

The bullets slowed to a lazy stop before they were even halfway across the platform.

"So," not-Esa said, turning to face me with half-lidded eyes. "You'd be Kamali, I take it? The mother *she* deserved, that I apparently didn't. I've wanted dearly to meet you, so that I could *take—*"

That was when someone—not Esa, Esa had dropped to her knees as soon as the work was done, a kind of desperate hopelessness in her eyes that hurt to see, but someone else entirely, someone I hadn't even known was *on* the goddamned platform—grabbed the clone from behind, wrapping a metal hand around her throat and spinning her around, so that the psychopathic would-be demigod was suspended above the lake of light and fire below.

"How about *me?*" the Preacher snarled into the lunatic's face. "Are you excited to meet *me*, you child-murdering little *bitch?*"

CHAPTER 22
Esa

Activating the Dead Furnaces—it took everything I had. Not everything I had *left*—it took more than that, even. Reaching my gift into the center of that machinery, finding the place inside that felt like it was made for exactly this, the place fitted to exactly my—*our*—abilities: it hurt, like something was ripping apart inside me. It hurt, but it felt *right*, too, like there was a purpose to it, a purpose to us, to being here, and together, Ase and I reached in—

—and then the forerunner-designed machinery started reaching back. Reaching back, and *taking*.

Suddenly I knew why Ase hadn't wanted to do this herself. Once it started, there would be no stopping—either the Dead Furnaces would come blazing back to life, or they would drain us both dry, well short of full activation. If the latter happened, we'd just . . . *die*, and the facility would sink back into stillness, but there was nothing we could do about it now: we were no longer in control, either of us.

Not that I had been, ever, not even before I reached into the heart of the machine designed for people like us, people with our gifts. I hadn't had any control since the moment I saw her, standing on the platform above. I'd thought I'd grown so strong, been so *proud* of myself, proud that I could take the Cyn on, that I could do something the others couldn't. In minutes, she'd shown me that all of that strength was a lie, that I'd never been in control, that I wasn't even the strongest version of *me* that there was.

And then Jane appeared, falling right into her clutches, just like she'd planned. The hate in her voice, when she called Jane my mother—hate and greed and even a kind of sad longing underneath it all, something that would have been pitiable, just a little, if she hadn't been such a goddamned *monster*—I could feel it, her envy, her loneliness, her rage, the emotions burning like a hot wind against my skin, racing along the connection forged between us when we'd reached into the machine, a connection still active, if fading.

"Run," I whispered, tears streaming down my cheeks, still on my knees, despite the fact that no one could hear me. "Jane, please, *run*—"

That was when the *Preacher* appeared, out of nowhere, an avenging angel wrought from copper and steel: she grabbed Ase by the throat, holding her out over the fiery furnace beneath the platform, where light and molten . . . *something* . . . made crescents like waves, blazing with stellar fury in the basin below.

How had she even . . . we'd left the Barious safely in Shell, she hadn't even been *on* the Dead Furnaces. How had she *gotten* here, how had she known, how had she made her way through the force fields and the Bright Wanderers, how had she made her way past the *Cyn*? She had new dents and burn marks on her chassis, wires sparking inside a rift under her abdomen, but—

It didn't matter. She was here, and she had her hand around Ase's *throat*.

"Just *drop* her, Preacher!" I screamed, finding my voice somewhere, the words coming out raw, a shriek of pure fury. "Just *do* it!"

"Can't," the Preacher grimaced, still holding Ace in a vice-tight grip even as the clone struggled, but there was nothing the psychotic, power-mad version of myself could do: stronger than me or not, activating the Dead Furnaces had left *her* drained as well, I could feel that much through the fading connection between us—that, and the constant blazing hatred that was an omnipresent thing in the back of her mind, a rot at the core of her soul just waiting for a target to spread its blight toward, a target it now found in the Preacher. Ase was already throwing everything she had left at the Barious, doing *something*, but I couldn't tell what.

"Why *not*?" I begged the Preacher.

"Because it's a stalemate." Even though the words had a dire implication, there was something of a grin in the Preacher's voice, a kind of grim satisfaction that she'd shown up the lunatic who was so much stronger than any of us. "She's using her gift to lock my servos in place, but that's all she can do, and she knows it. She's just like *you*, in that way—a whole lot of power, but shit at fine control." The grin on the Preacher's electronic mouth widened, as she turned her attention to the despot in her grasp. "So go ahead, Ase—start plucking at the strings inside me, try and make me walk you back to safety. See if you can do it without triggering something that won't carry us both over this ledge. Maybe you'll just make my hand tighten instead, just a little bit, and pop your twisted little head right off your shoulders. Try. I've got all the time in the world—Barious, remember? We don't so much *do* exhaustion. You, on the other hand, well—from that blue creeping into your lips, I'd say even gods need to *breathe*."

The hatred from Ase was a fiery, awful thing—I couldn't just feel it coming through the connection between us, I could see it on her face, all her sadistic impulses and her maniacal god-complex and her impenetrable surety fading before the towering survival instinct that had propelled her this far, the part of her—a part of *me*, one I'd felt myself, even as I pushed it to the back of my mind, didn't want to confront what it might mean—that *hated* the Preacher with an all-encompassing fury, not because she was threatening her, but simply because she stood in her way.

"All the good you could have done," the Preacher shook her head sadly, still clinging tight to Ase's neck, still implacable against her struggles. "One of your Cyn—just one—sent to eat the pulse around Requiem, around any of the Barious factory worlds . . . but you only ever thought of yourself, of what *you* wanted. Esa never would have done that. Esa thinks of *others*, not just of herself." Oh, god, Preacher, just . . . *stop*, please. *Stop*. Couldn't she see the hate in Ase's face, the desperate need to lash out, to find a way to hurt her right back?

But the Preacher continued, implacable, her voice rising into the fire-and-brimstone cadences of the sermons she used to give back home, four years and what felt like a hundred lifetimes ago. "You are just a poor imitation of the real thing," she spat at Ase, the web of light from the heart of the Dead Furnaces causing shimmers of radiance to slip across the reflective portions of her chassis; even the hand she held tight around Ase's neck was glowing, radiant, all that brilliance making it seem like the Preacher herself was a creature of avenging, cleansing fire. "A flawed copy that ought to be erased, and

I'm going to be the one to do it. It was my hubris that brought both of you into this galaxy, that *gave* you such great gifts—so it's fitting that I'm going to be the one to take you right . . . the *fuck* . . . back out of it. Cost be damned."

"Preacher, don't . . . don't . . . you *can't* . . ." My voice was working again, though I was rasping as though I'd been screaming at the top of my lungs for hours, and I was still on my knees. "You have to find a way to . . . what . . . what can I *do?*" I begged her. "How can I . . . how . . ." I was as weak as a kitten; I could barely hold myself upright. My arm was broken, I was bleeding from well over a dozen lacerations and contusions spread across my body, I had at the very least a major concussion, and my gifts were drained well beyond *any* reserves; even the capacitor in my intention shields had shorted under Ase's relentless assault. But even so, I had to do *something*—I had to help, somehow. Jane would have found a way—Jane would have—

—and then she was there, Jane was *there*, with *me*, getting my good arm over her shoulders, pulling me up into a kind of staggering, stuttering lurch of a walk. "Preacher?" she asked, but she wasn't heading toward the Barious— she was moving away, making for the door back into the facility, where Jack-Does and Meridian and Sho were waiting.

"Keep her safe, Jane," the Preacher said simply. "You know what this place is, right? What it can do? If you don't, Esa does. I did this—I did *all* of this; the experiments, the research, joining the Justified—to find a cure for my people, and this place is it. If this little monster manages to take me with her: finish what I started. Both with my work, and with Esa. You've already done a fine job with that part. I'm sorry I haven't said it more often. Jealous, I think."

"Preacher, you can—"

"Can't. *Go*, Jane. Get Esa out of here. Come back with every ship the Justified has, and tear the remnants of the Bright Wanderers out of the walls like the vermin they are. I don't think they'll put up much of a fight, not with their goddess melted to the floor down there." Jane was still half-carrying me toward the door—it seemed so goddamned far away—but I turned, even so, looking back over my shoulder. Ase was still struggling against the Preacher's grasp, and the Preacher was right—the clone *was* starting to suffocate, I could see it in her face, in the crazed, trapped-animal expression around her eyes. The Preacher herself was still glowing, bright and immortal, in the reflections of the Dead Furnace's fires. "If I can follow, I will. If I can't—I've been glad to know you, Jane Kamali. It's been my pleasure."

"Preacher, *please!*" I begged, the words gasping out of a throat that felt like it had been on fire.

"Esa," the Preacher said, turning her head to face me—just her head, the rest of her was locked ramrod straight, holding Ase above the fire—"I've wanted to tell you something for a while now." I could barely even see her face, lost in all that reflected light, but I could hear the smile in her voice: not the hard-edged, mean grin she'd had for Ase, but a kinder thing, gentle, almost sad. "That song—the one you hum to yourself, when you're not thinking of anything else? I used to sing it to you. When you were a baby. I didn't think you remembered. I didn't—"

And then Ase tore her apart.

She tore her apart, and I was watching as she did it.

The psychotic copy of me was *floating* just off the end of the platform, floating and gasping in shuddering breaths of air, gasping inside a cloud of metal and sparking wires that were all that remained of my friend.

I screamed—I couldn't help it—and Jane *heard* what had happened, lurched into a run, and then we were through the doors, and I was still screaming, still looking back toward the *nothing* where my oldest friend in the world had just been, and the last thing I saw before the doors slid shut behind us was Ase, haloed against the light of the infernal machine behind her, surrounded by the floating metal shards that had been the Preacher: Ase, just beginning to smile.

CHAPTER 23

Jane

Still half-carrying Esa in my arms—my own injuries be damned—I ran. Over the comms, Sho had called this Ase—the end result of the Cyn's insane experiments, broken and spoiled by their brutal attempts to create something malleable enough to carry out their vengeance—a "sadist," and he hadn't been wrong. She could have killed the Preacher at will: had likely never been in any real danger at all. But she'd let the Barious choke the life out of her, had come dancing right up to the edge of death, not for the Preacher's sake, and maybe not even her own: instead, it had been for *Esa*. All of it, to fuel her obsession with her lost "sister," to give her a taste of the pain Ase had always known.

She'd waited to respond to the Preacher's assault until that response would hurt Esa the most. Had waited just long enough to give Esa a glimmer of hope that maybe, just *maybe*, we could all make it out of this alive—mutilated and injured and unquestionably beaten, but still alive—so that it would hurt all the more when she reached out and ripped that hope away.

Along with the Preacher's life.

I hadn't always agreed with the Preacher—hadn't even necessarily always *liked* her, though we'd come to an understanding, eventually—but she'd deserved better than an ending like that. She'd been loyal, and brave, and cunning, and had always done what she thought was right for Esa, even if Esa herself didn't think so. She'd deserved better than to be shown a glimmer of hope for her people, only to have it—and her life—snatched away before it could manifest.

Now, Ase was in control of the Dead Furnaces—the facility now fully operational, ready to begin its task of purging entire worlds from pulse radiation, if Julia was to be believed—and she was still somewhere behind us. The fact that I *knew* she was a true-blue fucking sadist meant I knew every step we took toward our ships—every step that felt like freedom, that felt like safety, that felt like it was one step closer to getting the fuck away from the lunatic we'd left behind, the lunatic who might just be too exhausted by activating the Furnaces and all her wanton murder to give chase—might also just be another step she was simply letting us take, so that when she reached out and pulled us back, screaming, she could savor the greater hurt that would cause.

Still, that reach didn't come; I kept waiting for it and waiting for it as we followed the winding course back toward the docking bay, waiting for another trap to fall on us like a hammer, but there was nothing. Just the facility around us, humming back to life after eons of dormancy. We passed the breach in the walls—the bulkheads torn right through—where the Preacher had ripped her way through the facility; she hadn't landed at the docking bay at all, she'd come straight down, setting Shell onto the exterior of the Dead Furnaces and using Barious strength to tear herself a passage into the station.

She'd known, somehow, that Esa was in trouble. I'd never know how. But she'd known, and she'd come, and she'd saved Esa in the process—saved us both. And she'd paid the price.

I wondered if she'd known that was coming too.

Meridian and JackDoes were carrying Sho's weight draped across their shoulders, and Esa's good arm was similarly draped over my own: she was capable of stumbling, but that was about it. Whatever it was she and Ase had done to wake this place up, it had drained the hell out of her, maybe even more so than the savage beating she'd clearly taken beforehand; I kept waiting for her to give out entirely, so that I'd have to haul her over my shoulder in a fireman's carry.

Maybe that would have been better; even in her semi-conscious state, tears were pouring down her face. She was in . . . a great deal of pain, and it wasn't all physical. Maybe not even most of it.

She kept stumbling anyway, kept moving. Just like I'd trained her to do.

We made the docking bay. We *made* it. Maybe activating the Dead

Furnaces really had drained the hell out of Ase, the same way it had Esa: maybe the energy she'd used to destroy the Preacher had been the last strength she had left. Maybe she really wasn't capable of reaching out, of pulling us back.

Or maybe, in her own, twisted way, she was honoring whatever deal she'd made with Esa in the first place: some sort of fucked-up promise to let her and the others live, so long as Esa woke the Furnaces up, the only possible explanation for why Esa had worked with her to do so. The Preacher hadn't been part of that bargain—and maybe Ase, even then, had known she was there, had known she'd still get to *take* from Esa, even if Sho and Meridian were left alive.

Could be either. Could be both. Could be some horrible third option I hadn't thought of—and it *could* have been that she really was about to reach out, and haul us back, just as the bay came in sight. Whatever the truth was, I likely wouldn't ever know.

Javier and Marus were standing on Khaliphon's lowered ramp, double-checking their weapons; I'd told them earlier to wait inside the protective envelope of the ship's guns, so of course as soon as they'd gotten Sahluk sta-bilized they'd geared up again, preparing to head right back in after us. If they'd left a moment earlier, we might well have missed each other in the warren of labyrinthine corridors of the Dead Furnaces. "Get on board!" I shouted at them through the comms; we were close enough that they'd fi-nally come back to life. "We need to get the fuck out of here!"

They heard the desperation in my voice, heard the fear, and so they im-mediately did the exact opposite of what I'd asked: rushed forward instead, Javier to help with Sho, Marus to help with Esa, and we got them onto our ships, and only then did they return to their own craft, starting takeoff se-quences even as the great station around us continued to thrum back to life, recessed illumination spilling through the tangle of baroque architecture that made up the interior of the massive docking bay.

"Jane, what's *happened* to—"

"Not now, Schaz," I growled, sliding into the cockpit and grabbing the stick even as Scheherazade lifted us off from the surface of the landing plat-form. I was still bracing for one last blow, the hit the lunatic had been keep-ing in reserve—a missile, maybe, fired at close range from a surface-to-air launcher, one that could breach Schaz's shields and leave us vulnerable to being dragged right back into her clutches—but it still didn't come, she didn't reach out.

Maybe she was exhausted, maybe she was keeping her word, maybe she was operating some grander scheme: but there was a fourth option, as well. Maybe in all her plans, all her years spent obsessing over Esa, over activating this place, maybe she'd never imagined she could be beaten, that we would get this far away from her.

She'd prepared to fight Esa; she'd brought in Julia to take me off the board, long enough to buy her the confrontation she'd so desperately desired. She'd been prepared for Sho, and Meridian, for other gifted, and she'd counted on her Cyn to neutralize the others. But she hadn't seen the Preacher coming. She wasn't entirely invulnerable, her defenses weren't entirely impenetrable: even in death, the Preacher had proved that.

The ships made for the distant exit of the docking bay: I pushed the throttle up and we roared forward, following tightly on Bolivar's heels, making for the vast spread of the stars that was the mouth of the approach tunnel.

That's when I saw it.

The Dead Furnaces hadn't just come to life, hadn't just returned to function: they were fully operational, and already serving their purpose.

There was a single beam of light, soaring outward from somewhere above us in the complex, aimed directly at the world where the antenna tower had been built; it was light, but then again, it *wasn't*, seeming almost liquid, somehow, more like how the stars looked from a cockpit during a hyperspace jump than how light was supposed to work in normalized space. That ribbon of fluid illumination stretched all the way to the distant world, the only one in the system, where it actually seemed to splash across the atmosphere, suffusing the very skies with its glow—

—and then there were more beams of light, stabbing outward from the planet, the single bridge that had stretched from the Furnaces now shattered into half a dozen that streaked out-of-system in different directions, splinters of liquid illumination that turned the wheel of the cosmic ballet into fire, rather than void. The strange devices in the tower, the ones Sho and Meridian and Sahluk hadn't recognized: they were refractors, diffusing and aiming the energy generated by the Dead Furnaces, sending it outward, across the stars.

I couldn't help myself—even as we sailed clear of the station, I activated Scheherazade's instruments, scanned the distant world with our sensor package: it had held minor traces of pulse radiation earlier, but now, wreathed in that strange light from the stellar ring, they were . . . gone, had vanished entirely.

The pulse had been eradicated from the entire world, in an instant. And those beams of light, splintering off from the Dead Furnaces' original target: aimed at other worlds, whatever worlds the forerunners had last calibrated their tool to defend, a web of liquid fire, stretching out across the cosmos like cables held taut and singing.

Half a dozen beams, singing across the infinite darkness toward half a dozen different distant worlds. And somehow, the forerunners must have moved beyond that, beyond this place, to eradicate the pulse from the entire galaxy: the Dead Furnaces were just the first step.

"A firmament of flame"; that's what the forerunner writings had called their downfall. We'd thought it meant the Cyn. Maybe not. Maybe it had meant the very machine they'd built to try and better the galaxy, no different from how—once—the Justified had envisioned a far brighter future, with the weaponized pulse in our control. They'd learned the same lesson we had, somewhere along the line: nothing *stays* controlled, not forever.

"Jane, we need to go," Javier said through the comms.

"I know," I shook my head, breaking out of my reverie. "We need to—"

"No, I mean we need to go, *now*." I looked away from the distant world, toward Schaz's instruments, even as I knew what I was going to see: bursts of quantum radiation filling the screen, the tell-tale indicators of new arrivals from hyperspace. I'd known before I'd even looked because of the shadow that had suddenly cut between us and those distant spans of light: it was just a small thing, that shadow, but that was only a function of the great distance between Scheherazade and the form causing it. For us to even be able to see the newly arrived craft, haloed in silhouette from this far away, meant only one thing: the Bright Wanderers had brought one of their dreadnaughts to the Dead Furnaces.

And then there was another shadow, another burst of radiation on the scans, and then another. And another.

They just *kept coming*.

This place had never been unguarded; it had never been abandoned. They'd just moved all of their soldiers and all of their spacecraft to a nearby system, like hunters waiting in a blind to make sure they didn't scare their prey away, because Ase had *needed* Esa, needed her to activate the Dead Furnaces. It had been a trap, all of it: all of it according to her design.

And now that the trap had been sprung, the Bright Wanderers were reclaiming the system, dozens of dreadnaughts visible now between us and those pathways of fire, and more were still appearing—as well as frigates and carriers and smaller craft like ours, an intergalactic navy larger than any I'd seen since the pulse, maybe larger than any I'd seen before, as well.

It dwarfed the Pax armada that had assaulted Sanctum—dwarfed even the navies of the great corporate powers during the sect wars. The Preacher had told me to come back, to pry this system from the Bright Wanderers' hands, but even with every single Justified ship recalled to Sanctum for an assault, we'd never be able to make a dent in this much firepower.

"Jane, we need to—"

"Wait," I said to Javier, waiting for what I knew would happen next. As terrifying—even awe-inspiring—as the sight of all those dreadnaughts was, we weren't in any immediate danger: our ships had been docked on a station, hadn't entered an atmosphere, which meant we could jump to hyperspace any time we chose, heading to the nearby rally point we'd set before the mission even began. But what I wanted to see was—

It started, like a migration of birds following invisible magnetic lines, except these lines weren't invisible, they were searing paths of flame cutting through the cosmos: the dreadnaughts began aligning themselves along the beams of liquid fire, and then, one by one, they started jumping away, ready to take the Bright Wanderers' demands of submission to the worlds where the light was falling. "Join, for we are the ones who have cleansed the pulse from the skies of your world; join, or have our dreadnaughts pound your cities from orbit." The carrot, and the stick.

This wasn't the sect wars. It wasn't the Golden Age.

We were watching an *empire* begin to form, before our very eyes.

The same empire Julia had warned me about, the one that would be protected, once Ase found that final station of the forerunners, the one that could veil—or summon—the pulse across the entire galaxy. An endless cycle, where those who resisted the Bright Wanderers' creed were returned to the stone age, and the web of imperial ambition just grew larger and larger, stronger and stronger, until it covered every system, every shipyard, touched every life between the stars, in one way or another.

And the spider at the center: a brutal psychotic of a sadist whose only real desire was to torture anything she couldn't control.

I didn't know how, and I didn't know when, but even as I watched those dreadnaughts jump away, to begin the rise of her empire—not all of them jumped, of course; plenty stayed behind to protect the source of their power, still more than the Justified alone would ever be able to fight—I swore to myself that we weren't *just* watching the foundation of the Wanderers' hegemony, the beginnings of their sovereignty that would stretch from one edge of the galaxy to the other. We were also watching its downfall, the seed of its very end planted at the moment the whole thing truly began. That seed—that ending—was a very simple fact: *we were still here.*

And this universe wouldn't just knuckle under, wouldn't give in to her demands, wouldn't succumb nearly as easily as the would-be empress thought it would, because she didn't understand anyone motivated by anything other than fear, or pain, or rage; she couldn't. She thought everyone other than herself—even the cultists who made up her armies—were all just . . . prey, domesticated cattle, as easily manipulated as the Cyn had been, however she'd achieved that.

She was wrong; people *would* resist, they would fight. It was what they did. For better or worse, the history of all the sapient species was one of conflict—she could offer all the "freedom" she wanted, complete with the caveats of annihilation attached if they refused, and people would *still* fight back, fight just because of the very ultimatum she'd offered. It was just what we were.

The Preacher could have told her that.

"What now?" Esa asked; she'd clawed her way back to consciousness, had dropped, more than sat, in her chair behind the gunnery controls—was look-ing out at the arrival, and departure, of all those dreadnaughts, the expres-sion on her face just . . . tired, worn through, like she simply didn't have any more horror to give, not after what had happened to the Preacher.

She'd find more, again. More horror, more fear, more anger, more rage, more determination, more bravery. She was young. She'd recover from this. And then—like me—she'd fight the fuck back. When you're hit, when you're knocked down, you get up again, and you just start swinging. That's what you *do*.

I'd taught her that. And I'd taught her well.

"Now?" I asked her, even as I pulled Schaz's nose away from the launch of the Bright Wanderers' fleet, away from the pathways of fire carving an-cient and long-lost courses through the sweep of the edges of the galaxy. "Now, we find a way to fight, Esa. There's always a way to fight."

"And can we win?" Even now, a little bit of that spark was returning to her voice: a little bit of what she'd lost, finding its way back. It was a tiny thing, just a little bit compared to what she'd had taken from her, but it was there, all the same. Losing the Preacher—losing *to* Ase—wouldn't break her. Not my Esa.

"We can. Somehow. We'll do it together." I reached out, and took her good hand, squeezed it in my own.

It took her a moment, but she squeezed back.

And then we made the jump to hyperspace.

ACKNOWLEDGMENTS

The difficulty in writing the acknowledgments for the third book in a series is that you're really just thanking the same core group of people for a third time running, and by this point, there are only so many ways you can say, "Thank you; there's no way this book would exist without you, and even if it somehow did, it would be a far, far lesser thing if you had not helped it come into being." Still, there's a reason for that: that same core group of people are the ones who have their fingerprints on every page, the ones whose voices are just as integral to the work as my own, the ones who do the actual *work* when it comes to getting a ragged manuscript filled with half-developed ideas and bizarre flights of fancy ready for actual publication. So they're getting thanked again, whether they like it or not—the fact that you, the reader (who should always be first and foremost in terms of who gets thanked, because without you, there's no point for this book to exist), somehow found this book, and somehow made it all the way to the end, is a testament to the hard work and dedication of these people, much more than it is to my own private lunacy.

First, my family, who encouraged a love of stories in me before anything else—all of my first memories involve storytelling of some description or another, and most of my later ones do as well. The fact that *this* story joins, in some small way, such a wide, vast, deep pantheon as already exists is entirely a testament to your encouragement and support. Thank you.

For Sara, who's always the first person to listen to me complain, and is coincidentally the first person to tell me to *quit* complaining and just solve my problems already, and what do you mean I can't see how to solve it, the solution's right there: thank you. You have the best solutions, always. Even the ones that involve fire. *Especially* the ones that involve fire. Thank you.

For Chris Kepner, agent extraordinaire, who works tirelessly to make sure that I can cling to even the slightest shred of sanity, even when he knows my grip is always slipping—thank you.

For Devi Pillai, Rachel Bass, Desirae Friesen, Liana Krissoff, Deirdre Kovac, and the rest of the team at Tor: seriously, reader, you won't believe how hard these people work. It's insane; it's ludicrous. The fact that they manage to do all that work—large chunks of which are a direct result of me being an idiot—and still remain gracious, friendly, helpful, and dedicated speaks to their belief in their authors and their faith in the notion that what they do *matters*, and let me tell you: it does. It really, really does. Thank you.

For Anne Perry, Bethan Jones, Harriett Collins, and their colleagues at Simon & Schuster UK: The support, care, and attention you've lavished on me—and on *Firmament*—is a testament to your kindness, your compassion, and your dedication. Thank you.

For the innumerable other people in my life (okay, I lied when I said it was just a "core group" earlier) who have done everything you could—knowingly or not—to influence this work, in ways both large or small: thank you. If you think there's the slightest chance this thank-you is for you, then guess what—it is. Thank you.

And last, but certainly not least—like I said above: first and foremost—for you, the reader: thank you. Thank you for taking this journey with me; thank you for making it this far; thank you for making these characters part of your life, part of your imagination, part of your dreams. I'm so glad, so awed, so phenomenally humbled that you invited them in and made a place for them there. Thank you.

—Drew Williams
August 19, 2019